WONDERFULLY DREADFUL

A MEDICAL THRILLER

Copyright © 2020 by Roger Blevins
All rights reserved

2nd Printing

This is a work of fiction. Names, characters, and incidents are the product of the author's imagination or are used fictitiously. Any resemblance to actual persons, living or dead, businesses, companies, events, or locales, is entirely coincidental.

This book is dedicated to the victims of opioid addiction, past and present.

A substantial portion of the proceeds from the sales of this book will be donated to opioid addiction rehabilitation.

PROLOGUE

Gainesville, FL

The pain was excruciating and unrelenting. Judging from the collective gasp of the fans gathered that Saturday night at *The Swamp,* it was likely a career-ending injury.

Warren Reinhardt was the star quarterback of the Florida Gators. As a returning senior, he was high on the whisper list of candidates for the Heisman Trophy and, like Tim Tebow before him, was expected to lead the team to a repeat performance of the 2009 season. His near-religious dedication to working out in the gym, dating back to junior high school, maintained a physique that escaped the attention of only the most nearsighted of coeds. Despite his BMOC status, Warren was unassuming, almost bashful. He didn't date much and blamed that on having too little time, what with football and classwork. He was a good student and an even better bass player, but his future was pinned to the gridiron.

Now, clutching his left knee and biting down hard on his molars, all he could see was the garnet-and-gold jerseys of at least five Seminole linemen and all that came to mind was Jameis Winston, which only made the pain worse!

To Warren it appeared as though the paramedics were moving in slow motion. In fact, they were moving at Mach 1 as they approached the 40-yard line with their Ferno stretcher and lifted him carefully onto the padded metal gurney. Some wondered whether respectful applause would be proper. Others just looked on with concern as Warren was rolled off the field and into a waiting ambulance, its red and white lights ablaze but sirens silenced.

That fateful night more than two years ago would become even more fateful than Warren had imagined. In college, he had been courted by NFL scouts and provided the resources necessary to support an off-campus lifestyle that was enviable.

Now a college dropout, and arguably a life dropout, he sat on the threadbare sofa of a southeast Gainesville tenement he shared with four other sad stories. The pall of stale cigarettes filled the room, the centerpiece of which was an old wooden coffee table complete with stains and cigarette burns. On the table beside a dirty ashtray and within Warren's reach was an Afrin nasal spray bottle he had just filled with his own concoction of fentanyl in saltwater. As he stared at it with repulsive desire, he pondered the long list of those he had come to blame for his addiction to this *wonderfully dreadful* class of drugs known as opioids.

Perhaps he alone was responsible, unwilling to act on the pleas and the prayers of his concerned family and close friends. Or maybe like his alcoholic father, he just carried a gene that waylaid any choice he had in the matter.

Maybe it was that orthopedic surgeon who had done a great job repairing his knee and prescribed Vicodin for the post-operative pain. More likely it was the truly less-than-caring staff of the hospital-recommended Pain Management Clinic that continued to write his opiate prescriptions month after month, or the neighborhood pharmacist who continued to fill them without question.

Maybe it was the article he had read about Paul Gray of Slipknot, the bass player Warren aspired to emulate, who had died of an accidental overdose of morphine and fentanyl. Or perhaps it was his most recent "friend" who had sold him the fentanyl at an outrageous price and given him the weblink on how to prepare it for intranasal administration.

No, he finally concluded the one most responsible for his plight was the damnable drug company that overproduced, over promoted, and over sold the shit!

With a blast into each nostril, Warren sat back on the couch and waited for the euphoria he had come to hate. Within seconds he felt the bottle slip from his hand and heard it hit the floor. Suddenly his visual field was filled with bright ... white ... light.

Ahhh ... I'm back in the game!

1

Washington, D.C.

"I don't give a damn what the voters think, Jack! It's not in their best interest to 'drain the swamp' by imposing term limits on members of Congress," Bill Bassett blustered as he stabbed a pair of bacon-wrapped scallops with his fork and leaned as far forward as his ample belly would allow. He patted his lips with the white cloth napkin then hailed the waiter to pour the last glass from the first bottle of Opus One.

As the six-term senior Senator from Tennessee, William Bassett was the state's longest-serving Senate Republican in history. Only Edgar "Old Ned" Barnes, a Democrat who claimed to be a direct descendent of General Nathan Bedford Forrest, CSA, had served the state longer. Bill was the Senate Majority Leader and, while he agreed with the President on most issues, Congressional term limits was not one of them.

"Look Bill, I'm just telling you what the D.C. grapevine is saying about this President," Jack Powell replied. "He believes what's good for the Presidential goose is good for the Congressional gander."

John "Jack" Powell was the Director of the Bureau of Competition at the Federal Trade Commission. He had joined the law firm of Jones Day in Chicago following his graduation from Northwestern and began as an intern in mergers and acquisitions. Years later after a rather public falling out with one of the senior partners, the firm transferred him to its Washington, D.C. office. He worked there for only a year before trading in his private hat for the public sector. Jack had been courted by a couple of the big investment banks in New York, but he was a natural in the Division of Mergers III and quickly climbed its ranks. Jack finally made bureau chief after the latest cadre of commissioners were appointed and confirmed. This changing of the guard was a poor fit with his left-leaning ideology, but he kept his views to himself, for the most part.

"Fortunately, the President and I are aligned on most matters, but he's not a politician," Bill said, carving into a perfectly seared medium-rare 24-oz. Porterhouse.

"He thinks he is," Jack said with a smirk.

"Well, there's no denying he's a good campaigner, but he's no lawyer that's for damn sure, and he doesn't have a clue what it takes to make sausage."

The visual interfered with Jack's enjoyment of his Cobb salad. His vegan ways and morning jogs maintained a slim frame that sat in stark contrast to the overly consumptive Bill Bassett.

"Frankly, I think he's only beholden to the Republicans until after his re-election," Jack said as he pushed aside some of his bleu cheese crumbles. "Then assuming he wins you'll see him turn on both parties and pursue an agenda that includes Congressional term limits, a balanced budget amendment, and the line-item veto."

"Power to the people," Bill said sarcastically. "He may be the only one in this town with unabashedly anti-Federalist views. I'm certainly not the only one around here that says, 'you can't make sausage without a little pork.'"

The Palm restaurant was a third-generation family-owned favorite among D.C. bureaucrats and local celebrities, especially those with their caricatures on the wall. Bill did not fancy the place since there was more than one restaurant of the same name. He had outgrown his liking for chain restaurants three terms ago and much preferred the independent eateries owned by the local gourmet chefs. As the senior Senator from Tennessee, he was also disappointed that a cartoon of his mug did not yet adorn the walls of the Palm. Jack, on the other hand, could not have cared less. He was just another unchanging face of the Deep State, though he hated the President's use of the term.

Tonight, they dined in Booth 21 with its caricature of Wolf Blitzer staring over Jack's left shoulder, right at Bill.

"I spoke to Pam Bailey yesterday about the President's Commission on Combating Drug Addiction and the Opioid Crisis," Bill remarked, trying to maintain eye contact with Jack despite the distraction of Wolf in his peripheral vision.

"And what did our favorite Florida Attorney General have to say?" Jack inquired.

"Pam said the President is not just paying lip service to the subject unlike previous administrations. She said he is genuinely disturbed by the epidemic of opioid deaths that are making the COVID-19 virus look like the common cold."

"And what's he going to do, send the U.S. military over the border to take on the drug lords?" Jack asked rhetorically.

"In fact, that's one of the prongs of their plan," Bill said as he reached for his first glass of Opus One poured from the second bottle. "But the drug cartels are just part of the problem, albeit a big part. They traffic in the illicit opioids like heroin and counterfeit versions of fentanyl, as well as the non-opioid narcotics like cocaine, methamphetamine, and MDMA or Ecstasy."

"Drug trafficking across our southern border is big business," Jack acknowledged. "I know the Sinaloa cartel is the big dog and I was only half joking about sending in the U.S. military."

"The truth is, the Mexican government worked closely with our embedded DEA agents to bring down Joaquín 'El Chapo' Guzmán," Bill said. "After extradition and conviction for crimes, including murder, 'Shorty' is now serving a life sentence at the Supermax in Colorado, and the cartel hasn't missed a beat. It's a multibillion-dollar industry defended by a killing machine with tactical training and modern weaponry."

"And they're only part of the problem, you say?" Jack posed, taking a sip from his glass of tangerine flavored LaCroix. "What, pray tell, is the other part of the problem?"

"Prescription opioids," Bill replied, wondering whether cherry cobbler would pair well with Opus One. It would no doubt go much better with a cortado, with or without a shot of Jameson, but he was quite sure they would not let him out the door with the rest of the bottle of wine. "Today, prescription opioids account for well over half of all the drug overdose deaths in this country. In fact, 80 percent of all heroin users were initially abusers of prescription opioids. Think about that the next time you fill your prescription for Percocet after a dental extraction. Since the individual is no longer responsible or accountable for his or her own actions these days, the question is, 'Who is to blame'? Truth be told, there is plenty of blame to place at the feet of doctors, nurses, and pharmacists for over-prescribing and under monitoring the use of these powerful analgesics. However, and further exemplified by their courage during the COVID-19 pandemic, our healthcare providers have attained superhero status."

"Yeah, I love the picture of Superman, Batman, Wonder Woman and other superheroes lining the walls of a hospital and bowing to the gowned and masked doctors and nurses walking by, as if to say, 'you are the true superheroes,'" Jack added.

"Our newest first responders," Bill remarked. "Right up there with the public safety heroes of 9-11. It would be political suicide to go after the caregivers, especially now. No, the high ground is to go after the greedy executives and damnable drug companies that overproduce, over promote and over sell these narcotics, taking advantage of the least fortunate among us."

"So, just exactly what does the President have in mind that would involve the FTC, let alone my Bureau?"

"We have reason to believe - make that evidence - that the major opioid manufacturers have covertly formed a consortium and are colluding to protect their fiefdom in the multibillion-dollar prescription opioid business," Bill stated with some degree of disdain.

"What do you mean by *colluding*?" Jack questioned. "Since the Mueller investigation into election interference by the Russians, we have become acutely aware that collusion is not an illegal activity and, apparently, falls short of an impeachable offense as well. I really thought we had the guy on that one."

"Careful Jack, lest you find yourself deserving of the 'Deep State' moniker. Reliable sources are telling us that senior executives of these drug companies are colluding - make that conspiring - to collaborate on the labeling, marketing, and promotion of opioids for pain management that includes anti-competitive practices and price fixing."

"Can you say, 'Bureau of Competition?'" Jack quipped.

"Seriously, the President's Commission would like your Bureau to investigate any wrongdoing by these executives," Bill said with the game face of a seasoned politician. "Since our sources have not yet gone public with their allegations, there has been no retaliation by their companies to date, so there can be no protection under the whistleblower provisions. Rather, it is our hope that you can substantiate the allegations, so we can have the DOJ empanel a federal grand jury to seek criminal indictments without risk of failure."

Jack thought for a moment as he drank his after-dinner half-caf and half-decaf coffee. Just enough caffeine, he thought, to keep himself alert for the remainder of their conversation, but not enough to prevent a sound sleep that night. He had passed on dessert. Surprisingly, so had Bill.

"Listen, Bill," Jack began. "The Commission and the Bureau have a great record of accomplishment working together with the DOJ to successfully prosecute antitrust cases against drug companies and criminal conspiracy complaints against some of their executives. However, most of these cases have targeted a single bad actor, not half an industry. Some of the cases were settled for substantial dollar amounts that inured to the benefit of the federal government and not to those harmed, while others ended in prison terms for executives whose behavior was particularly egregious. Unfortunately, most cases are simply withdrawn for lack of evidence or loss of inertia. The fact is these cases are very costly and time consuming to pursue. Administrations come and go long before the fat lady sings, hence the loss of inertia when it looks like the opposition party will get the credit for the takedown."

"Well, that's disheartening," Bill said with all sincerity. "I can tell you this President couldn't care less which party gets the credit, as long as the American people are duly served. On the other hand, patience is not his strong suit, and you could find yourself bullied regardless of your pace or progress. He's a businessman that learned how to use a stick, not a politician that learned how to use a bottomless bag of carrots!"

"That's a bit cynical, even coming from the dark side, don't you think?" Jack chided.

"Maybe," Bill said, "But where does that leave me? Empty handed!" Looking over Jack's shoulder he could swear the dispassionate face of Wolf Blitzer suddenly grinned. He hoped it was just the Opus One.

"I'm a mergers and acquisitions attorney, M&A by training and experience," Jack exclaimed. "So, this is not my area of expertise and probably not my place to opine, but if it were my call, I'd give up the criminal pursuits and toss it over the fence to the junkyard dogs of tort. Support them in filing a class action lawsuit with multiple legal theories against multiple defendants. Wrongful death, negligent manufacturing, deceptive advertising, misbranding, fraud, and conspiracy. Hell, I'd even throw in the wrong-colored kitchen sink!"

"Sounds like the approach that brought down Big Tobacco," Bill recalled. "Billions collected from virtually all the major players in the sector with millions awarded in damages to the widows and widowers of former smokers."

"The difference, of course, is that tobacco is a vice, not a virtue," Jack observed. "On the other hand, Big Pharma and biotech opioid manufacturers are the purveyors of pain relief, which is a virtue if you're the one in pain. And not just pain, but a myriad of other conditions. Don't forget, these are the deities that developed the COVID-19 diagnostic tests in a matter of weeks and vaccines in a matter of months. Right alongside the other superheroes of the day. Going after this group can't look good on your resume."

With that, Bill put the check on his government-issued American Express card with a tip assuring that his caricature would be on the wall by his next visit. The two pushed back from the table and headed toward the front door.

"What did one alligator say to the other?" Bill asked as he put his credit card away and his arm around Jack. "If you're going to swim in this swamp, you need to keep your nose above the waterline!"

2

Washington, D.C.

Jack asked his secretary to get his boss the FTC Chairman on the phone. When Jack's secretary had the Chairman's secretary on the line, she patched the call through to Jack. As Jack picked up, the Chairman's secretary said, "One moment for Mr. Fitzsimons." It was the protocol that crystalized the pecking order in the minds of both parties, whether you were an executive in the public or private sector. After a few wasted moments of silence, establishing whose time was more valuable, he finally heard, "Good morning, Jack!"

"Good morning, sir!"

Jack proceeded to brief his boss on the conversation he had had the night before with the Senate Majority Leader. He conveniently omitted the part about the Palm, the Opus One, and Wolf Blitzer.

"Sir," Jack said with all due respect, "Bill Bassett said the President is dead serious about tackling the opioid crisis with more firepower than previous administrations deployed. He said they have evidentiary reason to believe the major opioid manufacturers are conspiring to engage in shared anticompetitive programs and price fixing."

"What kind of evidence?" Fitzsimons asked.

Ray Fitzsimons was a man of few words, but one who could bring a Fortune 500 company CEO to their knees. He was one of the forty-six Heads of Federal Agencies or Commissions, in addition to the fourteen Cabinet Secretaries, that reported directly to the President. Only the President and his wife called him "Fitz." All the others just called him "Sir."

Bad, Bad Leroy Brown, Jack thought.

"Well, sir," Jack answered. "The conspiracy is thinly veiled on the inside but well disguised from the outside. Fortunately, some of the more self-serving employees have come forward. Whistleblowers that have not yet gone public and have not yet been fingered by their respective companies. The price fixing is very subtle. Not overt collaboration on wholesale or retail drug prices, which could be easily detected, but things like information sharing on discounts, credits, wastage and breakage allowances, buy-backs, and a myriad of other creative ways to manipulate bookable net sales."

"And what about their anticompetitive practices?" Fitzsimons questioned.

Concise. Cut to the chase. It reminded Jack of the fabled story of when Fitzsimons went to the mat over some lame-brain Congressman's proposal to adopt Helvetica as the standard government font, after Apple concluded it was the most readable. Fitzsimons asserted that it would be unwise to abandon Times New Roman 14 since this font and size had been long recognized by the private sector as heralding an official government communication. Just its appearance struck terror in the eyes of its readers and commanded their compliance. Nothing more was said and nothing more was done.

"Most notable are the subtle omissions from the Chemistry, Manufacturing and Controls (CMC) section of the New Drug Application (NDA) for a branded drug that makes it nearly impossible for generic competitors to duplicate," Jack said. "Senator Bassett also implied that there were hard-to-find electronic files memorializing kickbacks to federal regulators that were made in exchange for favored treatment on matters of compliance or enforcement involving the FDA and SEC."

"Did you tell Bassett that these matters are very costly and time consuming to prosecute?" Fitzsimons asked. "He's a lawyer, and a damn good one from what I hear. He should know these matters are rarely resolved before the cards are reshuffled from the top of the deck. I'll call the President tomorrow just to be sure he concurs, but you need to go back to Bill and suggest that he pursue his options with the DOJ instead."

Badder than old King Kong and meaner than a junkyard dog.

3

Washington, D.C.

"One moment for the President," the White House secretary said.

One one-thousand, two one-thousand, three one-thousand, Ray Fitzsimons counted to himself while waiting for the President to pick up.

"Hello, Fitz!" the President said in a jovial tone.

"Good afternoon, sir," the FTC Chairman replied. "I won't keep you long. Just wanted to relay a little conversation Jack Powell had the other night with Bill Bassett."

"Remind me again, who's Jack Powell?"

"Chief of the Bureau of Competition over here at FTC, sir. His team is responsible for investigating anticompetitive practices in the private sector. If warranted, with the consent of the full Commission, I would call the AG to recommend empaneling a grand jury for further investigation and possible indictments. Or, with sufficient and irrefutable evidence, I might suggest moving straight to federal charges."

"Thanks Fitz," the President said. "It's a big damn organization you know. Don't get me wrong, I'm used to a big damn organization. Gave one up to sit in this chair. But the White House org chart looks like Secretariat's stud record."

"Yes sir, that it does," Fitz agreed. "For background, let me say that Jack and I are both lawyers. Mergers and acquisitions when we were in the private sector, but breakups on this side of the fence."

"Lawyers, yep," the President quipped. "Lots of lawyers in this town. Can't swing a dead cat around here without hitting a bunch of lawyers. Cats. That's what we need. More cats!"

"More cats. Yes sir," Fitz said. "In any event, the Senate has come across some whistleblowers in the opioid industry that claim to have evidence their companies are conspiring to share anticompetitive practices and fix drug prices. I don't need to tell you that drilling into something like that can take years and cost millions, and you can still come up dry. Your call, of course. But there's another path, and credit to Jack. It occurred to him to let the private sector handle this one. Keep our hands clean. No criminal charges, just civil suits by tort lawyers that we can claim to have no control over. They brought Big Tobacco down several rungs and the incidence of smoking is now just one in eight adults. Going after the Big Pharma opioid companies could have a similar effect on mortality rates from overdose."

"I like it," the President beamed. "We wouldn't be the bad guys going after the latest group of superheroes; the developers of testing kits and vaccines for COVID-19 standing up the first responders of healthcare."

"Precisely," Fitz said. "But there is a caveat. When Big Tobacco coughed up billions, pun intended, the only ones hurt were the stakeholders of an industry despised by the public and derided by the media. No shortage of folks willing to trade liberty and freedom for safety and security. Nevertheless, Big Pharma is a different animal. We're all stakeholders in a sense. If this industry is made to pay billions in damages, real and punitive, its allocations to pharmaceutical and biological research and development would be compromised for years to come. The negative consequences to public health would be immeasurable."

"Well Fitz," the President sighed. "Sounds like we're between a rock and hard spot on this one. I sure would like to reverse the ugly trend of deaths by overdose. Much like the homeless suffering from mental illness, these are folks that really need our help, and not just lip service. I'll need to give it more thought. Thanks, Fitz. Oh, and tell Jack that I'll have the White House staff send him an autographed portrait of me behind my desk in the Oval Office." On that note, he disconnected from the call.

I wonder who picks up first, the President or God? Fitz thought.

4

Durham, NC

Her breath was visible in the subzero temperature, and she became acutely aware of the hair follicles in her nose. On days when Mia was in the drug discovery laboratory at the Duke Center for Opioid Research (DCOR), she often made several trips into the walk-in freezer near the back of the laboratory. The perimeter was lined with stainless steel racks containing a myriad of opioid compounds; samples acquired over many years of research.

Mia saw that two of the samples were the naturally occurring opioids, morphine and codeine, isolated from the poppy seeds of opium plants. Other samples like hydrocodone, oxycodone, and hydromorphone were derived from morphine or codeine using different chemical reactions and synthetic pathways. Still others were the opioids like meperidine, fentanyl, and tramadol that were made from other starting chemicals. As a second-year postdoctoral research fellow, Mia knew them all by these chemical names, but she was also familiar with most of their prescription brand names like Demerol, Dilaudid, OxyContin and Duragesic. These were the opioid drugs that were FDA-approved as narcotic analgesics and designated Schedule II controlled substances because of their addictive nature and abuse potential. Prescribers were required to be registered with the Drug Enforcement Administration (DEA). Mia knew there were lots of other branded products like Percodan, Percocet, Hycodan and Vicodin that combined one of the FDA-approved opioids together with aspirin or acetaminophen, but there were no samples of these in the freezer because only the pure opioids were of research interest to DCOR. The freezer also contained hundreds if not thousands of other opioid derivatives that had been synthesized but less well characterized as analgesics and never developed as pharmaceuticals. The DCOR freezer was a veritable chemical library of the standards in opioid research.

Mia Reinhardt, PhD, had earned her doctorate from the University of Kentucky College of Pharmacy in Lexington. She had been more passionate about a career in research pharmacology than a more patient-oriented discipline like hospital pharmacy, so she elected the PhD track over the PharmD. Her graduate research had been in the field of opioids; less a choice and more a calling. A couple of years back she had lost her older brother Warren to a fentanyl overdose. He had been a star college quarterback at the University of Florida, but a knee injury ended his athletic aspirations, and opioids ended his life. His post-surgical pain had been managed with oxycodone which led to chronic addiction and ultimately, tragically, heartbreakingly, to a fatal overdose of fentanyl. Mia was intimately familiar with the *wonderful* analgesic effects of opioids and with their *dreadful* addictive properties. She vowed to honor his memory by discovering and developing something better.

Wonderful without dreadful.

Walking past all the well-known and lesser-known opioids in the freezer, Mia focused on a collection of 100 unknown compounds in the corner that had been made by RxFactor, a San Diego-based synthetic chemistry company in the business of creating designer molecules for universities and drug companies. The collection was referred to at DCOR as the *T-series*. Each unique sample was contained in an amber glass vial with a black screw cap and labeled T001-T100, unlike all the other samples in the freezer that had labels with chemical names.

Mia was fascinated by these newly synthesized molecules, all virtual unknowns but each hoping to contribute to medicine someday. They were in amber vials because it was not yet known whether any were sensitive to light and subject to photodegradation. They were stored in the freezer because subzero temperatures extended the shelf life of most compounds, including macromolecules like insulin, antibodies, and vaccines, just as refrigeration better preserves most foods.

She had already completed her initial testing of T001-T090 and was now ready for T091-T100. Lifting the white cardboard box containing these ten vials, she left the freezer holding the precious cargo with both hands. Using her backside to close the freezer door, she walked across the laboratory and placed the vials on a benchtop nearby. When the circulation returned to her fingers and nose, she pulled up a stool and began to arrange the vials such that each label was legible from her vantage point. Perfectly straight. Perfectly aligned. Perfect! Mia was aware of her obsessive-compulsive disorder (OCD), but hoped it was just a personality trait and not a full-blown nine-alarm neurosis. She prayed it would never come to Zoloft or Prozac.

Dr. Mark Oberon, the center Director, walked into the drug discovery laboratory unannounced as Mia was thawing the last cohort of the T-series and preparing it for testing.

"Dr. Reinhardt," Mark thundered. "What's on the agenda today that should have been on the agenda yesterday?" he chafed only half in jest. If she was borderline OCD, he was just one spending spree shy of certifiably manic. Mark was well regarded by his colleagues, students, laboratory technicians and postdoctoral fellows as a talented clinician and dedicated scientist, but his adrenaline levels were near pathologic.

"I just finished preparing the last ten compounds from RxFactor and I'm wondering if your Nobel Prize is among them?" she replied only half-jokingly as well. Mark was widely rumored to be a contender for the prestigious award, and a major clinical contribution in the form of a new drug derived from his research hypothesis would cement the deal.

Mark Oberon, MD, PhD was Chief of the Pain Management Clinic at Duke Medical Center and Director of the Duke Center for Opioid Research, and he was the principal reason Mia had chosen Duke for her postdoctoral studies. Mark was a Duke graduate, Blue Devil through and through, and he treasured the school's celebrated athletic department but rarely went to any of its sporting events. Whereas Mia was motivated by the memory of her brother, Mark was driven by a natural curiosity. He continuously questioned the world he knew with anxious anticipation of the next answer. And the world he knew as well as anyone on the planet was the world of opioids.

Mark was a pioneer in the field of opioid research. He had published on the pathways of pain signaling through nerve cells that communicate with the brain and on the mechanisms by which the brain perceives pain. He and others had shown that natural substances in the brain called endorphins were released in response to painful stimuli and reduced the perception of pain. These were the body's own natural analgesics, and opioids used the same pathways for pain relief. It was well accepted that there were at least three different opioid pathways and they had been named using the Greek letters mu, delta, and kappa.

Opioids such as morphine, codeine, oxycodone, and fentanyl preferred the mu pathway and were very effective analgesics but highly addictive. They were also associated with euphoria, or a mood-altering sense of well-being better known on the street as a "high" and had a propensity to cause respiratory arrest and death in the case of an overdose. Opioids such as ketazocine and pentazocine preferred the kappa pathway and were also very effective analgesics and highly addictive. But these compounds caused the opposite effects on respiration and mood, namely respiratory stimulation and dysphoria marked by a sense of uneasiness or frank hallucinations. As such, these had fallen out of clinical favor. Few compounds had been reported to utilize the delta opioid pathway and much less was known about its function.

The center of Mark's universe was his discovery of a fourth opioid pathway. He had named it using the Greek letter theta after finding it was the preferred pathway of tetracyclozine. This was an old compound retrieved from his extensive chemical library that he had found to be a very effective analgesic and surprisingly less addictive and euphoric than other opioids. Since he knew that all opioids, including tetracyclozine, were very effective analgesics but differed in terms of their side effects, it caused Mark to wonder whether all four pathways are mediators of pain relief, but not all mediators of opioid side effects. This was supported by his observation that the mu and kappa signaling pathways had opposite effects on respiration and mood. Mark's hypothesis was that a new opioid highly selective for the theta opioid pathway, with no predilection for the others, would be a *nonaddictive* opioid pain reliever. The perfect narcotic analgesic. And finding one became his mission in life.

"I'm glad you stopped by because I'm curious to know," Mia asked. "That's an impressive library of compounds you have in the freezer, including some opioid samples that I'm guessing are very rare. How did you come by them?"

"Many are simply samples of the opioid drugs on the market today. Some I purchased in their pure form from raw chemical manufacturers. Others I obtained by horse trading with colleagues from around the world, some of my opioids for some of theirs, much like numismatists trade coins."

"What about the box labeled *endorphins*?"

"It contains samples of the protein fragments called peptides that are released in the brain in response to painful stimuli and act as the body's own natural analgesics. These are the reason we can tolerate levels of pain that would otherwise be intolerable and may explain why different individuals and different species have different thresholds for pain."

"I also noticed a compound called *diamorphine*," Mia said. "It's apparently a morphine derivative, but I frankly don't recall having studied that one."

"Probably because it's not an approved therapeutic. It's the chemical name for heroin and it's derived from the simple acetylation of morphine. Diamorphine is a Schedule I controlled substance, so designated by the FDA because it is highly addictive and has no recognized medical use. Of course, the manufacturer, distribution or possession of these substances is illegal in the United States and most everywhere else."

"I'll give the DEA a call. You'll look great in pinstripe!" Mia mussed.

"I have a special research license. They know me well," he mugged.

"Are all the samples in the freezer single compounds? she asked.

"Most are individual compounds either man made or isolated from plants or marine life. But a few are extracts from the poppy seeds of opium plants and contain a mixture or tincture of morphine and codeine. One of the most interesting is a very rare unopened bottle of laudanum. It dates from the late 1800s and its formal name is Opium Tincture, USP. You know Mia, prior to 1914, anyone could purchase opium products from a neighborhood pharmacy or apothecary without a prescription. There's even good evidence that opium extracts were used for pain relief back in the days of Hippocrates around 400 B.C., but I haven't yet laid my hands on a sample from his collection!"

"I'll keep an eye out the next time I'm in Greece," Mia said smiling. "Although not literally or anatomically. That would be gross!"

Mia continued working while carrying on the conversation. Ever the multitasker. Verifying that the samples of T091-T100 had all thawed, she transferred a small quantity of each to an array of 10x10 plastic vials such that each row was a different compound. Then she used a multichannel micropipette to make serial dilutions of each sample, so each row now contained ten different concentrations of each compound. The concentrations ranged from nanograms at low end to milligrams at the high end per millimeter of aqueous solution.

"Tell me Mark," Mia asked. "I know each of these samples is a novel new molecule that is structurally related to tetracyclozine, but why did you select tetracyclozine as the starting molecule for synthesis of the T-series of opioids? Oh my gosh, I just realized that's why you named it the T-series! It's a big secret, I know, but my lips are sealed. Besides, among the many documents that I signed when I started my fellowship was a nondisclosure agreement. I think it gives Duke the right to my first born if I speak out of school, or out of laboratory as it were!"

"And your second born!" Mark said, wagging a finger. "As you know, my hypothesis is that an opioid that is highly selective for the theta opioid pathway will be a nonadditive narcotic analgesic. Unfortunately, tetracyclozine is not that selective, but it's a good place to start. Based on its structural differences from other opioids, RxFactor should be able to find a related compound that uses *just* the theta pathway. Just one new patentable molecule. The pièce de resistance!" Mark said with a perfect Parisian accent.

"So, we're basically looking for a needle in a haystack and the T-series of compounds is our haystack!"

"That's a terrific analogy!" Mark said. "And our newly patented assay is our metal detector!" Using the word "our" to characterize the haystack was as a sign of her shared commitment and was not lost on him. To reinforce her devotion, if not subliminally, he used the same word to characterize his assay.

Two pioneers with the same vision but different motives.

Mia gazed at the black plastic rack that contained the 10x10 array of vials and thought about how the different concentrations essentially represented a different dose of a potential drug. She knew the range was broad because they had no idea just how potent or impotent each sample would be with respect to its desired effect. Ultimately, the desired effect would be analgesia in whole animals and human subjects, but for now they were testing in human cells that were maintained alive in a nutrient-rich broth.

Since pain itself cannot be measured in cells, Mark had developed an assay that measured fluorescence in response to a test compound added to cells. To connect the fluorescence directly to pain signaling in cells, he had purchased a population of human cells that he then divided into four groups. Each group was then genetically engineered to over produce just one of the opioid pathways. Test compounds would then be added to each of the four cell groups, and their fluorescent responses to increasing doses would be observed under a specialized microscope. The brighter the green fluorescence the greater the potency and selectivity of the test compound for the opioid pathway of that cell group. Compounds of interest would be those that fluoresced brightly in the theta cell group with no fluorescence in the mu, kappa, or delta cell groups.

"I think your characterization of our assay as a metal detector is quite clever. Almost as clever as having named it the Fluoropioid assay, which is very descriptive of its utility. Is it trademarked?" Mia asked.

"It is, right along with a utility patent on the assay methodology and a new use patent on the tetracyclozine molecule," Mark replied.

"You know, in addition to your hypothesis, the Fluoropioid assay was another big reason that I applied to Duke for my fellowship. Do you plan to commercialize the assay?"

"Perhaps someday, but for now it's our competitive advantage. Lots of *opioidologists* out there, as I like to refer to our ilk, and the Fluoropioid assay gives us a big jump on the competition!"

"Now I appreciate why you had me spend the better part of my first year automating the assay for high-throughput drug screening. Your little manual benchtop assay was only amenable to viewing through a confocal microscope. Let's see, 100 different compounds at ten different doses run through four different cell groups ... hmmm ... that's 4,000 visualizations. If I didn't go blind, at the very least I would have developed a bad case of strabismus!"

"And that would be no way to treat a fellow now, would it?" Mark said with a smirk. "But you're right about automating the assay, and not out of a concern for your ophthalmologic health as much as the fact that visual observations of fluorescent responses are just *qualitative* and subject to the vagaries of interpretation. The automated method which integrates digital signals of fluorescence with computerized analyses gives us a precise *quantitative* interpretation of the results. And let me say again what a great job you did converting the manual assay to high throughput."

"Thanks, boss," Mia said endearingly. "I'll run the assay on T091-T100 through the night and we should have the results in the morning."

"What do you say we meet in my office this Friday morning around eight o'clock, if that works for you? By then you should have the Fluoropioid results for the entire T-series, and we can see what we have."

Mark looked back at Mia and, as she nodded in the affirmative, he raised his right hand and flipped her the middle finger crossed over the index finger, then headed out the door.

Good luck, indeed, she thought.

AFTER SETTING THE Fluoropioid high-throughput screening system on autopilot for the night, Mia drove her 10-year-old Subaru Outback a mere eight minutes to a contemporary three-bedroom ranch on Woodburn Road in Duke Forest. She had rented a room there since her first day in Durham and had selected the location based on its equal proximity to DCOR and the Duke University Golf Club. She had been on the high school golf team in Valencia, California and maintained a GHIN index of 4 during her two years at College of Canyons prior to transferring to the University of Kentucky. Her six-foot frame and athletic build made her a long ball hitter with a big arc to her swing and her approach shots were deadly accurate. It was her short game that put the LPGA out of reach. Regardless, she loved the sport and the recreation of walking a course with or without a caddie. She managed to get in a round at the Club now and then but quit keeping her GHIN score after she had moved to Lexington.

"Another day, another dollar," Mia said as she walked through the front door and tossed her car keys into a decorative sweetgrass bowl sitting in the alcove of the vestibule.

"A dollar a day?" Jillian questioned. "I knew they were paying you too much," she joked as she looked up from her reading of an animal study protocol that had been submitted to the Animal Care Committee at Duke. This was the University's veterinary equivalent of its Institutional Review Board for human research and assured the humane treatment of subjects.

Jillian Saunders, DVM, had become more of a friend to Mia than a landlord. Jillian had graduated from Michigan State University School of Veterinary Medicine in East Lansing and had been a staff veterinarian at DCOR for a couple of years before her promotion to Director of the small-animal laboratory last year. The two of them were looking forward to working together as soon as Mia had some lead compounds to begin testing in animals. Jillian was also the Chairman of the Animal Care

Committee at Duke which positioned her well to facilitate Mia's preclinical studies.

"What do you say we head to Spanos for a burger and a beer?" Jillian said with more enthusiasm than its menu deserved. "I hear there's a solo singer-songwriter there on Wednesday nights. Plays the guitar and heard he's pretty hot."

"Oh baby, swipe me right!" Mia said, revealing that she may have had some experience with online dating. "I'll tell you what. I'll join you for a less-than-nutritious meal, but I'll pass on the *hot* tonight. The last of my Fluoropioid test results will be ready in the morning and I'd like to be there bright and early for a quick read. Mark will be thrilled that we finished ahead of schedule. With any luck I'll be sending some preclinical protocols to your Animal Care Committee very soon."

"My fingers are crossed! Hey, if you'd like, I'll drive us to Spanos."

"Be my guest," Mia replied. "Your Audi RS 5 will catch more guitar players than my old Subaru Outback. Go Blue!"

"It's Go Green!"

"I know!" Mia said dismissively.

The two women jumped into Dr. Saunders' new racing-green Audi and headed for Spanos. Jillian was a Blue Devil by driver's license, but a Spartan by birth certificate.

5

Durham, NC

Mark was on his second cup of black Sumatran coffee and thumbing through the current issue of the *Journal of Opioid Management* when his phone rang. Looking at caller ID he saw it was Mia and picked up. "Good morning, Mia. Let me guess. You won't be ready by tomorrow."

"Au contraire, mon frère," Mia said with a little French twist. She knew Mark spoke French fluently.

"Est-ce que tu parles francais?" he replied with an accomplished accent.

"No, not really," Mia said sheepishly in English. "I did take two years of Latin when medical school was an option, but having gone down a basic science path, I don't think it did me much good."

"Trust me, it would not have helped much had you gone down a more clinical path either," Mark said reflecting upon his experiences.

Sedare dolorem opus divinum est, she thought, which translated, "alleviating pain is the work of the divine." It was one of the few Latin phrases that Mia could remember because it was one that inspired her.

"Listen," she said. "I know that Thursday is your day to be in the Pain Management Clinic, but I'm ready now with the Fluoropioid results for the entire tetracyclozine series made by

RxFactor, if you're available for a few minutes before you head over to the clinic."

"I'll be right down."

I had no doubt, she thought.

By the time Mia collected her laptop and notebooks and arrived at the drug discovery laboratory conference room, Mark was already there, second cup of black Sumatran still in hand.

"Caffeine?" she questioned. "In your case, isn't that like giving phenobarbital to a narcoleptic?"

Mark was amused by her reference to his manic ways and smiled as he took another sip of coffee. Then he watched as she began positioning her laboratory notebook left of and precisely equidistant from the top and bottom corners of her laptop. He had become familiar with the ritual, and let it pass.

"As you know," Mia said opening her laptop and launching a PDF file residing on her home screen, "we ran all the T-series compounds over a wide range of doses against the four cell groups each expressing a different opioid pathway. We know that tetracyclozine was the first compound discovered to utilize the theta opioid pathway."

Mark cleared his throat to remind her that he was the one who had made the discovery.

"Sorry," she said politely regarding his gesture. "Since tetracyclozine was the starting molecule for all the subsequent structural changes made by our chemistry partner, we would expect lots of them to utilize the theta opioid pathway and indeed the vast majority did. In fact, tetracyclozine itself was compound T001 and serves as a reference. In the series of 100 compounds, 87 were fluorescent green in the theta cell groups. Of those, 85 were also fluorescent to some extent in at least one of the other cell groups."

"Yes! Two!" Mark shouted, unable to contain his jubilation. "We found two needles in the haystack!" Mia just smiled with a big grin.

"T045 and T046 were positive only in the theta cell group," Mia said as she pointed to the screen. "The dose response data indicate that both are rather weak but clearly selective for the theta opioid pathway with absolutely no measurable activity vis-à-vis the other three opioid pathways. On the left is T045 with fluorescence that peaks at a medium dose. On the right is T046 with nearly identical fluorescence at the same dose. Disappointing that they are not more potent, huh?"

"Are you kidding me," Mark said. His enthusiasm was palpable. "All we needed was one, Mia. Just one structure that was highly selective for the theta pathway, regardless of potency, and we have two! All we need now is a little more synthesis around these two molecules to find one more potent. The right one. The perfect one! I'm no synthetic chemist but I do know they now use three-dimensional computer modeling to predict the best structures. Much like graphic artists employ computer animations that can be rotated and observed from different perspectives, chemists can use the same basic technology to conceive of new molecules composed of various atoms in three-dimensional space. Using the Fluoropioid data as a surrogate for analgesic activity, the chemists can look at the structure and activity relationships between the various molecules and opioid pathways. In this way they can predict what chemical groups or moieties need to be added to or subtracted from a given molecule to optimize its potency and selectivity for the pathway of interest.

"Designer drugs," Mia said. She was amazed.

"I know RxFactor has these data, but we should independently confirm the structures of T045 and T046. For this we'll need to ..." Mark said but Mia interrupted.

"To send samples to the Duke Chemistry Department for testing by gas chromatography with mass spectroscopy and nuclear magnetic resonance. I called them this morning, right after I called you!

We're two peas a pod, Mark thought.

"They told me they'll have both structures for us sometime next week," Mia said thinking that was reasonable. "What do you want to bet the two compounds are very similar?" she challenged as Mark was headed for the door.

"I won't bet against that," he said looking back.

When Mark returned to his corner office two floors above the drug discovery laboratory, he walked along the wall lined with wooden flip shelves that held the latest issues of the medical journals *Anesthesia & Analgesia*, *Anesthesiology*, and the *Journal of Pain Management,* as well as the basic science journals *PNAS* and *Nature*, and at least a dozen others like *JAMA* and *NEJM* which no self-respecting internist would be without. Flipping up any of the shelves would have revealed the last two years' worth of each. Old school, since they were all online.

Along the opposite wall was his teak credenza with a handsomely framed portrait of his family on one side and a three-dimensional model of the tetracyclozine molecule in colored tissue paper on the other side. A gift from RxFactor. He was hoping to replace it with a unique structure of his own someday. Above his credenza was an impressive collection of diplomas, licenses, certificates, and awards. In front was a large, highly polished teak and holly desk with a blonde leather high-back chair in the hue of the holly wood and two beautiful burnt-orange guest chairs in the hue of the teak. The minimalist motif was nautical. He took his seat behind the desk and pulled his phone out of his white coat pocket.

"Ron, it's Mark," he announced with no administrative assistance on either side of the call. Ron had answered on the second ring. Had he not it would have gone straight to voicemail.

Ronald Newberry, PhD, was Chairman of the Chemistry Department at Duke and a respected colleague of Mark's. The two had become better acquainted as Mark ventured ever deeper into drug discovery. Ron was notable for wearing a bowtie with matching suspenders every day and Mark could swear he never wore the same set twice.

"Listen," Mark said with no other pleasantries on this occasion. "I have a second-year research fellow here that sent over a couple of samples for structural confirmation. Your boys, or perhaps girls, told her that they would have the results to us sometime next week. Since you owe me one, any chance you can get them done yesterday?"

We need to get this boy on some lithium, Ron thought.

"I frankly can't recall who owes whom at this point," Ron said. "But look, we'll move those samples to the top of the queue. Should know what the little darlings look like in a day or two. How's that?"

"That's great! And thanks, you'll owe me one," Mark said.

That's not how it works, Ron thought.

6

Los Mochis, Sinaloa, Mexico

The air would have been stifling were it not for the old metal air conditioners hanging in a few of the windows. They could have used a fresh coat of paint years ago, but no one seemed motivated enough to lean into that job. On the other hand, it could have been worse. Much worse. The Albert K. Owen Colegio Bilingüe was a very private school in Los Mochis, a town of nearly 400,000 residents situated near the shore of the Gulf of California in the Mexican state of Sinaloa. It was a nice building surrounded by low-income housing. Its cinder block and white stucco facade had been freshly painted with royal blue, red and gold stripes. There were a few parking spaces in front along the street, but most of the children were dropped off by their parents.

Pedro was one of the lucky few to be a student there and a cheerful little dark-haired seven-year-old boy with deep dimples in both cheeks. He was also fortunate to have both a father and a mother at home, and both biological. His mother, Margarite Martinez, was an ex-patriot from the U.S. side of the border town of Nogales. She had met her husband, Miguel, when he was living on the Mexican side and working border patrol for the Federales. On his days off, he would cross into Arizona for a round of golf at the Tubac Resort and Spa with his patrol buddies. Margarite had been working the beverage cart for minimum wage and tips after having graduated from Nogales High

School two years earlier. One day Miguel had tipped her handsomely then returned on many subsequent occasions to do the same.

"Class," the profesora announced in perfect English. "Time to close your books, gather up your things, and don't forget to work on your assignments tonight." Salma Flores was a very attractive former Miss Mexico and the scholarship award had put her through the Universidad de Guadalajara. She had received her Bachelor of Arts in English along with a teaching certificate and was very well paid by the Colegio Bilingüe since her students were from the high society of Sinaloa. Most of the parents had significant business dealings with the U.S., so English was an important subject for her students. In fact, much of the classwork was taught in English. Pedro's father, Miguel, spoke very broken English, although he understood nearly every word he heard. He had little respect for the gringos and no interest in learning their language except for what he needed to get the job done, whatever it was. Margarite, on the other hand, was bilingual, having spent her youth on both sides of the border, and her vocabulary was expansive in both languages. Spanish was spoken at home.

"I see that some of your parents have already arrived," Salma said, peering over the heads of the students through the front windows.

Pedro lifted his black North Face backpack from the back of his chair and headed toward the windows. Coming down the busted concrete road was his father's white 1973 Ferrari Daytona Spyder. Mint condition. It pulled into the only available parking space right near the front door and Pedro rushed out. He rounded the front of the car and headed for the passenger-side door. Before Pedro could enter, Miguel got out. Dressed in a white sport coat with white beltless pants and a sky-blue T-shirt, he looked like a regular Don Juan Johnson. *Miami Vice* reruns were a staple entertainment for him when he wasn't preoccupied, which was rarely. He motioned the boy over and gave Pedro a hug, then asked him to wait outside for a few minutes while he went into the school.

"I'll only be a minute, son," Miguel said in Spanish. He opened the front door and headed inside. Pedro was not quite sure why his father needed to go into the school. He was not in any trouble, so far as he knew.

"Ms. Flores, so delightful to see you again," Miguel gushed in his best broken English.

"Ah, Mr. Martinez, so nice to see you as well," Salma said in a hushed voice so the others could not hear. "But please, call me Salma. In fact, call me whatever you'd like. Just call me!"

"The last time that I called you we didn't leave that hotel room in Culiacan for three days," Miguel quietly boasted. "Room service. The entire weekend. Oysters, caviar and champagne."

"I don't know if it was the oysters, or your, well ... you know," Salma purred. "But I'm guessing that's what all your women say about your, well ... you know."

"All my women?" he feigned disgust. "C'mon. You know you're my only squeeze, other than my wife, of course."

"Your wife?" she feigned surprise. "You never told me you were married!" They both snickered.

"Well, at least you know you're *my* only squeeze," she said with no sincerity.

As Miguel turned to leave, she smacked him on the backside, accidently flipping up the back of his coat and revealing the butt of his Kimber EVO SP Raptor 9mm with custom rosewood grips. It was his up-close-and-personal weapon of choice, and he used it frequently. As he took another step, the coattail flipped back down over the gun before she had a chance to mention it was exposed, but it was no shock to her. She had seen it many times. It was never beyond his reach, even in their most compromised of positions.

The white Spyder zipped down and around the city streets without much regard for pedestrians or authorities that may have been lying in wait. As for pedestrians, he had no empathy for human life whether family, friend, or foe. As for the authorities, he owned them.

As a young border agent in Nogales, Miguel had made a rookie mistake of opening the trunk of a rusted old Cadillac Eldorado, rather than having the driver do it himself. He never heard the shot fired from the trunk of the car. Later he had learned that it was because the muzzle velocity of a jacketed hollow-point 357 Magnum at 1295 fps is slightly faster than the speed of sound through ambient air at 1125 fps. He only remembered waking up in a hospital bed on a breathing tube with his mouth wired shut. The bullet had ripped through his right cheek and passed through his mouth to the other side, shattering his left jawbone and blowing out three molars before exiting his left check. Fortunately, a maxillofacial surgeon was able to reconstruct the mandible and repair the temporomandibular joint (TMJ), as well as the teeth, and a plastic surgeon had restored his cheeks. Miguel had been fortunate that his head was not another inch closer to the trunk. During his hospitalization they must have chilled his intravenous fluids because from that day forward he had ice in his veins. Stone cold. The only residual complication was a slight TMJ disorder. If he opened his mouth too wide, it would produce a clicking sound with slight pain. He quickly learned to avoid the discomfort by adopting a Marlon Brando-like speech pattern. However, when he got mad, he would do it intentionally.

His phone was held on the dashboard of the white Spyder by a magnetic mount, and the Bluetooth hands-free speaker was enabled. The GPS and location services were disabled for privacy, and the instrumental theme to *Miami Vice* blasted from the car stereo with plenty of bass. The tune always put him in a badass mood. About a mile from his coastal villa, the phone rang.

He reached for the volume control knob mounted on the radio rather than the steering wheel, which dated the vehicle. Typically, he would answer his phone with a simple "Si." Nothing more. Nothing less. But the caller's name appeared on his phone.

"Si, señor," Miguel answered, recognizing it was his boss.

Hector Morales nicknamed "El Enterrador" was not just the center of his universe, he was the Lord and Master. He was also the only man on earth that Miguel truly feared. Miguel had quickly climbed the ranks of the Federales to become a respected member of the Presidential Guard until his duties as a liaison with the cartel and bagman for the Guard led to a better offer in the private sector. In the months that followed the Federales' raid on a home in Los Mochis that resulted in the capture and arrest of Joaquin "El Chapo" Guzman, there had been a violent struggle for control of the Sinaloa drug cartel. El Enterrador had been Shorty's senior enforcer and personally responsible for a body count not seen since the days of Pablo Escobar in Columbia. However, Ismael Garcia, El Chapo's closest and most trusted associate, had been widely expected to assume leadership of the cartel. That never happened.

"Miguel," El Enterrador blared over the phone. "We're having a little trouble with El Contador. I'll explain later, but I need you and the boys to send him a stern message. Did I say stern? Let me be clear. Don't kill him. We need him. I don't give a shit about his goons but leave El Contador standing. Scared, but standing."

Miguel ended that call and made another, then deposited Pedro in the driveway of their beautiful three-story seaside villa. Wrapped in cobblestones from a local quarry with a baked clay tile roof, it could not be seen from the road. Any road. In fact, on the few occasions when El Enterrador had paid a visit, he came from the seaside and landed on the helipad near the tennis court.

"Tell your mother not to wait up for me," Miguel said to his son. "I think it's going to be a long night. Don't forget to do your homework." By all appearances, Miguel was a good husband, loving father, and capable provider. But inwardly, nothing. Stone cold.

He spun the car around the circle drive and raced back up the long black asphalt driveway. He had selected asphalt over concrete during construction because he liked the way asphalt grabbed the rubber tires of the Spyder. All torque. No spin. El Enterrador was The Gravedigger, and El Contador was The Accountant. Miguel aspired to an equally imposing alias, namely El Ejecutor, The Enforcer, and this was his opportunity to prove himself.

A few miles up the road, Miguel was joined by a convoy of khaki green and gray military surplus vehicles. In front was a Willys M38 Jeep with a mounted and manned Browning 50mm machine gun. Behind it was a late-model black Cadillac Escalade with armor-plated doors and bulletproof glass, followed by two canvas-covered personnel transport vehicles, each containing at least a dozen well-armed men. Falling in behind Miguel were two more personnel transports with another Willys M38 covering the rear. The white Spyder was sandwiched in between them all and looked a little cartoonish. Tubbs would have made some snide remark.

Miguel was now the enforcer for El Enterrador, not yet by title, but certainly by deed. The Gravedigger had been the enforcer for El Chapo before his capture and had taught Miguel a hundred different ways to kill a man. At least as many bodies were a testament to his training. Slowly and agonizingly, quickly and painlessly, thoughtfully and purposefully, or spontaneously and just for the hell of it. Miguel was good at all manner of death. The best.

There was no communication between vehicles. None was needed. This operation fell under thoughtful and purposeful.

After a 30-minute drive into the foothills near the town of Morelos, the complex came into view as they crested the last hill. Two large metal warehouses with rusted corrugated rooves were visible in the distance and several smaller buildings were scattered nearby, apparently residential. The area was surrounded by a 12-foot cyclone fence topped with rusted razor wire, and two old guard shacks were positioned near the gated entrance. Beyond the fence and rising all around were rocky tree-covered hills.

As the convoy approached without slowing, one armed guard came out of each shack and both opened fire with automatic rifles, but they were no match for the 50mm. As the Willys picked up speed and crashed through the front gate, it dusted both men and their guard houses. The white Spyder and one transport together with the Willys Jeep in the rear broke left and stopped near the center of the residential quarters. Miguel's men quickly exited the transport and positioned themselves around the perimeter of the housing complex. Miguel waited in the Spyder beside the Jeep.

The rest of the convoy had continued up the main road toward the warehouses. The three transports with well-paid mercenaries, the armored Escalade with a few lieutenants that served as the command-and-control post, and the lead Willys Jeep had stopped just short of the first warehouse. Miguel could hear the gunfire echoing through the canyon and it wasn't long before the noise drew several men out of the tin houses. Most were armed and prepared to fight but quickly surrendered when they realized they were outmanned and outgunned. Not a shot was fired. Miguel stepped out of his car and approached a man who had not yet laid down his weapon.

"Where's El Contador?" Miguel demanded. The man thought for a moment then pointed toward the warehouses. By now the sounds of the firefight had ceased, except for a few stray rounds. Miguel looked at the man in disgust and clicked his jaw then quickly drew the Kimber 9mm from his backside, put the weapon to the man's forehead, and fired two shots in rapid succession.

That goes under, "just for the hell of it."

Miguel left some of the boys behind to keep an eye on their captives while he and the others headed up to the warehouses. All was quiet now, but no one had come out of the buildings. The questions in his mind were, "how many are still standing," and "whose team are they on?"

Miguel and his men entered the nearest warehouse prepared to fight but there was no resistance. In fact, there was no motion or sound at all coming from the bodies strewn about the floor. As he and his men moved on to the second warehouse, Miguel noticed that most of his other men had already come outside. One of them told Miguel that his lieutenants were inside the second warehouse with El Contador and a few of his bean counters.

Miguel was buoyed by the words. He entered the warehouse and passed a couple of his foot soldiers before coming upon his lieutenants. The room was filled with modern stainless-steel equipment of all sorts, computers and monitors, glassware and bottles filled with solid chemicals and solvents used to produce fentanyl. The rusted metal exterior belied its expensive and contemporary innards. Looking to his left down the length of the main corridor, Miguel could see a few motionless bodies crumpled on the floor. Some dressed in green fatigues. Others in white laboratory coats. All splashed with various shades of red. To his right wearing a light gray suit and his trademark banker's green visor, slouched with his head back in a leather chair, was the bullet-riddled body of El Contador.

"Ah shit!" Miguel blurted out as he bit his lip. "Which one of you idiots is responsible for this? Did I mumble or stutter when I gave the order? Did I say, 'kill them all'?"

El Ejecutor, he thought. *Not a good start.*

One of his lieutenants sheepishly stepped forward. The others stood dumbfounded. Miguel approached the man and slowly drew the Kimber from behind his back. This time he placed the barrel to the man's temple. But this time he did not click his jaw and he lowered the pistol to his side.

"Maybe we'll just wait and see what El Enterrador wants to do about this," Miguel said.

As he stepped aside and headed back down the corridor, it became apparent to everyone there that the man was standing in an acrid yellow puddle on the floor.

7

Durham, NC

"You won't believe this," Mia said with unfettered zeal. "Our friends over in chemistry just emailed me the structural data files for T045 and T046. It hasn't even been 48 hours!"

Mark smiled knowingly, but she couldn't see since she hadn't used FaceTime. "Do you have any idea what time it is, Mia?" he asked in mock disgust. "I just finished brushing my teeth and haven't even had my first cup of coffee, let alone my second. But judging from your angst, I'll make a point of getting into the office as quickly as I can without getting a ticket. Will you at least tell me whether the structures are nearly identical since we didn't bet on it?"

"Nope," she said to the point.

"How about an email or text of the PDF or raw data files?"

"Nope," she said again.

"Fine. I get it. Big crescendo. I'll text you when I get there."

Once he was comfortably seated in his blonde leather chair with his second cup of Sumatran in hand, Mark sent a text message and invited Mia to come up to his office. She bounded up the two flights effortlessly taking two stairs at a time then sat in one of the soft burnt-orange guest chairs.

"Well, I was right," Mia said with indifference. "Actually, we were both right since you didn't take my bet. The two compounds are nearly identical."

"And you didn't guess, based on their assigned numbers being side by side?"

"Got me on that one," she said. "My bad! I circled back on the Fluoropioid data for T044 and T047, the compounds on either side of our two hits. Both are positive for the theta pathway, but both are positive for the mu pathway as well. Neither involved the kappa or delta pathways."

"Well, I'm no molecular chemist," Mark said. "But the structures of these two compounds compared to the structures of our two hits should give RxFactor some valuable information on the direction to head. In fact, they might find the entire Fluoropioid data set with dose responses for all the compounds most helpful. Let's have a look at the structural data for our two hits, T045 and T046."

Diamonds in the rough, they both thought.

Mia pulled her chair around and sat beside Mark, so they could share the view on her laptop. "Here," she said pointing at the screen with a rubber-tipped stylus. "Looking at the chromatograms, the only difference between the two compounds is a single methyl group. Just one carbon and three hydrogen atoms apart. In other words, if T046 is chemically X, then T045 is X-CH$_3$."

"Of course, a single methyl group is a very slight difference, so we shouldn't be surprised by nearly identical results. The challenge for RxFactor now will be to make further subtle changes to this same region of the molecules, like adding a carboxylic acid group rather than a methyl group.

"I studied up on diamorphine when I learned it was heroin and it differs from morphine by having two ester groups rather than two alcohol groups. Since heroin is three times more potent than morphine, maybe that's a change we can suggest to RxFactor."

"You, you, you're good, you!" Mark said stealing a line from Robert DeNiro in the 1999 movie *Analyze This* with Billy Crystal. "That's the right idea, but morphine and heroin are mu opioids, and their chemical differences may not behave the same as theta opioids. Besides, this is precisely what RxFactor knows best. Given their chemical database on the known opioids, when we tell them that T045 and T046 are the new starting points for synthesis, I'm guessing their computer modeling will tell them in seconds exactly what further changes to make."

"So, what's the next step?" Mia asked.

"Reporting your findings to RxFactor as soon as possible is job one but sending the chemical structures of T045 and T046 to the legal eagles at Duke, so they can draft and submit a composition-of-matter patent application to the United States Patent and Trademark Office (USPTO) is a high priority," Mark said with a sense of urgency. Nearly everything Mark said was with a sense of urgency, so Mia was never well guided by his nonverbal cues.

Mia had not taken any courses in patent law, though she had taken an undergraduate course in pharmacy school on the laws and regulations governing the manufacturing, marketing, sales, and distribution of pharmaceuticals in the U.S. It included the laws governing the practice of pharmacy in the state of Kentucky and would have been more important to her had she sat for the state boards to become a licensed pharmacist. Some of her classmates had done just that and put themselves through the graduate programs by working parttime as pharmacists. In fact, her roommate in graduate school had worked the midnight shift on weekends as a hospital pharmacist at UK Good Samaritan and her two 10-hour shifts paid her room and board, tuition and modest living expenses.

Mia knew it was the Pure Food and Drugs Act of 1906 that first recognized the privately produced *U.S. Pharmacopoeia* and *National Formulary* as the national standards for strength, quality and purity of drugs, and that the Harrison Narcotics Act of 1914 was the first to put a limit on the amounts of narcotics that could be sold over the counter by pharmacists without a physician's prescription.

She had learned the tragic story of when Massengill, a major drug company at the time, had used diethylene glycol, better known as antifreeze, as a solvent in their patented Elixir Sulfanilamide, resulting in the deaths of 107 people, mostly children. The product was quickly recalled and reformulated, but led to the Food, Drug and Cosmetic Act of 1938 as the first to regulate drug safety and labeling. Then another tragedy, birth defects associated with the introduction of thalidomide as a sedative, the so-called *thalidomide babies*, prompted the Kefauver-Harris Amendment of 1962 that gave authority to the FDA to regulate drug labeling regarding claims of efficacy. At one point Mia could have recited many of the relevant CFR code numbers, but she knew little about patenting a drug.

Mark was in a hurry to get to the clinic, but he briefly explained the process to Mia. "There are basically two types of drug patents," Mark said. "Composition-of-matter and use or utility. Once the chemical structure of a compound is published, the inventor has one year to file a patent. If no patent is filed, the compound is said to be in the public domain and no longer patentable."

"So, we need to be mindful of when we publish the structures relative to when we file the patent application."

"That's right," Mark said. "And we have no obligation to publish it on our own, but the USPTO will publish it for opposition prior to issuing a patent. By that I mean the office will give third parties a window of time to object to the issuance and assert that they conceived of the same structure on a date prior to our filing date."

"Sounds like that could be messy."

"Very," Mark said. "Then it comes down to who kept better records on the exact date of conception. Beyond just having a structure, the patent application must also include a statement of use. Some assertion as to therapeutic benefit must accompany a composition-of-matter application and must be supported by data or examples prior to issuance. Otherwise, chemistry or drug companies could produce an endless number of molecules with no regard to their potential clinical use or commercial value. The other type of patent is a use patent. This is for previously published compounds, referred to as *known in the art* but for which the inventor has discovered a new utility. In the case of a drug, this might be a potential new indication. Again, the inventor has one year from first public disclosure of the use to file a patent application."

"In the case of our molecules, wouldn't the folks at RxFactor be considered the inventors of record by the USPTO?" Mia asked.

"They would indeed, but our contract with them stipulates that all patent rights transfer to Duke without any further consideration, such as fees or royalties. The contract further specifies that they will skippy

search the chemistry literature to be sure that all compounds synthesized are patentable as new composition-of-matter, but of course the USPTO will do its own search before they issue a patent."

Mia was nonplussed. "It seems to me we're not quite ready to file a patent application, and we certainly don't want to publish yet and show our hand. The fact is, neither compound is a great development candidate. They are both rather weak with respect to the theta opioid pathway and we know that preference for a particular pathway may be dose dependent. If we need higher doses for pain relief, they may lose their selectivity for the theta pathway and begin to display undesirable effects associated with the other opioid pathways. We know this happens with some other classes of drugs such as the betablockers. At low doses, some are selective for the beta pathway useful in the treatment of certain irregular heart rhythms, but at higher doses they begin to block other beta pathways that can cause respiratory difficulties."

"You're absolutely right about dose dependency and selectivity. When we receive the next tranche of tetracyclozine-related compounds from RxFactor, we'll need a range of doses ..." he said, but Mia interrupted.

"You mean the first tranche of T045 and T046 related compounds!"

Precisely. Perfect. Nothing out of order.

"Technically yes, that's more correct," Mark said recognizing that her attention to detail was occasionally at odds with his interest in expediency. "If, or to be technically more optimistic, *when* RxFactor uncovers one or more compounds that are more potent, we'll need to make sure that they don't lose their selectivity for the theta pathway at higher doses. Go ahead and call our friends at RxFactor. Tell them that T045 and T046 were hits but only modestly potent. Share the Fluoropioid assay results for all 100 compounds, as the lack of pathway selectivity among the others will be a useful addition to their chemical database. Then ask them to use the T045 and T046 structures as their next starting point rather than tetracyclozine and design another 12 molecules. That should give them the flexibility to find at least a couple of better compounds without breaking the bank."

"So, when should we file a patent application?" Mia asked. "You think we should file now on T045 and T046, and I say we should wait until after we test the series of compounds derived from those. I know we have no obligation to publish at this point, and we should wait until after the patent application is filed, but the question is when to file? I know the sooner we file the sooner the clock starts on the expiration of an issued patent. But by the time a drug is developed and approved for marketing, there may be very little patent life remaining. Filing later can maximize the patent life and commercial value, but we run the risk that someone else discovers the same molecules and beats us to the USPTO."

"That is the conundrum," Mark said with frustration. "And there is no right answer. Only our best guess. On the one hand, we know that opioid research is very competitive and the financial incentive for better chemistry is huge. The opioid crisis has given the U.S. government a sense of urgency, but the *War on Drugs* is all but lost. Pursuits of antitrust by the drug companies and fraud by their executives has made little difference, and civil suits with big damages would only reduce the capital available for further research and development. Our battles with drug cartels and foreign governments may limit the supply of illicit drugs in fits and starts, but there will be no impact on demand until the problem of addiction is effectively addressed. These factors all motivate academia and industry to find a solution sooner than later, and the best solution in my view is the perfect narcotic analgesic devoid of addictive potential. For these reasons I think we should file a patent on T045 and T046 right now."

"Hold your horses, Mr. Let's-do-everything-yesterday," Mia said. "I think our Fluoropioid assay is a major competitive advantage, unless you get anxious and give it away, or publish. And what are the chances of that? *Never mind.* I did my due diligence before choosing Duke for my fellowship and I know that we are the only ones with this competitive advantage. Besides, RxFactor is well-funded and has the best equipment to rapidly synthesize small quantities of a myriad of chemicals. It's my guess they'll have our next 12 compounds in a couple of weeks, and I can have them run through the Fluoropioid assay in a couple of more. No one will beat us in just a month or so. We can have the patent lawyers prepare the application now and drop in the new structures when we have them. I think we should wait until then to file a patent application."

"Mia, what's a month? It seems like a big risk for such a short additional period of market exclusivity," Mark said.

"Last I looked the pharmaceutical opioid analgesic market was $30 billion annually worldwide, which translates to $2.5 billion monthly. I'll take a month of that. Might buy me a new Subaru! And that doesn't even consider the costs to society in terms of hospitalizations and lost wages due to addiction, another $60 billion annually. Or the black market for opioids, another $30 billion worldwide. In fact, I'd be inclined to sit on the patent application and slow-walk it through the process. Someone told me that drug companies are given 17 years from the date of issuance, so waiting until we get closer to FDA approval of a drug would seem to make the most sense."

"Who said you knew little about patenting a drug?" Mark asked with a raised eyebrow. "That was the Big Pharma patent strategy for years, but in 1994 Bill Clinton signed the Uruguay Round Agreements Act which started a 20-year clock from the filing date rather than a 17-year clock from the issuance date. The intent was to shorten the period of exclusivity and allow for earlier entry by generic competition to hold down the cost of drugs, and it did just that. Thankfully, we are more beholden to our grant-writing ability than to drug prices. But I'm okay with waiting before we start the 20-year clock. I'll give Austin Crammer a call over at the Duke University patent office and ask him to draft an application based on T045 and T046. We can pull the trigger on the filing when we have the next batch of compounds and data. And I'll make you a promise. The day our patent application leads to a drug approval by the FDA is the day I'll buy you a new Subaru Outback!"

Gee, I was thinking a Tesla ... and make it a Model S, she thought.

"I'll call RxFactor and ask them to get started," Mia said.

"Good, and I'll ask our administrators to work with RxFactor to extend our contract by another 12 compounds. I'm off to the clinic."

"Remember, *primum non nocere*," Mia said with a wink.

8

San Rafael, Chihuahua, Mexico

Miguel Martinez removed his black-and-orange headset as the crew chief opened the main cabin door of the black Sikorsky S-76C. The flight from the helipad of his seaside villa to this site deep in the mountains of Copper Canyon in the Mexican state of Chihuahua not far from the town of San Rafael took about an hour. Miguel feared no man, except the one he was about to visit, but flying was another matter. It didn't help that he was climbing out of the same model chopper that claimed the lives of Kobe Bryant, Bryant's daughter, and a few others up in California not long ago. On the other hand, El Enterrador was the head of the Sinaloa drug cartel, so he controlled the Federales and the airspace over the country. The air traffic controllers had been instructed to clear the corridor between Los Mochis and San Rafael while the Sikorsky was en route.

Two of El Enterrador's henchmen ducked below the whirling rotor blades when it landed and offered their assistance as the pilot cut the power to the twin turboshaft engines. Miguel waved them off. As he slowly regained his hearing, he looked around the well-manicured grounds leading to the main house and began to make his way up the inlaid cobblestone path. He had been there before on a few occasions and was always impressed but not surprised by the extravagance of the place. There were gazeboes, pool houses, guest houses, maintenance sheds and multivehicle garages, all handsomely landscaped with native Mexican firs and wildflowers that bloomed throughout the year. There were any number of nooks and crannies to conceal a man should the need arise. He was sure the place was staffed with a paramilitary force that could easily have handled the one he used to visit El Contador, but he saw no one. The hike up the steep grade to the front door left him slightly winded. Once there, he turned to admire the 360-degree view from the top of the ridge to the canyons below.

The Grand Canyon of Mexico.

Miguel heard the front door open and turned to enter. The house staff escorted him down the hall of a well-lit gallery with fresco paintings of Copper Canyon on the walls. They walked past a massive wooden bar stocked with various brands of Mexican tequila, cerveza, and vino, then through one of the many four-paneled sliding glass door walls that horseshoed around a colorfully tiled swimming pool. They continued under a red bougainvillea-laden trellis that led to an elevated patio with the pool and spa on one side and the most breathtaking view of the canyon on the other. Seated at a cocobolo wood table under a thatched roof was the man himself, Hector 'El Enterrador' Morales.

"Miguel," The Gravedigger said. "You're looking well. Please, join me. How about a cold lemonade?" he asked as he pointed to a large pitcher of the refreshment wet with condensation and sitting on a pewter tray with a couple of chilled glasses. "Or perhaps something livelier?"

Miguel simply nodded to the waiter nearby dressed in a white tuxedo who left and returned moments later with a glass of double distilled 100 percent agave Gran Patron Burdeos on the rocks. As always, Miguel's custom Kimber 9mm was in the waistband behind his back and he was dressed in his trademark white Don Johnson leisure suit, this time with a pink T-shirt. The Gravedigger, his silver hair still damp from a morning dip in the pool, was wearing a white boxer style swimsuit under a black silk robe with orange graphic print. He was unarmed.

"I suppose you heard about our little mix up with El Contador," Miguel opened hesitantly.

"Little!" El Enterrador said with some volume. "Mix up!" he said with a lot more.

"Sir, one of my lieutenants is a bit ..." Miguel said, but El Enterrador interrupted.

"Look, Miguel. You are responsible for whatever your men do. If El Contador was killed, it was by your hand! I'm assuming I was properly informed of his death, or did he somehow rise like a phoenix from the ashes?"

"No sir," Miguel said. "You heard right. He's as dead as my father's dick and that's pretty dead from what he tells me." Miquel tried but failed to introduce a little levity.

"And I assume your lieutenant is just as dead as *your* dick, do I have that right?" El Enterrador replied with a straight face.

Miguel felt the acid reflux and could taste the bile in the back of his throat, just a little. *I think the sonofabitch already knows the answer to that.* He was fighting back a full-blown heave. "Sorry, sir. He's not as dead as my dick, but he will be soon. You can count on that, sir!"

"Miguel," El Enterrador said in a fatherly tone as he took another sip of lemonade. "I taught you everything I know about killing. Everything about being El Ejecutor for the cartel. I did so because I know that one day, you'll take my place as head of the cartel. But I do hope that day comes not too soon, you know. The point is, you can't earn your men's respect if you tolerate disrespect. Fortunate for you, before your little mishap, it was already my belief that El Contador's days were numbered. I never paid him directly but allowed him to skim his share from the books. That was fine until one of his clerks informed me that his accounting technique had become 'two for me and one for you.'"

"I suspected that too boss. A real scumbag," Miguel said, delighted the man had focused his wrath on a new subject.

"I don't need to be no accountant to know that doesn't work. Fortunately, I saw this day coming and secured a backup. Juan Pablo Torres of the Michoacán cartel has agreed to join us. A very honest and very fair man. At first, he was, how you say, 'disinclined.' But I sent some of our men down to have a little discussion with him and, wouldn't you know it, now he's inclined."

"El Nuevo Contador. Very good, sir," Miguel said, relieved that his little case of ingestion had subsided.

El Enterrador stood, took one last sip of lemonade and spun on his heels. Looking back at Miquel, he said, "I need to fly to Michoacán this afternoon for a meeting with Juan Pablo and President Alvarez of Mexico. I think the President wants to discuss 'one for me and two for you,' so it will be nice to have Juan Pablo there. I'll be back in a few days. Feel free to stay here and make yourself at home. I'll have some of the men drive me out to our airfield, so the chopper is at your disposal."

Miguel stood, shook the man's hand, then sat back down as El Enterrador rounded the patio and headed into the house. Miguel sat by the pool a while and enjoyed another Gran Patron Burdeos on the rocks that the waiter had delivered unsolicited. Miguel heard the entourage of vehicles leave and decided to take the chopper back to his villa, then on to the warehouses near Morales to take care of business sooner than later. But first he would use the restroom.

As Miguel finished up and started to head toward the front door, he looked down the main hall and saw the beautiful former Miss Mexico emerge from El Enterrador's bedroom. She was wearing nothing but a sheer black negligee which fanned open briefly in the front as she spun around before noticing that Miguel was standing in the hallway.

"Salma! What the hell are you doing here?" Miguel said with mixed emotions. He was pleased to see her, especially half naked, but not coming out of El Enterrador's bedroom.

"Well," she said indignantly. "It's not like *you're* monogamous. We both know that. I'm quite sure you have a lady in every town you pass through."

"I'm not bothered that you see other men," Miguel said. "In fact, I don't care if you see them two or three at a time. Lord knows the thought's crossed my mind to be a part of that. But you're a fool for seeing El Enterrador while you're seeing me. If he learns of this, he'll kill us both. And he's very good at it, I assure you."

"You're the fool," she said. As she spun to slap his face, her negligee fanned open, and he again caught a glimpse of the body that most assuredly had won the swimsuit contest in the pageant that year. He blocked her blow and grabbed her by the wrist with his left hand, then reached around behind her with his right hand and pulled her negligee off in one move. He took her other wrist in his right hand and pinned them both to the small of her back. She bit him on the lip a little harder than she had intended and purred, "I didn't know you liked it rough."

He grabbed both cheeks of her naked bottom then forcefully pushed her back into the room and onto El Enterrador's bed. "If the man comes back to get something he forgot," Miguel said, "this will get a lot rougher than either of us like it."

9

New York City, NY

"Look, you little dweeb." Karl wanted to pull the guy through the phone. "I don't pay for rumors, innuendo, or graffiti written in ink on the walls of the executive washroom at UBS, I pay for information. Bona fide, verified, substantiated, validated, bet your wife's ass on it, information. And the only thing less I'd settle for is a printed copy of a corporate press release that found its way to a dumpster instead of PR Newswire, and only if you know the sonofabitch will be released tomorrow!" He listened as the caller began to reply, then disconnected in the middle of it.

Karl was the wild half of the infamous Fischmann Brothers, notorious as short sellers on Wall Street.

"Pam," he said over the intercom to the receptionist just outside his office door, "The next time that idiot Frank Baldwin from the WSJ calls, tell him I'm out to lunch ... with his girlfriend!"

"Hey, Geoff," Karl said into the private two-way headset that made them electronically conjoined twins. "What was the name of that research analyst that used to be with DLJ before Credit Suisse took them out? Guy was an MD, or PhD, or some kind of D." Karl was holding his phone and frantically typing search words into the office's contact app. "Guy knew a lot about viruses. Put us onto that big GenoVax play. Last name started with an H, I think, but he's not coming up under the H's." Karl re-entered an H progressively harder each time as if the phone might respond differently. Karl had little patience for most people and even less for uncooperative inanimate objects.

"Did you try looking under the O's for *On-The-Dole*?" Geoff said with a toothy grin. It was a term in the office directory abbreviated "OTD" and was more covert in the event of a hack or subpoena by the SEC. "His last name was Heimer. I believe you called him Doc Wisenheimer."

Geoff was the more reserved half of the team. Known on Wall Street simply as "The Brothers," they had amassed one of the largest fortunes in trading history by short selling public stocks, most recently Big Pharma and biotechnology companies. Early on as young hedge fund managers they would *buy on the rumors and sell on the news*, as the adage went. They became quite adept at beating most of their peers by staying on top of the wire services and appreciating the market implications sooner than most. But their real competitive edge was inside information and their ability to stay one step ahead of the SEC and the DOJ.

Several years back Karl had gotten a tip from an insider that one of the largest investment banking firms on Wall Street was quietly planning to file for bankruptcy amid the subprime mortgage meltdown because they were highly leveraged and dangerously exposed. The Brothers shorted the stock and made a killing when the news broke. They could have made a few bucks just selling the handful of shares they were long before the stampede. But this was the first time they had real inside information and borrowed shares for a potentially larger gain, essentially selling shares they did not yet own with the obligation to buy them back in the open market. In the world of high finance, this was called a *short sale* and not unlike a *put option* in commodities trading. Both were bearish strategies intended to speculate on a decline in the value of the underlying securities. In this highly leveraged trading scheme, not unlike the situation in which the investment bank had found itself, the potential gains were huge, but the losses were theoretically infinite. The Brothers had made hundreds of millions shorting that investment firm and Karl never named his informant.

Karl and Geoff had decided that the SEC disclosure requirements for the hedge fund, together with their fiduciary obligations, was more heat than they wanted in their kitchen. Life was good, so they took down their public marquee and quietly continued trading for their own account as Fischmann Brothers Investments.

At the peak of the HIV/AIDS crisis, Karl again had gotten a call. This time from a research analyst with a great contact in the compliance office at the FDA. He had had inside information that FDA inspectors had uncovered sterility issues with the injectable formulation of GenoVax's vaccine for the HIV/AIDS virus that would soon trigger a non-approvable letter on their pending New Drug Application. The setback would crush GenoVax enthusiasts and its stock price. The Brothers quickly built a short position in the stock that would have alarmed the GenoVax shareholders had the collapse not occurred before the SEC's required reporting of their short position. After an unreasonable delay that would create even more trouble for them down the road, GenoVax announced the bad news and their stock tanked. The Brothers covered their short position all the way down. Another nice day.

"Yep, here it is," Karl said after entering the correct name. "Wilhelm Heimer, and it's MD. One of those guys that changed his mind after medical school and joined his father's world at Wall and Broad as a technical analyst specializing in science and medicine plays. Nice to have an unbiased guy on the inside that knows when he's being fed horseshit by the corporate scientists. I think I'll give Ole Doc Wisenheimer a call. Maybe see what he knows about the ViroSelect vaccine."

"What do you know that I don't?" Geoff asked, curling one finger at a time palm up.

"I had a call from Ty Dixon. He's that PhD biostatistician from the University of Michigan that the FDA often calls to serve on those outside independent Advisory Committees. Anyway, turns out ViroSelect has contracted his statistical group to conduct a futility analysis on the pivotal trial of their vaccine for COVID-19."

"What's a futility analysis?" Geoff asked, surprised that Karl had any level of sophistication in biostatistics.

"Getting a heads up on a *bad day* for a Phase-III clinical trial always portends a *good day* for us, so I've done my homework. Since pivotal trials are so expensive and take so long, companies are opting to contract for an outside independent so-called *interim analysis* in the middle of a clinical trial. The company remains blinded to the results, and they pay a small statistical penalty for their contractor taking an early look. The trial may then be stopped prematurely for safety, efficacy or futility. Safety or efficacy are obvious. It means these endpoints were met statistically and continuing the trial would be unnecessary and arguably unethical. A futility outcome, however, means there is an extremely low likelihood that the efficacy endpoint will be met, so the sponsor is most likely wasting time and money by continuing."

"What's the upshot of all this with respect to ViroSelect?"

"Ty said they just completed the interim analysis on the COVID-19 vaccine trial and if the company encounters just one more death in the treatment group before there's another death in the placebo group, there's no chance for statistical success and the trial will be terminated as a failure. Since only his group is unblinded as to treatment, he'll be the first to know."

And we'll be the second, Geoff thought.

Karl had been so impressed by the guidance Doc Wisenheimer had provided to DLJ and Credit Suisse that he convinced Geoff they needed their own in-house expert analyst. They hired Carlos Martinez, MD, a very bright and conscientious young man who had graduated from St. George's University School of Medicine on the island of Grenada. It was among the oldest and best of the offshore medical schools scattered about the Caribbean. Most were accredited and staffed by adjunct faculty from the U.S. looking for sabbaticals in the sun.

In the short period of time that he had been with The Brothers, Carlos had provided valuable technical analyses that had led to some very nice returns. The Brothers compensated him well, but not quite as well as those listed under OTD. His hometown was somewhere in Mexico, but The Brothers didn't know any more than that and didn't ask. Their policy was not to get personally involved with anyone on their staff and the practice had served them well on occasions when personnel changes were needed.

"Carlos, would you mind coming down to my office for a moment?" Karl asked over the phone. Moments later, Carlos walked in and had a seat on the other side of Karl's massive African Blackwood desk. "This may be more of a regulatory question than a medical one, so feel free to get back to me, but in your opinion would a sterility problem on an injectable product preclude an NDA approval?" Getting back to Karl would not be necessary.

"Absolutely," Carlos said with no hesitation. "Injectable products go directly into the bloodstream whether by the subcutaneous, intramuscular or intravenous route. So, they bypass the gastrointestinal tract which is the first line of defense against impurities or contaminants. For this reason, the FDA requires additional testing of injectables for pyrogens, foreign substances and other potential contaminants. How long the approval is delayed depends upon the nature of the contaminant and the diligence of the manufacturer to correct the problem, but it's generally no small task."

"Hmmm," Karl pondered. "I had a call from an OTD by the name of Ty Dixon. He shared that the pivotal trial for VSLT's COVID-19 vaccine will be terminated for futility if there's just one more death in the treatment group. The most likely explanation would be inefficacy. Failure to save lives. But an alternative explanation could be a toxin, like we saw with the GenoVax vaccine for HIV/AIDS. Perhaps one that's *increasing* mortality and thereby offsetting any survival benefit."

"Theoretically," Carlos replied. "But a life-threatening contaminant would be extremely unusual. GenoVax just had a sterility issue that set them back, but the vaccine was ultimately effective and approved. Besides, the bad news of ending a trial for futility will bury the stock in the short-term even if they can resurrect the vaccine and recover later."

"You're right," Karl said. "Let's wait to hear back from Ty."

10

New York City, NY

Whenever the market was expecting good news, whether favorable clinical trial results, drug approval, or sales exceeding expectations, if The Brothers were on the other side of the trade, it was *buyer beware!* Some called it luck, but the ancient Greek philosopher Seneca was quoted, "Luck is what happens when preparedness meets opportunity." There was always opportunity on Wall Street, on one side of a trade or the other, so preparedness was the only differentiating factor. In the case of the Fischmann Brothers, most suspected it had more to do with their connections at the FDA, USPTO, or SEC than it did with any sort of preparedness.

"Hey Geoff," Karl said into his headset. "I have a 4 p.m. meeting on my side of 'The Bar' with the Director of Investor Relations for VSLT. Her name is Jayne Gillis. I want to hear what her company is shoveling ahead of the news on the pivotal trial for their COVID-19 vaccine. I bought a handful of shares just to put us on their mailing list."

"That may be the first long position we've taken in years," Geoff said wryly.

"Don't worry," Karl said. "It was well below the threshold for public disclosure and if word gets out it certainly won't be market-moving."

Just for giggles, The Brothers had purchased the top five floors of the 60-story Woolworth Building at 233 Broadway in Manhattan, known in the local real estate market as the Pinnacle Penthouse. When the neo-Gothic structure was erected in 1913, complete with gargoyles, it was the tallest building in New York City until 1930, when the Chrysler building assumed the honor. The Brothers spent $80 million on the place and spared no expense on renovations. Living quarters on the top three floors included every luxury imaginable. Offices occupied the first two floors and were organized around the perimeter with a two-story garden atrium and waterfall in the center. Key features were African Blackwood desks and conference tables and a full-wall OLED display of all the major stock, bond, commodity, and cryptocurrency markets around the world. Just walking by the "Big Boards of the Pinnacle Penthouse" was like taking a nighttime stroll through the Ginza. There were displays of 24/7 news channels and business news crawlers scattered about, and a map of the world with a real-time LED display of daylight and darkness.

Karl and Geoff each had their own office with a lavish board room between them. All three rooms had privileged access to the wrap-around portico with expansive views of City Hall Park directly below, just a few blocks from the 9/11 Memorial and Museum. The board room included an African Blackwood conference table that seated 20, with additional capacity around the perimeter, and all manner of audiovisual equipment neatly concealed.

Just outside the board room, facing the first floor of the atrium and running its length from Karl's office to Geoff's was The Bar. It was a formal yet inviting affair with a collection of furniture in a dark Gothic motif. The full-wall bar was black mahogany with a rack of wines glasses above and wide variety of liquors, liqueurs, wines, and beers on the back bar and in the refrigerators below. For his side of The Bar, Karl had gone to a Sotheby's silent auction and purchased the original barstool from Aristotle Onassis' yacht the *Christina* that had been upholstered with the tanned leather foreskin of a sperm whale. Karl never disclosed what he paid for the barstool. He would only say it was priceless.

Not to be outdone, Geoff had purchased the less conversational but equally audacious original Claude Monet *Haystacks* (1890) for the outrageous sum of $26 million. It was framed in 18k gold, and he had hired an armed guard to watch over it during business hours. Their extensive security system and support services were belts and suspenders.

Geoff showed up on Karl's side of The Bar precisely at 4 p.m. to find that Karl was running late as usual. An attractive young woman in black was already seated and having a drink. Geoff introduced himself and she said her name was Jayne Gillis from ViroSelect. Geoff couldn't help but notice her raven hair, investment-inspiring cleavage and black Old English script tattoo peering out from under the edge of her sleeve. Her lips and nails were finished in black. Goth. Not Geoff's cup of tea but right in Karl's wheelhouse.

The Brothers were both confirmed bachelors. Geoff was in a long-term relationship with a woman his age; equally conservative and refined but he was reluctant to commit. Karl, on the other hand, played the field with women half his age. Jayne fit the mold, but he preferred tattoos on the small of their back for better viewing on special occasions.

When Karl finally showed, he nodded to Geoff, then sat beside *Ms. Goth*. He introduced himself as the better-looking half of the investment team. Geoff just glanced at Jayne and shrugged. Karl was stealing glances back and forth between the tattoo and the cleavage like a metronome set to allegro.

"So, Ms. Gillis," Karl said now focused on her eyes. "What's the good word at ViroSelect?"

"Well, first let me thank you both for being our newest shareholders, albeit a rather modest position given your capability," she said sarcastically, as she took in the motif on Karl's side of The Bar. "Who was your decorator? Marquis de Sade!"

Just the first name to come to mind, was it? Geoff thought.

Geoff headed back to his office shortly after Karl arrived. Karl chatted with Ms. Gillis a while longer but spent more time wondering what her tattoo read than whether ViroSelect was a good investment. He had heard what he needed to know about the company in the first five minutes. ViroSelect was expecting the approval of their vaccine for COVID-19 any minute now and there was nothing in the tea leaves to suggest anything else. The read on The Street was *green light go* and the company was giving no other signals.

"Let me ask you, Jayne. May I call you Jayne?" Karl asked, though the subordinate remark seemed awkward.

"Why, of course," she replied as she adjusted her chair to give him a better angle of endearment.

"By the way," Karl redirected the conversation as he slid his stool a little closer. "You may not believe this, but you're sitting on the foreskin of one of the largest penises on earth!" She was still stammering when Karl told her the story about the barstool, the *Christina* and how Aristotle Onassis had used the same line on Elizabeth Taylor in the presence of Richard Burton. "This very stool." She almost slid off.

"Jayne, do you know what a hockey stick is?" Karl answered his own question before she could embarrass herself not realizing that he had changed the subject. "It's a term used to describe the typical stock chart of a public company that requires government approval to introduce a new product. There's the run-up to a pre-approval peak or the *buy on rumor* phase, then the downward slide to a post-approval trough or the *sell on news* phase, followed by a typical post-launch period of price recovery and stabilization giving the chart the appearance of a hockey stick. The slope of the handle is dictated by the extent to which product sales meet market expectations. Since I'm not into hockey sticks Ms. Gillis, and I'm not a fan of flat, what can you tell me about VSLT's sales forecast for its vaccine compared to the market's expectations?"

"Well," she said intentionally taking a deep breath and holding it for a beat. "We don't give sales guidance and the market is free to buy or sell as it sees fit. All we can tell you is that COVID-19 is a pandemic virus with a level of virulence and mortality not seen since the 1918 Spanish Flu, and the FDA is about to say we have the first and only safe and effective means of prevention."

I think I'm in love!

For the next half hour, the conversation had little to do with VSLT. It was getting late, and Jayne decided it was time to call it a day. As she was leaving, she looked back at Karl and said, "By the way, it reads *audaces fortuna juvat*, which translated means, 'fortune favors the bold.'"

It was the end of another long day, the kind The Brothers thoroughly enjoyed, and most of the office staff had cleared the building a couple of hours earlier. Karl and Geoff met near the elevator bank and waited for the ride up three floors to their living quarters. When the historic brass elevator of the old Woolworth Building stopped, there was no indication that it could go up any higher. Very exclusive. Very private. Their sanctuary.

Karl was retrieving his key card for the upper floors when the massive door opened and standing in the elevator were two Hispanic men in brightly colored garb. Neither made a motion to get off, indicating they were continuing up to the residential quarters. One had a thick black mustache with dark glasses and was wearing a Yankees ballcap. The other had a shiny bald pate and a diamond stud in one ear while wearing an open purple silk shirt that exposed two pierced nipples. There was a cleaning cart between them, and Geoff had a look of terror in his eyes.

"I guess you haven't met our new housekeepers," Karl said as he put a hand on Geoff's shoulder. It was no comfort. "Apparently you didn't notice but they've been here every day for a week. Let me introduce you to Eduardo Fernandez," Karl said as he gestured in the direction of the guy with the ballcap.

"Pleased to meet you, señor," Eduardo said in a very feminine voice, and Geoff's eyes widened. "I've lived in New York most of my life but came from Guadalajara with my mom and pop. Spain, not Mexico. We're Spanish, so my friends call me 'Span.' You can too," he said as he flipped his hand palm up.

"And this is Raul Sanchez," Karl said as he nodded in the direction of the bald guy with the pierced nipples.

"Pleased to make your acquaintance, señor," Raul said with an even more effeminate voice than Eduardo, as he offered his hand with the pinky ring to Geoff palm down. Geoff didn't budge. "I'm from Guadalajara, too. Imagine that. But Mexico, not Spain," Raul said. "I was raised in Puerto Rico though, so my friends call me 'Spic.' I'm not offended by it. I think it's rather endearing. Please call me 'Spic,'" he said as he winked at Geoff.

Spic and Span? Really Karl?

"Jesus, it's been a long day. I don't need this!" Geoff snarled.

"What, *this*?" Karl said a little miffed. "We're not inviting them to dinner, they're just cleaning our damn house!" Raul looked at Eduardo like a kid that just had his ice cream cone stolen. Geoff wondered if they were a number or if Karl had hired them separately.

"So, how shall *we* refer to the two of *you*?" Raul said with a puzzled expression while waving a finger first between himself and Eduardo then between Karl and Geoff.

"Mr. Fischmann, and Mr. Fischmann," Karl said. "And if we happen to be standing together, I guess we'll both answer!"

11

Durham, NC

PACKAGE FROM DEL MAR, CA AT SHIPPING AND RECEIVING. MARKED URGENT.

Mia headed for the mail room on the first floor at DCOR to retrieve the package after receiving the text message. On the way, her phone rang, and caller ID was no help. She answered anyway.

"Mia, this is Paul Harris with the Lead Optimization group at RxFactor. Just wanted to follow up on the package we shipped out yesterday. May not have arrived yet, but it's on dry ice and needs to hit the freezer when it does. We've had some shipments thaw before reaching our clients lately, not many, but all manner of excuses from ..." Paul said but Mia interrupted. Unfortunately, she knew the type.

"Sorry Paul. Just wanted to let you know it arrived before you spend the next five minutes telling me why it might not." *Dang, that didn't come out quite right,* she thought. "I'm headed to retrieve it now. If anything is wrong with it, I'll call you."

"Thanks Mia, but please call when you get back to your office regardless. There's a couple of items I'd like to go over with you."

"You bet Paul," she said, and ended the call.

The Styrofoam container was wrapped in cellophane with a packing slip attached. The outer label included a white diamond shape with black and white stripes on the top and 9 on the bottom, the labeling symbol for dry ice. She unwrapped the package and left it lying on the bench at room temperature near the freezer, then went to her office to place the call.

"Hello Mia," Paul said. "Thanks for calling back. DCOR ordered 12 compounds, but you'll note we sent 15. Only charged you for 12. First, thanks for sending the Fluoropioid data on all the previous compounds. Very helpful. After we made the 12 new compounds using T045 and T046 as a starting point we noted a couple of other key structures that should utilize the theta opioid pathway exclusively. We didn't want to miss anything, so we made three more compounds. Gratis. We're scientists too, and value the opportunity to contribute, even though we don't always get much background from our clients on their objectives."

"Gee, Paul. I guess sometimes we just get so wrapped up in our work that we forget there are others with an interest in our success. Briefly, we're hoping to find the perfect opioid analgesic. One devoid of addictive potential. It would be a major contribution to pain management and reduce, if not eliminate, deaths due to opioid overdose."

"Wow," Paul said with an academic rush. "Guess you think those liabilities are associated with mu, kappa or delta opioid pathways, huh? That was rhetorical. I know the answer. Don't worry, I also know the terms of our nondisclosure agreement. That's really exciting." He waited momentarily for her response.

"Tell me," Mia said shifting the conversation. "I was lucky enough to have visited San Diego once and even luckier to have stayed at the Hotel del Coronado for a few nights. I'm not familiar with Del Mar, but I've heard it's not far from downtown."

"That's right," Paul said. "About thirty minutes north on the I-5 freeway. A real biotechnology hub now. Lots of great science going on with the likes of UCSD, Scripps and Salk." A little pressed for time he ended the pleasantries. "Give me a call when you have the Fluoropioid data on the new compounds. I'm genuinely as anxious as you are to see what we have."

"I certainly will," she said, embracing his shared interest.

Mia ended the call and went back to the drug discovery laboratory after sending a brief text message to Mark letting him know the compounds had arrived. She had not taken the new samples to the freezer because she intended to assay them as soon as they thawed.

She withdrew a micropipette with disposable tips from the bench drawer and transferred a small quantity of each sample to separate amber glass vials. She repackaged these in the same Styrofoam box in which they had arrived, added fresh dry ice, then called the campus courier to have them delivered to Dr. Newberry's laboratory ASAP. She relabeled the package 'Urgent,' then sent a text message to alert him it was on its way and to request that his staff confirm the chemical structures at their earliest convenience. He acknowledged the text and promised to have the structure files emailed to her the next morning.

Mia then prepared the four different groups of cells and various doses of the new compounds for the Fluoropioid assay. She also included samples of T045 and T046 for comparison. Once the automated drug screening had been initiated, the laboratory technicians would monitor the progress and call her if there was a problem. She knew the results would not be available until morning.

Anxious as a long-tailed cat in a room full of rocking chairs, Mia decided to head to the Duke University Golf Club to play a round and relax. On a Tuesday afternoon there was a good chance she could play alone, and wouldn't mind that, but decided to give Jillian a call on the off chance she could join her.

"Hey Jill, it's Mia. I just put the latest compounds from RxFactor on autopilot and won't have the results until morning. I'm suffering from a bad case of anticipatory anxiety that I'm sure only a round of golf will cure. Any chance you can join me at the club?"

"I was just about to review some of the protocols submitted to the Animal Care Committee for its meeting next week, but nothing that can't wait."

"Great. Let's meet at the Fairview on the clubhouse patio for a tea before we head out to the course. They have oolong on the menu that's incredible."

"As I recall, the only beverage on their afternoon menu is tea. I was hoping for a beer from a beverage cart boy, but I'm fine with a tea. Meet you at the Fairview in twenty minutes."

Mia and Jillian sat outside the Fairview at an umbrella-covered wrought-iron patio set. Mia enjoyed her cup of blueberry hibiscus tea and raved about how well the Nigerian hibiscus complimented the blueberries, apples and hints of rosehips. Jillian had the Acai green tea and was pretty sure it was just being wasted on her herbal palate.

"So how many compounds are you screening now?" Jillian asked.

"RxFactor sent 15 new ones, including three they made gratis," Mia answered. "I sent samples to Ron Newberry for structural confirmation then initiated the automated Fluoropioid assay which is running as we speak. The results will be in my hands tomorrow morning. I'm so pumped that I'll probably overshoot most of the greens. I'm guessing my GIR will be less than 50 percent and that's usually the strongest part of my game."

"Remind me again," Jillian asked. "What's GIR?"

"Greens-in-regulation. The easy way to remember is that 72 strokes is par for most 18-hole courses. Half should be putts and half should be strokes from tee-to-green. It's basically your long game versus your short game. Lately I've been playing about six strokes over par with four missed putts and two missed greens. A better long game than a short.

Sorry I asked, Jillian thought.

12

Durham, NC

The black metal mesh K-cup rack held a nice assortment of Bigelow teas. Constant Comment was her favorite in the morning, but Mia had already had a cup of that before leaving the house, so she selected a Ginger Lemon for her second cup. In twenty seconds, she had the brew in hand and took a seat at her office iMac with its 27-inch Retina display. She powered it up and waited for the desktop to populate with her favorite weather widget, then launched Mail from the dock which opened to the inbox of her DCOR email address.

The most recent email was time stamped 7:47 a.m. and was an advertisement from a local department store to which she had given her business email address in exchange for a five percent discount on her last purchase. Now she regretted having shared it as she marked the email as junk. The next was stamped 7:36 a.m. from the Duke Chemistry Department and attached was a PDF file with the chemical structures of the 15 compounds from RxFactor.

Mia was grateful the data had arrived when Ron Newberry said it would, despite the early hour, and she made a note to do something special for his group. She opened the PDF, along with the one previously received containing the structures for T045 and T046, and merged the two files, creating a single PDF with the 17 relevant structures. She then attached this file to an email she composed and sent to Austin Crammer at the Duke patent office asking him to add the compounds to the claims of their draft patent application. She also included a list of the supporting references and citations from RxFactor establishing that none of the 17 had been previously disclosed in the chemical or patent literature. She closed the email to Austin by saying that she and Mark would meet with him at 3:30 p.m. to make any final corrections before putting the patent application in the mail to the USPTO. She copied Mark on the email and asked them both to acknowledge the appointment.

Next Mia selected an email from the Information Technology (IT) group at DCOR that managed all the internal data, analyses and reports for the center. She was impressed by the visual display on the first page of the report. The IT group had generated a color graphic that summarized the Fluoropioid results for the 17 compounds. It was a 4 x 17 matrix with the four columns representing each of the four opioid pathways and the 17 rows representing the 15 newly synthesized molecules plus T045 and T046. Each square in the grid was either white or a shade of green ranging from very pale to very dark. It was obvious to Mia that this was a visual summary of the peak fluorescent response of each compound with respect to each opioid pathway, and she knew that the darker the shade of green the more potent the compound.

Instantly, Mia could see that the squares for T045 and T046 were all white in the columns representing the mu, kappa and delta opioid pathways, but the same intermediate shade of green in the column representing the theta opioid pathway. This proved once again that the two reference compounds only involved the theta pathway and were only moderately potent. She then observed that every row representing a new compound was also green in the theta column and white in the others, with one lone exception. One of the new compounds was pale green in the mu column. *Fourteen hits and just one miss*, she thought. She noted that, among the 15 green squares in the theta column representing the new compounds, five were a darker shade of green than the squares for T045 and T046, and the one labeled T113 was a deep emerald green.

EUREKA!

Mark read the text message from Mia and called her immediately. She answered without looking at caller ID.

"Come on down," she said in her best gameshow voice. "You're the next contestant on *The Price Is Right!*"

"How about if you come on up?" Mark said and chuckled.

Taking the stairwell up two flights and two stairs at a time as always, she walked into his office with laptop in hand. She gave Mark a quick nod and a big smile then noticed that one of his diplomas above the credenza was slightly askew. She walked over and straightened it then stepped back to have a look. Mark wondered if that was her OCD or just his failure to attend to matters less important than those at hand.

"It's a nice morning," Mark said. "What do you say we have a look at the data out on the balcony?"

Mark was fortunate to have not only a corner office but a private balcony with a small collection of outdoor furniture where he could catch some fresh air while continuing to work. *Fortunate* was probably the wrong word. *Well-deserving* was probably the right one. Mia sat on the end of a wicker chaise lounge and Mark pulled over a matching chair from a four-piece table set. She placed her laptop on the ottoman nearby and they both adjusted their seats for the best view of her computer screen.

"Here's the colored summary chart produced by our IT guys," she said proudly, as she opened the laptop and launched the data file. "Creative, don't you think? I haven't yet gone through the raw data and dose-response curves, but we obviously have five compounds that are better than our previous two, and one appears to be very potent."

"Five needles in the haystack and one might be made of gold! I think you have the Midas touch, Mia," Mark said, and the words lingered like the finish of a fine wine.

They ordered lunch in from a local deli and continued to review the data to be sure nothing had been overlooked as they dined on Mark's balcony. Heart-healthy soups and salads.

"Did you receive my email this morning about our 3:30 p.m. meeting with Austin at his office?" Mia asked.

"Yes. Sorry I didn't reply, but I knew I'd be seeing you this morning and didn't have a scheduling conflict. I also noted that you said we would finalize the patent application so that Austin could drop it in the mail. Fortunately, patent applications are filed electronically. No need for snail mail. Whether it's an application for trademark, service mark, composition-of-matter or use patents. Even copyright applications are submitted electronically with document files for printed material and audio files for singer-songwriters and proprietary sounds."

"How do you know about copyrights for singer-songwriters?"

"I once tried my hand at it," Mark said bashfully as he leaned back in his chair on the balcony and took in the fresh air. "I was surprised. It was like some others have said, all the lyrics came to me in an hour or so. Then a short while later, I banged out a melody on my Taylor 914ce and used Garage Band to add a percussion track. I went online to the USPTO, paid a small fee, and uploaded the music and lyrics in their acceptable digital formats. It didn't take long before a certificate of copyright appeared in my inbox. Now I'm a bona fide singer-songwriter!"

"Well, I'll be. A left-brained guy with some right-brain talent. What's the genre and name of the song?'

"It's a country music tune titled *My Redneck Girl Loves Her Red Man.* Catchy little tag line, don't you think?"

"I just hope the only thing you know about chewing tobacco is the name of a popular brand!" Mia said only half-jokingly.

Mia offered to drive them to Austin's office in her old Subaru Outback, hoping Mark would counter with his black BMW 7 Series. He accepted her offer.

They arrived shortly before three-thirty and gathered around a conference table in Austin's office. Mia mentioned that all the structures characterized by the Duke Chemistry Department were identical to those reported by RxFactor. No discrepancies.

Austin used his laptop to redraft the claims with a detailed description of the synthetic process that started with the T045 and T046 structures that led to the T101-T115 compounds, including T113 which they believed would become their drug candidate. He also redrafted the disclosure statement and mentioned that a comprehensive review of the chemical literature revealed no previous publications of these specific molecules, and the relevant references were cited. The application speculated that these compounds would be useful in the practice of analgesia, as pain relievers, and possibly sedatives or hypnotics. It would be updated as additional supportive data became available. When the three agreed that everything was in order, Austin submitted the application electronically.

"HOW LONG HAVE YOU been home?" Jillian asked as she closed the front door and found Mia reading on the couch in the living room. It was unusual for Mia to be the first one home, although they both put in long hours on most days.

"Long enough to cook us dinner, which should be ready in a few minutes. We filed our patent application this afternoon. I was catching up on some reading in my office and figured I would just bring it home. Much more comfortable and spacious here. My office in the drug discovery laboratory at DCOR is a little spartan."

"Spartan? Go Green," Jillian said with a smirk as she walked over to the coat closet and pulled out two big green-and-white pom poms. "Give me a P!" Give me an A!" After an uplifting cheer that spelled out PATENT, and a few very professional moves with the poms, she gave Mia a big smile.

"Are you kidding me? You were a Michigan State cheerleader?"

"High school, actually. The Alpena Wildcats! They have the same school colors as MSU."

"Where's Alpena?" Mia asked with no clue.

Jillian flipped her left hand over palm down making the mitten shape of the lower peninsula of Michigan then pointed to the tip of her left index finger like any good Michigander would do. "Right there," she said, pointing with her right index finger. "About 200 miles north of East Lansing."

Mia went to the kitchen and brought out a decorative bowl of spaghetti and meatballs that she placed on the chrome and glass dining room table with a setting for two she had laid out earlier. Jillian retrieved a bottle of Lambrusco from the wine chiller in the Butler's pantry and they enjoyed the meal together.

"The Fluoropioid assay results came in this morning," Mia said, then twirled some spaghetti noodles using her fork and spoon. "We have five highly selective compounds that utilize the theta opioid pathway exclusively, even at very high doses, and compound T113 looks to be very potent. I'm guessing it will be the best performer in the animal studies and will become our drug candidate for clinical trials. I have a meeting with Mark first thing Monday morning to talk about our preclinical plan. What compounds? What animal studies? Budgets and timelines." She set aside the fork and spoon for a moment as she tore a piece of garlic bread from the loaf and placed it on her bread-and-butter plate.

"Speaking of budgets," Jillian said taking a swig of Lambrusco from a crystal wine glass that was an overstatement for the occasion. "What is your plan for funding? Animal studies are much more affordable than human clinical trials, but they're not cheap. You'll also need a supply of the compounds in a form or formulation suitable for use in the animal models you select." Jillian jabbed a fat meatball with her fork while she pursed her lips and sucked in three long spaghetti noodles from beginning to end. She had plenty of social graces for any occasion, but this occasion called for none.

"Funding?" Mia pondered as she poured a second albeit half glass of wine. "Mark hasn't mentioned funding but I'm sure it will be among the topics we discuss tomorrow. To date we've been funded out of the DCOR general operating budget, and I know Mark was recently awarded a small NIH grant from the National Institute on Drug Abuse to offset some of the costs of the animal studies. I'm not exactly sure of all the preclinical testing the FDA will require before clinical trials."

"After you meet with Mark tomorrow morning, you'll have a good idea of the studies you'll need," Jillian said. "If you'd like, I'll block out the afternoon. Maybe give you a tour of the small-animal laboratory on the top floor of the DCOR building and introduce you to some of our staff veterinarians and technicians."

Jillian and Mia pushed back from the dining room table and retired to the Great Room, the centerpiece of which was a massive limestone fireplace with a driftwood mantel. Alone on the mantel was a hammered copper urn containing the remains of Phoebe. Jillian had lost her beloved tricolor Cavalier King Charles Spaniel the year before and could not yet bring herself to get another. Maybe someday.

Mia chose to recline on the white leather sectional well suited to her long frame and shapely legs. Jillian climbed into her teardrop-shaped clear acrylic hanging chair with its colorful cushion and sat with her legs folded underneath her. Wearing faded jeans and a colorful tie-dyed shirt knotted at the waist, she looked like a parrot in a plastic egg.

"Incidentally," Mia said unprovoked. "It occurs to me that you never said anything about that hot singer-songwriter that was playing at Spanos the night I left early."

"His name is Shaun McKinney," Jillian said. Immediate recall. Present tense. "He turned out to be a ballad-singing-one-more-Guinness-beer-drinking Irishman. Great personality. Good sense of humor. Looks like Luke Bryan. We've been hanging out a little."

"Really," Mia exclaimed. "When do I get to meet him?"

"When you're married," Jillian panned.

13

Durham, NC

Mark used the Keurig coffee maker in the kitchenette adjacent to his office to make Mia a cup of Constant Comment tea and himself a cup of black Sumatran coffee. Not his first cup of the morning, and maybe not his second, but he never counted. He handed Mia her cup of tea as she sat in one of his burnt-orange guest chairs while he took a seat in his blonde leather high back with the beautiful teak and holly desk between them.

"The series of 15 compounds derived from T045 and T046 yielded five good leads," Mia opened. "Namely T107 and T112-T115. Of course, T113 was clearly the most potent among them."

Mark chuckled.

"What's so funny?" Mia asked curiously.

"Your use of the word 'namely' to describe a bunch of alphanumeric characters. Struck me like a reflex hammer on my patellar tendon."

"Just exactly how many cups of coffee have you had this morning?" Mia gestured with a backhand. "Don't answer that. Now then, with five good leads, the first order of business is to confirm that they are all pain relievers, right?

"Yes," Mark agreed. "They are opioids by definition because they utilize the theta opioid pathway, but we'll need to prove that their pain-relieving properties persist despite no other opioid pathway involvement."

"Of course, there's no way to assess analgesia in cells or tissues or even organs, so we'll need to test for pain relief or the prevention of pain in whole animals. Are their animal models for analgesia?" she asked.

"There are, indeed," Mark said. "Since there are many types of pain, such as inflammatory pain, acute post-operative pain, neuropathic pain that patients call *nerve pain* and chronic pain often associated with cancer, there are many different models. We could test all five leads in lots of different models, but that would be time-consuming and costly. The more efficient approach would be to test them all in a couple of the standard models and use those results to pick a lead candidate. We could then go back and test the lead candidate in the other models to more completely characterize its analgesic profile before we start clinical trials."

"Makes sense to me," Mia said. "I'm curious though. Patients can tell us when they are in pain, and we can ask them to score the pain as a measure of its severity. We can't ask the critters, so how do we gauge their pain?"

"For clinical trials, there are FDA-recommended pain scores to quantitate pain relief. This may be a numerical score, typically 0-10 with ten being the worst pain imaginable, or it may be a visual score where the patient is asked to place a mark somewhere along an unmarked line indicating their level of pain when told the right end of the line is the worst pain imaginable. This method takes out some of the bias introduced by ten prepositioned intervals. There's even a method called the Wong-Baker Scale involving *smiley faces* with a range from extremely happy to crying. Probably no more accurate than simple scoring from 0-10, but creative."

"These are all subjective measures requiring patient interpretation, and some patients may be more tolerant of pain than others," Mia remarked. "In fact, I'm aware of studies indicating that pain thresholds may be related to endorphin levels in the brain which may vary between patients. Isn't there a more objective measure of pain?" Mia asked.

"Well, there are instruments called dolorimeters that can measure pain thresholds and pain tolerance. Depending on the instrumentation or technique, these apply pressure, heat, or electrical impulses as the stimuli for pain. We will employ one of these in our animal studies, but they are not used in human trials."

"Ouch," Mia said with genuine empathy. "Seems cruel. I'm guessing PETA would not be happy to hear about this."

"PETA knows all about this. In fact, they are credited with the activism that led to all such studies now requiring the approval and oversight of an Animal Care ..." Mark said but Mia interrupted.

"Animal Care Committee. Yes, yes, I know. Your head of the Small Animal Laboratory upstairs is also the Chairman of the Animal Care Committee here at Duke."

"Jillian Saunders. Yes. Of course. Do you know her?"

"Jillian happens to be my landlord. I'm renting a guest room at her very nice house over in Duke Forest."

"That I didn't know!" Mark exclaimed. "Well, the reason we need to use these really-not-so-cruel techniques to measure pain in animals is precisely because they can't tell us when they're in pain like humans can. Dogs are notorious for tolerating a great deal of pain without obvious distress. Hopefully, God or the supreme being of your preferred belief created animals with more endorphins than man, and there's real data to suggest this may be the case."

"The God part, or the endorphin part?" Mia said slyly.

"Well, if you believe in evolution rather than creation, then I hope God created evolution to put more endorphins in dogs!"

"That's good," Mia said. "I'll need to spring that on my atheist and agnostic friends. She paused for affect, then continued.

"I'm actually meeting with Jillian upstairs this afternoon to discuss the protocols for the animal models of analgesia and drug addiction."

"In that case, let's take another moment and review what we know about drug addiction," Mark said scholarly. "Addiction is a compulsion to engage in a rewarding behavior despite potentially serious or even life-threatening consequences. It is believed that certain neurotransmitters in the brain are involved in the reward pathways, including dopamine, adrenaline, serotonin, acetylcholine, endorphins, cannabinoids, and others. In addition to these natural substances, there are a host of drugs with addictive potential apparently involving some of these same pathways, including caffeine, nicotine, alcohol, amphetamine, marijuana, opioids, and other substances of abuse."

"I seem to recall that tolerance and dependence are the twin pillars of addiction and that these are inextricably linked," Mia exclaimed.

"You're right. We know there is physical addiction and psychological addiction, and these may or may not be inextricably linked. Setting aside psychological addiction for the moment, we know that physical addiction, at least to drugs of abuse, is characterized by tolerance and dependence. Physical tolerance is defined as diminished drug effects upon repetitive dosing which explains why addicts require higher and higher doses to achieve the same affect. It's also the reason why many go on to use more potent drugs or begin combining two or more. Tolerance is a major contributor to unintentional and frequently fatal overdoses in addicts."

"How many doses are required to develop tolerance?" Mia asked.

"Tolerance is a cumulative-dose effect and the higher the cumulative dose the greater the tolerance, but the rate at which tolerance develops varies depending on the drug and the subject. Similarly, dependence is characterized by the physical symptoms of withdrawal when the subject stops taking the drug or addictive substance. The manifestations include body aches and pains, fatigue, nausea, vomiting, stomach cramps and diarrhea, even delirium tremens or the so-called *DTs*. We also know that withdrawal can be life threatening."

"This is why detoxification should only be attempted under medical supervision and why drugs such as buprenorphine or methadone are typically used to lessen the severity of the symptoms," Mia stated.

"Even alcohol and tobacco are in this category, although nicotine withdrawal is generally not life threatening," Mark said. "It is interesting however that some of the drugs used in smoking cessation are associated with suicidal ideation and it's not unlikely that nicotine withdrawal is a contributing factor. Dependence is also associated with the biofeedback loops of drug-seeking behavior or cravings; the body's effort to avoid the symptoms and risks of withdrawal."

"Are there animal models of addiction with measures of tolerance and dependence?" Mia asked.

"Indeed. We can use the same measures of pain but with repetitive dosing to determine whether progressively higher doses are needed to achieve the same level of pain relief; that is, whether the subject has developed tolerance. Again, the cumulative dosing requirement will depend upon the specific drug and subject or species. Other models are used to assess dependence, such as continued drug-seeking behavior after the drug, or *reward*, has been removed."

"The physical addictions you've described all relate to drugs or other substances of abuse that must be exogenously administered. Is it possible for subjects to become addicted to the endogenous neurotransmitters?"

"That's a great question Mia, and an area of considerable research. We've all heard about *adrenaline junkies* and those seeking an adrenaline rush or *natural high*. Whether by adrenaline or dopamine or some other neurotransmitter or combination, the extremists often describe activities such as hang gliding, mountain climbing or bungee jumping in much the same way that drug addicts might describe their addiction."

"Is tolerance and dependence a factor with these neurotransmitters in individuals at the extreme end of the spectrum?" Mia asked.

"Maybe," Mark replied. "Many describe the need for higher mountains, deeper canyons or greater speeds. Is this an indication of tolerance? Is their endless drive for greater challenges a result of physical dependence? Perhaps. Some of them have experienced the manifestations of withdrawal when their extremist activity is denied for a period."

"If not physically addictive, can the brain's neurotransmitters be psychologically addictive?" Mia posed.

"Another interesting question," Mark pondered. "There are certainly people that seem to be psychologically addicted to activities such as gambling or sex, yet I don't believe there's a component of physical withdrawal if these activities are denied for any length of time. There is also a growing body of literature to suggest there may be a genetic basis for an addictive personality trait or disorder. Of course, it can be difficult to know where to draw the line between a desire or compulsion and a habit or addiction. Most would make the distinction when the behavior becomes uncontrollable or interferes with normal daily activity, or worse."

"That all speaks to the endogenous brain neurotransmitters, but what about the drugs of abuse?" Mia asked. "Is there a psychological component to addiction that is not associated with the physical addiction of tolerance or dependence?"

"I'm not sure we know yet Mia," Mark answered. "Many describe a *euphoria*, a sense of well-being or pleasure, especially with the opioids, which can occur with the first dose. Perhaps the pathways of physical pain are linked to the pathways of emotional pain, and emotional pain relief may be described as euphoric. Others describe no sensations at all beyond pain relief and have no interest in taking the drugs after the pain is gone. Still others describe sensations beyond pain relief as an unpleasant feeling of lightheadedness, dizziness or a frank sense of impending doom as described in the literature."

"Well, I hope our drug candidate provides potent pain relief with no physical or psychological addiction. The gold needle in our haystack!"

"Before you head off to meet with Jillian, mark your calendar for a meeting this Wednesday at 9 a.m. with a friend of mine by the name of Robert Taylor. Bob has a PhD in molecular biology from UCSF and an MBA in finance from Duke. He's a serial entrepreneur of some local renown here in the Research Triangle Park, having started, grown and sold a couple of biotechnology companies. He did very well and now, together with some of his high-net-worth associates, runs an angel investment fund that specializes in biopharma spin-offs with technologies out of Duke, UNC and NC State. Perhaps you can put together a brief presentation of our Fluoropioid study results, along with an outline of our preclinical plan, approximate costs, and timelines. And be sure to use the keywords *haystack, metal detector* and *gold needle*. He'll love it!"

"No problem," Mia declared. "I anticipated the need to present sooner than later and already have a PowerPoint file in the fairway. The budget and timeline are still in the sand trap but not buried. You'll also be pleased to know that I'm an accomplished speaker in front of sizeable audiences. I failed to mention during my interview for this fellowship that I was on the high school debate team. My partner and I took first place in the California state championship held at the Hotel del Coronado in San Diego and placed seventh in the nationals at Independence Hall in Philly. Passed up several scholarships to Ivy League colleges with guaranteed admission to their law school if I had joined their debate squads. But opioid research became my calling."

Their loss, Mark thought.

14

Durham, NC

The Duke Center for Opioid Research, affectionately referred to as DCOR, resided in a modern seven-story brick building not far from the iconic Duke Chapel. The top floor with its optimum ventilation housed the resident canines and rodents that were used in the animal studies conducted on the floors below. The facility could accommodate other species such as guinea pigs, felines, porcine or primates as needed from time to time. Most of the guests were wild-type specimens, meaning they were genetically natural or normal. Some, however, were genetically engineered or modified to study a particular disease or disorder.

DCOR had its own café on the ground floor with an outdoor patio which was open from 7:00 a.m. to 3:00 p.m. on weekdays, serving breakfast sandwiches and light lunches. It was called the "High Five "and, given the opioid interests of its occupants, the double entendre was not lost on many.

Mia finished her meeting with Mark in his office then took the stairwell down four flights to meet Jillian at the High Five for lunch. After lunch, Jillian gave Mia the nickel tour of the top three floors of the facility and introduced her to most of the staff. Then the two women sat at a small conference table in Jillian's office on the sixth floor and discussed the animal studies they would soon conduct.

"Tell me more about the compounds you plan to test in animals and how they will be supplied," Jillian asked.

"We have five leads designated T107 and T112-T115. T113 was the most potent in our Fluoropioid studies which may or may not be the case in whole animal models. RxFactor has agreed to supply the necessary quantities of these compounds delivered frozen as they have been to date in concentrated aqueous buffer solutions and packaged with dry ice."

"That will be fine," Jillian said. "We can administer the drugs by intravenous injection in the initial studies and deal with oral formulations later. We can dilute the samples as you did in the Fluoropioid studies to determine whether higher doses produce greater pain relief in animals just as they produced greater fluorescence in cells."

"Jill, what animal models should we use to test for analgesia? Mark thought the tail flick and hot plate studies in rodents may be the best."

"I would agree," Jillian said as she searched her laptop and found the files containing the study protocols. "Those are certainly two of the standards, and efficacy in these models alone would support proceeding to human trials. Of course, that presupposes there are no other effects, side effects or toxicities that would preclude this."

Jillian printed two copies of the protocols and together they reviewed and commented back and forth on the materials, methods and required statistical analyses. Jillian mentioned that DCOR had the necessary instrumentation and experience for both. She said the tail flick study at DCOR involved an automated apparatus in which a mouse would be placed with its tail exposed. A high intensity beam of light would be directed at the tail and a timer would be activated. When the thermal stimuli reached the mouse's pain threshold, the tail would flick, and the timer would stop. The elapsed time was noted as the *latency interval* and a thirty second limit would be used to avoid excessive exposure to the heat. A few measurements would be averaged for a baseline then increasing doses or different analgesics would be administered. Higher doses or more potent analgesics would prolong the latency intervals.

Jillian then described the hot plate study in which a mouse would be placed on an apparatus preheated to 55°C, then covered with an open-top clear glass cylinder to prevent escape. The latency interval to first hind paw lick or jump would be noted, and again a thirty second limit would be used to avoid injury. Baseline, drug testing and interpretations would be the same as for the tail flick test.

"Jill, why does this protocol say to use naïve mice for each new test?"

"Because a mouse tends to become conditioned or *learns* that the test is over when it jumps. As such, a previously studied mouse will jump the moment the glass cylinder is lowered! I learned that the hard way the first time I conducted a hot plate test. The professor was very amused while I went about trying to catch the mouse! The lesson was that naïve or uninitiated mice are not preconditioned."

"Pavlov's dogs!" Mia recalled from her undergraduate classes in psychology. "Next we need to show that our compounds are nonaddictive by demonstrating that tolerance and dependence do not develop. Is there an animal model for drug addiction?"

"The classic model for this is the drug *self-administration* protocol and again DCOR has the experience and instrumentation. Basically, an indwelling catheter is positioned into the jugular vein of a rodent for intravenous drug administration. Dosing is triggered by a proactive behavior such as a lever press or nose poke. The behavior is reinforced using rewards, typically food, given during training sessions. After the behavior has been *learned*, the reward is withdrawn and replaced with drug or placebo infusions. If the drug is addictive, self-administration continues or even increases in the absence of reward as an indicator of dependence or endogenous reward. If the drug is nonaddictive or placebo, self-administration subsides and eventually ceases."

"Are these models all dose-dependent?" Mia asked. "That is, do higher doses or greater potency yield more pain relief or more dependency?"

"They are and that's an important element of our of proof of efficacy and lack of addiction." Jillian said. "Ideally, our most potent pain reliever even at the highest cumulative doses would not be associated with addictive behavior."

"These will need to be controlled studies," Mia postulated. "We will need to include placebo as a negative or no-effect control, but also at least one FDA-approved opioid as a positive control for comparison. Hopefully, our compounds will be at least equipotent as pain relievers and devoid of addiction. What FDA-approved opioids should we use as positive controls?" Mia asked.

"Probably morphine or fentanyl, and both are available as clear intravenous formulations, so blinding the studies would be easy. Fentanyl is one of the most potent opioids and 100 times more potent than morphine, so the two would essentially span the therapeutic range for approved narcotics."

"It would be nice if we can prove that our compounds also lack the potential to cause respiratory depression," Mia remarked. "Is there a test for that in animals?"

"There's a validated animal test for nearly every drug effect or side effect, and respiratory depression is no exception. We would again use mice and measure arterial blood oxygen saturation and respiratory rates with repetitive dosing of the test drug compared to placebo or the opioid standards. Opioids are notorious for depressing both respiratory parameters, presumably via the mu pathway. It will be interesting to see if your theta opioid compounds lose their respiratory depressant effects with their loss of mu pathway involvement."

"As I understand it, respiratory arrest and death is the inevitable product of tolerance and dependence; the twin pillars of death," Mia said pensively as she reflected on what must have been the final moments of her brother Warren's demise. "On the one hand, dependence drives the addict to an uncontrollable need for more, as the body ironically attempts to avoid potentially life-threatening withdrawal symptoms, then tolerance drives the addict to an uncontrollable need for higher and higher doses to satisfy the dependence. It's a vicious cycle. Death spiral. And the only way off the treadmill is medically supervised rehabilitation."

"Or an entirely new and novel *nonaddictive* narcotic analgesic," Jillian said emphatically, as if reading the mind of her new friend.

15

New York City, NY

Wally Cooper had been a patent examiner at the U.S. Patent and Trademark Office for years. He enjoyed his job and gained a working knowledge of both chemistry and medicine, though as a lawyer he had no formal education in either. When the chemistry literature came online a few years back, he was thrilled that it made him more productive. He could access resources like PubChem and ChemSpider to search for chemical structures and related molecules with no need to consult a chemist.

When the patent application for a novel new group of opioids was submitted by the Duke Center for Opioid Research (DCOR), Wally was assigned as the examiner. Upon his initial review of the so-called *patent file wrapper*, he knew it didn't take a PhD to appreciate the value or implications of the discovery. He recognized that any one of the new DCOR molecules, if proven safe and effective to the satisfaction of the FDA, would revolutionize pain management, ultimately reduce or eliminate opioid addiction and related deaths, and eventually destroy the black market for opioids. He knew this information was valuable and he knew just whom to call.

Carlos looked at caller ID and saw that it simply read OTD. He accepted the call on the first ring. "Carlos Martinez, Fischmann Brothers Investments. How may I help you?"

"Carlos, this is Wally Cooper over at the patent office. I just completed my first read of a file wrapper by some investigators at Duke and I thought you and The Brothers might want to know about it."

Wally had been a valuable source of information at the patent office on a few occasions in the past and The Brothers had shown their appreciation in each case. Once, Wally and his wife enjoyed a two-week luxury cruise around southeast Asia that began with a three-night stay at the Marina Bay Sands hotel where they enjoyed the views of Singapore from the world's largest and highest infinity pool. Another had been a private guided safari through East Africa with viewings of the Great Migration from luxury canvas tents on the Serengeti and a trek into the Bwindi Impregnable Forest of Uganda for a visit with the endangered Mountain Gorillas.

"What do you have for us Wally?" Carlos asked as his salivary glands contracted like he had just bitten into a lemon.

"Seems that one Mark Oberon, MD, PhD and his co-inventor Mia Reinhardt, PhD have designed some new molecules that may be opioid analgesics without the risk of addiction. Given your background as an MD, I don't need to tell you what this could mean."

"Fascinating," Carlos replied. "You're right. It could be very big. But you know we don't bet on success, abhorrent as that is to my sense of altruism. We bet on failure, or well-timed setbacks."

"I know that. So maybe I just slow walk their application. Maybe a very slow walk. Of course, there could be pressure from the top to move this thing along at some point, especially if there's demand from the medical community."

"We appreciate the heads-up Wally. Unfortunately, Duke is not a business entity with securities traded on an exchange, so there's really no opportunity for us, long or short. But let's stay in touch on this one."

"Thanks Doc and let me know if there's anything I can do for you here at the USPTO. Happy to interfere in any way I can!" Wally said with a grin as he ended the call.

Carlos made a note of his conversation and the patent application filed by DCOR. Since it did not represent a near-term opportunity for their investment style, he didn't feel compelled to share it with The Brothers. Rather, he searched his contacts and found the name of the compliance officer at FDA that Doc Wisenheimer had mentioned. Carlos had dealt with Jim Panow during the GenoVax short play and felt very at ease calling him directly rather than using Dr. Wilhelm Heimer as an intermediary. He placed the call from the comfort of his office in the Pinnacle Penthouse.

"Hello Jim, Carlos Martinez at Fischmann Brothers Investments. How are things in compliance at FDA these days?"

"Same ol' same ol'," Jim said. "Still chasing the bad guys that can't seem to keep their food production or drug manufacturing facilities clean and tidy. Watching out for our supply chain, you know."

"Jim, there's a company by the name of ViroSelect currently conducting a pivotal trial of its vaccine for COVID-19. We caught word that your folks over in biologics may be seeing a *higher* mortality rate in the treatment group on this one. Not many explanations for a *poorer* outcome, but a pathologic contamination would be one."

"Since they have not yet filed a New Drug Application for marketing approval, there has not been a pre-approval inspection of the production facility," Jim explained. "There are periodic inspections of every facility with products on the market, but these are general facility inspections. There would not be a product-specific inspection prior to a marketing application unless it was for cause. Let me check with the folks over in biologics to see if there's been a request for cause."

"Thanks Jim," Carlos said. "We'll keep you in our hearts and minds, and on our Christmas list!"

"On another note," Jim continued, remembering the Super Bowl tickets he had been given last year. "You and The Brothers might be interested in this. We just completed our review of the abbreviated NDA for the first generic drug company looking for approval on the heels of yet another innovator losing its market exclusivity. As you know, generic companies are not required to conduct their own safety or efficacy studies, since the innovator has done so in its NDA. The generic company only needs to demonstrate that a sample of its drug product is *bioequivalent* to the innovator's branded product. In this case, we learned that the generic company XenoMed submitted a sample of the innovator's product rather than its own. Clever, but fraudulent. Drafting a letter now indicating that FDA is suspending the review of all its pending applications and demanding a halt to the distribution of all its generic products until we confirm the bioequivalence of verifiable samples of its own drug products. Letter goes out early next week."

"Ouch," Carlos said as he whistled and leaned back in his chair, then put his feet up on his desk. "One of the biggest generic drug makers out there. Public company. NYSE: XMED. As my brother Miguel down in Mexico would say, 'That's a good Juan!' Thanks for the heads-up on that Jim. By the way, when's your birthday?"

"Not until November. But my anniversary is next week. I think it's our ninth."

"Done," Carlos said. "And tell the wife we said congratulations. Oh, and Jim, we won't need a copy of your letter to XenoMed in our files."

"Didn't think you would. Tell The Brothers that I said hello, and thanks," Jim said as he ended the call.

Those boys sure are a thoughtful bunch.

Carlos stood up and tossed the burner phone in the trash. He took comfort knowing The Brothers paid extra each month to be sure the trash was collected nightly, then incinerated every morning in the basement of the old Woolworth Building. Whatever number appeared as an inbound call on Jim's phone record would never appear as an outbound call on any phone record.

Carlos called The Brothers' administrative assistant, Pam. She told him Karl was out of the office, then put him through to Geoff who invited him down for a chat.

As he passed the Big Boards of the Pinnacle Penthouse on his way to Geoff's office, he paused briefly to tap out NYSE: XMED on a wireless keyboard nearby.

Currently $233.43. Near its all-time high $235.45 last week. Market cap $286B. Company News: First generic version of Humira pending FDA approval.

Carlos put down the keyboard and continued down the hall to Geoff's office. He regarded Geoff briefly then went straight to the window for a spectacular view of the Manhattan skyline.

"Just another glorious day, isn't it?" Carlos said with a smile.

"What's the ticker symbol?" Geoff asked.

"What do you mean?"

"Every time you've walked into my office, gone to the window, looked out, and said, 'another glorious day,' it's always been followed by your sharing a conversation you just had on a phone you just threw away, and a ticker symbol that led to another glorious day!" Geoff noted.

"NYSE: XMED" Carlos revealed.

"No kidding?" Geoff whistled. "That's one of the thirty companies in the Dow Jones Industrial Average. Maybe the biggest generic drug manufacturer in the world, and purveyor of a ton of healthcare products. Let's see, what's their current cap?" he said as he entered the ticker symbol into the stock market app on his phone.

"$286 billion," Carlos answered, coincident with the same number appearing on Geoff's screen. "I just checked before I came in. About $233 per share and near its all-time high."

"Gracious," Geoff exclaimed. "That's a big cap alright. Frankly, I can't imagine anything disastrous enough to move that juggernaut up or down much."

"How about a letter from the FDA going out early week citing fraud for submitting a sample of the innovator's product as their own resulting in FDA suspension of all further review of their pending generic drug applications and a halt to all further production and distribution of their marketed generic drugs, including a recall of everything on the shelves, until the FDA declares them rehabilitated. Stay tuned for the hoops they'll need to jump through for that!"

Geoff withdrew another a burner phone from his desk drawer. "What we really need is some stock in the company that makes these damn things," he said as he nearly dropped the untraceable phone twice from excitement while trying to speed dial their NYSE floor trader.

"Ben," Geoff said with more volume than necessary. "Listen. Put us down for a million on NYSE: XMED," listening for a moment as Ben responded. "Yes, short. Of course, short. How long have you been working for us Ben?" he asked rhetorically. "No, not dollars, shares! What's it at now, about $233 per share? Probably lots of daily volume on this big boy. Should be able to work it in without moving the market. Much. Take your time. We have until early next week. If you haven't filled the order by the close on Friday, let me know and I'll get a little more fidelity on how much more time we have before the drop-dead date."

Carlos threw a thumbs up to Geoff and headed back down the hall toward his office. As he passed by the Big Boards of the Pinnacle Penthouse, he stopped for a moment to watch the NYSE ticker scroll by. Lots of green numbers. A good day in the market for most companies. Then a red one scrolled by. *XMED $231 down $2.17 (-0.93%).*

I wonder who's hitting that, Carlos thought knowingly.

Just as he walked back into his office and closed the door, his phone rang. "Carlos Martinez, Fischmann Brothers Investments. How can I help you?"

"Carlos, bro, how goes it?" Miguel Martinez said as his brother answered the phone. They had not spoken since Carlos had left Grenada to do his internship and residency at NYU Langone on the East River not far from the Pinnacle Penthouse. Carlos didn't care much for the company Miguel had been keeping in Sinaloa and Miguel had been envious of the success Carlos had had without breaking any laws. They had basically stayed in touch through their younger sister Catalina who lived in the Mexican border town of Matamoros across the Rio Grande from Brownsville.

"Miguel, you Chamuco! How have you been?" Carlos asked, but not quite sure he really wanted to know. He couldn't make out the music in the background, but it sounded like Jan Hammer.

"Good, bro. Real good. Bought a terrific little seaside villa in Los Mochis. Big swimming pool. Tennis court. Bought me a 1973 Ferrari Daytona Spyder. White. Same as the one Sonny Crockett drove on *Miami Vice*. It might even be the one he drove! Mint condition. Dropped a coin. Don't recall anyone getting hurt, so I must have paid for it!"

I thought I recognized the tune, Carlos thought. "Listen Miguel, that's all good. I'm happy you have nice things, but how's Margarite and little Pedro?"

"Fine," Miguel said. Stone cold. "Pedro's teacher is Salma Flores!"

"Who's that?"

"C'mon, bro. Where you been? Under a rock? Miss Mexico from a few years back. She's one hot tamale! With or without jalapeños!"

"So, tell me Miguel. What do you do for a living these days? How is it you can afford a seaside villa, swimming pool, tennis court and a white Spyder?" Carlos heard a clicking sound that he hadn't heard before and didn't recognize, but it sounded like bone-on-bone.

"Look, bro. I told Catalina, and I know she told you, that I'm a very important dude down here now. I have whatever I want. I do whatever I want. And I do whoever I want. Sometimes I do them with my eyes closed. Sometimes I do them with my eyes open. And sometimes I have other people do them for me. You should come down sometime for a visit. Anytime. I can show you around. Meet the guys. Catalina tells me you're a money guy now. We can always use a good money guy. We just lost a good money guy the other day. Not even sure yet if El Nuevo Contador is going to work out."

"What do you mean you 'lost' him?" Carlos was puzzled by the choice of words, as if the man had been misplaced.

"It's a long story," Miguel said. "Come down for a visit and I'll tell you all about it. Show you where it happened. Gotta run, bro. Buy a ticket. Any dates are good for me. I go wherever I want. Whenever I want. Adios, bro."

Show me where what happened?

16

Durham, NC

From a drone's view, the circular fountain formed the sound hole of the guitar-shaped front driveway as it curved around the multi-terraced front lawn. Mia drove her old Subaru Outback along the curves and took in the splendor of the Versailles-style home that was one of the largest private residences in the Raleigh-Durham area. She pulled under the granite columned port cochere and parked behind Mark's black BMW. She wondered how long he'd been there since it was exactly 9 a.m. He was always early. She was always right on time.

The front door opened as Mia stepped onto the porch, and a butler escorted her across the marble foyer. He guided her under a double staircase then through a double French door that led to the stately home office of Dr. Robert Taylor. Mark was seated at an elegant antique conference table next to a man with more-pepper-than-salt hair and a perfect five o'clock shadow. Both men stood as she entered.

"Mia, let me introduce you to my good friend Bob Taylor," Mark beamed as he put a hand on Bob's shoulder.

"Very pleased to meet you, sir," Mia said warmly extending her hand.

"It's Bob, please, and the pleasure is all mine," he said as he gently but firmly shook her hand. He was awestruck by the fact that they were nearly eye to eye. Bob was every bit of six-two and looked down on most women as a matter of altitude not attitude. "I'm sure you've heard this before but you're a doppelgänger of Lexi Thompson. She's the ..."

"Yes. I know. The long-legged $10 million LPGA pro," Mia interrupted, flattered by the comparison. "We happen to be the same height and about the same age, but she has me by a few strokes and a lot of dollars! I do play, but she's out of my league," Mia said demurely and looked down at her shoes for effect before looking back up at Bob. "And you've no doubt heard this before, but you're the spitting image of Phil ..."

"Phil Michelson," Bob interrupted, having heard that comparison more than once. "He has me by lots of strokes and a few years. Probably a push on the dollars!" At 50 years of age, Phil Michelson had become the oldest player to win a major championship, while Bob was barely into his forties. "I swing the mashies and niblicks myself. My short game is usually pretty good, strong putter, but tee-to-green is a struggle on any given day."

"That's funny," Mia said engagingly. "I'm just the opposite. My GIR percentage is ..."

"Are we going to play a round of golf here or do a little business?" Mark interrupted, his manic side coming to fore.

Bob invited Mia to connect whatever device she was using to a USB port on the center console of the conference table then lowered a 10-foot screen from the ceiling and turned on a compact projector suspended from the opposite side of the room. Mia had the PowerPoint presentation on her phone and found the projector discoverable by Bluetooth. She asked Bob for his network password then launched the file.

Not just a scientist and golfer but a technophile, he thought.

Bob offered his guests refreshments sitting on a credenza nearby with a bucket of ice. Help-yourself-anytime-style. He drew the curtains on the bay windows behind his desk and dimmed the lights, using an app on his phone for both.

Not just a scientist and golfer but a technophile, she thought.

"Please, Mia," Bob said as Mark sat beside him. "I'm all ears!"

Mia had been trained to begin formal presentations with a light-hearted introduction, perhaps a cartoon, funny photo, or humorous short story, and to tailor it to the audience or occasion. Since there were three PhDs and one MD in a room of three people, she thought she would keep it medically oriented.

First slide please.

"Gentleman, I was told to keep this talk under an hour, but I couldn't get it below 400 slides. That's about one every ten seconds. So, if either of you have photogenic seizures, I hope you're well medicated!"

Bob had a good laugh.

"Are you for real?" Mark said, looking as if the Starship Enterprise had just landed in the room. It made Mia wonder whether he might have a subclinical touch of Asperger syndrome on top of his slightly manic ways. She knew that a failure to appreciate sarcasm was nearly pathognomonic for the condition, if not the trait.

"Of course, I'm not for real." Mia looked at Bob and grinned as she advanced to the second slide. It was titled *Mia Reinhardt, PhD* and contained about 12 lines of small font text.

"I'm Mia Reinhardt. I was born on March 25, 1992, at Los Robles Regional Medical Center in Thousand Oaks, California, and went to Glenwood Elementary School." Mark began to fidget in his seat as he squinted to read the text on the screen. "Our family moved to Valencia when I was 14, so I graduated from Valencia High." The double entendre brought a smile to Bob's face, but Mark was still trying to read the tiny lines on the screen while tapping his fingers on the table. "I was on the debate team in high school and the topic my senior year was 'Resolved: That the federal government should ...'"

"Oh, for God's sake," Mark interrupted and walked over to where Mia was standing in front of the screen. "Mia, we'll all have plenty of time to get better acquainted. Trust me, Bob's a busy man and a brilliant scientist. He'll appreciate our discovery and grasp its importance in thirty seconds if we can just put his nose on the right slide." Mark took her phone and fingered past several slides. He stopped on the colorful 4 x 17 summary grid of the Fluoropioid study results. "Here it is. Beautiful. Let's take it from here." Mark walked back and took his seat beside Bob.

A touch embarrassed that she had not prepared an elevator pitch, she continued more concisely. She mentioned the tetracyclozine-derived series of compounds from RxFactor and referred to it as their *haystack*. She briefly described the patented Fluoropioid assay and called it their *metal detector*. She pointed out the five compounds that had fluoresced a bright green, likened them to needles in a haystack, and suggested that T113 may be a *needle of gold*. Mark could not have been more pleased, and Mia breathed a sigh of relief.

Nice save.

"Finally, let me review the preclinical plan for the project," Mia said as she called up the next slide. It was a project management-style summary of the many preclinical studies, tasks, and costs along a timeline. "Of course, we have not yet had a pre-IND meeting with the FDA, but we do know there are several ..."

"I've heard enough," Bob interrupted as he leaned forward in his chair. "I'd be the court jester in this town if I hadn't heard the rumor that this might be Nobel Prize winning stuff. Let me just say that I'm thrilled and grateful you're asking me to join you both on this journey. Lord knows there are plenty of other deep pockets around here, and I know you can and should approach others. But let me say that most are businessmen or lawyers that I eat for lunch. I'm a scientist and you won't need to tell me twice about your status and plans going forward. How about $5.1 million on $10 million?"

Bob looked anticipatingly at Mark and waited for a reply. Mia set her phone aside, perturbed at having been interrupted again, but pleased that Bob was already making an offer.

"Let's see," Mark replied, tweaking his chin with his thumb and forefinger. "If you were to invest $5.1 million on a $10 million post-money valuation, that would give you a 51 percent share. A controlling interest in the company. Hmmm. Truth is, we don't need $5 million at this time," Mark continued. "When we do, we can raise it when the company is more valuable. That would mean less dilution to the shareholders which would be me and Mia, and even you at that point. Barring any unexpected requests from the FDA, we should be able to get through all the preclinical pharmacology and toxicology studies for less than $2 million. How about $2 million for a 5 percent share?"

"That's a $40 million valuation and all you have is a few cells that glow green when you add your special sauce!" Bob mugged and whistled. "Tell me you didn't take some of that T113 stuff of yours before you came here!"

"Very funny, Bob. You know the size of the opioid market, to say nothing of the cost of the opioid crisis, so you know as well as we do what the value will be if we can prove we have the perfect narcotic analgesic."

"If, if, if," Bob said. "Many a slip from the cup to the lip! Look, I'll need to clear this with my partners, but I think I can twist their arms to go 2-on-10. But rather than $2 million upfront, we would propose to pay in tranches. Equal installments of say, $500,000 each based on achievements. Maybe the first upfront, but the other three tied to mutually agreeable development milestones. That's a 20 percent stake when fully invested.

"Deal!" Mark said, but Mia cleared her throat. "Oops. Is that okay with you?" Mark looked at Mia as if asking for forgiveness rather than permission. She shrugged her shoulders and pensively nodded her head in the affirmative.

"Just so you know, we like the phrase *on-time-and-under-budget* around here," Bob said. "I also like to name things ...

companies, drugs, slogans, tag lines, even titles of country music songs. In fact, I already have a name in mind for the company. I mean *our company*. How about *Theta Opioid Therapeutics, Inc.*? We can use the abbreviation TORX. If you'd like, I'll ask our attorneys to file the forms. A Delaware C corp. NASDAQ: TORX when the time comes!

"Got the exit strategy mapped out already, eh, Bob?" Mark said slyly.

"I kind of like the name," Mia said and winked at Bob.

"Well then, I do too!" Mark said.

All three smiled and shook hands.

17

Durham, NC

"Morning Glory," Jillian said with a bright smile as Mia pulled out a stool from under the white-and-gray speckled Cambria countertop that horseshoed around the kitchen. Mia was still in her red-and-white silk chemise while Jillian was dressed in a navy-blue pantsuit and ready to meet the day. "I found some K-cups of oolong tea on Amazon. Arrived yesterday. Want me to make you a cup?"

"That'd be nice. Thanks Jill. Since we're spending the day together in the animal laboratory, what do say we ride in together? I'm happy to drive for a change."

"Sure. I'm not planning to go anywhere else," Jillian said as she retrieved the cup of tea from the Keurig one-cup and handed it to Mia.

"We agreed to a $2 million A-round of funding for the company the other day on a post-money valuation of $10 million," Mia said as she took a sip of tea. "One of Bob Taylor's private equity funds. We're calling the company Theta Opioid Therapeutics, or TORX for short. Bob's idea. I like it. We already have a P.O. Box in RTP and a Bank of America account with the first $500,000 installment, minus some of the startup costs that Bob deducted prior to the deposit."

"That's exciting. If you don't mind my asking, how's the company ownership split between you and Mark?"

"We talked about that and signed an ownership agreement prior to meeting with Bob. I thought he would want a majority interest, but he insisted on a 50/50 split. Down the middle. Any unresolvable issues to be settled by arbitration. He doesn't want lawyers to be enriched if we can't agree on something. He thought 50/50 was fair since I will be doing most of the heavy lifting under his tutelage. Mark's employment agreement with the University gives him a significant stake and controlling interest in his work and he is vesting the company with all the intellectual property related to the Fluoropioid assay, including the issued patent and DCOR's rights to the compounds under its contract with RxFactor. Bob put up $2 million for a 20 percent stake together with his partners, so that dilutes Mark and I down to 40 percent each and gives Bob the tie-breaking vote on any disagreements. Of course, every subsequent round will dilute all of us."

Jillian backed away from the stool where she had been sitting next to Mia and bowed deeply at the waist as she took two or three steps back in formal Japanese fashion.

"What's that all about?" Mia questioned.

"Have you stopped to figure out what you're worth now, at least on paper?"

"Not really," Mia said. "I've been too busy to think about it."

"Well, let me run my bionic calculator for you. Bob's $2 million for a 20 percent stake in the company puts your 40 percent at about ... no ... at exactly $4 million dollars. Give me a T ... Give me an O ... Give me an R ... Give me an X. What's that spell? Go Green!"

"Crazy, I know. But don't forget that's the fully diluted valuation, at which point we would have positive proof-of-efficacy in man and the last tranche in the bank. At this point, we only have the first tranche in the bank which puts my current stake at just $1 million."

"Oh, excuse me, Little Miss One Million!"

Mia changed into something more appropriate for work and the women bantered back and forth all the way to the DCOR parking lot. Mia pulled her Subaru into a spot near the back of the lot because they both enjoyed the walk. They stopped at the High Five for another coffee and tea, then sat out on the patio to talk shop without distractions.

"By the way," Jill started. "Your animal protocols were all approved by the Animal Care Committee, and you won't need written informed consent from any of the subjects." She giggled at her own joke despite having used the line dozens of times. "Should be able to get things rolling with my staff upstairs today. We could have all the results in a couple of days with that first big check you wrote to DCOR."

"That's great Jill, and thanks for helping me get the protocols through your committee. I spent some time yesterday with Anne McCarthy going through all the preclinical requirements for filing an Investigational New Drug application (IND) to obtain FDA authorization to begin testing in humans. Do you know Anne?

"Yes," Jillian replied. "I know her well. She's head of Government and Regulatory Affairs at the Duke Center for Translational Research and a former staff attorney at the FDA. Anne and her colleagues at the center help faculty move their research from the laboratory through clinical trials and into commerce."

"She was very knowledgeable and helpful. I described the studies we have planned to prove efficacy or pain relief and demonstrate a lack of drug addiction or respiratory compromise in animals. Anne mentioned that, while these would suffice for preclinical proof of efficacy, we also need a myriad of general pharmacology and acute toxicology data in at least two species, one of which must be nonrodent. She said the pharmacology studies were intended to demonstrate safety across a range of organ systems and would include physical examinations, blood tests, EKGs, X-rays and a battery of others. She said the toxicology requirements vary depending on the intended dose, route and duration of use but felt that 6-week so-called *acute studies* should be sufficient in the first instance."

"Duke has plenty of general pharmacology and toxicology testing capability that we can tap," Jill proffered.

"Anne said that your Small Animal Laboratory at DCOR is in full compliance with Good Laboratory Practices as required by the FDA, so we're in good shape for the proof-of-efficacy testing here. But she thought it might be quicker and easier to contract with an outside vendor for the other studies. She suggested a local group called Research Triangle Partners."

"I'm familiar with that group," Jillian said. "Most of their staff are former pharmaceutical or biotechnology scientists or medical researchers from the RTP area. I'm told they do great work for a fair price and always deliver on time."

"Anne was kind enough to give me a complete list of the studies we'll need for the IND submission, along with the approximate cost of each, as a sanity check on a bid from Research Triangle Partners. I think I'll toss a call into them when I get upstairs. A key component of the IND will be the protocol for the first clinical trial."

"I haven't had much experience with clinical trials," Jillian admitted. "However, your partner, Dr. Oberon, will nail that. As Director of the Pain Management Clinic at Duke Medical Center, he has a sizeable patient population, and he frequently collaborates with UNC and NC State when more patients are needed for a particular study."

Mia and Jillian finished their morning beverages and headed up to the animal laboratories on the top floors of the DCOR building. Jillian gathered her staff for a short meeting and brief review of Mia's animal protocols, then enlisted several of the veterinary technicians to assist with the studies. The instruments and equipment were retrieved, and Jillian personally reviewed the inspection and calibration records of each. Mia had gone downstairs to the drug discovery freezer and returned with quantities of the five test compounds from RxFactor and together with a couple of technicians prepared the necessary doses for intravenous use.

Once the experiments commenced, Jillian and Mia wandered about the laboratory, sometimes together, sometimes separately, assisting with some of the tests while just supervising on some of the others.

"Hey, Mia," Jillian spoke out from across the room. "Come check this out." Mia strolled over and Jillian had just placed a white mouse on a hot plate apparatus then quickly covered the rodent with a glass cylinder that was open at the top. The mouse immediately jumped up on the edge of the glass cylinder, then leaped onto the laboratory benchtop. It took a couple of the technicians to corner the critter and put it back in its cage. "Apparently, this one is no longer naïve," Jillian remarked. Everyone shared a belly laugh and the women named the mouse "Harry Houdini."

Mia excused herself and headed down the stairwell four flights to her office. There she placed a call to Research Triangle Partners. She was transferred to the person in charge of contracts and briefly described the preclinical work that Anne McCarthy had outlined. Mia indicated that she would send an email itemizing the studies she needed, essentially the list provided by Anne sans any cost estimates and asked that they get back to her ASAP with a quote and a timeline.

Next Mia called Paul Harris at RxFactor. "Hey Paul, this is Mia Reinhardt from the Duke Center for Opioid Research. How are you?"

"Fine Mia. Good to hear from you. I was just thinking that you've probably had a chance to run our second tranche of compounds through your fancy little fluoroscopic assay. If that's the case, I'm anxious to hear the outcome."

"We have, and that's why I'm calling. I thought you'd be happy to learn that 14 of the 15 compounds were fluorescent in the cell group for the theta opioid pathway with absolutely no fluorescence in the cell groups representing the other pathways at any dose. Five of the 14 were more potent than the T045 and T046, and one was extremely potent."

"Tell me Mia," Paul implored. "What are the numbers of the five lead compounds?"

Mia required no notes to reply. "T107 and T112-T115, and T113 was the one most potent. I mean the fluorescence was a dark emerald green even at a medium dose. A thing of beauty."

"Well, I'll be," Paul said. "You may think there was no rhyme or reason to the number assignments. But there was. I can tell you the exact functional group differences between each of them, just based on their numbers. You may recall that T045 and T046 differ by a single methyl group. By adding or subtracting some other functional groups, we made 12 new compounds as DCOR had requested. In addition, there was one other region of interest we wanted to probe, so we made three more. Sounds like we were right because the three additional compounds we made were T113-115. Three of your five leads, including your emerald!"

"And I thought it was just the luck of Irish! You drug designers have some powerful new technology at your disposal these days. Won't be long before we have little programmed nanobots running up and down these cellular signaling pathways mapping all the exact molecules and their functional groups that maximize responses and give us the capability to manipulate every behavior from empathy to lawlessness."

"Do you have any proof of efficacy for pain relief yet, or studies of addictive potential?" Paul inquired.

"Not yet. We're conducting the studies upstairs as we speak. We should have the data in a couple of days. I'll give you call when we do."

"Please do," Paul said, and they disconnected.

Mia then called the Southern Season gift shop and ordered a North Carolina-shaped basket with an assortment of cheese, crackers, chocolates and nuts. She asked that it be shipped to the Duke Chemistry Department c/o Dr. Ronald Newberry and to include a little thank-you card signed simply Mark and Mia. She reached into her purse and pulled out the Bank of America VISA embossed with the name Theta Opioid Therapeutics, Inc. She read the account numbers, expiration date and security code over the phone to the clerk and authorized the charge of $39.99 plus tax. As she ended the call, she felt good about having sent a token of their appreciation to the chemistry group, but not about having used the corporate credit card.

Just as her remorse was subsiding, Mia's phone rang, and caller ID announced it was Mark. Her remorse returned as she answered the call. The thought quickly went through her mind to mention having used the company card for a non-business purchase but just as quickly dismissed the thought because it was only 40 bucks, and it was in fact a legitimate business expense.

"Hello Mark," Mia answered before he said a word, signaling that she had used caller ID and that he was not *persona non grata*. "I was just headed back upstairs to continue helping Jillian supervise the technicians with our animal studies. We have a series of tail-flick and hot-plate tests in progress in one portion of the laboratory and self-administration tests for drug addiction in another."

"That's terrific," Mark replied. "When will you have the studies completed and the data analyzed?"

"I should be able to finish the analyses and report over the weekend. I'll arrange a meeting between you and me and Jillian to discuss the results Monday morning."

"I have a better idea," Mark said. "If Bob's available, and he usually has some flexibility, how about a foursome round of golf Monday afternoon at Duke? You and Jillian can share the results with us between putts. He and I just need the bottom line. We'll trust you two with the details."

"It's a date!" Mia said, imagining a match play between Lexi and Phil.

"Before I let you go," Mark said quickly. "I've been reviewing my catalogue of protocols for analgesic proof-of-efficacy clinical trials. The Pain Management Clinic has been involved in several sponsored by some of the major manufacturers of opioid pain relievers, so we have a good idea of what is acceptable to the FDA. If you're open Monday morning, let's meet at my office over at the clinic. Maybe after I finish my morning rounds. Let's say around nine-thirty to be safe. We can discuss the highlights of a clinical trial, then take a brief tour of the surgical recovery ward before we head to the links."

"Works for me," Mia said, and ended the call.

She took the stairwell back up to the animal laboratory and tracked down Jillian who was observing a tail-flick experiment being conducted by one her technicians. Mia gently placed a hand on her shoulder to avoid startling her since she was intently focused on the study at hand.

"Oh, hey Mia. Did you get your calls made?" Jillian asked.

"Yep. Good shape," Mia answered as she peered over Jillian's shoulder. "Looks like you're ready to nuke another mouse tail. Oh, look. This mouse's tail is tapered at end. Not pitchforked like yours!"

"That only happens on Friday nights," Jillian shot back. "At Spanos!"

"Guess what? Today's Friday," Mia said invitingly.

"We'll see. Look, Mia, I wanted to show you the dose-response data," Jillian said as she pointed at the technician's laboratory records on the counter. "Each successive dose is higher than the last and you can see that the latency intervals, that is, how long the mouse leaves its tail on the hot plate, increases with each dose. Of course, we don't yet know if it was treated with morphine or fentanyl or one of your compounds because it's a blinded study, but it's not placebo. Each dose level is an average of five tests and each test uses a fresh mouse. Since we don't yet know how long a single dose of the drug stays in the body, we retire the mice to their cages for at least a few days between tests. Let's go check on the self-administration tests in the back, then we can we cut out for the day."

The two strolled through the laboratory glancing at the many tail-flick and hot-plate studies in progress. At the other end they sided up to one of the technicians running an addiction test and observed a rat with an intravenous catheter attached to a swivel positioned from above to allow freedom of movement about the cage. Jillian asked the technician if this animal had already been trained and she indicated that it had. Then she asked if the reward had been water or food and whether it had been withdrawn at this point. The technician answered that the reward had been food recently withdrawn.

"See Mia," Jillian said pointing at the rat that was repeatedly poking its nose into a hole in the cage and alternatively sniffing at an empty food tray nearby. "This animal is no longer being rewarded with food, but the behavior has continued indicating the drug is rewarding and addictive. If this were placebo, or a non-addictive drug, the behavior would have subsided and then ceased. It's a pretty definitive test for the addictive potential of drugs."

"I wonder how many trips I would make to the Keurig machine in the morning if you took away my Constant Comment?" Mia said not even jokingly.

"Even more than you do now," Jillian said with a laugh.

The two finished up for the day in their respective offices and headed together through the parking lot toward Mia's old Subaru. As they walked Mia received an email alert on her phone and noticed it was from Research Triangle Partners. She stopped and took a moment to read the attachment then sent a reply that the price quote was fine and to proceed with the complete list of preclinical studies.

On the drive home they talked about how helpful Jillian's staff had been with the experiments and how the two of them would likely need to work through the weekend to have the results compiled and ready to discuss by Monday morning. Mia mentioned they would be sharing the results with Mark and Bob on the golf course at Duke on Monday afternoon, if that fit with her schedule. Jillian found the invitation delightful and said she would clear her calendar of whatever else was scheduled.

The Subaru passed up a street that was on their usual route home and Jillian took note.

"Where are we headed?"

Mia did her best imitation of Elwood portrayed by Dan Ackroyd in *The Blues Brothers*. "It's 6:30 p.m. on a Friday night. We've got a half a tank of gas, half a pack of cigarettes, it's dark and we're wearing sunglasses. I'm hungry for a burger and a beer, and Spanos is right around the corner."

"Hit it," Jillian said, recalling Jake's line from the movie as she began to squirm and reposition herself side-saddle in the passenger seat.

"What on earth are you doing?" Mia asked.

"I'm getting my tail out!" Jillian replied devilishly.

It was only twilight, but Spanos was dark on the inside, day or night. Jillian guided Mia around the bar then toward the back of the main room. They were interrupted along the way by waitresses in matching green tops and plaid skirts who just wanted to say hello to Jillian. The other patrons must have thought she was the owner given the attention. The two women slid into a dark pinewood booth near the stage and one of the waitresses took their drink orders. Mia ordered a Miller Lite in the can while Jillian asked for a Guinness draft in a chilled mug.

"Must be Irish night," Jillian said as the waitress was leaving.

"Every night is Irish night when I'm playing, darlin'," Shaun said, coming up from behind them as he slid into the booth beside Jillian and gave her hug.

"Shaun, this is my roommate Mia Reinhardt," Jillian said with a gesture. Mia was delighted that Jillian had introduced her as a roommate rather than a renter or tenant. "And Mia, this is my ..." Jillian paused. "This is my friend Shaun McKinney." Shaun and Mia were both surprised by her characterization of their relationship. Mia was surprised it was more than she thought. Shaun was surprised it was less.

The three chatted briefly and it was mostly a getting acquainted back and forth between Mia and Shaun. Just as the burgers and fries arrived Shaun announced it was time for his first set.

"What make of guitar do you play up there?" Mia asked Shaun as he was getting up from the booth.

"It's a Taylor. Why? Do you play?"

"No," Mia replied. "But I know a couple of guys that wouldn't play anything else." Shaun tossed a thumbs-up as he climbed on stage and tapped the microphone to hear if it was hot. Then he strapped on the guitar and adjusted a couple of strings that were slightly out of tune.

"Seems like a nice guy," Mia said to Jillian and meant it.

"He is, but he's always broke, and he can be very moody," Jillian said a little disheartened.

"You know what they call a guitar player without a girlfriend, right?"

What?" Jillian allowed the set-up.

"Homeless!"

18

Teterboro, NJ

The two ounces of caramel-colored Jack Daniels suddenly formed a column above the shot glass, then just as quickly receded. The turbulence was extreme but short lived just 14 nautical miles from takeoff. Nothing the Hawker 800XP business jet couldn't handle. Carlos was always more than a little nervous when he flew, so he quickly downed the liquid sedative before it had a chance to escape the glass permanently. Several minutes later at cruising altitude the ride became smoother, and the copilot came back to check on him. Carlos asked for another two-ounce shot, and the copilot courteously complied then returned to the cockpit and closed the door.

The Saturday morning flight from Teterboro to a private airfield in Sinaloa just outside Los Mochis took almost five hours. The in-flight service provided by the copilot and the array of in-flight audiovisual entertainment made the time pass comfortably.

Carlos was pleased his brother Miguel had invited him for a visit to Mexico and grateful he had sent a private plane for the trip. He wasn't sure whether it was chartered or owned outright. Frankly, he was afraid to ask. The brothers had not seen one another in years and neither really knew what the other had been up to in the meantime. Miguel knew Carlos had completed medical school in the Caribbean and had taken a job with an investment firm on Wall Street. Carlos recalled that Miguel had been running with a very rough crowd in Mexico for years and suspected that his acquaintances had not gotten any better or brighter.

As the pilot announced his approach and requested that his only passenger take his seat and buckle up, the Hawker quickly descended toward the tarmac. Moments before touchdown Carlos looked out his tiny window and noticed a white convertible sports car chasing alongside the jet and keeping pace nicely despite a landing speed of 130 mph. After the jet had come to a stop the pilot made his final announcement.

"Good afternoon, Carlos. This is your pilot, Manuel Hermanos. I'd like to welcome you to Los Mochis, Sinaloa. The local time is 12:15 p.m. and the temperature a pleasant 92 degrees. Have a safe visit."

The copilot opened the cockpit door and entered the cabin, then lowered the side door. Carlos disembarked and was warmly greeted by his brother.

"Welcome to Mexico, bro," Miguel said enthusiastically, as they briefly embraced. "How was your flight? Sorry that your copilot was a steward and not a hot-tamales stewardess," making assumptions about both the gender of the copilot, whom he had never met, and the preferences of his brother, whom he hadn't seen in years.

"Good to see you too, Miguel," Carlos said sincerely. "It will be good to spend some time with you and Margarite and little Pedro. It's been too long for sure. Catalina tries to keep us informed, but difficult for her I'm sure what with living in Matamoros."

Miguel took the leather weekender from Carlos and tossed it into the trunk of the Spyder. Then the two men climbed into the car and left the two-man jet crew as they taxied to a hanger nearby. Miguel dialed down the volume on Jan Hammer as they sped away with the top down.

It was very warm but dry and Carlos enjoyed the ride as much as the flight. The breeze was exhilarating as they traveled along the outskirts of town, then several minutes down a private asphalt road until the villa came into sight on a bluff overlooking the Gulf of California. Miguel parked under a columned port cochere on the oceanside of the stone mansion and the two entered through a set of double glass doors at the side of the house.

"Margarite!" Carlos said unable to constrain his regard. "It's been too long," he said taking each of her hands in his and a step back to admire. It had been many years since she played beer babe at the Tubac Golf Resort up in Nogales, but she had not lost a second of her charm or appeal. Wearing her favorite rattlesnake banded white Western hat and a colorful fiesta print gingham dress gathered at the waist and tied in a bow at the top, she was coastal Mexican á la mode.

Margarite escorted the two men into the home and Carlos noticed a sizeable business office behind twin saloon-style wooden doors on the right and a large billiard room with a full wet bar on the left. They continued down a gallery with spot-lit artwork in the alcoves along the way past a gourmet kitchen with Spanish tile and a myriad of commercial-grade appliances, including two subzero freezers. She said the master suite was down the hall to the right and that a matching guest suite was down the other hall to the left. Both had covered cabanas facing the swimming pool out back. The Great Room in which they were standing had a massive two-way stone fireplace that a person could have walked through to the pool patios beyond and balconies on three sides with several en suite rooms for guests and staff. Pedro's bedroom was even further down the hall just beyond the master suite.

A few caretakers wandered about, but Carlos had to look hard to notice. Through the fireplace he could see just a portion of the swimming pool. Splashing about and having all manner of fun, although alone, was the little one he had never met. Just as Carlos was about to go out and introduce himself to Pedro, the sounds of sirens grew louder, and he saw a pair of Federales patrol cars rounding the circle drive just outside the front door.

"Assholes," Miguel blurted. "How many times do I need to tell them we don't find their little sound and light show funny? At all!"

"Is everything alright, Miguel?" Carlos asked with concern.

"No worries, bro," Miguel said dismissively. "This shouldn't take too long. Enjoy your visit with Margarite. Maybe put on a swimsuit and join Pedro in the pool. He's quite the fish."

Miguel went outside and shut the front door. After a few loud words he came back in with the Mexican law enforcement officers and escorted them down the long gallery to the billiard room bar. Margarite showed Carlos to the guest suite on the first floor where he tossed his bag on the bathroom countertop. He quickly changed into the swimsuit that he was now glad he had packed and headed out his patio doors to the pool.

"Pedro, come here and see El Tío!" he implored. Pedro swam to the pool steps and climbed out, then approached his mother and Carlos relaxing in a pair of pigskin Spanish Equipal chairs.

"Pedro, this is your padre's brother, Carlos," Margarite introduced. "Say hello."

Pedro didn't speak but did take Carlos by the hand and shook it firmly. His big grin exaggerated the dimples in his plump little 7-year-old cheeks. His wet black hair looked like Armor All on a car tire. He turned toward the pool and was about to dive in when he looked back over his shoulder and said, "Very pleased to meet you, señor." Then he dove into the water. Headfirst. Very little splash.

"He's a good boy," Margarite said. "Bright boy. Studies hard. Maybe he'll take after his Uncle Carlos someday. Maybe the University of Arizona in Tucson. He speaks English as fluently as Spanish. His teacher at the prep school in town is terrific. Her name is Salma Flores, and you'll have a chance to meet her soon.

She comes here every Saturday afternoon about three-thirty to tutor Pedro. Advanced coursework. How can he miss?"

"Sounds like he has the bull by the ..." Carlos said but Margarite interrupted.

"By the balls! I know you, Carlos. You were going to say *by the horns!* This is Mexico, not Wall Street. Here the picadors get the horns. The matadors get the balls!" Margarite said quietly with Pedro nearby.

"So, tell me Margarite. We haven't seen one another in years. On the one hand, I'm happy for you and Pedro, but concerned about how Miguel can maintain such a lifestyle. Even more concerned that the Federales show up with lights ablaze and he tells us not to be worried. That was his word. Worried. I was thinking more like petrified, stupefied or mortified."

"He's in no trouble," Margarite said positively, as she repositioned herself in the chair for more comfort. "Remember, he was a simple border patrol officer when we met and married. He was making a very comfortable living then and has climbed the ranks with the Federales ever since. He doesn't talk about it much, and I mostly keep to myself here with Pedro, so I don't hear much about it from others. But Mexican state police and government officials come and go at least a few times a month, so it's hard to believe he's in trouble. Other men and some women come and go as well, even using the guest rooms upstairs quite often. I don't venture up much since we have a house staff, but some of the guests are very well dressed. Others slovenly. I'm guessing most are local politicians or proprietors. I wouldn't worry. Pretty quiet here, really. Except for the hippos out back.

Say what? Carlos couldn't even imagine.

Margarite stood up and stripped off her gingham dress to exhibit her still stunning figure in a brightly colored and refreshingly modest one-piece swimsuit. She dove into the deep end of the pool creating even less splash than Pedro had and began to swim laps using a slow but deliberate sidestroke.

"Carlos, my brother," Miguel said as he arrived poolside. Carlos turned in his chair and could hear the patrol cars as they were leaving. Miguel was wearing his trademark white polyester beltless pants and a pale-yellow T-shirt sans sport coat. As he turned to sit in the Spanish Equipal chair previously occupied by his wife, Carlos noticed the Kimber 9mm in his brother's back waistband. He could not have recited the make, model or caliber but he thought the wooden grips were *sporty.*

"I have something I'd like to show you," Miguel said a bit secretively, "We'll need to wander down past the tennis courts. Not far really. It's a collection. Some very rare items."

The exotic pet zoo down the hillside from the villa should have told Carlos his instincts were right. Miguel shared the story of when El Chapo was arrested and found with a collection of nearly 80 big cats. Most went to zoos throughout Mexico and the U.S., but many went to El Enterrador who gave a few of them to Miguel.

What Miguel did not share was that this feline menagerie had been his entrée into the underworld of illegal trafficking in exotic animals which complimented his trafficking in illicit drugs. The same cadre of characters that shepherded metric tons of the cartel's illegal drugs over the southern border of the U.S., were the same bunch of bums that transported exotic animals that were equally illegal for private exhibit. Miguel took pleasure in showing Carlos and other guests from time to time his well-kept collection that included white Bengal tigers, Asian snow leopards, East African lions, South American black jaguars and a breeding pair of hippopotami that were a gift from El Cocinero, the cartel's chief fentanyl cook hired away from Janssen Pharmaceuticals. The entire time he was walking Carlos through the exhibits, Miguel brandished his Kimber, perhaps for safety but more likely for show.

When they returned to the villa, Salma Flores was there working with Pedro on a school assignment under a cabana near the pool. The former Miss Mexico wore a bright orange string bikini as though she were prepared to jump in and cool off at any minute. Miguel introduced Carlos briefly and the two men continued to the billiard room bar. They shot a few games of pool and had more than a couple of drinks while they spent the rest of the afternoon reminiscing about their childhood.

"Now that neither one of us can shoot straight, perhaps it would be fun to invite Margarite down for a little cutthroat," Carlos said suggesting the eight-ball game for three players.

"Trust me, I've thought about that more than once but the version that I have in mind does not involve billiard balls or cue sticks!"

"Seriously?" Carlos questioned with genuine surprise. "I thought you both were getting on just fine."

"Not really. In fact, she left earlier this afternoon. Spends most Saturday nights in town with her folks. Usually doesn't come home until Sunday morning. My only regret is that she comes home at all. Fortunately, Salma is as much a mother figure to Pedro as she is a teacher and watches over him whenever Margarite is gone. In fact, Salma and I are going out on the town tonight. A little private club that rocks."

"And what about Pedro?"

"He frequently stays home with the house staff and does just fine. Would you like to join us tonight? Plenty of babes and blow!"

Carlos sensed that the invitation was insincere and jumped at the opportunity to spend more time with his nephew.

Salma had taken a shower and came down from one of the upstairs guest rooms wearing a black mamba snakeskin club dress with a plunging neckline. Miguel came back after going into his room and had exchanged his white leisure suit for a white T-shirt with a black leather jacket and black jeans. As the two headed out the side door for the Spyder, Carlos was reminded of John Travolta and Olivia Newton John in *Grease*!

The house staff prepared a gringo style Mexican meal for Carlos and Pedro that was a smorgasbord of fajitas, tacos, tamales, black beans and rice. Afterwards, Carlos and the boy retired to the great room where they watched a couple of shows on the U.S.-broadcasted version of the Disney Channel. Pedro was familiar with most of the shows and a few of the songs which he sang in perfect English. Later he asked Uncle Carlos to read him a bedtime story from an eBook on his iPad and fell asleep on his uncle's lap. Carlos carried the boy to his room and laid him in his bed. Then he headed to his own guest room for a hot shower and hit the sack.

Perhaps having had too many drinks that afternoon, Carlos awoke in the middle of the night. The clock on his nightstand read 2:45 a.m. He went to the bathroom and relieved his bladder then noticed his tongue was parched and stuck to the roof of his mouth, so he went to the kitchen for a drink. After pouring a small glass of apple juice he returned the jug to the refrigerator and left the kitchen. He was about to turn up the hall toward his suite when he heard muffled sounds coming from the gallery in the direction of Miguel's office. As he quietly and hesitantly made his way down the gallery hall it became clear the voices were those of a man and a woman hushed and coming from the billiard room bar. Carlos peered slowly around the corner and could barely make out the silhouettes of Miguel and Salma on the pool table in various stages of undress and positions of passion. Miguel's Kimber was on the edge of the pool table well within reach of his right hand. All they needed was a *Miami Vice* soundtrack to match their rhythm and a small cannon to mask their cries.

Carlos gingerly retreated to his suite and decided to relax by the pool for a while before heading back to bed. He came out his patio door and caught the pall of cigarette smoke, then noticed someone sitting in one of the Spanish Equipal chairs.

When he recognized it was Margarite, he whispered her name. She regarded his presence and invited him to sit in the matching chair next to hers. Carlos saw she had a cigarette in one hand and a cocktail in the other, and there was a half-bottle of tequila and a half-pack of cigarettes on the table beside her.

Once his brain allowed his eyes to process the poolside images in the dark, it permitted his ears to process the sounds that were coming from beyond. Unfortunately, Salma and Miguel's throes of passion were not masked by cannons and were easily heard by Carlos and Margarite, and probably by the hippos down below.

19

Los Mochis, Sinaloa, Mexico

Carlos Martinez watched the seaside villa grow smaller and smaller in his passenger sideview mirror as Miguel raced the Spyder back down the same road they had traveled up the day before. The Sunday morning sunlight reflected brightly off the highly polished chrome, but it didn't lift Carlos' spirit as he pondered the plight of his sister-in-law Margarite and little nephew Pedro.

"Why so glum, bro?" Miguel asked looking at Carlos and taking his eyes off the road for more than a glance. "If you need another drink, man, there's a full bottle of Patron in the glovebox."

"Thanks, I'm fine," Carlos lied. "Just sorry we didn't have more time together. I still feel like we barely know one another. I'll make a point to come back again soon. Or perhaps the three of you can visit me in New York. Maybe give you and Margarite a chance to patch things up. It's a terrific city with great people and a lot of things to do."

"I'd like that, bro. If you don't mind, I need to make a little stop here before we continue to the airfield. No rush. The plane won't leave without you. Unfortunately, I need to ask you to stay in the car because the men here don't know you and some are the nervous type, you know. We don't want anyone getting hurt. If you don't like *Miami Vice*, feel free to surf the stations."

The white Spyder pulled into the front driveway of an old two-story clapboard bungalow. There were a few older-model cars already in the driveway and several nearby in the street. The houses on either side were a few hundred feet away and Carlos could see no one else as Miguel disappeared around the side of the bungalow wearing his white leisure suit and a black T-shirt. Carlos was about to change the radio station when he heard the blood-curdling scream of a man that was quickly followed by his muffled cries. Despite Miguel's instruction to remain in the car, Carlos got out to investigate. He followed in his brother's footsteps up alongside the house and positioned himself quietly behind a parked car, so he could observe the activities in the backyard without being seen.

There was a sizeable gathering of men. Carlos focused on the object of their attention and to his horror saw a naked man with a solid steel rod entering his body through the apple in his mouth and exiting through his anus. The rod was suspended horizontally over a firepit, and his skin had begun to cook. Carlos was hopeful, if not certain, the man was already dead as the metal spit would have skewered his brainstem leaving him with no primordial functions.

Facing the firepit were three heavy-set shirtless men kneeling with their hands tied behind their backs and all wearing white cloth blindfolds. Each man was being held by two large men on either side. Standing beside the one on the spit, Miguel began to speak.

"Gentleman," Miguel clicked his jaw a few times. "Moments ago, you heard your friend and business associate scream. Now, you can no longer hear him, but you can smell him." Miguel's men lifted the blindfolds off their three captives who were still kneeling. "This is what we do to greedy pigs that try to sell their shit on our turf. We roast them. We will not tolerate Los Zetas anywhere near Sinaloa. Now you go back and deliver this message to your boss El Gran Credo. But before you go, we want to give you something to remember us by. I thought maybe we would give them to you all at once, but it may be more fun, at least for us, to give them to you one at a time."

While two men held the first captive tightly, Miguel reached down and lifted a hot poker from the firepit. With it he branded the letter 'P' into the man's forehead, and everyone heard the brutal scream. He then branded the forehead of the second man with the letter 'I' and the third man with the letter 'G.' The volume of the wailing first doubled, then tripled. Carlos fell to his knees out of sight behind the car and regurgitated everything that he had had for breakfast.

"Boss!" one of Miguel's men shouted over the screams. "Maybe we should take the hot poker and put their eyes out. That way they can be the Three Blind Mice and the Three Little Pigs!"

Miguel's men all laughed, and the wailing grew louder.

"That would be nice but then we would have to drag their asses back home ourselves. This way, we can just turn them loose and they can find their own damn way home. I'm just not sure if we should let them take their amigo here back on the spit or just give them his head? You decide. I need to get my brother back to his plane."

Carlos managed to scramble to his feet and back to the Spyder before Miguel returned. As Miguel climbed into the driver seat the pungent smell of vomitus belied Carlos' attempt to look innocent.

"Oh, bro. You didn't stay in the car, did you? Now you know what your little brother does for a living. He's El Ejecutor of the Sinaloa drug cartel! He's rich and powerful and respected. So long as drug companies keep making addictive narcotics and doctors keep prescribing them, people like me will keep living a *wonderful* life and people like that asshole back there on the spit will keep dying a *dreadful* death."

20

Durham, NC

The cup of oolong tea seemed almost too hot to drink, so she pursed her lips and blew gently over the edge of the cup before taking a sip. Mia thanked Dr. Oberon's secretary and continued waiting on the couch in his office. It wasn't unusual for Mark to be running late after his Monday morning rounds at the Pain Management Clinic. Mia gazed about the room impressed by his decorative palate and the nautical theme like that of his office at DCOR.

"Morning Mia," Mark greeted as he breezed into the room. He took a seat behind his desk and spun around to face his iMac sitting on the back credenza. "Sorry I'm late. I spent some time this morning looking through the recent protocols of company-sponsored studies in which our Pain Management Clinic has participated. But it seems to me we have a different challenge."

Mia rubbed her eyes and took another sip of tea as she wondered whether Mark had had one too many cups of coffee this morning or was just on another one of his manic runs.

"What do you mean we have a different challenge?" Mia asked.

"Let's say T113 is a good drug candidate," Mark speculated, but Mia didn't flinch. She was keeping it a secret to share with everyone later at the golf course. "We will need to prove that T113 is a pain reliever, at least as good as any other opioid, but the real question is whether it is nonaddictive unlike the others. Addiction occurs with repeated dosing. Patients become progressively more dependent and tolerant. We can prove pain relief in an acute setting but proving the absence addictive potential will require longer-term exposure to oral medication in an outpatient setting."

"Wouldn't we want to prove that it's a *better* pain reliever?"

"For opioids better is only a matter of safety, not efficacy. They are all equivalent pain relievers in equipotent doses. They just differ in their potency. For example, fentanyl is 50 to 100 times more potent than morphine, so it only takes 1 mg of fentanyl to match the pain relief of 100 mg of morphine. It's not superior it's just more potent. Likewise, sufentanil is a derivative of fentanyl that is used in the operating room as an adjunct to anesthesia and it's 5-10 times more potent than fentanyl and 1,000 times more potent than morphine. Clinicians refer to morphine-equivalent dosing charts to switch between opioids while maintaining the same level of pain relief."

"How do we establish the morphine-equivalent dose for our drug candidate?" Mia asked.

"I would propose we begin with intravenous trials. First, establish safety over a range of doses in heathy volunteers, a so-called *Phase-I dose-finding study* in perhaps 200 subjects. Then establish efficacy in patients with acute post-operative pain, a so-called *Phase-II comparative study* in perhaps another 200 subjects. In this trial, we would treat half the patients with intravenous morphine and the other half with various intravenous doses of our drug candidate to establish its morphine-equivalent dose."

"Why would we pursue the approval of an intravenous formulation for the treatment of inpatient pain when addiction is primarily a problem with the chronic use of oral formulations?" Mia posed. "I know there are intravenous drug addicts, but most were hooked on oral medications first. In fact, I believe the statistic is that 80 percent of heroin addicts began with prescription opiates like Vicodin. Given that morphine is safe, effective and inexpensive in the hospital setting, I see no market for an intravenous drug even if its nonaddictive."

"I agree. We wouldn't pursue an intravenous indication, at least not initially. Rather, once we have the morphine-equivalent dose from the intravenous Phase-II trial, we would use this dose to produce an oral formulation, then repeat the studies in outpatients with pain. Of course, the critical or pivotal trials would be the Phase III randomized double-blind studies of at least 1,000 patients with half receiving our drug and half receiving oxycodone or some other approved narcotic for oral use.

"So, you're thinking 400 subjects in the intravenous Phase I-II trials followed by 400 patients in the oral Phase I-II trials, then at least 1,000 patients in the oral Phase-III trials," Mia speculated.

"That's what I would propose," Mark said. "The literature suggests an incidence of addiction with currently marketed opioids as high as 20 percent after the completion of a 10-day course of oral therapy for any indication. Among those given an initial eight-day supply, 13.5 percent were still users after one year and this climbed to 30 percent for those given an initial 30-day supply. As such, we should be able to prove that our drug is nonaddictive with fewer than 500 patients in a Phase III trial given a 30-day supply of the drug, although I'd want the statisticians to confirm the sample size."

"Let's say we show equivalent pain relief and no cases of addiction in 500 patients, and let's also say the FDA grants fast-track status because of the opioid crisis. Would this be enough for approval?

"Not likely," Mark replied. "I think the Agency will still want to see safety in at least 1,000 patients but they would probably allow the additional cases to come from an unblinded or open-label safety study running in parallel with the double-blind comparative trial."

"If we encounter no cases of addiction in at least 500 patients, it is intuitive that there would be no cases of death by overdose, and that would be an important claim to make," Mia said thinking of her brother.

"It should be intuitive, but I believe the FDA will want us to prove that as well, and it usually takes lots of patients and many years to establish a survival benefit. Regardless, such a claim would not be necessary for initial approval."

"Given the program that you've laid out, what's your best guess on the budget and timeline to approval?" Mia asked.

"I think we're looking at a minimum of two years and $100 million," Mark speculated.

"With 130 opioid addicts dying every day in this country, that's 95,000 more souls lost during clinical trials. I would hope the FDA can work with us to be more expedient," Mia bemoaned.

"Me too, but we're getting ahead of ourselves," Mark walked it back. "I think the intravenous Phase I-II trials will take three to six months and cost maybe $20 million. We should ask Bob if he's good for that or if we need to bring additional sources of capital to the table. I would work with Anne McCarthy to file an IND as soon as possible with at least the intravenous Phase I-II study protocols we would propose. It should include the general pharmacology and toxicology from Research Triangle Partners and the chemistry from RxFactor, as well as our own Fluoropioid data. It should also include your efficacy studies in Jillian's little rodents, assuming the results are favorable, which I look forward to hearing more about on the golf course this afternoon!"

Mia just winked.

Mark took Mia on a brief tour of the Pain Management Clinic which managed patients with chronic pain such as cancer patients, most of whom were on opioids and essentially addicts under medical supervision. Then they toured the surgical recovery suites where the intravenous Phase I-II trials would be placed. While Duke had a sizeable surgical volume, Mark intended to recruit his close colleagues at UNC and NC State to better assure a speedy enrollment. When they finished their tour, Mark and Mia jumped into his BMW 7 Series and headed for the Fairview Dining Room at the Duke University Golf Course.

"GREAT TO SEE YOU again, Mia," Bob said as he stood and gave her a cordial hug, ignoring Mark altogether, though not intentionally.

"And very nice to see you too, Bob," Mark said with sarcasm that Mia thought he was incapable of generating. Perhaps she needed to rethink her diagnosis of subclinical Asperger's. Maybe his mind was just so focused that he didn't always pay attention to what others were saying.

"Hey Jill," Mia tossed her a smile and looked at Bob. "Shall we join you both for tea and discuss the animal study results here, or would you rather catch bits and pieces of it around the links?"

"For God's sakes, Mia," Mark said with exasperation. "I've waited patiently all morning without choking you, and heaven knows my golf game can wait. Let's join these two lovely folks right here, right now, and have it out."

Mark and Mia took the remaining two seats at the patio table under a covered umbrella. It was an overcast day and somewhat cool, but more than comfortable. After ordering a round of teas from the outdoor server, Mia got the ball rolling.

"Bob, let me know if you want more details on any of the objectives, materials, methods or statistical analyses. Since Mark and Jillian know the protocols, I thought I'd jump right into the results and conclusions." Mia outlined her remarks in the same order as they would appear in a scientific publication.

"First, both the tail-flick and hot-plate studies in mice essentially measure the same thing," Mia continued. "That is, the prevention of pain observed as a latency in the time it takes for the animal to withdraw from painful stimuli, in this case heat. There was a clear dose-dependent relationship in all treated cohorts, meaning the higher the dose, the longer the latency. In this series, all five compounds, namely T107 and T112-T115, were 50-100 times more potent than morphine and T113 was at least 100 times more potent in every individual test. This means 1mg of T113 was equivalent to 100 mg of morphine in terms of pain prevention. Similarly, it was essentially equivalent to fentanyl milligram for milligram."

"Nice!" Mark said preceded by a whistle, and the sterling results were not lost on Bob. Though Bob was not an "opioidologist," a quasi-discipline coined by Mark to describe his ilk, he held a PhD in molecular biology and probably could have regurgitated most of the methodologies without reference. "So, our lead compound is at least as potent as one of the most potent in the practice of medicine today. Now, what about addiction?"

"Next," Mia continued, "we explored the addictive potential of our compounds compared to morphine and fentanyl using the classic and well-accepted self-administration protocol in rats. In these studies rats are trained to perform a modest task, such as poking their nose through a hole in the cage to receive a reward, in this case food. At some point after the animal has learned the behavior, the reward or food is discontinued, and drug or placebo is continued in its place. If the drug is addictive, nose pokes will continue in the absence of food and may even accelerate. If the drug is nonaddictive or placebo, the nose pokes will subside and then cease. Across the board, when food was replaced by morphine or fentanyl, the nose pokes continued or accelerated, a clear indication of addiction. On the other hand, all our compounds were mirror images of the placebo response. There was rapid and complete cessation of the reward-seeking behavior as soon as the food was removed in the presence of drug."

"Bingo, Bango, Bongo!" Bob said, using one of his favorite golf expressions. "It doesn't take an MD, PhD or any other kind of D to know that we may have ourselves the first nonaddictive opioid pain reliever. That satisfies the requirements for the second investment tranche in my book. I'll transfer another $500K into the TORX account right after our round of golf today. That leaves the third tranche when the first subject is enrolled in the first clinical trial and the last tranche when the study is completed regardless of the outcome, good, bad, or indifferent, although not to exceed accounts payable in the event we have nothing, which I now highly doubt will be the case. In fact, I'll tell you what," Bob said looking at Mark. "I'll give you another $2 million right now for another 20 percent."

"How about another $2 million right now for two percent?" Mia jumped in. Mark was pleased his newest protégé was getting the hang of the business side of things and Bob was falling hard!

"Bob," Mark cut back in. "Mia and I discussed the clinical path we plan to propose to the FDA, and we'll probably need $20 million to get through the first phase of the clinicals. Of course, we'll have more fidelity on that after we discuss it with the Agency."

"When will that be?" Bob asked.

"Anne is filing the IND and requesting a meeting very soon."

"Let's wait and see what they have to say," Bob suggested.

The foursome gathered in the pro shop and Bob picked up the tab for everyone, then they all headed for the golf carts. Mia was paired with Bob and Jillian was paired with Mark. No one would admit who was responsible for the pairings.

As they gathered on the practice green for a few putts to get a read on the speed, Mark approached Mia with another question. "I forgot to ask about respiratory compromise. It's not necessarily a showstopper and it's always dose dependent, so maybe it's just important that we don't see it at therapeutic or analgesic doses?"

"*Mea culpa*," Mia said with the intentional play on her name. "You'll be pleased to know that there was not the slightest effect on blood oxygen saturation or respiratory rates associated with T113, even at the highest dose tested which was well beyond the expected therapeutic dose. There was slight depression of both with a couple of the other compounds and quite frankly I can't remember which, but it goes without saying that T113 was our best performer across the board and the clear choice as our drug candidate."

Bob caught the tail end of the conversation as his practice putt raced past the hole near Mark and Mia. "Sounds like T113 is our baby, eh?" he said, interrupting as he chased his putt off the backside of the green.

Jillian sank one from ten feet away, and everyone watched as the ball disappeared and rattled in the cup. She gathered it up, then headed toward the others now standing just off the green. "I'd give it a nine, maybe a ten, on the stimp," she said as she joined the group.

"I concur," Mia said.

The guys had no clue and were too proud to ask.

As they waited for the foursome in front of them to head to the first tee box, Mark asked yet another question of Mia. "You know, it didn't occur to me until the other day, and I had since forgotten to mention it. It's fine and dandy that our Fluoropioid assay indicates that our compounds only utilize the theta opioid pathway. But one could argue we haven't proven that other pathways are not involved; just that our assay didn't detect any. And that's a fair concern. Even the slightest involvement of another opioid pathway would compromise our conclusions since no one knows the relative contribution of each opioid pathway with respect to analgesia. However, there is one way we can ..." Mark said but was interrupted by Jillian.

"The use of genetic knockout mice!" she said, causing Mark to raise both eyebrows. "Don't look so surprised. We use genetically modified animals every day in the laboratory for one investigator or another. There's a whole range of medical conditions and disorders that can be reproduced for the purposes of research by deleting or *knocking out* a specific gene that encodes for a specific protein. Most of these knockouts or KO models can be purchased from suppliers of animal specimens for research."

"That was my thought," Mark said. "I wonder if there are KO rodent models of the various opioid pathways?"

"There are!" Jillian exclaimed. "Since each of the opioid pathways involves a different protein, there are KO mice for each. You can pick and choose the pathways that are present in each mouse. So, we purchased some for additional testing. In one group of mice, the mu, delta, and kappa opioid pathways had been knocked out, leaving only the theta pathway for pain relief. Upon conducting the hot-plate and tail-flick studies in this group, our compounds retained their full analgesic effects, proving that the theta opioid pathway was responsible for pain relief with no involvement of the other pathways. We then repeated these experiments in a different group of mice in whom the theta pathway had been knocked out, while the others had been preserved, and the analgesic effects were lost completely. These studies prove, with or without the Fluoropioid data, that our compounds are utilizing only the theta pathway to impart pain relief. I hope you don't mind but we used the TORX credit card to purchase the KO critters since these studies were not budgeted."

One of these days DCOR is going to lose her to TORX, Mark thought.

The foursome in front had just left the first tee box and headed down the fairway to chase their drives. Mia and Bob stepped up to the blue tees since he and Mark had decided earlier that the men's tees should also be fine for the ladies given their youth and talent. Mia looked at the scorecard and noted that the total yardage from the blue tees was 6,562. Although she no longer maintained a formal GHIN index or handicap, she typically played to more than 6,500 yards and shot somewhere around six strokes over par which was just six shots more than the average pro golfer for 18 holes. The fact was, even playing as little as she did, 6,562 yards would be a walk in the park.

"Hey Bob," Mia spoke softly since the other foursome was still in the fairway but loud enough to get his attention. "What's the deal with that guitar-shaped driveway of yours?"

"I'm a singer-songwriter of sorts. Guitar player. Enthusiast of Taylor guitars. I have a collection of no fewer than a dozen and made a trip once to the factory in El Cajon just outside San Diego. There I had the pleasure of meeting the Bob Taylor who happens to be the founder and still chief luthier of the guitar that bears his name. At my request and expense, he made me a custom 914ce Grand Auditorium with an African ebony body and Sitka spruce top. We both signed it. Probably the only one with two Bob Taylor signatures! I also bought a 914ce off the shelf for Mark. He loves it."

"Very kind of you," Mia said sincerely. "You must be good friends. But don't you think a guitar-shaped driveway is a bit over the top?"

"I had thought about a swimming pool in the shape of a four-piece drum set. Now *that* would have been over the top!"

"In that case, I won't ask if the master bed is shaped like a baby grand piano!" Mia remarked.

Don't even go there ... yet, he thought.

The foursome in front had cleared the fairway and were headed for the green. Bob offered the tee box to Mia. She positioned her tee at precisely the right height and always resisted the impulse to measure it with a ruler. She took just a couple of full practice swings then stepped behind the tee to pick a spot slightly ahead of her ball and in line with her target. Then she addressed the ball with her six-foot frame and leaned into a beautiful swing. The ball traveled in a deep arc with a slight draw and finished with a nice roll out to about 260 yards mid-fairway.

"Fabulous drive," Bob whistled. "Not only does she look like Lexi Thompson, but she also swings like her!"

Mia stepped aside and yielded the box to Bob. Without much ado, he positioned his ball on the tee, stepped up without a practice swing and sliced one into the woods.

"The rule here is you get a breakfast ball on the first tee box. That's a free swing with no penalty stroke."

"Yes, yes. I know what a breakfast ball is. That's fine," Mia said.

Bob reached into his pocket for another ball and another tee since he had broken the first one. He positioned them both again with even less consideration and drilled another one precisely down the same path as the first.

"Guess I'll play the mulligan on that one," Bob said as he bent down to retrieve the tee, quite sure that she had heard *that* term before.

We call it lying three and hitting four, she thought.

Bob and Mia both stepped back and yielded the box to Mark and Jillian. After their relatively uneventful drives, the foursome walked back toward the golf carts.

"I've been thinking," Bob said, and everyone wondered what was next. "I'm pretty good with names. Kind of a hobby of mine. Company names. Brand names and trademarks. Even titles and tag lines to country music songs." Everyone was waiting for the other shoe to drop. "I think I have the perfect name for T113.

Always better to go to clinicals with a tradename. Best to establish brand recognition and loyalty early in the game. What do think about *Narcogesic*?

Narcogesic. Not bad. Not bad at all.

21

New York City, NY

The hollandaise sauce paired nicely with the egg whites and yolk as he cut through and into the toasted English muffin. Karl preferred a full breakfast every morning and this one was complete with bacon well done, stone-ground grits with salt, pepper and butter, V8 juice, and coffee all served by the house staff on white linen. Geoff rather enjoyed his bowl full of strawberries, raspberries and bananas with a little light cream. No sugar added. This morning was no different than most as they dined on their balcony breakfast table four floors above the Big Boards of the Pinnacle Penthouse. A stroll to the edge and they could have looked straight down on City Hall Park below.

"Another gorgeous Thursday morning in Manhattan," Karl noted as he pushed his empty breakfast plate aside and grabbed a copy of the *Wall Street Journal* that the staff had retrieved from the lobby before dawn. They also subscribed to the online edition, but he preferred to read the print version at breakfast. Old habits die hard.

"Let's see what asshole made the *Wall of Shame* on the right column of the front page," Karl said as he looked and sighed, thankful it wasn't either one of them this time. He knew this was the section reserved for the CEOs, financiers, politicians, government officials and other high rollers that had been arrested, served a subpoena, or indicted by a federal grand jury after the ink presses had stopped the day before.

Karl was busy reading the *WSJ* business gossip when Geoff's phone alerted him to a press release just hitting the wires.

"Would you look at that," Geoff whistled and read aloud. "Released at 8:31 a.m. Before the opening. 'XenoMed, NYSE: XMED announced today that they received a letter from the FDA citing fraud in the submission of their marketing application for the first generic version of Humira, an $18 billion monoclonal antibody approved for ulcerative colitis, rheumatoid arthritis, etc.' It goes on to say '... FDA has suspended its review of all the company's pending generic product applications,' and here you go '... calling for a halt to all further production and distribution of their marketed generic drugs and a recall of everything on the shelves until the company is successfully rehabilitated. The FDA did not define the terms or the timeline for rehabilitation.' Happy days are here again!"

"Does it mention what the fraud was all about?" Karl asked.

"Let's see," Geoff continued. "Yes. Here it is. Submitting a sample of the innovator's product rather than their own for bioequivalence testing by the Agency. Chutzpah! I wonder how they were caught."

"Maybe they forgot to remove the drug from the Humira-labeled autoinjector, or submitted it in the box stamped AbbVie," Karl said almost choking on his V8 as he laughed at his own joke.

"Listen," Geoff said, pushing back from the table. "We need to get downstairs and get our NYSE floor trader Ben on the phone. This thing's going to tank at the opening, and we'll want to guide him through the big block trades. I placed an order for a million shares with him late last week when Carlos received the heads-up from Jim Panow while you were gone. Ben called me Friday after the close. Said he managed to fill the entire order with one million shares sold short at an average share price of $230. Sometimes that much selling can drive the price down, but there was still lots of buying on the expectation that their latest product would be approved imminently, so we didn't move their market much at all."

"Well, this news will move their market!" Karl exclaimed.

"And their bowels!" Geoff added for effect.

The Brothers were already dressed and ready for a busy day. Karl was wearing his gray pinstriped suit by William Fioravanti with a paisley tie and pocket square. He had gone to the haberdasher off Sixth Avenue a block from Central Park for the fitting. Geoff had on a dark olive herringbone suit by Caraceni and not to be out done had flown to Milan for his fitting. Both men could afford the finest but, on the scale, Geoff was class and Karl was crass.

As the two trading mavericks stood by the elevator waiting to go down and get their day started, the doors opened, and their effeminate Hispanic housekeepers Eduardo and Raul came out with their cleaning cart and supplies in hand.

"Well, Spic and Span," Geoff said. "Perfect timing. Sorry we can't stay and visit but we were just leaving," he said with sarcasm that was not lost on Karl, but it made the boys' heart's flutter not wanting to believe his remark was insincere.

"Not as sorry as we are," Raul said with his hand over his heart and perfectly accepting of his nickname Span as labeled by his Spanish friends. "Maybe we'll still be here when you return, working our little fingers to the bone for you. If it's not too late when you get home, maybe we can all go out for dinner. We don't have to call it a double date. But we could!" Geoff couldn't believe his ears as the elevator doors closed.

The Brothers descended two floors to their offices in the Pinnacle Penthouse while Eduardo and Raul proceeded with their daily cleaning of the three residential floors above the offices. Eduardo started in the gourmet kitchen which would take nearly two hours all by itself as Raul headed straight for Geoff's bedroom and started snooping through his closets and drawers. After twenty minutes of finding nothing that didn't belong to Geoff, Raul took the stairs down two flights and went to the kitchen to confront Eduardo.

"You know, Spic," Raul said. The boys liked their nicknames and enjoyed using them. "I look through Geoff's bedroom every morning and I have never found a single article of clothing or item in the trash that would reveal his orientation one way or the other. If the choices are LGBTQI or A, then I think he's an A. I don't think I even know anyone that's asexual with no interest in either sex."

"Funny you should say that Span," Eduardo replied. "I've been investigating Karl's room for the same purpose and A is my choice for him as well. So, now we know of two!"

"That Geoff," Raul cooed. "I'd give a whole week's wages for just ten minutes with that Chiquita!"

———————————————————

BY 8:50 A.M., THE BROTHERS were in their respective offices, checking their morning emails for any that required immediate attention. The only one of note was to Geoff from Carlos.

"Just checking to make sure you saw the XMED release this morning, but I have no doubt you did," Carlos had sent.

Geoff smiled to himself, reassured that he was still on his game, and then replied.

"Come on down to Karl's office at 9 a.m. and join us for the fun at XMED's expense," he sent.

At precisely 9 a.m., Geoff walked into Karl's office, which they called the "War Room" on a busy trading day. Carlos arrived a moment later and the three strategized about their XMED moves then called Ben on the floor of the NYSE at exactly 9:15 a.m.

"Ben, it's Karl. I have Geoff and Carlos in my office, and we have you on speaker phone."

"Oh, hey guys," Ben said. "I was expecting your call. Looks like we're in for a wild ride today. Better than the Cyclone and a lot more than ten bucks," he said with reference to the famed roller coaster on Coney Island. "Of course, XMED will crater at the opening. They closed yesterday at $233.32. You're in for a million short at $230, so let's see where this goes. I think we're in the driver's seat."

"Hey Ben," Karl said. "If you don't mind, Carlos is still a bit new to short selling. Can you walk him through the basics on this one? And keep it simple, he's just an MD!" Karl snickered and Carlos took it in stride.

"Sure," Ben agreed. "In this case, The Brothers borrowed one million shares of XMED from the accounts of a few willing brokers and we sold those shares last week at an average price of $230 per share. That put $230 million in the plus column of our ledger and one million shares of XMED in the minus column to be paid back to the brokers. That means we are short one million shares in the account. We agreed to return the million shares to the brokers when we buy them later and hopefully at a lower price. Now then, if the share price of XMED falls today as we predict and we buy a million shares at an average share price of, let's say $180, we can return the million shares to the brokers we owe and pocket the $50 million difference in profit. Of course, that's gross profit. We still must pay the brokers their fees for loaning the shares, and the trader his commission, that's me! Everybody wins, except XMED."

"This may be a bad example," Carlos pondered. "But what if XMED announces that the FDA made a mistake and rescinded its letter? In other words, what happens if the share price goes up and not down?"

"You're right. Bad example. The FDA doesn't make mistakes like that. But if the stock of a company you shorted goes up, you lose by the same amount you would have gained had it gone down that amount. In our XMED case, let's say the stock price goes up to $280. If we buy one million shares at that price to cover our short position, we can return the million shares to the brokers, but now we've lost $50 million."

Carlos thanked Ben for the tutorial and the NYSE opening bell rang at exactly 9:30:00 a.m. EST as it had every day for over 100 years, with orders placed from around the world and filled on the floor of the exchange at the corner of Wall and Broad. NYSE: XMED opened at $175.24 per share, down 24 percent from its close the day before on the bad news of its letter from the FDA.

"You could close your position right now boys and pocket a cool $55 million," Ben offered, as excited as if the shares were his. They were not, but his commission on this ticket would be substantial. He never forgot The Brothers on their birthdays. Even bought Karl a brand-new gold-colored Mercedes once, which Karl promptly gave to his niece. "Not many of us on this side of the trade, boys. A lot more sellers than buyers. It's a feeding frenzy. Hold or fold? What do you want to do?"

"Their generic products are at least 50 percent of their business," Karl said, having done his homework. "If we start buying now with a million shares to cover, it may slow the bleeding. Might even drive the price back up a tick. But if we hold out, it could be a complete exsanguination with a price of $115 per share by lunch. I say we hold."

"Don't forget the old saying," Geoff said as Ben listened in on the speaker phone. "Sometimes bulls make money, and sometimes bears make money, but pigs always get slaughtered!"

It reminded Karl of Cody, the taxidermized Kodiak brown bear that greeted visitors in the lobby just down the hall. It was The Brother's mascot and their answer to the bronze Charging Bull that stood further down on Broadway near Bowling Green. Someone had stuffed Cody's mouth with a "Snort the Bull" Beanie Baby they had borrowed from Karl's office, while "Blackie the Bear" Beanie Baby remained in Geoff's office for inspiration. Cody had been a gift from an appreciative client in their heyday as hedge fund managers, and the Beanie Babies had been a joke between the two of them one year for Christmas.

"The XMED chart over the next few days will take on a hockey stick appearance, as they almost always do," Karl projected. "The market knows at least 50 percent of XMED's earnings are now at risk. It will oversell them in the horror of the news to somewhere south of $115 then settle into a trading range that reflects the real expectations once the dust settles."

"It's at $145.50 now boys," Ben announced. "For your benefit Carlos, at this price it would cost The Brothers $145 million to buy back and return the one million shares they borrowed. Since they have $230 million on the ledger for this transaction, they would walk away with a paltry $85 million minus fees. Wait a minute. I'm starting to see a little weakness in the volume. What do you want to do, boys? Pass or play?

"We'll fold," Karl said looking at Geoff who concurred with a nod. "Go ahead and walk us out of the entire position as cleanly as you can and call us with the bottom line when you have it."

"What do we say when the SEC calls asking about our trades today?" Carlos asked nervously not having played the game before.

"We tell them what we always tell them," Karl said. "We thought the XMED stock price had gotten to a level of *irrational exuberance* to quote the former Fed Chairman Alan Greenspan on the prospects of its generic version of Humira. And who could have known it would collapse today on this kind of news?"

We could have, Geoff thought.

Carlos and The Brothers then left Karl's office and went around the corner to Geoff's side of The Bar for a celebratory toast. Kingsley the bartender had seen them coming and had their usual midday drinks waiting on the counter when they arrived. Karl had a shot of 18-year-old Talisker single-malt scotch straight up. Geoff had an ice-cold bottle of Tusker lager imported from East Africa. Carlos had a double Campari on the rocks. Just as they touched glasses Geoff's burner phone vibrated in his pocket. He took it out and caller ID announced Ty Dixon.

"Geoff, Ty Dixon here. How are you?"

"Just fine, Ty'" Geoff replied. "What's up?"

"Just had another case fatality in the ViroSelect COVID-19 vaccine trial. Broke the blind and it was an active treatment case, not placebo. I'm sure they'll be announcing a premature termination of the study based on our futility analysis up here at the University of Michigan. No chance of achieving efficacy with any statistical confidence and no sense spending more money needlessly. I also heard they produced several million doses at risk. Not sure what that cost but it will only compound the bad news."

Geoff shared the news with Karl and Carlos. The first thing Karl thought of was the call he had gotten last week from Jayne Gillis, the company's Director of Investor Relations. Little Ms. Goth had been so excited that her 10,000 shares of qualified stock options had vested just as the VSLT share price hit an all-time high of $106.24. She had a right to purchase shares at $80.25 each and was in the money for a cool $260,000 but holding out for $200 per share on the launch of their COVID-19 vaccine.

Poor kid will be crushed, he thought.

As the three men downed their drinks, Carlos said he had checked this morning and NASDAQ: VSLT opened around $103 per share on light volume. They all walked around the corner to Karl's office, shut the door and got their NASDAQ floor trader Max on the speaker phone.

"Max, it's Karl. We'd like to short NASDAQ: VSLT. Let's say 200,000 shares if you can keep the selling price north of $100." He looked at Geoff who winked, and Carlos who tossed a thumbs up. "Let us know when that's in the book. Volume's been light, so it may take a couple of days to fill the order and that's fine. Shouldn't be hearing shit hit the fan until sometime next week."

"Will do," Max said.

Karl disconnected from Max on the floor of the NASDAQ and called Ben over at the NYSE for an update.

"We closed out your NYSE: XMED account a few minutes ago. One million shares bought back at an average share price of a buck thirty. Put a cool $98,516,880.00 net in the win column for the Fischmann Brothers. Enjoy!" Ben said and disconnected.

Geoff called their driver who met them downstairs at the curb of 233 Broadway. He drove them up FDR Drive across the George Washington Bridge to Teterboro, where they boarded their Gulfstream V. Everyone at the general aviation facility knew that N4632FB was owned by the Fischmann Brothers and never chartered. The refrigerator in the galley was stocked with a few bottles of Dom Perignon just for such occasions. Karl ordered his straight up in a fluted crystal glass while Geoff wanted his with a splash of pomegranate juice. They had no destination in mind when the jet took off and changed their minds twice in flight. They also had no luggage onboard but buying whatever they needed whenever they got to wherever they were going was half the fun.

Paris is lovely this time of year.

22

Beltsville, MD

Jillian and Mia sat in the middle seat while Anne and Mark sat in the rear as the shuttle departed Ronald Reagan Washington National Airport for the offices of the FDA. The van was comfortable with no luggage since they had a return flight scheduled for later that afternoon. It was also private and theirs for the day. The group was looking forward to their 10:00 a.m. meeting with the Division of the FDA that would be responsible for reviewing the Investigational New Drug application (IND) that Anne McCarthy intended to submit on their behalf when they returned. She was a seasoned veteran of regulatory affairs at Duke and had defended many an IND at the Agency. She also had many friends at the Agency from the days when she was a staff attorney there.

Anne had sent a packet of the information she intended to include in their IND submission and had requested this pre-IND meeting. It was their opportunity to ask the reviewers specific questions to be certain they had all the preclinical data and drug production specifications needed for the FDA to authorize human trials of their new pain reliever Narcogesic.

They could have saved some money and rode the Metro Green Line from National Airport to Greenbelt via transfer at L'Enfant Plaza then Ubered to the FDA annex on Ammendale Road, but their financier Bob Taylor told them to be miserly, yet comfortable. They figured the van qualified as both.

They arrived at the annex a little after nine-thirty and grabbed a table near some vending machines just inside the lobby. Mark offered to buy. Mia and Jillian asked for a tea, Anne passed, and he added a cup of coffee for himself, not sure if it was his second or third of the morning. They chatted a bit with some time to kill but not about shop. Anne had taken them through a Q&A session in the days before, so they were well prepared.

Shortly before ten o'clock, they took an elevator to the lobby of the Office of Neurosciences, Division of Anesthesiology, Addiction Medicine, and Pain Medicine (DAAP). The receptionist led them to a small conference room down the hall and told them to make themselves comfortable. He also asked if they needed any refreshments and they all said thanks but declined. Moments later they were joined by Charlene Hopkins, MD, Division Director, and Jayden Banks, PharmD, Associate Director for Opioids.

After introducing her colleague, Dr. Hopkins began. "It's your meeting Ms. McCarthy. Please proceed," she said curtly yet nicely. She knew Anne had been an attorney at the Agency a few years back, but she was not in the habit of addressing lawyers as doctors despite their Juris Doctorate degrees.

"Thank you for inviting us today," Anne opened. "Joining me are Drs. Mia Reinhardt, Mark Oberon and Jillian Saunders, all from the Duke Center for Opioid Research. Also joining us by speaker phone is Dr. Paul Harris from RxFactor, our contract supplier of Narcogesic. Let me begin by giving a brief overview of the contents of the IND we intend to submit. First, we have summary results from the use of our patented …" Anne said but was interrupted by Dr. Hopkins.

"Please, Anne. I'm sorry to interrupt but we're all very busy, I'm sure. Everyone on this side of the table has reviewed the summary documents you submitted, and we are prepared to move right to the Q&A, if you don't mind."

"No," Anne said, taken aback but welcoming the efficiency. "Fire away."

"Dr. Oberon," Charlene began "First, let me say that we are all aware of your reputation in the field of opioid research and pleased to have this opportunity to review and, perhaps in some small way, to critique your work. Lord knows and this Administration appreciates that the opioid crisis is real. Unfortunately, it's been next to impossible to do anything more than put our finger in the dike. As you eloquently stated in your pre-IND meeting package Ms. McCarthy, addressing the problem from the supply side has been and will continue to be ineffectual. There are just too many sources and too much financial incentive on the supply side. No, the answer must come from the demand side. We have some very effective anti-opioid derivatives like naloxone to reverse an overdose and methadone to manage withdrawal under supervised rehabilitation. But the real answer will come from a novel new drug that provides narcotic pain relief without the risk of addiction. This may not be the answer to helping addicts kick the habit, but it is the answer to keeping opioids for pain relief from leading to new addicts. We hope as much as you do that Narcogesic is that drug and we're here to facilitate your efforts. Don't mistake what we say here today as being anything other than a genuine interest in your success. Having said that, I'll ask my colleague Dr. Banks to begin the questioning from our side. Oh, and feel free to ask your own questions and interrupt us for more clarification at any time. We want this to be a dialogue that ends with a mutual understanding of what's required. Dr. Banks, please."

"Thank you, Dr. Hopkins."

"Let's dispense with the proprieties and have a relaxing exchange, shall we," Dr. Hopkins interrupted. "Sorry, Jayden. Go ahead."

"Thanks Charlene, and I'll direct my first question to Paul," he said as he learned closer to the speaker phone. "The pre-IND documents indicate that RxFactor will be providing both the *drug substance* as we refer to the chemical compound and the *drug product* as we refer to the drug in a formulation for its intended route of administration. First, let me ask if your facility there in Del Mar has a certificate of compliance with current Good Laboratory Practices (cGLP)? This would be most relevant to the drug substance."

"We do," Paul answered with certainty. "We will send a copy to TORX, so they may include it with their IND submission."

"Good," Jayden replied. "Now, more relevant to the drug product, let me ask if you have a similar certificate with respect to current Good Manufacturing Practices (cGMP)?"

"No, I doubt it," Paul answered. "We're not manufacturers per se. We're synthetic chemists. Some might call us molecular architects. We use computer-assisted design software and three-dimensional molecular modeling to create ..." Paul continued but Jayden interrupted. Mia felt badly for Paul as she could relate to his borderline OCD.

"Paul, the reason I asked is that RxFactor supplied the Narcogesic in aqueous solubilized concentrated form frozen and packaged in dry ice for shipping. It was then thawed and diluted by TORX and administered to animals intravenously. Is that right?

"It is," Paul answered.

"And is this the intended route of administration and approximate concentration range proposed for the first human trial?

"It is," Paul again answered.

"Even in the absence of a cGMP certificate, which you could obtain if the facility qualifies, the question is whether RxFactor has the capability of producing a sterile product which could be authorized by the FDA for parenteral use in humans. Production must be under certifiably sterile conditions and the finished product must be tested and free of particulate matter or other contaminates, including toxins and pyrogens. RxFactor is probably a perfectly acceptable supplier of drug substance, assuming it produces a valid cGLP certificate, but unlikely to be an acceptable provider of finished drug product for intravenous or oral use in humans."

"Point well taken, Jayden," Anne conceded. "We will ascertain the capability of RxFactor in this regard and secure an alternative supplier if needed prior to filing the IND."

"We would accept RxFactor as a placeholder and simply require a suitable substitute, if necessary, prior to enrolling the first patient," Charlene said. "In this way you can move in parallel on the myriad factors that need to come together without losing time by moving sequentially."

"Thank you, Charlene," Anne said, intrigued by the concession.

"That's really all I had on Chemistry, Manufacturing and Controls (CMC) for the IND," Jayden said. "Paul let me just compliment RxFactor on some high science and great work defining the chemical groups that appear to be responsible for selectivity with respect to the various opioid pathways. We share your hope that Dr. Oberon is correct in his hypothesis that the theta pathway is the key to success." Mark smiled and nodded with humility.

"With that, let's move to the preclinical studies," Charlene said. "Unless Jayden has any issues, I found the general pharmacology and acute toxicology results as reported by Research Triangle Partners to be within acceptable limits to proceed to human trials. Of course, you will need to continue the toxicology studies to support longer durations of drug exposure, but what you have now is adequate for up to six weeks of dosing in man. Your vendor's use of canines as the non-rodent species for testing was reasonable and there were no observations of concern. With one exception. We are bothered by the incidence of nausea and vomiting reported in their studies of rodents, and not by the nausea as much as the vomiting."

Jillian and Jayden snickered, and Mark laughed out loud. On the other hand, Mia sat puzzled. She finally looked at Mark and asked, "What's so funny? Nausea and vomiting are well known and dose-dependent side effects of narcotics. I was hoping Narcogesic would be devoid of these, but we shouldn't be surprised or disappointed to encounter a few episodes."

"Was the meeting beginning to bore you, Charlene?" Mark regarded her with a wink. "Did you find the need to spice it up a bit at the expense of my postdoc?"

Before she could answer, Jillian spoke up. "I'm the veterinarian in the crowd, so allow me the honor of admonishing my friend. Maybe she'll teach me to be a better golfer! You see Mia, rodents apparently lack the physiological capability of vomiting, so they would be a poor choice for testing the efficacy of antiemetics." Mark chuckled again. Jillian smiled and continued. "I'm not sure we know exactly why, but some suggest they have musculature that's not conducive to the contractions necessary to affect regurgitation. However, we do know this holds true for the three major species within the Rodentia order, including mice and rats, squirrels, and guinea pigs. That's as far as my comparative mammalian physiology will take me, other than to say that horses are also incapable of vomiting. As for nausea, that's a little difficult to establish in rodents since they tend not to volunteer that information! Charlene, you should be ashamed of yourself," Jillian smiled and wagged a finger at her.

"Well, that's embarrassing," Mia said. "Thanks for waiting until our meeting with the FDA to share that with me Jillian. Seems you and I and Harry Houdini could have had that conversation back in the laboratory." Mia sat back and hoped the discussion would take a new direction.

"I have no issues with the general pharmacology or toxicology either." Jayden said. "In fact, I found all the proof-of-efficacy studies in rodents, both single-dose and multiple-dose in the tail-flick, hot-plate and self-administration studies to be very compelling. I was pleased that, in addition to morphine, you included fentanyl as a positive control since it is one of the most potent narcotic analgesics we use in humans. There are some more potent, but these are reserved for anesthesia or veterinary use, isn't that right Jillian?"

"That's right. For example, sufentanil and carfentanil are both chemical derivatives of fentanyl and prescription medications. Sufentanil is 5-10 times more potent than fentanyl and used as an anesthetic, while carfentanil is 100 times more potent. Just a small amount of the powder on unprotected fingers can be deadly. It is primarily used as a large animal tranquilizer, which is why my only experience with it is on Saturday nights when my dates misbehave! Sorry, just a little veterinary humor."

"I too found the animal studies compelling," Charlene added. "On the one hand, Narcogesic was slightly but consistently more potent than fentanyl and, as Jayden mentioned, that's one of our most potent narcotics. But it's also one of our most addictive and most abused. I was particularly struck by the fact that Narcogesic displayed no tolerance or dependence in the animal test for drug addiction, whereas this tendency was marked with fentanyl and morphine. This is a classic and well-accepted model for drug addiction and should give us a great deal of confidence that we're on the right track. I know you expended considerable effort on these studies, and I'd love to spend more time on the details of each, but it would not advance the discussion beyond where we are now. The fact is, as soon as you sort out the certification issues with your drug supplier, I think you're on your way to the clinic. The remainder of our time today would be better spent discussing the clinical path and protocols."

"Thank you, Charlene," Anne said. She was surprised again by the expediency and concluded that the Agency was clearly behind their effort. "There are two protocols in the pre-IND package. One is titled *A Phase I Open-Label Safety Study of Intravenous Narcogesic in 200 Healthy Human Volunteers*. The other is titled *A Phase II Safety and Preliminary Efficacy Study of Intravenous Narcogesic versus Morphine in 200 patients with Acute Post-Operative Pain following General Surgery.* We intend to form a Narcogesic investigative consortium between Duke, UNC, and NC State to facilitate recruitment and Dr. Oberon will serve as the Principal Investigator. As such, I will defer to him for a discussion of the trial designs. Mark, please."

"Thank you, Anne," Mark began. "The first is simply a safety study in 200 healthy subjects. These volunteers are not in pain, so there is no assessment of pain relief or efficacy. That will be reserved for the Phase II trial, and I look forward to discussing the Agency's current posture on pain scores and the one most appropriate for use as a primary efficacy endpoint. But first, let me highlight the eligibility criteria for the Phase I study."

"Mark, let me ask," Charlene interrupted. "I assume these single dose studies of intravenous medication in hospitalized patients will be followed by multiple dose studies of oral medication in outpatients, since that's where we see addiction. Is that right, or are you seeking an indication for intravenous use without regard to addiction, at least in the first instance?"

"No," Mark replied. "We have no plans to pursue the approval of an intravenous formulation. Morphine is an inexpensive and very effective opioid for intravenous use, and we don't see much need there. The goal is, as you say, to prove pain relief without addiction in outpatients on oral medication. But first we need to establish the morphine-equivalent dose in man, and that will require an intravenous study in patients."

"No, it won't," Charlene said assuredly.

"Pardon me?" Mark said somewhat puzzled.

"You already have excellent data in rodents consistently showing that 1 mg of Narcogesic is equivalent to 100 mg of morphine. That's your morphine-equivalent dose. That was further confirmed by that fact that Narcogesic was equivalent to fentanyl, mg for mg, and it's well established that fentanyl is 100 times more potent than morphine. There is also considerable data showing that the analgesic dose in rodents is equivalent to the dose in man on a mg/kg basis adjusting for differences in total body weight. If you don't mind, we would like you and the others to set aside your protocols, and I'll ask Jayden to distribute copies of two others.

Mark and his colleagues were taken aback as Jayden passed out copies of two very detailed protocols. Charlene regarded Paul on the phone and immediately emailed a copy that allowed him to follow along. You could have heard a pin drop as Charlene continued.

"The first protocol is titled *A Phase I Randomized Open-Label Placebo-Controlled Safety Study of Oral Narcogesic in 200 Healthy Human Volunteers*. The other is titled *A Phase II-III Randomized Double-Blind Efficacy Study of Oral Narcogesic versus Oral Oxycodone in 400 Patients Requiring Outpatient Pain Management*. We would ask that you not recruit any patients to the Phase II study until the first 50 subjects have completed the Phase I study, as a precaution."

"Are we to understand that these parallel track studies would form the sole basis for an NDA submission? Anne asked hesitantly.

"Not quite, but nearly so," Charlene said. "With respect to efficacy, our statisticians tell us that the Phase II-III trial is adequately powered to establish equivalency between oral Narcogesic and oxycodone. In terms of safety, 300 subjects will have been exposed to Narcogesic in the two comparative trials. Not bad, but not enough to characterize the safety profile. We would like to see another 700 patients in a Phase III open-label safety study that we would allow you to run in parallel with the other two trials. This will give us 1,000 cases for safety and some indication of whether the drug is nonaddictive."

"A very elegant investigative plan," Mark belauded, ready to pack up and leave with no further discussion.

"Mark, Mia, Jillian, Anne, and Paul," Charlene continued slowly for emphasis. "We have discussed these protocols internally with the Center Director, Office Director, and the Commissioner of the FDA, and I'm certain he has discussed it with the President of the United States. Assuming your raw data is consistent with your summary documents, we are all in agreement that Narcogesic is a potential game changer in the opioid crisis and worthy of fast-track status by the Agency. We believe these trials can be completed quickly and we're committed to an equally prompt review and approval of Narcogesic, if it performs as expected. We do plan to empanel a scientific Advisory Committee to assist with the review, but we assure you it will not matters."

"I'd say you shortened the timeline that we had contemplated by at least a year, and that will save many additional lives," Mark patronized.

Mia raised her hand, as if she needed to be acknowledged by Charlene, and Mark looked at her like a teacher ready to throw an eraser at his pupil. "Charlene, it's unlikely there will be any overdoses or related deaths in these trials, and not unexpectedly if Narcogesic is nonaddictive. What proof is needed to support labeling and advertising of superior safety in terms of the risk of overdose and death?" The question was less commercial and more personal for Mia.

"As we all know, there were 47,600 deaths attributed to opioid overdoses last year alone in the U.S.," Charlene declared, and could have recited the exact number of cases for the current year to date. "That's 130 a day, every day, with no vaccine! It's the reason we're all motivated to get Narcogesic to market as quickly as possible and to make sure the market knows its attributes. Let me give your question some thought, and confer with my colleagues, but I would say, if there's no addiction, it follows there can be no addiction-related overdoses or deaths. No further proof would be needed, in my opinion."

23

Durham, NC

Mia parked her gray Subaru Outback near the fountain next to the Duke Center for Translational Research and took the elevator up three floors to Anne McCarthy's office. Their meeting with the FDA the day before had gone exceedingly well, but they now had a laundry list of items to scrub before they could file an IND to begin the clinical trials of Narcogesic.

Mia took a seat at the small conference table in the corner and was enjoying the last of the Constant Comment that she had poured at home. Anne preferred her ergonomically more comfortable X-Chair and pushed it from her desk to the table. Its red mesh fabric complimented the red-and-gray décor of her office and the Ohio State pennant on the wall next to her sheepskin from the Moritz College of Law. After a brief exchange of pleasantries, Mia tapped the call button on her contact list for Paul Harris at RxFactor and tossed her phone on the table with the external speaker enabled. It was shortly before 10:00: a.m. in Durham, NC, which made for an early morning call to Del Mar, CA, but she knew the company had many business dealings on the east coast and arranged its business hours accordingly.

"Paul, it's Mia Reinhardt and Anne McCarthy here. Sorry for the early bird. Just trying to catch us a worm."

"Good morning, Mia," Paul replied politely. "Hello Anne. No problem. I'm always here early. First, let me apologize for not having sent you a copy of our cGLP certificate before the FDA asked for it. After our call yesterday, I went to the ..." he said but Mia interrupted to spare him the unnecessary monologue.

"I received your PDF of the certificate yesterday in the shuttle on the way back to the airport. You could not have been more prompt. Thank you. And don't take it so hard. We would have had that box checked before we filed the IND. I think the FDA just wanted to make the point that a boutique drug designer, while cutting edge in terms of drug discovery, is probably not the right partner for clinical trial materials or commercial manufacturing."

"We don't disagree," Paul said. "In fact, we recognize the limitation, and our CEO is contemplating some vertical integration into those capabilities since that's the next logical step for most of our clients. Let me suggest that you call Brantley Corbin over at TheraPeuTex. I'll text you with his number. They are right here in Del Mar, and we pass a lot of business their way. They have a sizeable contract manufacturing business, and they can produce virtually any formulation from small batch or commercial scale. They even have a fledgling generic business but may divest of that since sales and marketing are not among their core competencies.

"Do they have experience producing clinical trial materials?" Mia asked. "As you heard on the call with the FDA, we will need look-alike oral formulations of placebo, oxycodone, and Narcogesic for the double-blind studies, and quantities of open-label oral Narcogesic for the Phase-III safety study.

"TheraPeuTex works for clients in clinical trials all the time," Paul said. "That's half of their business, and the other half is commercial supplies. They even have a formulation development group. Very sophisticated and probably expensive. I'll just warn you that you'll avoid a lot of headaches if you use the same formulation in the clinical trials that you plan to introduce to the market. Might cost you a little more time and money upfront, but you won't regret it. Swapping formulations after an

NDA is filed causes the FDA a lot of grief. And FDA grief runs downhill. Trust me!"

"I know that well," Anne said. "I used to shovel grief downhill! I'm sure TheraPeuTex has a cGMP certificate, but do you know if they offer full-service Chemistry, Manufacturing and Controls (CMC) support for both INDs and NDAs?

"They do," Paul replied. "They can be your supplier and wholesale distributor from soup to nuts. After the NDA is filed, all you will need is a salesforce, and I'm guessing Narcogesic will sell itself. I'll tell you what. I know your compound as well as anyone, and Brantley Corbin is a friend of mine. I'll give him a call on your behalf right now. I know he's there. He's a closet day trader, so he's always in the office before the opening bell, which is 6:30 a.m. on the left coast! I know exactly what you need, and you have other fish to fry."

"Thanks Paul," Mia said warmly.

Anne and Mia knew that engaging TheraPeuTex for clinical trial materials would likely be the rate-limiting step to starting the Phase I safety study. They also knew that, with Mark's directory of local volunteers, the first 50 subjects could be enrolled very quickly, and they would soon be into the Phase II-III efficacy trial. Mia committed to follow up with Paul and Brantley on a supply contract. Together with Anne, she would also develop a budget and timeline to discuss with Bob. They weren't sure how much he was good for, as he palmed that coin like a magician, but the FDA had just made it more affordable.

"Back of the envelope," Anne said. "Let's assume that TheraPeuTex will want $10 million for formulation development and clinical trial materials." She had considerable experience with research budgets, both basic and clinical, so Mia trusted her judgment. "Our investigators and their institutions will require an average of about $15,000 per completed case, multiplied by 600 cases across the two double-blind trials, and that's $9 million. Then, I would add another $5 million for the open-label Phase-III study of 700 cases, and $2 million for a pre-approval batch of Narcogesic for FDA testing and initial commercial supplies. Toss in another $2 million for long term toxicology studies in animals to support chronic use, and maybe $1 million for SG&A. What's that 29? Call it $30 million."

"How long from now until we file the NDA?" Mia asked.

"Timeline is tougher. Lots of moving parts, but maybe nine months to NDA submission. Let's say we're off by 20 percent on the costs, and I'm sure we're not off by that much. Bob would need to be capable of $36 million to avoid putting you on the road to raise more dough before the trials. What do you think?"

"Your guestimates seem reasonable," Mia said with little confidence. "Let me call Bob and propose a meeting to discuss his interest and capability. That will also give me a chance to brief him on the outcome of our meeting with the FDA and maybe put him in the mood to take a bigger bite of the apple. If you don't mind, I'll call him right now."

"Be my guest," Anne said, happy to eavesdrop.

Mia launched the call from contacts and Bob answered on the first ring. She was pleased not to be on his send-directly-to-voicemail list.

"Hello, Bob. It's Mia Reinhardt."

"You can dispense with the Reinhardt routine. You're the only Mia that I know."

"Yeah, I'm usually the only Mia anyone knows, at least personally. So, our meeting with FDA yesterday went swimmingly and we have a much better understanding of our capital requirements and timeline through clinical trials to NDA submission for marketing. Wondering if you can squeeze me in today. We need to know if you and your partners want the whole enchilada, or if I need to hit the road in whatever direction you send me."

"I'd love to meet today, but I'm slammed here," Bob lied. "Maybe we can discuss it over dinner tonight at the Angus Barn?

If not, I'm available next Tuesday late morning, or early afternoon on Thursday. But the sooner the better, especially if your needs exceed my endowment."

"I'm guessing you're adequately endowed, and dinner at the Angus Barn tonight would be my pleasure, and my treat."

"Nonsense," Bob rejected. "It's a legitimate TORX business expense and I'm the one that audits the books! Give me your home address and I'll put it in my GPS to pick you up at six. I'll make the reservations and we'll get the conversation started over a drink. The bartender there makes a great Lynchburg Lemonade!"

Robert Taylor was a member and frequent guest of the University Club, a private dining club in Durham located on the 17th floor of the University Tower. He had considered the club for dinner, but decided on the legendary steakhouse in Raleigh, established in 1960 by Thad Eure, Jr., son of the late and long-time North Carolina Secretary of State. Bob reserved the private dining room in the basement adjacent to the fabled wine cellar. No prices on the menu. Just a cozy little dinner for two.

"See you then, Phil!" Mia said, evoking the name of Phil Michelson, the PGA tour great. Bob resembled the man, and it was the recreation that he and Mia shared as pastime and passion.

Anne teased Mia about mixing business with pleasure, but knew Bob was a great guy and thought the two of them might be well suited. Anne committed to file the IND as soon as TheraPeuTex was onboard, and Mia would let her know when a supply agreement had been executed.

Mia headed back down the elevator and proceeded to keep her meeting with Austin Crammer at the Duke patent office. His secretary announced her arrival and Austin invited her to join him at his small conference table. She opened her laptop and began to take him through the highlights of the proof-of-efficacy results for Narcogesic.

"Here, Austin, are the summary results for T107 and T112-T115, which includes T113, now referred to as Narcogesic," Mia said, pointing to the relevant sections of the open file."

"Terrific! Mark mentioned you had a great meeting with the FDA yesterday. Congratulations! As an aside, we filed a trademark application for *Narcogesic* after a search indicated the name should be available for use in medicine. I'll go ahead and add these proof-of-efficacy data in animals to the patent application. This is exactly what the patent office will want as evidence to support our therapeutic claims."

Mia spent the rest of the afternoon with Mark and his research staff at the clinic preparing for the Phase I study, then headed home to get ready for her dinner meeting with Bob. After a quick shower, she slipped into a sleek navy-blue, mid-thigh-length dress accented with a white leather belt that complimented her narrow waist and long athletic legs.

Jillian arrived home just as Bob and Mia were leaving and greeted them both in the driveway. Bob had brought his 1990 black Jaguar XJS convertible, one of four classics in his collection, and the first model year after Ford's acquisition of the British car maker. He hoped that Ford's influence on future models would be felt under the hood and not between the doors. At Mia's request, Bob left the top down and backed out of Jillian's driveway.

The light breeze made for an enjoyable drive from Durham to Raleigh. After arriving at the Angus Barn, with the Jag in the capable hands of the valet, the maître d' escorted Bob and Mia to the private dining room below the lobby and seated them at a table for two alone in a room that could have accommodated a hundred. Shortly thereafter, he returned to give them a private tour of the wine cellar, one of the finest in the country, then served them a vintage bottle of Altamura chilled to 18°C prior to their arrival at Bob's behest. It was one of his favorites. He had visited the vineyard on his last trip to Napa Valley and had not been surprised to learn that the vintner had been a winemaker at Caymus. The Lynchburg Lemonades at the Angus Barn were refreshing, but Bob felt that a fine cabernet sauvignon on this occasion would be more, well, impressive.

"Have you played any golf since our foursome last week," Bob asked. The waiter poured them both a half-glass of the Altamura, and Bob performed the ritual of a wine aficionado, then lightly aerated a swig across his palate and swallowed. Mia copied all the moves, then lampooned the aeration with as much noise as possible. Bob thought it was classy in a funny sort of way.

"I've been way too busy for golf," she said with a sigh. "But I'm ready to play a round whenever you are."

"Is there a space between the 'a' and the 'round,' or no?" Bob asked. She smirked. "Of course, I'm fine with it either way," he said with a wink. "Tell me about your meeting with the FDA."

"It was my first trip to the Agency. I've heard they are among the toughest regulators in government, but I found them to be exceedingly cooperative. To our universal astonishment, they pushed our protocols aside and basically said, 'Here, do these studies and, assuming the results are favorable, we'll promptly approve your drug.'"

"Why do you think they were so accommodating?" Bob asked as the waiter prepared two small Caesar salads with croutons and anchovies tableside.

"Honestly," Mia replied, staring at her salad as Bob started in on his. "Two reasons. First, I think they have a great deal of respect for Mark and were compelled by the preclinical data. Second, I think they're under some pressure to address the opioid crisis and curb the number of related deaths. I think this challenge for the FDA is second only to COVID-19 which is likely to remain a priority with the emergence of more contagious variants. However, unlike the coronavirus, there's no vaccine for opioid addiction. Never will be. So, they hope Narcogesic is the next best thing, and no one's more hopeful than I am," Mia said as she jabbed a healthy piece of Romaine lettuce but flipped a crouton laden with Caesar dressing off her plate and onto the white tablecloth. They both tried to ignore it.

"What path forward did the FDA propose and do you have a cost and timeline estimate?" Bob asked anxiously.

"They agreed to grant us fast-track status if we accepted their plan, which I thought was elegant. Essentially three parallel trials involving oral dosing in outpatients. One is a double-blind placebo-controlled safety study in 200 volunteers. The second is a double-blind oxycodone-controlled efficacy study in 400 patients. And the third is an open-label safety study in 700 additional patients. They did however ask that the first 50 healthy volunteers be enrolled and reported before we begin the patient trials."

Mia finished her salad then used her thumb and index finger to put the lonely crouton back on her now empty salad plate. She resisted the temptation to lick the dressing off her fingertips and instead smudged her wine glass as she took another swig, then gave the glass a look of uncertainty as to whether she had selected the lesser of the two evils.

Lexi Thompson and Sandra Bulloch. Gotta love them, Bob thought.

"What happened to the intravenous studies?" he asked.

"They accepted the morphine-equivalent dose data from the rodent studies for the purpose of oral formulation and we agreed there was no other reason to do an intravenous trial. I thought their rationale was very sound."

"What about the cost and timeline?" Bob asked as the waiter cleared their salad plates and poured them each another glass of wine.

"I met with Anne this morning and her best guess was $30 million and maybe nine months to NDA submission. Seems reasonable to me. She said she's not likely off by more than 20 percent, so $36 million and one year should be a worst-case scenario. Are you good for that, or am I hitting the road?" Mia said coyly as she took another sip of Caymus.

"You're hitting the road if you still insist that I only get 2 percent for $2 million!"

They both ordered the Grand Marnier Parfait for dessert.

24

New York City, NY

Her black lace Gothic choker had been left on his nightstand and her size-five silk crotchless panties had been cast in a bunch beside his bed. Karl still didn't know what the tattoo on the small of Jayne's back read in English, but now he knew what it looked like.

Dinner for two on the balcony of the Pinnacle Penthouse the night before had been a success as the kitchen and wait staff had outdone themselves once again. The sky had been filled with stars competing with the lights of Time Square for their attention. Their conversations had been light and mostly personal, except for the fact that Ms. Goth had told Karl about a recent death in the ViroSelect trial of their experimental vaccine for COVID-19. She said company executives had found it was due to a production problem but quickly corrected the issue and were back on track at the plant.

"Dammit," Eduardo cursed discovering the telltale signs of mischief near Karl's bed. He gathered the items and scurried down the hall to where Raul had just completed his daily sweep of Geoff's bedroom.

"Would you look at this, Span," Eduardo said, tormented as he held the crotchless panties over an outstretched index finger like a venomous snake on a stick for Raul to see. "The personal effects of a woman! And crotchless, no less!" he snorted. "Why bother taking them off?" he questioned rhetorically with disgust. "If my Karl is a member of our LGBTQIA community at all, at best he's a 'B.' Which would be of no interest to me!"

"He's a 'B' all right," Raul said, putting a hand on his hip. "He's a B-I-T-C-H! I still haven't found anything telling in Geoff's bedroom, but after your little discovery, I don't hold out much hope."

Karl and Geoff had gone downstairs to their offices right after their morning breakfast on the balcony. They had missed Eduardo and Raul who had gotten on the elevator at street level just as The Brothers had passed Cody in the lobby of the Pinnacle Penthouse. Karl and Geoff were now in their offices communicating with one another via wireless two-way headsets.

"I heard Jayne as she left *very early* this morning," Geoff said. "Must have been four-thirty or five o'clock. Did you enjoy yourself with her?"

"Never mind," Karl said dismissively. "Listen, she let it slip about the death that occurred in the VSLT COVID 19 vaccine trial that Ty Dixon had called us about early last week. She said there had been a problem on the production line but that the matter had been resolved, so they elected not to make a disclosure. I'm not sure why they're waiting. Futility is futility."

"Let's get Jim Panow on the horn over at FDA compliance and see what he knows about any manufacturing issues at VSLT. I'll patch him in right now."

"Hey Geoff. How are you?" Jim said having looked at caller ID. "What can I do for you?"

"Hey, Jim. I have Karl on the phone with me. You weren't aware of any compliance problems at VSLT last we spoke but wondering if you've heard anything since."

"Your Ouija board is working for you today," Jim said. "I don't have firsthand knowledge, but I'm told there was a life-threatening impurity of some sort. Toxin. Apparently, they fixed the problem in less than 24 hours and our office cleared them for continued production. Since there's no issue now, I figured there was nothing to report to you guys."

"Okay, thanks Jim," Geoff said. "Gotta run. Another call coming through. We'll touch base later."

"You bet. Take care," Jim said, then disconnected. Geoff cleared the call and took the next.

"Hello, Geoff. Ty Dixon here. Biostatistics at the University of Michigan."

"Oh, hey, Ty. I have Karl on the phone with me. Great timing. We were just about to call you."

"I figured as much. It's the darndest thing!" Ty said. Karl cringed, knowing the idiom was typically followed by the messenger being wrong, but faultless. "Right after we spoke, there was another death in the VSLT COVID-19 vaccine trial. This time in the placebo group. I thought, okay, that can happen by chance. Futility analysis still holds. But then there were three more deaths reported in the placebo group. Same day, right in a row. What are the odds?"

You tell me, Karl thought.

"I've served on many Advisory Committees and know many of the FDA's statisticians personally, so I called a few. They told me that VSLT had a deadly sterility problem in manufacturing process. Some sort of toxin that could have been masking a survival benefit in the active treatment group. They corrected the problem immediately and, since COVID-19 vaccines have been granted fast-track status, the Agency allowed them to continue the trial with a small statistical penalty that we call an *alpha penalty*."

Oh, is that what we call it, Karl thought.

"I'm guessing they'll be reporting positive trial results very soon, and pending approval of their vaccine."

"Shit!" Karl shrieked with no attempt to mask his lividity.

"Sorry, Karl," Ty said, having heard him over the phone. "I know how much you hate good news."

Remind me to take you off our Christmas list, Karl thought.

They thanked Ty insincerely and disconnected from the call. Karl tossed his headset on the desk and walked over to Geoff's office, then took a seat in one of his guest chairs. They talked about how this explained why VSLT had not announced the outcome of a futility analysis and wondered what to do.

Max had filled their entire order, so they were now 500,000 shares short on VSLT at an average share price of $102. Geoff checked and the last trade was at $124. There had been some upward movement over the past few days and Karl had correctly assumed that there had been some insider trading. Friends of federal regulators and corporate executives exercising stock options that were in-the-money.

A complication for The Brothers was that VSLT would soon be filing its Form 10-Q quarterly report with the SEC via the Electronic Data Gathering, Analysis and Retrieval (EDGAR) system. Then the entire world would know that The Brothers were 500,000 shares short on VSLT. That could trigger a *short squeeze* where investors buy more shares to drive up the stock price, putting pressure on The Brothers to buy sooner rather than later, which in turn drives the price up further. An upward vortex of death for a short trader! Regardless, it was getting late based on the new information from Ty, and The Brothers would be lucky to lose just an arm and a leg if they got out today.

"Max, how's it looking for us on VSLT?" Geoff asked. "I have you on speaker phone and Karl's in my office."

"Hello, boys," Max replied. "The good news is that I managed to cover your entire position in VSLT. The bad news is that I had to do it at an average share price of $135. There's been some upward drift lately and our buying only compounded the momentum. In at $102 and out at $135 on 500,000. What's that, a $16.5 million bad day, plus costs. Had better. Had worse."

Who's had worse? Karl wondered, knowing Max collected his fees win, lose, or draw.

The Brothers decided to head to The Bar just outside Geoff's office for some noncelebratory drinks. The atrium waterfall came into view as they rounded the corner and wandered through The Bar down to Karl's side. Seated there on the *Cristina O* barstool was Jayne Gillis dressed in her favorite color black with yet another plunging neckline. This time a shorter sleeved blouse revealed her entire forearm tattoo. Karl approached to give her a hug, but she planted a long kiss on his lips as she peered over his shoulder at Geoff and winked.

"Hello, Jayne," Karl said. "Surprised to see you here in the middle of the week and middle of the day. What gives?" He took the barstool beside her. Geoff excused himself and headed back down the hall to visit Carlos.

"I'll tell you in a minute," Jayne said. "I'm so excited! But first, I think you should rename this barstool. Instead of the *Christina O*, I think you should call it the *Janie O!*

Done, he thought.

"What's so exciting?"

"I know you're not a big shareholder, and that's an understatement, so you probably haven't been following the VSLT stock closely," Jayne said as she checked the stock app on her Apple Watch. "We're at $136.34 now. My options are at $80.25. That's $560,900! But I think we're going to $200, and that'll make me a millionaire!"

Her enthusiasm was contagious, and it took some of the sting out of his losing $16.5 million on the same security just moments ago. She finished her Black Russian, which paired nicely with her fingernail polish and lipstick, then told Karl she needed to run along back to VSLT. She gave him a big hug and blew Cody a kiss as she waited for the elevator, while Karl headed back to his office.

Geoff was in Carlos' office and the two were bemoaning the VSLT loss when Carlos received a call. "Carlos Martinez, Fischmann Brothers Investments. How may I help you?"

"Carlos. Wally Cooper here. USPTO. How are you?"

"Oh, hey Wally," Carlos greeted. "Just fine. Listen. I have Geoff here in my office. Let me put you on speaker phone. What's up?"

"We just received an update on the patent filed by the Duke Center for Opioid Research. It's the proof-of-efficacy in animals they needed to support the use of their compounds as pain relievers. I went through the data and it's very convincing. Their lead compound designated T113 was at least as potent as fentanyl."

"What's fentanyl?" Geoff asked.

"It's only one of the most potent narcotics known to man," Carlos answered given his medical background. "It's also one of the most abused and deadly."

"So, what's the big deal. Just another narcotic for addicts to abuse. FDA probably won't even approve it." Geoff scoffed.

"Here's the ringer," Wally continued. "They did studies in animal models of drug addiction." Carlos perked up. Geoff was lost. "This is where rats are trained to receive a food reward for poking their nose through a hole in the cage. Then the food reward is replaced with doses of drug or placebo. With morphine and fentanyl, the nose poking continued, even increased, but with T113 and placebo, the behavior stopped. Strong evidence that T113 is not addictive despite serious pain relief on par with fentanyl."

"Wow!" Carlos exclaimed. "Groundbreaking. There's a $30 billion worldwide market for prescription opioids and a similarly sized black market. This could wipe out the pharmaceutical market for opioids overnight and the illicit market in time as the source of new addicts dries up. But like I said before Wally, there's no public security here. Even if there was, we don't bet on success."

"Yeah, I know that Carlos," Wally said. "But I was thinking. The FDA will fast-track this drug because of the opioid crisis. There's no doubt it will become the narcotic pain reliever of choice and will destroy the worldwide market for opioids almost overnight. That's a $30 billion market and a significant percentage of the bottom line of some very big companies. You know the ones. If I had your money, I'd short them all. Just trying to be helpful. The wife and I haven't been on a vacation in a while!"

"Hopefully we can do something for you real soon, Wally," Geoff said then ended their call.

After Geoff left his office, Carlos spent some time online searching various subjects related to opioids, addiction, drug abuse and opioid research. It wasn't long before he noted several publications from the Duke Center for Opioid Research with most authored by Mark Oberon, MD, PhD. He read about the various opioid pathways and wondered just how Mark had solved the riddle of opioid addiction, then pondered the implications.

Suddenly Carlos' phone rang and vibrated on his desk. Caller ID announced it was his brother Miguel calling from Los Mochis in Sinaloa, Mexico. He thought about his recent visit and answered the call.

"Carlos, bro. What's happening?" Miguel said.

"Just trying to make my contribution to mankind," Carlos replied, although it caused him to reflect on the fact that he really made nothing, produced nothing, and frankly contributed nothing to society. He simply redistributed capital between the haves and the have mores. Once he was among the have mores, maybe he would join the full-time faculty at St. George's University School of Medicine in Grenada and pay it forward.

"I want to thank you again for visiting us down here," Miguel said. "Margarite and Pedro really enjoyed seeing you. And I did too, bro. I was happy you got to see my collection of kitty cats and hippos. Makes me want to go on a safari and shoot something, you know."

"I have the sense that you're already involved in enough shootings," Carlos interjected only half joking. Maybe not joking at all.

"Yeah, well. About all that. I'm kind of sorry you saw what you did. On the other hand, I'm glad it's out in the open between us. I worked my way up through the ranks of the Federales from border patrol to Presidential Guard. I was a bag man and liaison between the Guard and the cartel. Risky stuff. El Enterrador invited me into the organization when he was the enforcer for El Chapo. When Shorty was captured, El Enterrador took control and I've been The Enforcer ever since. El Ejecutor. He taught me everything he knows Carlos and now I know a hundred different ways to kill a man. I don't enjoy killing, but you'd be amazed what you can accomplish with just the threat. I can make things happen, or I can keep things from happening. Someday you'll need one or the other Carlos, and when you do, I'm your man! There isn't anything that I wouldn't do for you, big brother!"

Maybe there is something you can do for me when the time comes.

25

Durham, NC

His cheeks and forehead stung a bit as the wind blew the sand back in his face. He wiped a few grains from his eyes then spit some off the tip his tongue. Unfortunately, some had lodged in his molars, and he had to listen to a crunching sound for the next several minutes.

Bob Taylor wasn't much of a sand trap player. In fact, he wasn't much of a golfer at all. But he loved the game, and Mia's company, and it was a lovely morning at the Duke University Golf Club. It was his second attempt out of the greenside bunker of the 18th hole. His first had caught the lip and rolled all the way back, leaving him a few feet further away from the hole than he had been on the previous shot. This time his ball landed on the green without checking up and rolled well beyond the hole. Mia stood near her mark by the pin and watched his ball raced by.

"Another green-in-regulation for you, Mia?" he asked as he passed her on the way to his ball. There was no need for him to mark. He was still away with a downhill putt coming back.

"Yeah, but I missed three today," Mia said matter-of-factly, as she checked her line for the upcoming birdie attempt. Bob sank his 14-footer. All luck. It would have crossed the green again and rolled down into the fairway had he missed, but it hit the back of the cup, jumped straight up, and fell directly into the hole.

"Bingo," Bob said, delighted as he listened to the ball settle in the cup. "That's a double. Oops. No. A triple. It took me two to get out of that trap over there."

At least he's honest, Mia thought.

She took one more look from the opposite side of the hole, then stepped up to two practice strokes and nailed her birdie from six feet. "Yes," she said with a demure fist pump. "Six over for 78. Not my best here but I'll take it. How'd you do, Bob?"

"73, I think," Bob said with a straight face.

"What?" Mia questioned his incredulous calculation.

"Oh, you mean score. I thought you meant lost balls!"

Bob gave Mia a big hug after he had replaced the flag and the two strolled back to their golf cart. They changed their shoes and dropped their clubs into the trunk of Bob's car. After returning the cart they wandered up the path to the Fairview for afternoon tea on the patio.

"I spoke to my partners last night about a B-round for TORX," Bob said reaching for a tall glass of ice-cold lemonade with a fresh lemon slice hanging off the side. "Given the budget and timeline that you and Anne crafted, our proposal would be to give you $40 million in four tranches again based on milestones."

Mia took a sip from her cup of oolong tea. "That's a lot more than the $30 million and nine months that Anne thinks we'll need. Where are you on valuation? We now have animal data, not just Fluoropioid data, and the FDA has granted fast-track status with the requirement for just three parallel-track trials. I think we're at least 20 times more valuable than before. That would put us at $200 million now."

"It's still just animal data, Mia. It's good, but animal data is not always predictive of the human experience. We were thinking maybe an eight-fold increase in value. That would bump you from $10 million on the A-round to $80 million on the B-round. Let's see, $40 million on $80 million would give my partners another 50 percent for a total of 70 percent when fully invested.

You and Mark would each have 15 percent on a fully diluted basis.

Mia had told Mark that she planned to have lunch with Bob after golf and they would likely get involved a B-round discussion. He agreed to be available by text, so they could bounce the numbers back and forth.

I TRIED A 20X INCREASE IN VALUE, BUT HE'S AT 8X. WANTS ANOTHER 50% FOR $40 MILLION AND SAYS HE'S GOOD FOR MORE. PROBABLY DON'T NEED THAT MUCH, BUT ANNE'S $30 MILLION ESTIMATE COULD BE LIGHT.

Mark replied with a text message of his own.

TELL HIM $30 MILLION ON $100 MILLION, OR WE SHOP IT.

Mia shared the counteroffer with Bob.

"You two are tough. I'll be glad when our interests are fully aligned. Okay. We'll give you $30 million for another 30 percent which gives us 50 percent of the total fully invested. We'll make it payable in five tranches with $5 million upfront, $5 million upon completion of each of the three trials and the last $10 million upon NDA submission."

Mia sent a text message to Mark, and he tapped back with a thumbs-up emoji. Mia told Bob they had a deal. They caught each other halfway to a fist bump then stood up and gave one another a hug.

"I hate negotiating with friends," Mia whispered.

Is that all we are? Bob thought.

"Let's talk about exit strategy for a minute, then I need to run," Bob said as he finished his lemonade and bit the lemon. She pursed her lips and wrinkled her nose at the sight.

"What's an exit strategy?" Mia asked naively.

"Money in is great, but money out is what it's all about," Bob said. "Assuming the trials go well, and we have an approvable NDA, we basically have two options. Pass or play. To pass we would simply sell TORX to another company that would then make, market, and sell Narcogesic. In exchange, we get cash or shares of their stock, or a combination. We essentially give our newborn up for adoption."

"My brother never stopped short of the goal line and I'm not going to either," Mia said. "I owe him that much."

"Then to play we'll need to raise enough money to take Narcogesic to the market ourselves. Given the cost of hiring or otherwise acquiring all the operations of a fully integrated pharmaceutical company, it takes a very promising drug to make the numbers work.

"Narcogesic is more than promising and I'm sure the numbers will work just fine," Mia insisted.

"Wild guess, I'd say we'll need $500 million easy," Bob estimated. "That's in the range of a typical initial public offering or IPO, but there's plenty of private equity guys out there that could write that check. Not me or my guys mind you, but they're out there. I'll make a few phone calls and take their temperature."

"And I'll update our slide show with a commercial plan and budget," Mia committed.

"We'll need to embark on a roadshow for a $500 million equity offering the minute we have the trial results. Given the short timeline from financing to product launch I'd say the more viable option will be to acquire whatever companies or operations we'll need rather than to grow organically from scratch. For that reason, we're probably better off with an IPO and investment banker with expertise in mergers and acquisitions rather than another round of private equity."

Mia left the Washington Duke Inn and Golf Club and returned to her office on the second floor of the DCOR. She had sent a text message earlier to Paul Harris at RxFactor and arranged to talk by phone at 4:30 p.m. EST, which would be just after lunch in California.

"Hello, Mia. Good to hear from you and again great job at the FDA the other day," Paul said.

"Thanks, Paul. We were all very pleased and frankly a little surprised at just how accommodating the FDA was at the meeting. But they have a job to do, so their indulgence will have its limits. I'm sorry we must replace RxFactor but I'm grateful you recommended TheraPeuTex. We did our homework. They are a well-qualified commercial manufacturer. Just a question of whether they're within our budget and timelines."

"Since they are literally around the corner from us here in Del Mar, I went over and had a nice discussion with Brantley Corbin about the TORX meeting with FDA. They are sending a draft supply agreement to your legal department as we speak. It details the production of identical- looking oral caplets of Narcogesic, oxycodone and placebo for your clinical trials and proposal for the first commercial batch of Narcogesic for FDA testing and product launch."

"It will be rewarding to see our logo on the caplets," Mia exclaimed. "I'm imagining something like NARCOGESIC on one side and TORX on the other."

"Brantley told me the TheraPeuTex bid came in at $9.2 million and includes full document support for your IND and NDA. Oh, and Mia. Don't worry about bumping us from the project. Confidentially, RxFactor and TheraPeuTex are in discussions, and I think you'll be hearing about a merger soon."

"So, we won't be getting rid of you that easy," Mia poked.

The draft supply agreement from TheraPeuTex was sent to the law office of Richard Blair, a local business attorney retained as outside counsel by TORX. Mark and Richard had asked for some minor changes and renegotiated the contract to $9.0 million. Mia executed the final agreement electronically then noted the date on her digital calendar for investigational drug deliveries to the clinical sites. She was hopeful the first volunteer of the Phase I study would be dosed the very next day.

"Hey Jill, it's Mia," she said, calling from her office. "I just signed my first TORX business contract as its President and CEO. How about a small celebration? You up for Spanos?"

"Sure," Jillian replied. "I'm actually through here for the day, so I'll just meet you there in 20 minutes."

The women sat across from one another in an old wooden booth at Spanos and crunched a few empty peanut shells on the floor below. Mia ordered a patty melt with fries and a coleslaw while Jillian asked for a burger medium, mustard, onion, and dill pickle with a side of onion rings. Over in the corner was a raised wooden platform covered with well-worn black carpet that the performers called *The Stage*. On it was a tripod stool and a tower-shaped amplifier connected to a cordless microphone on a boom and a Taylor acoustic-electric guitar cradled on a stand. There was a poster on the wall near their booth.

Shaun McKinney – Tonight @ 7:00 p.m.

Jillian looked at her phone. It was 6:36 p.m.

"I didn't know you liked Guinness," Mia commented as she took a long pull on her own Miller Lite.

"I don't usually, but it's Irish and there's a good-looking Irishman playing that guitar up there tonight," Jillian said, showing her devilish tail. "He'll sit with us between sets. We've come to be friends."

"Just friends?" Mia probed.

"We'll see."

As Mia was thinking about how good Shaun and Jillian must look together, she noticed the general manager making his way around the establishment with a handful of posters and pushpins. When he arrived at their booth, he excused himself then reached over and replaced the poster of Shaun.

Derrick Ryder – Tonight @ 7:30 p.m.

"Shaun's not playing tonight?" Jillian questioned the manager with disappointment in her voice. "Did he get a better offer across town?"

"I'm sorry," the manager said hesitantly. "Shaun's roommate Steve just called. Apparently, Shaun overdosed about an hour ago. Paramedics gave him a shot of Narcan and took him to Duke Medical Center. Steve said he was in bad shape when they picked him up."

Jillian dropped her burger mid-bite and bolted for the front door. Mia told the manager they would cover the check later. He flashed her an okay sign as she chased after Jillian. Mia drove them quickly but safely to the Duke Medical Center while Jillian sobbed uncontrollably. She was evidently more attached to Shaun than she had confided.

THE RHYTHMIC CONTRACTIONS of the ventilator made the hair on Mia's forearms stand straight up as she tried to comfort Jillian. Shaun was in the ER and surrounded by a small medical team. One of the doctors left his bedside and approached the women.

"I'm doctor Ryan Williams, the attending ER physician this evening. I'm told Shaun McKinney has no immediate family in the area but that you two are good friends of his."

"I am," Jillian said somewhat hesitantly. "I'm Jillian Saunders and this is my friend, Mia Reinhardt. I'm a staff veterinarian here at Duke and Mia is a postdoctoral research fellow. I don't know Shaun all that well but he's a nice guy. A real gentleman. I didn't know he had a drug problem."

"It's more than a problem, ma'am," Dr. Ryan said with concern. "Shaun is very lucky the EMS team correctly identified his condition as an opioid overdose within moments of arriving on the scene. They said he required more than one dose of naloxone to reverse his respiratory depression and loss of consciousness. This suggests that he has developed significant tolerance and dependence over a prolonged period of abuse."

"Ironically, Jillian and I are both from the Duke Center for Opioid Research, so we are more than a little familiar with substance abuse," Mia said trying to relieve Jillian of some of the conversational burden. "Let me ask if you know what drug it is that Shaun took?"

"We did a stat drug screen which tests for all the common drugs of abuse. It was positive for opioids and negative for all other substances. His favorable response to naloxone is further confirmation it was an opioid. We sent a blood sample to the DCOR laboratory to determine precisely what opioid was in his system, and the results will be available tomorrow. It is strange though. He is our third opioid overdose tonight and sadly the first two arrived DOA earlier this evening. It's not uncommon for us to get a case or two in one day, but three in a couple of hours is very unusual."

Mia and Jillian heard the rhythmic hiss of the ventilator suddenly stop. Their hearts skipped the same beat. With terror in their eyes, they looked back over their shoulders just in time to see Shaun cough two or three times. They breathed a sigh of relief as they saw the senior resident place the discarded endotracheal tube on a tray and heard Shaun mumble something about being more comfortable without the breathing tube.

"Once we know what opioid was in his system, we'll have a better idea of how to proceed," Dr. Williams continued. "Regardless, we'll put him on patient-controlled analgesia with a morphine pump for the next 12 hours to estimate the severity of his tolerance and dependence. Then with his consent I'd like to take him through acute detoxification right here and right now using sublingual buprenorphine as needed to manage his symptoms."

"What will he experience during withdrawal?" Jillian asked. She was didactically familiar with the symptoms but neither woman had ever experienced withdrawal themselves or vicariously through any of their family or friends. This was going to be a first.

"The next 24-48 hours will be the roughest," Dr. Williams said. "We'll probably transfer him to the ICU for monitoring during the acute detoxification phase. Initially, he'll experience growing anxiety and fear along with strong cravings and drug-seeking activity."

"Make sure he doesn't try to break into your drug cabinet!" Mia said to the ER physician with no way to know how foretelling the wisecrack had been.

"These anticipatory symptoms will be followed by a myriad of others such as nausea, vomiting, sweating, stomach cramps, muscle spasms and body tremors," Dr. Williams said. "Again, a dose or two of buprenorphine should help take the edge off."

"What's the plan after the acute detoxification phase?" Jillian asked.

"Well, it's not the cheapest option and there may be some financial assistance available, but the one with the highest probability of success in my opinion would be the inpatient opioid rehabilitation program right here on the Duke campus. Depending upon the severity of his addiction, it would be a 30-, 60-, or 90-day inpatient program."

"Clear sailing after that!" Jillian expounded.

"Not exactly," Dr. Williams said ruefully. "It's a lifelong albatross. Not unlike smoking cessation. I smoked all through medical school and quit during my ER residency because of the inconvenience of constantly going outside 100 feet away from the building. I don't really think about it much anymore, but if I'm diagnosed tomorrow with a terminal illness, I'm buying a pack of Marlboro Red! Seriously, he'll need to stay highly motivated and committed for the rest of his life."

"We'll have that discussion with him right now," Jillian said.

"It's critical, Jillian," Dr. Williams emphasized. "Unless he gets off opioids, and I mean immediately and permanently, your next visit with him might be very one sided!"

Jillian approached Shaun's bedside with Mia close behind as the ER staff cleaned up and moved on. She spoke softly and held Shaun's hand as Mia held hers. Shaun told Jillian how embarrassed he was about his addiction and how sorry he was that he hadn't confided in her but that he had been planning to tell her everything very soon.

No time like the present, he thought.

Just as he was getting to the part about fentanyl, turmoil erupted as another young overdose patient was rolled into the ER. This time female. As she was transferred from the stretcher to the bed next to Shaun, the advanced cardiac life support in-progress was passed from the EMS team to the ER staff. After several more minutes of every heroic attempt to save her life, the code was called by Dr. Williams and the pulseless, lifeless woman was declared deceased.

"Dammit!" Dr. Williams said puzzled as much as disgusted. "What the hell is going on? That's the fifth OD in one night and it's not even nine o'clock yet. Fortunately, we have one save. Mr. McKinney over there. But we have four fails. Four. Usually, Narcan is the drug of Lazarus, but it's failing us tonight."

26

Durham, NC

The little 14-week-old black and tan Cavalier King Charles Spaniel was in the foyer looking out the screened door when Jillian's racing-green Audi pulled up in the driveway. She wasn't expected home for another half hour and the puppy was supposed to be a surprise. Mia picked up the dog and quickly put her back in the cage on top of the kitchen counter in plain view from the foyer.

Despite having been at the hospital with Shaun late into the evening the night before, Mia had driven to Farmville, VA, early that morning to purchase the puppy from a reputable breeder. It had been more than a year since Jillian had lost Phoebe, her precious tricolor CKCS. There was no replacing Phoebe, but Mia felt Jillian was ready for the love of another companion. She knew that comparisons would be inevitable yet unfair to the new pooch, so she intentionally avoided another tricolor to give the new pup one more degree of separation. It would be tough enough on her with a gorgeous portrait of Phoebe hanging in the great room. Mia had named her Penelope, pending the approval of her new owner.

"Oh my gosh, she's adorable!" Jillian exclaimed unable to contain her joy as she saw the puppy in the cage from across the room. "No, you didn't." She rushed over and retrieved the dog without reading the note on the cage.

EVERY VET SHOULD HAVE A PET!

After the dog had licked a couple of salty tears from Jillian's cheeks, she held the pup out at arm's length. "Another girl. She's so cute. Look at that face! What will we name her?"

"Check her tag."

"Penelope! That's perfect," Jillian said.

The three beautiful ladies retired to the great room and began the process of getting acquainted. Mia had purchased a purple collar and a heart-shaped name tag along with some chew toys that the little dog knew instinctively were hers. Jillian quite unintentionally glanced up at Phoebe's portrait and, maybe for the first time since her passing, felt a bit more at peace.

Penelope and Jillian were playing tug-of-war with a toy rope when Mia's phone rang. Caller ID announced audibly that it was Dr. Mark Oberon.

"Hello, Mark. What's up? You still at the office?" Mia asked, not expecting his call.

"Mia. When was the last time you were in the freezer of the drug discovery laboratory?" Mark queried without pleasantries.

"I don't know. Not since the Fluoropioid assays that I ran on the last batch of tetracyclozine compounds. A few weeks ago. Why do you ask?"

"I was putting together a presentation of our work and asked one of the laboratory technicians to take a photo of our T-series collection. While in the freezer, she noticed that the box of fentanyl compounds on the opposite shelf had been left open. As you know, this is a collection of fentanyl-based compounds, including fentanyl, sufentanil, carfentanil, and at least a dozen others that are not FDA-approved for general use. She looked inside the box and noticed that a few of the amber glass vials were missing. Would you happen to know their whereabouts? No one else on the staff has a clue."

"Oh, Mark," Mia said with a quiver in her voice. "I have no idea. That's terrible. It's always locked after hours. If the lock wasn't broken, it must have happened during the day."

"All those samples are highly concentrated," Mark noted. "Some are many times more potent and deadlier than fentanyl itself. I shudder to think how many lives are at risk if our repository hits the streets of Durham. The detectives are on their way here. I'll tell them what we know, which isn't much."

Mia recalled Dr. Williams telling her that there had been an unusually high incidence of opioid overdoses the night before and she began to think the worst. She waited long enough for Jillian to uncouple the call from her next few words then said she was going to the hospital to check on Shaun. She suggested that Jillian stay with Penelope since the puppy was not yet familiar with the house and promised to report back on Shaun. Jillian asked Mia to pass along her well wishes and to let him know she would visit in the morning. Mia gave Jillian and Penelope a hug then headed out the door.

She arrived at the Duke Medical Center around 5:30 p.m. and went straight to the ICU desk that served a dozen hospital beds fashioned in a circle around the perimeter. She could see Shaun's bed across the room and could tell he was awake and alert. She recognized Dr. Williams in his starched white coat sitting in a small side room reviewing a patient chart. When he looked up, she caught his attention, and he came right out.

"Dr. Reinhardt, if I recall correctly," Dr. Williams regarded her. "I was actually just reviewing Shaun's chart."

"Good to see you, Dr. Williams," Mia replied. "How's our patient?"

"He's doing as well as can be expected. Let's see here. Vital signs normal. Blood chemistries within normal limits. The patient-controlled analgesia record shows 30 mg of morphine use in the last 12 hours. That's enough to warrant a supervised acute detoxification that shouldn't be too rough. It's only a moderate degree of addiction, so a 30-day inpatient rehabilitation program might be sufficient, again with a lifetime of dedication to sobriety. Did you and Jillian happen to discuss this with him yesterday and get his consent? It's less a legal matter and more a gesture of commitment to the program."

"No, but we will," Mia responded. "Did the opioid toxicology report come back yet?"

"Yes, it did," Dr. Williams answered. "In addition to naloxone, which was given by the EMS team as Narcan, his blood sample contained 6.2 ng/ml of fentanyl. Not that high, really. The Artist Formerly Known as Prince was found to have had a fentanyl blood concentration of almost 70 ng/ml, although that was a post-mortem finding. Shaun's report was negative for all other drugs, including sufentanil and carfentanil which are related to fentanyl but much more potent as you well know. But here's the strange part, there was also a trace amount of an unknown fentanyl derivative in his blood. Since there's no specific assay for this substance in the drug screen, the amount was simply noted as <1 ng/ml. That's a miniscule amount. But if it's more potent than fentanyl, that could explain his life-threatening symptoms despite a fairly low level of fentanyl in his blood and a modest level of opioid addiction."

"I guess there's also some chance that it's a laboratory error or false positive artifact," Mia probed.

"I suppose," Dr. Williams said dubiously. "Frightening to think there's another fentanyl derivative out there and heaven forbids one more potent than what we already have."

Heaven forbids indeed, she thought.

Mia left Dr. Williams scratching his head at the nurse's station and walked across the room with determination to Shaun's bedside. On his nightstand she noticed a bouquet of flowers and a box of candy. The card on the flowers read *Get Well Soon* and was signed *Jillian*. The card on the candy was simply signed *Steve*.

"Who's Steve?" Mia asked after they exchanged a few pleasantries.

"Oh, that's my roommate," Shaun replied. "He stopped by last night after you and Jill left. I was out of it, but he said I was in much better shape than I had been a few hours earlier. I suppose that was an understatement."

Mia didn't know Shaun well since Jillian hadn't talked about him much. In fact, she was beginning to think that he and Jillian weren't much more than acquaintances. She liked guitar players and he liked blondes, brunettes, and redheads. Mia managed to get Shaun to talk about his drug abuse going back at least the last couple of years with a claim that it helped him to be more creative at songwriting.

"That's a bunch of crap and you know it," Mia said scornfully. "Dr. Williams said that the amount of morphine you just used in the last 12 hours indicates a level of tolerance and dependence that will require a medically supervised withdrawal, if you have *any* intention of quitting this high-wire act of yours."

"I'd like to. Really, I would. This was my first bad trip. I'm normally very careful, but I must have gotten a hold of some bad shit. Oops. Sorry."

"Don't worry, I've heard worse," Mia said. "They found fentanyl in your blood on the drug screen."

"Yep. Guess that's what you call my drug-of-choice," Shaun said imprudently.

"That's not funny! And it's no longer a choice. It's a compulsion that you have no control over. It's called dependence and together with the tolerance you've developed it's a death sentence. Besides, I'm not so sure you were careful this time."

"What do you mean by that?" Shaun asked more out of curiosity than concern.

"Dr. Williams said your drug screen also detected the presence of an unknown fentanyl derivative. It was just a trace amount but who knows how potent it might be. You may have been much luckier than you realize. Four others last night were not so lucky. Any idea what ..."

Suddenly, Mia was interrupted by a WRAL news bulletin that came over the television set suspended from the ceiling.

The station logo appeared in the lower left corner of the screen as the reporter announced, "The Durham County Sheriff is reporting this hour the theft of several vials of experimental narcotics from the laboratories of the Duke Center for Opioid Research. A spokesperson for the center said the drugs are all chemically related to fentanyl, a popular drug of abuse, and that some could be many times more potent and deadlier. It is not yet known whether this discovery is related to the recent series of deadly overdoses reported by the Duke Medical Center. Anyone having information about the theft or the whereabouts of the unlabeled amber glass vials is asked to contact the Sheriff's department, and recreational drug users are advised to be on high alert."

Shaun turned a lighter shade of pale than his hospital bed sheet and Mia just glared. She moved a little closer to his side and spoke quietly. "Is that something you know something about?" she asked with one eyebrow raised.

Shaun explained how he had stolen the vials from the freezer on the one and only occasion he had visited Jillian at the DCOR. She had taken him on a brief tour of the building and mentioned that the freezer was a repository of opioids for medical research. She hadn't known about or even suspected his addiction. She had mentioned to him with no reason to be distrusting that the freezer was generally unlocked during day but locked after hours. A policy that would soon change.

"I don't know what I was thinking," Shaun said with genuine regret. "It's gotten to the point where I'm buying more drugs than food and it just seemed like a cheap way out. I recognized the name fentanyl and I had heard of sufentanil and carfentanil. I didn't recognize the names on the other three vials that I lifted although they all ended in fentanyl or fentanil. I figured they might be more potent, so I just dabbed a little on a toothpick. I guess I was hoping the stash would last a while and cost me nothing."

"Well, it almost cost you your life," Mia scolded. "And it may have cost the lives of others already. We need to retrieve those vials before anyone else gets hurt, or worse. Are they at your house?"

"No. Gus stole them."

"Who's Gus?"

"He's a friend of Steve's. A real dirtbag!"

Have you looked in the mirror lately? she wondered, no longer seeing any resemblance to Luke Bryan.

"Listen, Mia. Do me a favor and keep quiet about my involvement in this," Shaun pleaded as he unknowingly employed the Benjamin Franklin Effect. "I'll have Steve call Gus and ask that he turn himself in, or at least turn the stuff in. I'm sure he has no idea how dangerous it is."

"I'm no cop," Mia responded indignantly. "But if those four bodies in the morgue downstairs died from any of the drugs in those vials, then Gus may be complicit in their deaths. And quite frankly, so may you."

"Yeah. Well, if your research center had kept its freezer door locked, those drugs would still be there!"

Mia thought Shaun may have a point, although she knew it was typical for addicts to blame everyone but themselves. Still, her priority was to do whatever she could to retrieve whatever remained of the stolen vials. She thought she would start by contacting Steve to track down Gus. Shaun gave her Steve's phone number and she left to make a call or send a text. As she walked by the guest elevators on her way to the ICU waiting room, Dr. Williams emerged from the service elevators.

"Dr. Reinhardt. I'm glad you're still here," he said. "I guess you heard the news about those drug samples that were stolen from your research center."

"I did. I can't believe it. There were some very rare and very deadly fentanyl derivatives among those that were stolen."

"Well, at least now we have an explanation. I checked the toxicology reports on the four fatal overdoses from yesterday and three of the four had an unknown fentanyl derivative in their blood. Same as Shaun. Sounds like the stolen samples found their way to the streets of Durham."

"Heavens," Mia exclaimed. "I can't help but feel responsible."

"Mia, they were stolen," Dr. Williams consoled. "You are no more responsible than the staff of a hospital pharmacy robbed of its supply of morphine ampules or fentanyl transdermal patches."

"I suppose," she said, not convinced entirely.

"Incidentally, while I was down in the ER, we had another opioid overdose about thirty minutes ago. DOA. Name was Gustav Lundberg."

Gus!

27

New York City, NY

The business class flight on American Airlines out of RDU that morning had been comfortable if not enjoyable. Dr. Mark Oberon had reminisced of the days when even a short flight from RDU to LaGuardia would have been accompanied by a full-service meal and a complimentary cocktail. Drs. Mia Reinhardt and Robert Taylor were both a bit too young to have recalled those days.

Bob had thought seriously about having a Bloody Mary, but he and Mark had settled for a coffee. Mia had enjoyed a cup of tea. By the time the flight had landed just beyond Rikers Island, the Carey service black Lincoln Town Car was already curbside at arrivals and the driver was holding up a sign that read, 'Dr. Robert Taylor.' Mark was chagrined it was not in his name since he was the senior academic in the group. However, he knew Bob also wore the hat of a biotechnology corporate executive with a few fund-raising trips to Wall Street under his belt. Mia sat beside Mark in the car contemplating her upcoming sales pitch to Goldman Sachs while Bob rode up front with the driver.

"Mia," Mark said as he tapped her on the knee. "I forgot to mention that the Durham County Sheriff called me early this morning. Apparently, they found our missing fentanyl compounds at the home of an addict whom they knew well. He overdosed yesterday afternoon and was DOA at the Duke Medical Center. His name was Gustav Lundberg."

She knew he was as a friend of Shaun's roommate but didn't let on that she had any connection. "Probably hit the sufentanil or carfentanil without realizing they are 10x and 100x more potent than fentanyl, respectively," Mia said.

"They also have reason to believe that this Gustav character was the one who stole the vials from our freezer," Mark said. "So, as far as the authorities are concerned it's case closed. I sent out a staff memorandum this morning that the freezer is to remain locked at all times unless occupied and I reassured Sheriff Hodges that our collection of *street candy* would never grow legs again."

Mia harkened to the hospital bed confession by Shaun and thought about telling Mark the whole story but decided to wait and tell Jillian first when she returned. She didn't believe Shaun was guilty of anything more than the original theft since the drugs were subsequently stolen from him by Gus. On the other hand, the threat of turning him in to the police might be the very wakeup call he needed and the leverage she needed to get him into rehabilitation and off drugs *immediately and permanently* as Dr. Williams had put it. A clean and sober Luke Bryan look alike with a velvet voice and a gift for lyrics would be reward enough for her silence. But she'd let Jillian be the judge.

The Lincoln Town Car pulled up to the curb alongside the greenway at 200 West Street in Manhattan and Bob told the driver he would text when they were ready for the ride to their next appointment. The security guards inside the street level lobby of Goldman Sachs requested their photo identifications and called upstairs to confirm their appointments.

"Grant Sawyer is a senior VP here," Bob mentioned to everyone, said as the elevator doors closed behind them. "He's an old friend of mine from business school. He too has an MBA from Duke. I think he interned at Lehman before the nuclear winter, and Goldman sucked him up. He'll have a small tribe of bankers, lawyers, and research analysts up there, but he's the Indian Chief. Make no mistake. He will have done his homework, and the only real question on his mind will be how many more bankers we're scheduled to meet with while we're here in New York!"

Grant Sawyer's assistant met them in the lobby of the 16th floor and escorted them to a large conference room down the hall from the reception desk. He invited them to refreshments in the back of the room and instructed Mia on the connection of her laptop to the big screen in front. She fired up her PowerPoint presentation and left it open to the title slide.

Theta Opioid Therapeutics, Inc. — Narcogesic: Coming Soon!

Bob and Mark stood beside Mia as Grant and his entourage filed into the room. Everyone shook hands as Grant introduced his team to his guests. They all took their seats with each group on opposite sides of the table like the Teamsters about to renegotiate their contract with GM.

"As a Duke alum myself, I'd like to welcome our guests from Durham this morning," Grant opened. "Dr. Oberon, your reputation precedes you and I join the rest of the civilized world in hoping that your road soon leads you to Stockholm." Mark nodded with humility. "Bob. What can I say other than you should have gone into banking!" Bob snickered and the others smiled politely knowing that Bob had done quite well for himself, thank you very much. "Mia. Please. Let's hear all about Narcogesic: Coming ... how soon?"

Mia preceded to make a very polished presentation and her skills as a former high school champion orator were on full display. She took them on a tour of Mark's work, down the pathways of pain signaling and the opioids that mediate pain relief. She described the patented Fluoropioid assay as their metal detector and the tetracyclozine compounds made by RxFactor as their haystack. She talked about naming their lead candidate Narcogesic and how well it had performed in their animal models of pain relief and opioid addiction, and she shared the surprisingly supportive pre-IND meeting they had had with the FDA.

"Mia," Grant interrupted. "When you say, 'surprisingly supportive,' why would you characterize it that way and what does it imply?"

"Frankly," Mia responded, "that was my first meeting with the FDA. But I'm familiar with its reputation as one of the toughest regulators. They are primarily responsible for ensuring the safety of our food and drug supply chain and usually demand more than the suppliers expect. In our case, they are clearly bothered by the safety profile of current opioids and hope as much as we do that Narcogesic is the answer. As such, they granted us fast-track status and put forth an expedited path to market."

"What do you mean by expedited?" one of Grant's associates asked.

"They proposed just three trials that we can run in parallel rather than using the more conventional sequential approach. One is a Phase I safety study of Narcogesic versus placebo in 200 subjects and the other is a Phase II efficacy study of Narcogesic versus oxycodone in 400 patients. Both are randomized, double-blind comparative studies. They also asked for a Phase III open-label safety study of an additional 700 patients. They committed to a quick review and approval if the trial results are favorable.

"What's the timeline and how much are you looking to raise for the trials?" one of the Goldman bankers asked.

"Actually, we already have the funding we need for the trials," Bob interjected. "We are about to begin enrollment and expect to have the results within the next 6-9 months. What we need is an investment banker to manage an IPO, so we can gear up to make, market, and sell the drug ourselves. In terms of timing, ideally, we would like the IPO to be booked, priced, and trading on the NASDAQ right after the trial results are announced and revenues are inevitable."

"Do you have any revenue projections?" he asked.

"We were hoping your research analysts could help us with that," Bob replied. "Some market research reports put the global opioid market at nearly $30 billion annually with morphine and codeine accounting for more than 50 percent. We can see no reason why Narcogesic would not take the entire market in a short period of time."

"The entire market!" Grant repeated, then whistled. "How much are you looking to raise?" he asked directing the question to Bob. Of course, Grant knew the answer. Their plan and capital needs were all detailed in the documents they had sent in advance of the meeting. He just wanted to start the dialogue. Mia took her seat. She was disappointed she hadn't gotten to her great closing slide, but knew the discussion was going in the right direction. Mark gave her a pat on the shoulder as she sat down.

"As outlined in our strategic and operating plans for the company, we will need about $500 million to commercialize Narcogesic," Bob said. "We will need all the operations of a vertically integrated single-product public company. One option would be to grow the operations organically but that would be very time consuming, and our runway may be very short if the FDA expedites the approval. The better option would be to acquire whatever companies or operations we will need immediately post-IPO. We would focus on acquiring these capabilities in the U.S. and would license the Narcogesic rights overseas to one or more foreign partners. The proceeds from these licensing agreements would be used to further finance operations and growth in the U.S. We would envision growing the company over time with a research pipeline and initial focus on pain management."

"Of course, you won't net $500 million," Grant said. "Maybe $475 after deducting our fees and expenses. We'll handle the S-1 registration process, red herring prospectus, and a roadshow that we'll schedule for right after the trials. As the underwriter we can't guarantee research coverage by Goldman despite the JOBS Act and a Chinese Wall, but our analysts rarely miss an opportunity to cover a good company in a promising sector," he said with a wink.

"Maybe you can ask your staff to send us a breakdown of the IPO costs. We'll have a look when we get back home and compare them to the others," Bob said coyly.

"Others? What others?" Grant asked anxiously, suddenly aware of the perspiration on his palms.

"Oh. Well. We have some other meetings while we're here in New York," Bob said like he was fly fishing in Montana.

"Look. We're not interested in being just another chef in your little bake-off. There's nothing about TORX or Narcogesic that Goldman Sachs can't handle. Alone!" Grant said tempestuously. He loosened his tie and unbuttoned his collar. Everyone saw Grant's hand tremble as he reached for a drink of water. Mark was about to ask if he felt alright but didn't want to embarrass him. Besides, it was probably just the excitement of the business deal.

"NASDAQ: TORX. Has a nice ring to it, don't you think, Grant?" Bob goaded.

Grant thanked his guests for coming then rushed out of the room as the others stayed back and schmoozed. He walked briskly down the hall to his office and loosened his tie some more along the way. Once in his office with the door closed, he opened a side desk drawer and withdrew a bottle of Visine and a bottle of Afrin. The Visine cleared the redness from his eyes and the contents of the Afrin nasal spray bottle stopped the perspiration and shaking.

If only my orthopedic surgeon could have prescribed Narcogesic, he thought as he settled back in his chair for another unproductive afternoon.

Mia, Mark, and Bob exited the building through the revolving front doors and walked up the street. Mia suddenly pushed Mark aside to keep him from stepping on a homeless man lying next to the building with an empty syringe by his side. She was comforted when Mark stopped and confirmed that he was just sleeping and not unconscious or worse, then depressed to think that the opioid crisis could claim a victim just outside one of the wealthiest investment banks on the planet. Little did she know it had also claimed at least one victim on the inside as well. It was a scourge that crossed all classes, categories, and creeds.

The three of them grabbed hot dogs from the street vendor and sat on one of the knee walls nearby to enjoy the classic New York steamed treat. Their sodas rested by and between them. Bob called the Carey driver and they all reflected on how well the meeting had gone with Goldman Sachs as they waited.

"They're in, if we want them," Bob said confidently, as he washed down his last bite of hot dog with a swig of Dr. Pepper under the shade of a greenway elm tree. "Their fees would be a little higher than most, but we would be well served, and there's none better. We can shop if you'd like, but I'm good with Goldman Sachs, at least for a public equity offering."

"You leave the science to us," Mark said, wagging his finger between himself and Mia, "and we'll leave the financing to you."

Mia commented on how much better she thought the New York franks were compared to the red dyed hot dogs back home.

"Next stop, Keystone Capital over on Wall Street," Bob said as the black Lincoln Town Car pulled up beside them. He jumped in the front seat, and Mark and Mia climbed into the back.

"Nice job on the presentation, Mia," Bob lauded as he looked over the back of the front seat. "I wouldn't change a thing. This next group I don't know personally, but they are well regarded and very capable. They manage about $20 billion in private equity assets, including a portfolio of several high-tech and biotech companies. They must be very well connected because we have not made any disclosures and they called me. I like their style already."

"What are the major differences or concerns for us between private and public equity? Mia asked. Mark hadn't asked but the question was on his mind too.

"Your fiduciary responsibility to your shareholders is the same. The big negative for a public company is the SEC reporting requirements, including quarterly and annual financials, material transactions, and insider stock trades. Corporate communications and investor relations tend to be more expensive and time consuming since there are typically more shareholders. However, these are easily managed with an adequate staff. The big positive for a public company is liquidity. There are lots of capable buyers in the public equity markets, but far fewer in the private markets."

"I'm going to miss our investor relations," Mia said. "One text message with one cc:" Mark and Bob chuckled.

The driver pulled up to the offices of Keystone Capital and after clearing security the group waited for the next elevator. The ground floor appointments were nice but nothing special. No doubt shared by several corporate tenants of various means. When the elevator doors opened on the 24th floor, it was a different story. A massive Ziegler Mahal Persian rug adorned the marble floor and twin crystal chandeliers each the size of a small Buick hung from the ceiling. Mia marveled at the two life-size terra cotta warriors that stood guard on either side of the elevators.

"They're on loan from the Chinese government," Hank Watson whispered in Mia's ear from behind. She turned a bit startled. "One of our major investors is a good friend of General Secretary Xi Jinping. I say on loan, but they've been here for 12 years now. Originals from the Qin Dynasty discovered outside Xi'an, China in 1974. I'm Hank Watson, one of the senior partners here at Keystone," he said as he extended a hand to Mia, then to Mark and Bob.

Hank escorted his guests to the large conference room around the corner from the elevators and introduced them to his waiting team of associates. Mia once again presented the background and plans for Narcogesic and never lost eye contact with her audience as she advanced through the PowerPoint slides. After fielding a few technical questions and giving Mark an opportunity to expound on a few more she sat down, and the group engaged in a productive discussion of the financial plan for TORX.

"Very elegant work," Hank said and meant it. "We really have done most of our due diligence at this point, so it's just a question of whether Narcogesic performs as advertised in the trials."

"Let's assume the trial results are stellar," Bob said. "That Narcogesic is the perfect nonaddictive narcotic analgesic. Where would you be on pricing?"

"I'll ask Norm Brady to answer that," Hank said. "Norm is a CFA, certified financial analyst and has been with us for a few years now. But let me just say that we will be competitive with any other option you consider in terms of pricing and valuations, whether public or private. While an IPO and investment banker can bring cash to the table, we can also bring relationships. All our investments are in the pharmaceutical and biotechnology sectors, so we have connections in every operational area of the business around the world and within the government agencies that regulate these businesses, such as the FDA and USPTO and their foreign counterparts. Norm."

"Thanks, Hank," Norm acknowledged. "In terms of valuation, we would get at that from a couple of different angles. First, we would use a discounted cash flow method making some assumptions about the future cash flow, especially from operations. Second, we would look at valuations commanded by similar companies in the same sector. Finally, we usually apply some probability weightings. But again, as Hank said, we would be competitive with any other option you have, and our relationships would be a bonus."

"I do have just one final question," Mark spoke up as Bob sent a text message to the Carey driver indicating they would soon be outside and ready for their next appointment. "We have been very careful not to publish anything related to the tetracyclozine-based compounds we had synthesized, or the results of Narcogesic in our animal models of pain, or for that matter our recent pre-IND meeting with the FDA. As such, I'm curious as to how you happened to call Bob with an interest in financing the company?"

"As I mentioned earlier, we do our homework," Hank said. "If we do a deal, we will certainly lift the kimono on all matters of mutual interest, but for now I'll simply say that the Del Mar biotech community is small and gossipy. A private investment of $500 million compels us to turn over some rocks. And that we did. Norm, go ahead and share your story."

"Money is certainly a great motivator," Norm said. "But we like to invest in people whose motivation goes beyond money. In the case of Mark, we see someone like Alexander Graham Bell or Steve Jobs. People driven by a thirst for knowledge and technological advance. Had we the opportunity, AT&T and Apple would have been in our portfolio. In the case of Mia, we see someone driven by deeply personal motives. I will share with you that I lost my 23-year-old daughter to a cocaine overdose two years ago. I know Narcogesic would not have prevented her addiction since cocaine is not an opioid. I also don't have the medical training or skills to create something so profoundly transformative as Narcogesic. However, I can help to allocate resources in the direction of those with the necessary skills and motivation. Mia, I'm very sorry for your loss."

"And I for yours," she said sincerely, impressed by the extent to which he had done his homework.

As their limo slowed in the rush hour traffic the question was whether to keep their reservations at the Waldorf Astoria and their appointments with other bankers and investors over the next few days, or decide now between Goldman and Keystone, and head to LaGuardia.

"In my not-so-humble opinion, there's none better than Keystone on the private side nor Goldman on the public," Bob posited. "Frankly, I'm fine with either. No need to see anymore."

"So, the question is, public or private," Mia surmised. "What do you think?" Her question was certainly directed to Bob, but Mark spoke up as he pondered out the window without much attention to the conversation.

"I'd like to keep our reservation at the Waldorf, but more for nostalgic reasons than business. The last time that I stayed there was the only time that I stayed there, and it was many years ago. I was having lunch in the dining room on the top floor one day when a colleague drew my attention to an elderly woman dining alone across the room. He knew her well and wanted to introduce me. Upon approaching her he said, 'Ma'am, I would like for you to meet Dr. Mark Oberon.' The woman smiled politely and extended her hand. 'Pleased to meet you, young man,' she said. 'I'm Mrs. General Douglas MacArthur.' Wife of the WWII hero of the Pacific Theatre. Turns out she had been a resident there for many years. One of those moments you never forget."

"Nice story Mark and wish we could indulge your reminiscence a while longer, but I vote for Goldman and an IPO," Bob said. "Hank tried to make a point of having relationships that Keystone can bring to the table after closing, but Grant has a much deeper bench. Our clinical plan is solid and with the help of Goldman we can develop and execute a commercial plan that will ensure the success of Narcogesic."

With everyone in agreement Bob called Grant to request an IPO engagement letter and Mark called to cancel their hotel reservations and other appointments as they instructed their driver to head for LaGuardia.

28

Washington, D.C.

Above the mantle over the fireplace was the equestrian portrait of Theodore Roosevelt titled *Rough Rider* by Tade Styka. Across the room was Teddy's 1906 Nobel Peace Prize on display. The Roosevelt Room was directly across from the Oval Office and the President used it frequently for staff meetings.

"Thank you all for being here this morning," the President said, wearing a silly green sequin bowtie in celebration of St. Patrick's Day. "Our Commission on Combating Drug Addiction and the Opioid Crisis meets again next week, and I just wanted an update from some of you on our efforts in advance of the meeting. As you all know, I have declared the opioid crisis a Public Health Emergency and we've taken several steps that should make a big difference. Let's first hear from our Attorney General Mort Boyer on the progress being made over at the DOJ. So, Mort, who's winning your little game of cops and robbers?"

"I am sir," Mort said. "I mean we are sir, sort of. So far, our office has successfully prosecuted four drug companies and seven executives associated with those companies on charges of conspiracy, fraud, and racketeering. These have all been relatively small manufacturers or distributors dedicated almost exclusively to opioid narcotics. The prosecutions have put these companies out of business and their ring leaders behind bars for a very long time."

"How about the big boys?" the President asked, then smiled and added, "... and big girls."

"Well, sir," Mort replied. "Big Pharma have much larger and more sophisticated legal teams than the little guys and they do a much better job at towing the line on marketing, advertising, and promoting. Afterall, these drugs are approved for pain management and a great many patients have a legitimate medical need."

"I thought the plan was to encourage the private sector to file class action lawsuits against some of the bigger players in the opioid business, like the suits that brought down Big Tobacco and reduced the prevalence of smoking and its health consequences."

"Sir, I spoke with Senate Majority Leader Bassett about that," Mort said. "He implied that you had agreed that unbridled enthusiasm by plaintiffs, attorneys, judges and jurors could result in awards that would cripple the ability of these companies to reinvest in the research and development that's vital to public health."

"How much opioid research are these companies doing?" the President probed.

"Not much, sir." Mort replied. "Most of the recent FDA approvals have been for reformulations such as sustained-release, sublingual tablets, transdermal patches, and lollipops, or combinations of more than one drug. Frankly, there has not been a new chemical entity introduced as a narcotic analgesic in more than a dozen years. It seems Big Pharma is satisfied resting on its laurels when it comes to serious pain management."

"So much for our domestic efforts," the President remarked. "How about our interdiction efforts south of the border?"

"We continue to operate with undercover DEA agents together with the Mexican government and continue to meet with some success in this regard, but it's very slow, very spotty and not impressive. However, on your orders to deploy some U.S.

Navy assets, we have had considerable impact offshore. Several metric tons of illicit drugs have already been seized just in the last few months."

"Were these opioid shipments?" the President queried.

"Some were cocaine or marijuana, but many were opioids like heroin and illicit fentanyl. In fact, one very substantial seizure was a large shipment of homemade fentanyl that turns out to have been laced with large quantities of carfentanil. Any unsuspecting addicts, which would have been everyone preparing to take their usual dose, would have died suddenly with no opportunity for a Narcan rescue. These days the big cartels brand their so-called *products* with tradenames and logos to compete with one another and have largely eliminated the small-time operators. The carfentanil-laced shipment was marked with the Sinaloa cartel brand. Clearly an effort by a rival cartel to taint the Sinaloa brand and its network. No concern for humanity whatsoever."

"It sounds like our interdiction program is having a terrific impact, is that right?" the President asked almost rhetorically.

"Honestly, sir," Mort responded, "the concern now is that these shipments are being redirected and brought across our land border which remains porous."

"Don't get me started on that!" the President retorted, and the room agreed with empathy.

"Mr. President," the FDA Commissioner Arthur Armstrong jumped in with a nod from the Secretary of Health and Human Services. "Unless you have more questions for Justice the FDA has some information that may brighten your day."

"Go ahead and brighten my day," the President beseeched. "Heaven knows we already have throngs more interested in bad news than good."

"Yes sir, and if you don't mind, I'd like to introduce Dr. Charlene Hopkins our Division Director for anesthesia, addiction, and pain medicine, and invite her to tell you all about it. Charlene, please."

"Mr. President," Charlene began. "I first became aware of this work when I received a call from the Director of the National Institute on Drug Abuse who informed me of a modest NIH grant that was awarded to the Duke Center for Opioid Research (DCOR) to study a novel new narcotic analgesic in animal models of pain. I should tell you that DCOR and its director Dr. Mark Oberon are well-regarded in the opioid research community and his accomplishments could well lead to a Nobel Prize. Since he's much more familiar with the animal models of pain than I am, let me introduce Dr. Jayden Banks and ask him to highlight the research."

"Thank you, Charlene," Jayden regarded. "I won't bore you with the precise mechanism of action, but I will simply say that Dr. Oberon developed a theory that he believes will lead to a nonaddictive narcotic analgesic. Based on data not yet published, DCOR with the help of a synthetic chemistry partner designed a series of molecules that they subsequently tested in the classical animal models of pain. I will spare you the details but suffice to say they showed that their lead compound called Narcogesic was just as powerful as fentanyl in terms of pain relief. Further, in a well-regarded animal model of drug-seeking behavior there was not a single case of addiction at any dose. Truly amazing!"

"We embrace your mandate in dealing with the opioid crisis, Mr. President," Charlene added. "As such, we granted fast-track status to Narcogesic development and recommended a facilitated path for clinical trials sponsored by Theta Opioid Therapeutics, Inc., the little company they formed to develop and commercialize the drug. These should be underway very soon and assuming the drug is safe and effective it should be on the market in less than a year."

"Let's keep our fingers crossed," the President said. "I don't need to tell you the numbers. More than 150 million opioid prescriptions written last year, a decline over recent years, but still absurd and unacceptable for a population of 330 million. Last year there were nearly 70,000 drug overdose deaths, two-thirds of which were opioid related. It was the single leading cause of death, and exceeded all other causes combined, among those 44 years of age or younger. For all the fund-raising and protesting and outrage over other types of deaths, why is so little attention paid to the most prominent cause by far? It's a scourge that knows no ethnic, religious, or socioeconomic boundary and claims those in the prime of their life. Unlike a virus, there is no herd immunity or vaccine for opioid addiction. There is only rehabilitation or death. Let's do what we can to support this little company Theta Opioid Therapeutics. They just may be the goose that can lay the golden egg."

"Golden egg indeed, sir," Wally Cooper interjected with the permission of his boss the Under Secretary of Commerce for Intellectual Property. "Sir, I'm the primary examiner of the patent application that was filed by DCOR not long ago which was subsequently assigned to TORX. We have not yet published their application for opposition, but I can tell you that there is nothing in the literature that would preclude their claims to these derivatives of tetracyclozine. In addition, they recently supplemented their application with the results of the animal studies that Jayden just described, and these are more than adequate to support their claims for utility as nonaddictive opioid pain relievers."

"Unless the company has any objection, and I don't see why it should, let's get the application published as soon as possible, so we can rest assured we're dealing with the rightful owners of the technology, though I have little doubt," the President instructed.

"Sir, this is just my opinion," Wally added, and his boss held his breathe. "But I've reviewed hundreds of medical patents over the years, and I've never seen one positioned to cannibalize an entire class of drugs. I'm no market analyst but I learned that the global market for prescription opioids is valued at about $40 billion with the U.S. market about half that. Given 20 years of market exclusivity that started when they filed the patent application, TORX could rival the likes of Microsoft, Apple, and Amazon in no time, as it should for making such a profound contribution to society. In fact, once Narcogesic is on the market, I might argue it should be criminal to prescribe any other."

Now there's something worth considering, the President thought.

29

Los Mochis, Sinaloa, Mexico

Miguel Martinez tried desperately to remain expressionless as Salma Flores ran her naked toes up his shin under the poolside table as she sat beside El Enterrador. If the one they called The Gravedigger was wise to her game, he didn't show it. Miguel sat across from them in a pair of white swim trunks and a lime green T-shirt with his Kimber 9mm resting on the cocobolo wood table near his right hand. The former Miss Mexico wore an Aztec print bikini that dared Miguel to pay less attention to El Enterrador than he should. As the three enjoyed tall glasses of ice-cold lemonade, some with tequila and some without, El Enterrador reached for the morning edition of the *El Debate* newspaper that lay on the table.

"What's this shit?" El Enterrador expounded as he stood. He began to pace near the pool and continued to read aloud. "It says here, 'The U.S. Navy today confirmed that the Sinaloa cartel shipment of illicit fentanyl that was seized off the coast of San Diego last week had been laced with substantial quantities of carfentanil. This chemical derivative of fentanyl is 100 times more potent and fatal to unsuspecting street addicts. Word on the street is that Sinaloa may have been the target of a rival cartel and their drug supply is now suspect.' Bastards!"

"Bastards?" Miguel questioned.

"Michoacán cartel. Little bastards!" El Enterrador repeated. "They are still pissed off that El Contador Juan Pablo left them to join us. So, they sabotaged our drug supply. Bastards! I'll kill them! I'll kill them all!"

"How do you know it's the Michoacán cartel?" Salma questioned. Miguel was hoping she would ask to spare him the impropriety.

"I'm just guessing, but I'm damn good at guessing," El Enterrador retorted. "They probably compromised one of our batches made up in the canyon where your idiots knocked off El Contador Numero Uno."

"I'll take the chopper up there right now," Miguel said quickly, not wanting El Enterrador to linger on that sore subject for long. "I'll find out what they know at the laboratory and report back."

"Take some of our men with you," El Enterrador said. "I don't think it's an inside job but watch your back just in case."

"Does El Cocinero, our fentanyl cook, make carfentanil up there?" Salma explored. "Maybe it was a case of unintentional contamination. Crossing over from one batch to the other without thoroughly cleaning the equipment."

"Not just another pretty face, eh boss?" Miguel said with a look of lust that was poorly disguised. "Maybe I should take her along for the ride. What do you think?"

Salma and Miguel quickly headed to the guest bedroom off the pool to change back into their street clothes before El Enterrador could respond to Miguel's question about bringing her along. Hearing no gunfire, they assumed they had his permission. Miguel stepped out of his swimsuit and lingered long enough to give Salma a show before putting on his white beltless pants and matching sport coat. Not to be outdone, Miss Mexico dropped her swimsuit and posed then slowly slinked into a floral print gingham dress. Sufficiently aroused but not alone at the palatial estate, they headed down the gallery hallway through the massive front doors and along the path to the helipad. A half dozen of El Enterrador's men met them there along with the pilot and copilot. Miguel marveled at the 360-degree view from the top of the ridge as the black Sikorsky S-76C headed out over Copper Canyon.

Thirty minutes later the chopper descended to its gravel landing pad near the warehouses of the cartel's El Cocinero in the foothills outside Los Mochis. The pilot cut the twin engines as the copilot assisted Salma, then Miguel, out the cabin side door. His men dressed in full combat apparel quickly exited behind them and formed a human shield around Miguel and Salma as they approached the warehouses and entered the offices of the Sinaloa cartel's new accountant, Juan Pablo Torres.

"El Nuevo Contador," Miguel said as he embraced the man. "First, allow me to introduce Salma Flores." Juan Pablo regarded the woman for more than a moment. "Now that I don't have your attention, let me ask. Is El Cocinero on the premises?"

"No," Juan Pablo said, now redirecting his attention to Miguel. "I'm afraid he's in China negotiating a new agreement for the starting materials he uses in the synthesis of our fentanyl. I think he called it NPP. Anyway, he's not expected back for a few more days. Is there something I can help you with?"

"Perhaps," Salma said, catching Miguel a bit off guard by answering. "As El Contador, you might know whether there are any other drugs or chemicals manufactured here. I'm thinking specifically of any fentanyl derivatives like sufentanil or carfentanil. Would you happen to know?"

Juan Pablo looked like he had just seen a three-headed Gila monster. "Is she a cook?" he asked Miguel.

"Actually, she's an English profesora and a former Miss Mexico. Now if you're finished with your questions, maybe you can answer hers," Miguel said with bravado.

"Sorry," Juan Pablo said. "No. No, there's nothing made here except fentanyl. El Cocinero has his own process that he developed when he was at Janssen Pharmaceuticals. The quality is every bit as good as anything manufactured by the multinational drug companies. Maybe better. In any event, no sufentanil, carfentanil or anything else."

"Well, then," Miguel said contemplatively. "Do you happen to know if there's any surveillance video of the warehouses, inside or out?

"Yes," Juan Pablo replied. "Yes, of course. Both inside and out. What would you like to see?"

"Do you have the fentanyl batch records and dates?" Miguel asked.

"Yes," Juan Pablo said. "Yes, of course."

Juan Pablo fired up his desktop computer and Salma was impressed that it was a late model iMac with a 27-inch Retina 4K display. He launched a desktop resident spreadsheet and clicked the tab for production dates. "Looks like there's approximately one batch a month. The last batch was about three weeks ago. On the 24th of last month."

"That would be about the right timeframe," Salma noted.

"The right timeframe for what?" Juan Pablo probed.

"My goodness you ask a lot of questions," Miguel said bluntly. "It's the right timeframe for you to tell me whether you have any surveillance video on or about the 24th. I'm not interested in normal business hours when there's lots of staff wandering around. I'm interested in afterhours when no one should be around."

"Without knowing more, I can't help you, but I will tell you that the security cameras include motion sensors. Assuming your footage of interest involves motion, we can quickly scan just the sections of the video that detected motion."

"Pretty sure I'm not interested in footage with no motion, you idiot, and *we* aren't scanning anything. If you don't mind, launch the video files on your desktop then move your ass aside, so Salma and I can have a look."

Juan Pablo did as he was told. He was aware of the hierarchy within the cartel that placed El Enterrador numero uno, El

Ejecutor dos, El Cocinero très and himself El Contador as quattro. He knew that every man at the facility was aware of the pecking order and only hoped that whatever it was they were seeking on the video did not involve him. After all, he was just the bookkeeper, but he had heard that being El Contador at that facility could be hazardous to your health. Very hazardous.

"Here's something," Miguel said as he and Salma watched the video footage of a man sweeping with a broom around the main tank then disappear off screen. "Damn, that was nothing."

"There. What's that?" Salma said as two figures appeared and moved quickly toward the main tank. Their genders could not be discerned from the footage, but one figure climbed a ladder up the side of the main tank while the other opened a sizeable briefcase and withdrew a clear plastic bag. The person on the ground handed the bag to the one on the ladder who then opened the lid and emptied the contents into the tank. It appeared to be a white powder of some sort. They put the empty bag back in the suitcase and hurried off. The time stamp in the lower left corner read 2:14 a.m.

"Is there more?" Salma asked anxiously. "Is there more footage from other cameras? Other angles, or outside? It looked like those individuals left down the central hallway and probably exited out the backdoor. Is there an outdoor camera on the backdoor?"

"There is," Juan Pablo said.

Salma gave Juan Pablo the date and time and he proceeded to sort through the tabs of the video files until he located the footage of the backdoor for that date and time. Comfortable that Juan Pablo was probably not involved and could be helpful they invited him to watch over their shoulder. As the time stamp in the lower left flipped to 2:16 a.m., the backdoor of the warehouse opened, and the figures emerged. They briefly paused under the bright overhead light then quickly disappeared into the night."

"Zoom," Selma shouted excitedly. "Zoom. Can you zoom in on their faces?" Juan Pablo reached over her shoulder and worked the mouse until the footage zoomed in tight. The 4k resolution was superb and color was a bonus. The two were both dark-haired Hispanic males. One with no facial hair. The other with a heavy mustache. A facial recognition database that included these two individuals could have made the match with no probability of error. Since they didn't have such a database, it was time to ask around.

Juan Pablo looked carefully and confirmed that neither man was an employee of the fentanyl laboratory facility. As such, he brought everyone into his office one by one to have a look at the best quality still shot they could find of the two unknown men. About a dozen employees were marched in and out with no one recognizing either man. Then, the next worker to view the screen had a favorable reaction.

"Sí," the man said. "I know them. I know them both. That's Rodrigo and Angel. Sorry, but I don't know their family names. I do know they're always together."

"How do you know them?" Miguel questioned with urgency.

"We grew up in the same neighborhood but went our separate ways as teenagers. I hung out with guys that joined the Sinaloa family. Rodrigo and Angel became Michoacán."

"El Enterrador was right," Miguel declared. "Do you know where Rodrigo and Angel are living these days?"

"I do," the man said. "They actually live together in a house on Gabriel Leyva Solano in Los Mochis. I know the house. I can show you."

Miguel and Salma returned to the Sikorsky with their entourage and the two strapped on headsets, so they could privately converse on the short trip back. Miguel shared his plan with Salma and insisted that she return to El Enterrador's mountaintop estate with his men and not be a part of this evening's festivities. Besides, Miguel was certain that his boy Pedro and wife Margarite would be at the villa. He didn't really care what his wife might think about his keeping company with Salma, but he didn't need the drama while taking care of business.

The chopper touched down without cutting the engines and the copilot assisted Miguel out the cabin door. As Miguel took off his headset and tossed it on the seat next to Salma, he was clicking his jaw in a way she hadn't heard before. Bone-on-bone.

RODRIGO AND ANGEL clambered out of the car and up the porch steps. It was nearly one o'clock in the morning and the end of another long night of drinking tequila and grabbing skirts at the neighborhood watering hole. It was a blessing they both had had too much to drink. As they opened the front door three large men jumped up onto the porch and pushed the two inebriated men through the front door. Before Rodrigo and Angel could appreciate their ill-fated circumstance, the door closed behind them and the men outside held the doorknob tightly. There was no escape.

Suddenly, deafening roars emanated from within instantaneously followed by hair-raising screams and wails occasionally interrupted by the sounds of bones crunching and tendons snapping. Eventually the cacophony of agony faded into moans and groans that gradually subsided. After 15 minutes of silence the men on the porch cracked the front door open just enough for one of them to raise a dart gun and fire twice.

Moments later the three men calmly entered the house and carried out two tranquilized white Siberian tigers that they loaded into a waiting van for the return trip to Miguel's exotic collection. The blood and bones would take some time to wash from the clothes of the men and from the mouths of the big cats. What little remained of Rodrigo and Angel was gathered up into a plastic bag and tied, then placed into a wooden box no bigger than a one-drawer file cabinet. As instructed by El Enterrador, it was taken to the kingpin of the Michoacán cartel by one of his own men who had been compelled by the Sinaloa to make the delivery in person. The wooden box included an envelope with a card.

We found these two assholes in our cook's kitchen!

30

Durham, NC

"I used Necco wafers to help me get off cigarettes.
I quit China white cold turkey and have no regrets.
But leaving you is something that I just can't do.
Cause baby I know there'd be no getting over you."

The applause and dog whistles were deafening as Shaun lifted the leather strap over his head and carefully placed his all-mahogany Taylor 514ce guitar back on its stand in the front of the room. It was only about ten o'clock in the morning, so raising a mug of coffee wasn't out of place. But playing his guitar without a beer nearby was as strange as most of the people in the audience. Entertaining his classmates at the Duke Center for Opioid Addiction and Rehabilitation had helped him get through the 30-day program and proved to him that his songwriting did not require a snort of fentanyl or a shot of whiskey.

"That's not how that song goes," one of the inpatients said indignantly, as Shaun stepped down from the stage.

"That's exactly how it goes," Shaun retorted. "And I should know. I wrote it!"

The man walked away puzzled but impressed.

Shaun knew he needed some new friends, and new habits, so he had intentionally kept his distance from those in the program. In fact, the only ones in the room he really knew were two women sitting in the back row. Jillian and Mia.

"Hey, thanks for coming, you two," Shaun said as they came up front and gave him a hug.

"We didn't want to miss your graduation from the program," Jillian said. "Besides, you probably don't remember that you didn't drive here, so we thought you might need a ride home."

"I don't remember much about those first couple of days," Shaun said. "Probably a good thing too because what little I remember I'm trying hard to forget. Oh. Write that down. Good tag line for another song!"

"Your incorrigible when it comes to songwriting," Jillian said. "But you really are good at it. Hopefully, you'll be one of those musicians that keeps writing and performing to a ripe old age and not one that ... Well, let's not go there."

Shaun put his guitar in its case and retrieved his belongings from the room he had occupied during his stay then the three headed out to Mia's Subaru Outback. Jillian's new Audi RS 5 was only a two-door sports coupe, so Mia's 4-door SUV was a better choice for this morning even though it was much older and frankly not as cool. Shaun put his things in the rear compartment then climbed into the backseat next to Jillian.

"Let's stop by my house before we take you home," Jillian said to Shaun as Mia drove. "There's a lady there that I'd like you to meet."

Shaun agreed but had no clue what she was talking about. A lady? He was still holding out hope for the two of them. He really had no interest in another lady at this point, strange as that may seem given his history of womanizing. When they arrived at Jillian's contemporary ranch home in Duke Forest, Mia pulled into the driveway but stayed in the car.

"Listen," Mia said. "I need to head on over to the Pain Management Clinic to meet with Sue Holbrook. She called me yesterday and said that our investigational drug supplies had arrived. If that's the case, we may be enrolling our first subjects into the Phase I trial tomorrow."

"That's exciting, Mia," Jillian said. "Let's see. That's the safety study that's enrolling healthy volunteers if I recall correctly. How long will it take to complete the recruitment?"

"Actually, we have a directory of healthy volunteers of all ages for studies like this. College students, homemakers, part-time workers, or folks temporarily unemployed and looking to supplement their incomes a little. There are restrictions on what we can pay them because we're not allowed to induce participation with excessive remuneration. To answer your question, about 70 subjects will be enrolled at each of the three clinical sites and we should have the study results in six weeks or so."

Shaun was lost on the conversation and Jillian said she would tell him all about it over lunch. Jillian exited the car and walked to the house while Shaun held back a moment before getting out.

"Say, Mia," Shaun whispered as he leaned over the front seat. "You didn't tell Jillian about my little rendezvous with the drugs in your freezer at Duke, did you?"

"No Shaun, I didn't," Mia said. "And I won't, provided you keep your commitment to me and to her. Staying clean and sober. If you fall off the wagon, I swear I'll run you over with it. Forward and reverse!"

Shaun was grateful that he finally had a couple of friends that truly cared about his well-being. His parents had cared but he had left home after high school and contact with them had been minimal ever since. His older brother would care but the last Shaun heard he was somewhere in Europe, so any caring would be distant at best. He didn't resent Mia for threatening to expose his thievery but his desire to keep Jillian in his life was a far more important motivator. To lose her would probably bring an end to his sobriety and a whole new beginning to his songwriting.

Shaun got out of the car and headed up to the house, looking back briefly to toss Mia a thumbs up as she backed out of the driveway and drove off.

Jillian was in the kitchen holding Penelope and let her down just as Shaun came through the front door. "There she is, Miss America!" Jillian said as Penelope ran into the foyer and jumped up at Shaun wanting to be held. He obliged.

"Oh my gosh," Shaun said as he looked into the dark eyes of the little black-and-tan dog. "Look at that face. Isn't she the cutest?" Jillian held the back of her hand to her forehead and feigned dejection. "Present company excluded, of course," he said, rolling his eyes as she smiled.

Mia left Jillian and Shaun back at the house to entertain Penelope and drove to the Pain Management Clinic where she took the elevator up to the clinical research department on the fourth floor.

"Hello Sue, good to see you again," Mia said pleasantly to Mark's research nurse coordinator. "So, our drug supplies from TheraPeuTex arrived safe and sound?"

"They did," Sue replied. "Come with me to our investigational drug supply room and we'll have a look."

Sue led Mia down the carpeted main hall to the last door on the left then punched in a digital code and unlocked the door. The room was lined with shelves full of experimental drug supplies. She went to the section assigned to the Narcogesic studies, lifted the first drug supply box, and withdrew an orange prescription bottle labeled TORX-A001. She then put on a thin latex glove and withdrew a single white film-coated caplet that looked like any other, but this one had a navy-blue imprint that read 'TORX.'

"Very cool," Mia said thinking how creative Bob had been to select Theta Opioid Therapeutics as the company name with an abbreviation that incorporated the symbol for a prescription.

Sue returned the caplet to its bottle and the bottle to its respective box then tossed the glove in a wastebasket nearby. "We have a research pharmacist on staff that maintains the drug dispensing logs and accounts for every dose of every experimental drug in this room," Sue said. "We also have a team of certified clinical research associates, some of whom have been assigned to your studies, to help with patient evaluations and data gathering."

"How are the data analyzed?" Mia asked.

"Data entry associates are responsible for maintaining electronic files that can be accessed online. Marvin Goldberg is our PhD statistician, and he will coordinate and conduct the computerized data analyses across the three clinical sites.

"Let me ask about patient compliance," Mia said. "How will we verify that the subjects are taking the study medication as directed?"

"Good question," Sue said. "Among the blood samples we draw at each weekly visit for routine chemistries, one tube will be sent to the DCOR laboratory for opioid blood levels. If the patient is on Narcogesic or oxycodone, then detectable levels of these drugs will be present in their blood. If the patient was randomized to placebo or is noncompliant, then of course these drugs will not be present. In the event of noncompliance, the subject will be removed and replaced. I recall a study once when the test drug was present in the blood of a patient that had been randomized to placebo. Turns out the active drug had accidentally been dispensed rather than placebo. I won't share the name of the institution, but it wasn't Duke!"

"If patients really want to cheat, I imagine it would be easy to dispose of the drugs rather than consume them," Mia speculated.

"Patients that do are usually those having side effects they believe are too embarrassing to discuss who simply stop taking their medication. Fortunately, phones with cameras now offer another option."

"What's that?" Mia asked.

"Two-way scheduled dosing alerts with every patient taking a short video clip of every dose to confirm placement on their tongue, swallowing and clearing. The video clips are time stamped and reviewed by the research staff. It would take a lot of effort and know-how to fake a dosing video, so it's a pretty reliable method."

"Sounds like we're ready to roll," Mia said with enthusiasm.

Suddenly, Mia's phone rang, and caller ID announced it was Austin Crammer from the Duke patent office. Mia said she wanted to take the call and Sue ducked out of the drug supply room to give her some privacy.

"Hello Austin. What's up?" Mia inquired.

"This is kind of exciting, actually. At least it's never happened to me before."

"Okay, you have my attention," Mia said.

"I just had a call from Wally Cooper at the USPTO. He said they had a meeting the other day at the White House. Apparently, the President's Commission on Combatting Drug Addiction and the Opioid Crisis has taken something of an interest in Narcogesic."

"How did the Commission learn about Narcogesic?" Mia asked.

"I'm guessing someone at the FDA gave them a heads up after your meeting with the Agency. The D.C. grapevine is pretty efficient."

"When you say they've taken something of an interest in Narcogesic, what do you mean by that?" Mia questioned.

"I'm not sure, really," Austin said. "Perhaps nothing more than the mere fact that it could put an end to the opioid crisis.

Maybe they just want to make sure the FDA is as cooperative as they can be in assisting you."

"I can't imagine them being any more cooperative than they've already been without it becoming questionable, or worse," Mia observed.

"Regardless, the President has asked the USPTO to publish our patent for opposition ASAP and, if we have any objection, to let them know right away. I don't know about you or Mark, but I see no reason to object. If there is an opposition, and I doubt there will be, they would have 90 days to notify us. The sooner we know, the more time we will have to respond. If there's no opposition, then the patent office can move quickly to issue the patent, and the timing might coincide well with our IPO. Just another box for the institutional investors to check."

"I'll call Mark and Bob right now to see if they have any objections. If you don't hear from me soon, call Wally back and tell him they are free to publish. If either Mark or Bob has a problem with that, we'll let them explain it to the President!"

Austin chuckled as he disconnected, believing with certainty that he wasn't going to hear back from Mia anytime soon. She immediately called Mark and Bob and managed to reach them both with little delay. They were pleased the President had expressed an interest in facilitating their work and invited her to join them for dinner that night to talk more about it. Importantly, they also wanted to talk about the TORX organizational structure, titles, and roles. Bob said he and Grant Sawyer had executed the engagement letter and that Goldman Sachs was already running hard down the flight deck.

Dinner was set for 6 p.m. at the University Club, a private dining room on the penthouse floor of the University Tower in Durham. This was a favorite haunt of university faculty and local entrepreneurs, and both men were members. She placed a bet with herself on which of them would pick up the tab. Fortunately, she wasn't a member, so she could leave her purse at home.

Mia left the investigational drug supply room and met briefly with Sue in her office. She mentioned to Sue how impressed she was with the resources and staffing of the research department at the Pain Management Clinic. The two agreed that it spoke volumes about Mark's ability to command working capital for his opioid research whether by grant writing, sponsored research funding, Duke alumni schmoozing or faculty browbeating. Mia was once again reassured that she had picked the right postdoctoral program and mentor.

31

Durham, NC

Bob didn't miss the opportunity to pick up Mia for dinner. This time he pulled up in front of Jillian's house driving his two-tone black-and-tan 1932 Duesenberg Model J. Jillian came to the front door first and as she opened the door Penelope lunged out. She was still a puppy and not well trained, but she was instinctively well behaved. She trotted down the steps and out to the Duesy then sat politely near the driver's door and waited patiently for the occupant to emerge. It was a Hallmark card photo op. Matching black and tans, and it didn't escape Mia's attention as she headed for the passenger seat. Jillian picked up the pup and waived a paw as Bob backed out of the driveway. At six feet tall, the top of Mia's head gently brushed the ragtop ceiling, and at six-two, Bob needed to slouch a bit. But the antique ride, along with his favorite passenger-seat cover on a splendid Tuesday evening, was well worth a slight kink in his back.

The University Tower was only a couple of par-5s away from Jillian's house on Woodburn Rd in Duke Forest. It would have made for a disappointingly short ride in the Duesenberg, but Bob stretched the legs of the old girl for a while before heading to dinner.

He parked the Duesy right outside the front door at the University Club and the valet needed no special instructions or encouragement. Mia assumed Bob had taken care of him before.

The elevator ride to the 17th floor offered an exquisite view of the UNC campus on one side and Duke University on the other. At the top, Mia got her bearings and led Bob to the proper window for a view of Jillian's house.

"Oh look," Mia said in her best rendition of Tina Fey imitating Sarah Palin. "I can see Duke from my house!"

Bob gave her a polite squeeze around the waist then noticed that they were standing eye level with one another. He looked down as discreetly as he could and noticed that she was wearing a pair of black shoes with two-inch heels. That's all it took. Six-inch pumps and he would have been craning his neck all night. She quickly glanced away as he looked back up.

"Oh, there's Mark," she said spotting him already seated at a table. "Hope he hasn't been here long but our little ride in the Duesy was worth his wait!" They both snickered. "So, a 1990 Jag and 1932 Duesy. I can't wait to ride whatever's left in that four-car garage of yours."

"The others are less impressive," Bob said with some remorse.

Mark stood as Mia sat down then the men followed suit. He already had a nice bottle of red wine on the table and had waited for his guests before having a glass. The waiter poured three goblets each half full, and Bob raised is glass.

"To the President of the United States of America taking an interest in Narcogesic!" Bob toasted as *Hail to the Chief* played in the back of his mind.

"Do you think there's a chance that someone else discovered our novel new series of compounds before we did?" Mia asked reticently.

"No way," Mark rebutted. "Mia, I didn't discuss my concept of targeting the theta opioid pathway with a soul other than you, and we can document proof of concept and reduction to practice all the way back to my first discussion with RxFactor."

The waiter wore a black tuxedo and politely interrupted their conversation to take their appetizer orders. The men wanted beef tartare and Mia asked for the butternut squash ravioli. He topped off their wine glasses before heading back to the kitchen. Bob required the largest pour to bring his glass back up to four ounces. Mia required the least.

"Look," Bob continued the conversation. "There's 150 million opioid prescriptions written every year in this country, many of which are new orders for post-operative or other forms of acute or chronic pain. Many of the patients are frightened that they might become addicts, so they choose pain over comfort. It's disquieting at best. Who knows? Maybe the President is thinking one day it may be him or his family struggling with the issue. I'm guessing he's just a compassionate guy in a position to help the people in a position to make a difference. The same reason the two of you are involved. Me, I'm in it for the money!" he said as he raised his glass.

"So, you signed an engagement letter with Goldman Sachs?" Mia changed the subject as she savored her first bite of the ravioli. She was more a connoisseur of herbal tea than pasta, but the roasted squash nuts sprinkled over the top was a nice touch.

"Yes, indeed," Bob said. "My little ploy of suggesting we had other meetings in New York worked like a charm. He pushed his team hard prospecting for this one and now has it on the launch pad like a Falcon Heavy. We covered a lot of ground on the phone, and I provisionally agreed to some outstanding items that we should discuss."

"What were the outstanding items? Mark asked before carving his last piece of bright red tartare into two more delicate bites.

"One was whether any of us are planning to sell into the offering," Bob began as he stared at his empty plate of beef tartare then glanced briefly at the waiter. The look was polite and unhurried, so the waiter took his time approaching the table to take their entrée orders. Mark wasn't sure what Bob meant by the phrase, but he waited a beat for clarification, and it followed. "I assumed we're all standing pat and told him so. That none of us wanted or needed to sell any of our shares into the offering. He was pleased since any selling by the founders can be a signal of concern and a red flag to potential investors. We then reviewed the current cap chart. I told him that my partners and I were not yet fully vested but would be by the time the IPO closes. I said that we would have 50 percent when fully invested and that you would each have 25 percent when fully diluted. Is that fair? No sellers here?"

Mark and Mia nodded, and the waiter mistook that as a sign they were ready to order. No worries. Ladies first. Mia selected the sea bass bouillabaisse and Mark chose the seared duck breast. Bob picked the center cut filet and ordered it rare.

Nice pairing with steak tartare, Mia mused.

"Grant asked how much longer before the trials are underway and I wasn't exactly sure," Bob said.

"Sue and I met today and the first cohort of ten subjects for the Phase I trial are scheduled for their initial visit tomorrow," Mia answered.

"She told me there are cohorts of ten subjects scheduled every day for the next seven days in a row," Mark added. "I've cleared my schedule together with one of the junior anesthesiology residents, so we can evaluate all the volunteers at their first visits."

"It will run like clockwork," Mia said. "UNC and NC State are on identical schedules to ours. The first 50 subjects will be completed 32 days from today and Marv Goldberg will have the preliminary results 24-48 hours later. I've marked my calendar. We will email the safety report for this cohort to the FDA for clearance to begin enrollment into the other two trials. We expect that it will then take another three or four months to complete these studies, including the one month of treatment."

Mia paused long enough for the waiter and his assistants to present their entrées. She invited the men to begin eating as she continued where she had left off.

"That means that we'll have the complete compliment of study results about five months from now," Mia said. "Source documentations, validations and final reports to the FDA will take a bit longer and the NDA can be filed on the heels of that."

"Grant's team is working on the red herring prospectus now and will send that out to prospective investors right after they file the S-1 for the IPO. We'll use your target dates to calendar out the roadshow."

"Who will be on the roadshow?" Mia asked as she scooped out a shrimp and clam from the seafood broth using a silver spoon large enough to have doubled as a ladle.

"I think all three of us should hit the road together," Bob said, setting aside his filet no longer than necessary. "Mia, you have the presentation down pat. As for the Q&A, Mark and I can backstop on the science and business. Grant will certainly join us and I'm guessing he'll bring one of his healthcare analysts over the Chinese Wall to opine on the opioid markets and sales potential of Narcogesic. This will prevent him from reporting on us until after the IPO, but there will be no shortage of coverage by other analysts with Goldman in our corner."

Mark was thoroughly enjoying his duck breast with cherry port reduction, as well as the conversation, but decided to interrupt with an important concern. "The one thing weighing heavy on my mind is the time it will take to hire or otherwise acquire the capability of producing, promoting, launching, and distributing Narcogesic in the U.S., to say nothing of product registration and sales overseas. It's going to be a monumental task and the timeline from cashing the IPO check to NDA approval could be very short, especially if the President has his way."

"That's been of equal concern to Grant as I mentioned briefly to Mia on the phone today," Bob said with some anxiety in his voice. "This really goes to our use of proceeds post-IPO. One option would be to grow the business organically, but I think that would take far too long."

"And our learning curve would be nearly vertical in so many different areas of the business," Mark observed.

"I agree," Bob said, and Mia nodded. "We have science and finance covered but we're weak on manufacturing, sales and marketing, legal and regulatory affairs, and so many more. Another option would be to outsource everything, but this can be very expensive, and you give up a lot of control over important operations."

"We would also need to hire lots of experts in lots of different areas just to manage the contractors," Mia said, and the others agreed.

"No," Bob said. "As I told Grant, I think our only real option is to acquire what we need through a merger or acquisition of one or more companies to give us all the pieces we need. One stop shopping might be to buy a small drug company with a salesforce and distribution network. If they have analgesics or anti-inflammatory products, that would be ideal. Goldman Sachs has a sophisticated M&A group and Grant said he would ask them to explore acquisition targets. He thought the idea of buying the right boutique drug company might be a great play. Since we want to control the destiny of Narcogesic, at least through its infancy, we'll want to be the acquirer and not the acquired, and that requires that we don't cede control to the institutional shareholders right out of the gate. If they could sell us to a larger company for a quick profit, they probably would."

"That reminds me," Mia paused from her meal. "Paul Harris called me to confirm that RxFactor is being acquired by Thera-PeuTex. They will have lots of formulation development and manufacturing capability and they already make Narcogesic. I don't know if merging with them would make sense, but we would still need the other parts of the puzzle."

"I'll mention that to Grant," Bob said. "I think his team has already identified at least a couple of boutique drug companies that would be a perfect fit and allow us to control the growth of Narcogesic. He said our discussion on the use of proceeds in the prospectus would need to be very clear about this but not name specific companies."

"I'm surprised he didn't tell us we need a CFO and internal legal counsel right away," Mark said with more business acumen than most scientists possess.

"Grant is okay with outside counsel for now but did recommend that we hire a CFO sooner rather than later to guide us through the finance and accounting matters and to mitigate the risks of an acquisition. Which brings me to the final topic that he and I discussed." Bob repositioned himself in his chair, put down his silverware and finished the last of his wine. He was clearly uneasy with where the conversation might go from here.

"Let me say that Goldman Sachs in general, and Grant in particular, are uncomfortable with the organizational structure of TORX as it stands today. They obviously have the greatest respect for the two of you in terms of the science and medicine. Without either of you, the deal would be DOA. They are also confident with me on the strategic and business side of the equation. But I'm not an operational insider at this point. Sure, I'm a major investor and shareholder and I tossed out the possibility of becoming a nonexecutive Chairman, but Grant said that would be *insufficient,* to use his word."

"You're beating around the bush, Bob," Mia said forthrightly.

"Sorry," he said more sincerely than she appreciated. "Frankly, Grant said Goldman will have nothing to do with the deal if I'm not at least the full-time Chief Operating Officer." He swallowed hard, averting Mia's gaze, and looked at Mark as he delivered the next line. "In fact, he said, it would be their strong preference for me to function in title and duty as the company's CEO." He paused and glanced back at Mia, half-expecting to be soon wearing the rest of her bouillabaisse.

"Well, that wasn't so hard now, was it?" she asked, catching him off guard. "I thought you understood that my only concern is doing whatever I can, whatever I must, to get Narcogesic in the hands of patients that will become addicts without it. That may die without it. Money and monikers are not even secondary to me. Not even tertiary." Looking him in the eyes Mia said, "Bob, believe me when I say, between the two of us, it really doesn't matter to me whether I'm on top or you're on top."

She's very good at jerking my chain, he thought.

32

Beltsville, MD

His government email account notified him of a new submission to the Narcogesic IND sponsored by Theta Opioid Therapeutics, Inc., RTP, North Carolina. Dr. Jayden Banks had been at the pre-IND meeting, along with his boss Dr. Charlene Hopkins, both representing the Division of the FDA responsible for reviewing the company's application to market the drug. He had been expecting the submission, but not this soon. He opened the attached file on his desktop and noted the document titled *Preliminary Report on the First 50 Subjects Completed under the Phase I Safety Study of Narcogesic versus Placebo in Healthy Volunteers.*" Jayden sent a text message to Charlene.

> JUST RECEIVED THE REPORT FROM TORX ON THE FIRST 50 SUBJECTS IN THE SAFETY STUDY OF NARCOGESIC. I'M SURE YOU HAVE A COPY. HOW LONG WILL YOU NEED TO REVIEW IT AND WHEN DO YOU WANT MEET? I KNOW WE'RE ALL ANXIOUS TO GET ON WITH THE PHASE II EFFICACY STUDY.

Upon reading the message she pulled up her copy of the submission, quickly scanned the summary and noted the length of the document. Just eight pages plus appendices, tables, and references. Not unlike a typical scientific journal article in length and format. It could have been a manuscript ready to submit for publication. She then replied with a text message of her own.

GIVE ME AN HOUR THEN COME DOWN TO MY OFFICE.

Charlene and Jayden spent the next hour in their respective offices reading the submission in its entirety. The results included several data tables and key among them was the one that showed there were 25 subjects in the Narcogesic group and 25 subjects in the placebo group. It compared the incidence of withdrawal symptoms between groups that occurred up to 72 hours after the last dose. There were only a couple of patients in each group with non-specific complaints, but these differences were not statistically significant. There was also no difference in the incidence of side effects noted during the four-week treatment period. The report concluded that there was no difference between Narcogesic and placebo in terms of side effects or addictive potential. At least not in this cohort.

Jayden finished reading the report then grabbed his government-issued digital tablet and headed up the hall to Charlene's office.

"Amazing," Charlene said sincerely, as Jayden walked in and sat in one of her guest chairs. "Narcogesic is as innocuous as placebo. Of course, there's always a small incidence of spontaneous complaints in a population of otherwise healthy adults. A runny nose here, a headache there, and clearly there were some of these in both groups. But nothing unexpected."

"If this is any indication of the final results, they have an exceedingly safe drug and clearly one that is not addictive," Jayden said in near disbelief. "I also looked through the myriad of other safety tests, including the X-rays, EKGs, and blood chemistries, as detailed in the appendices, and there were no findings of any concern."

"If the Phase II study shows that Narcogesic and oxycodone are at least equivalent for pain relief, and the safety profile for

Narcogesic holds, they have themselves a winner." Charlene commented.

"I guess it shouldn't come as a surprise," Jayden remarked.

"Why is that?"

"I spent some time looking into RxFactor," Jayden said. "You may have seen the announcement a couple of weeks back that they merged with TheraPeuTex."

"I did. TheraPeuTex is a contract manufacturer in the San Diego area. They were recently inspected by the FDA and found to be in full compliance. A good choice for TORX as a supplier of Narcogesic."

"I think the reason Narcogesic is so highly selective for the theta opioid pathway is because of the sophisticated molecular modeling used by the synthetic chemists at RxFactor," Jayden continued. "I think they have built an extensive and proprietary database of the compounds and chemical moieties with some degree of activity against various disease targets. This allows them to generate new molecules that are focused only on the effects of interest and devoid of other effects or side effects."

"Designer drugs," Charlene said. "Assets with no liabilities."

"Spoken like an accountant!" Jayden ribbed.

"I'll send a note to all the other internal reviewers," Charlene said. "Unless they have concerns that need to be discussed as a group, I'll call Dr. Reinhardt and tell her that TORX is free to initiate the other studies."

"Are you still inclined to empanel an Advisory Committee to review the New Drug Application for Narcogesic then ask for its opinion as to whether we should approve the drug?" Jayden queried.

"I am. If the drug behaves as advertised, it's not just another narcotic analgesic. It will be the first in a new class of drugs. The first and only nonaddictive opioid pain reliever. Such a drug could destroy the market for all other opiates. The impact on the drug industry will be seismic. As such, I think it's important to have a panel of independent scientific and medical experts advise and consent on the NDA rather than for the FDA to act alone on this one."

"And what if the Committee doesn't recommend approval?" Jayden said, tongue-in-cheek. Charlene chuckled at the absurdity then dialed Ty Dixon and laid her phone on the desk with the external speaker enabled.

"Hello Ty, Char Hopkins here at the FDA. I have you on speaker phone with Jayden in my office. How are things up at the University of Michigan?"

"Always more numbers to crunch than hours in a day. What can I do for you?"

"We thought we would give you a heads up on a new drug that's coming our way. Pivotal trials are ongoing for acute use and the NDA will probably land here in a few months. I'll send you a copy of everything under our existing confidentiality agreement. Suffice it to say that it may be an opioid analgesic as potent as fentanyl but nonaddictive."

"No kidding," Ty said, then whistled. "Too bad you can't let me guess the name of the company, so I can buy some stock before you send me the documents and lock me out!"

"Very funny," she said. "It's actually a private company, so nothing in it for you except your usual outrageous fees. Listen, the company is called Theta Opioid Therapeutics and the drug is called Narcogesic. As the first nonaddictive narcotic analgesic it will be a first-in-class drug, so we've decided to empanel an Advisory Committee and I'd like you to head up the Committee and search for members. Of course, your expertise would cover the study design and statistical analyses, and we'd like you to recommend some other academics in the fields of anesthesia, analgesia, pain management and drug addiction. The Committee should consist of researchers, healthcare providers and at least one consumer advocate."

"You said the pivotal trials were for acute pain," Ty repeated. "There is certainly a substantial population of patients requiring the management of acute pain, especially post-injury or post-surgery and these patients are at some risk of addiction, no doubt. But there are also lots of patients with chronic pain and a large percentage of them are at risk of addiction, if not already addicted. Why is the company not conducting trials in chronic pain? Do they think the drug will be ineffective or addictive in this setting?"

"To the contrary," Jayden replied. "There's supportive animal data and every reason to believe it will be equally safe and effective in such patients. It's just that the sponsor is a very small and modestly funded company at this point. I'm sure they'll use the results of these acute studies to raise more money for longer-term trials and expanded claims."

"Well, that's exciting," Ty said with sincerity. "I know the biologics group at the FDA has empaneled an Advisory Committee for the COVID-19 vaccines although I'm not a member of that committee. However, my statistical group here at the University of Michigan has been contracted by ViroSelect and they are one of several companies with a COVID-19 vaccine in development. They had some production problems recently, but they're back on track and I think you'll see their NDA submitted very soon."

"We'll let the Center for Biologics solve the COVID-19 crisis, and we'll solve the opioid crisis," Charlene said. Her shared ownership of the Narcogesic effort would not have escaped the attention of Dr. Oberon.

33

Durham, NC

The morgue in the basement of the Duke Medical Center just off the service elevator from the ER was lined with metal hospital gurneys. Most were vacant but some had occupants covered by a blue sheet from head to tagged toe. Dr. Williams, a staff ER physician, guided Jillian to the nearest stretcher as Mia stood back. He reached up and uncovered the torso, enabling her to make a positive identification.

"That's him," she said. "That's Shaun McKinney."

Dr. Williams could have made the ID from his previous encounter with Shaun a few months back when he was admitted for an overdose of fentanyl. Jillian had regained her composure but had wept almost the entire way to the hospital. He guided both women out of the morgue and back upstairs to a private room along the corridor of ER staff offices.

"Jillian, and Mia, I'm so very sorry for the loss of your friend," Dr. Williams said with repose. "After his transfer from the ICU to the step-down unit for acute opioid detoxification, I unfortunately had no further contact with him. I recall he had agreed to participate in our 30-day inpatient program at the Duke Center for Opioid Addiction and Rehabilitation. I'm guessing now that was unsuccessful."

"Actually, quite the contrary," Jillian said, but Dr. Williams looked puzzled since failure was obvious. "His detoxification in the hospital was rough and his 30 days in the rehabilitation program was not a cakewalk, but he did fine. He did great. Not a single setback as far as I could judge. Until now, of course. Are you certain he died of an opioid overdose?"

"The first responders said he displayed all the signs and symptoms consistent with an opioid OD, but he was unresponsive to Narcan. We did a stat drug screen when he arrived and it was negative for all drugs of abuse, except opioids. Of course, that could have been the Narcan, which is also an opioid. So, I had a blood sample delivered to your biochemistry laboratory at the DCOR for more specific testing. We should have confirmation as to the specific opioid very soon."

"I'll text them," Mia said. "That's a rapid test and they should have the results of a stat request by now." Dr. Williams had marked the sample *stat* because he knew Jillian and Mia were on their way and would appreciate the information, but the situation was clearly not stat since nothing more could be done for the deceased.

The DCOR laboratory replied to her text message almost immediately. "In addition to naloxone, Shaun's blood sample was positive for fentanyl," Mia said as she highlighted the text reply. "The concentration was 6.7 ng/ml, only slightly higher than it was when he overdosed before, but no fentanyl derivative this time."

"What do you mean 'no fentanyl derivative'" Jillian asked.

"Shaun had asked me not to tell you, so I didn't. But I see no reason to keep it from you now. He told me that, on his one-and-only trip to see you at DCOR, he had wandered off to our drug discovery freezer and had stolen a handful of vials from our fentanyl collection. Among them were fentanyl, sufentanil, carfentanil, and a few of other fentanyl derivatives equally potent and deadly. A long-lasting supply of potent narcotics, free of charge. He unwisely snorted a miniscule amount of one of them and ended up in the ER. Although, he survived, others were not so lucky. The drug cache was stolen again, this time by a friend of Shaun's roommate who, along with several other addicts, ended up in the ER DOA by opioid overdose. They could not have guessed a non-fatal dose of these potent derivatives. Fortunately, the Durham County Sheriff recovered the unused drugs and returned them to Dr. Oberon."

"So, at the very least, Shaun contributed to the death of those other addicts," Jillian said.

"Not really," Mia said. "He was no more liable for the criminal misuse of his stolen property than DCOR. But he certainly could have been charged with the theft. I would have surrendered him, but the drug supply had been recovered by the time I learned of his misdeed. I was hoping a little forgiveness might lead to a life of sobriety rather than crime."

"I think you did the righteous thing, Mia," Dr. Williams said. "It sounds like he was on the right track but fell off the wagon. I see it all the time, but I'm not sure I can explain it."

"Explain what?" Jillian asked.

"Shaun's fentanyl level was about the same as it was previously, with no fentanyl derivative contributing to his overdose. I'm guessing he just contacted his usual supplier in a moment of weakness and took his usual dose. This is what most recovering addicts do when they relapse. Of course, this would not be a toxic dose for addicts displaying their usual level of tolerance. But after a period of abstinence, it can be deadly."

"There is a pharmacological explanation for that," Mia said. "You can think of tolerance as a growing resistance to the drug. You become *desensitized* to its effects. It's caused by a down-regulation of the signaling pathway for the drug or substance. I won't bore you with the cellular details, but abstinence reverses this process and subjects become *hypersensitized*, such that the same dose produces a toxic response. This also occurs with certain medications and explains why they must be stopped slowly or tapered rather than discontinued abruptly."

"Someday, when I'm not on duty in the ER, you can bore me with the cellular details," Dr. Williams said and meant it. "I'm sure it's fascinating."

Jillian had been in no condition to drive when they left the house earlier, so Mia had driven them to the ER in Jillian's racing-green Audi. Now more composed, Jillian drove them home, and both were looking forward to lunch with Penelope.

The little black and tan pup greeted them at the front door when they arrived. She was only a few months old but housebroken, so her metal cage had been relegated to a shelf in the garage. Jillian took her out for a long walk around the neighborhood every morning and every evening, and more often if she had the time. Mia agreed to make lunch while Jillian attached Penelope's purple leash and headed out the door for a walk. When they returned, the women sat at the breakfast table and enjoyed butternut squash soup and garden salad. Penelope sat at their feet and patiently waited for any fallout.

"Jill, I feel badly about withholding Shaun's dishonesty from you," Mia said. "I think the dependence and drug-seeking nature of addiction can turn an otherwise honest person into a thief of drugs, or drug money. I was hoping that honesty would follow sobriety, and I wasn't sure how serious your relationship may have been."

"Shaun was a talented guy, and he didn't deserve an early demise," Jillian said. "But we weren't that close, really. Just friends, and very different in many ways. He was right brained, and I'm left, although I don't necessarily ascribe to the pop psychology. It's also been said that opposites attract and, while that is certainly true of magnetics, I'm not sure it makes for the best of relationships. Maybe in business, where complementary strengths and weaknesses can be an asset. But I think friendships are better forged from commonalities. Shared interests and beliefs. I will miss Shaun, but we weren't soulmates. You and

I on the other hand have much in common and that's why we make such good friends."

Glad that her friend did not feel betrayed, Mia told Jillian that she had a 1:30 p.m. meeting at DCOR with Mark Oberon, Anne McCarthy and Marvin Goldberg to review the results of the clinical trials of Narcogesic. It had been nearly four months since the FDA had received their report on the first 50 subjects and authorized them to continue. Jillian asked if she could join them since she had nothing more pressing and wanted to get her mind off Shaun. She was also genuinely curious to know how well the animal data had predicted the clinical results. Pleased that Jillian's interests went beyond her animal laboratory, Mia invited her to join the discussion, but suggested they drive separately since she and Mark and Bob had a subsequent conference call scheduled with Goldman Sachs.

The women met the others in the main conference room on the first floor of the DCOR building and Marvin was already upfront with his laptop open and mirrored on the big screen.

"I don't need to take this audience through anything more than the bottom line," Marvin said. Without further ado, he flipped through several introductory slides and landed on the first data table of interest. "Here's the Phase I safety results for all 200 healthy volunteers split 50/50 between Narcogesic and placebo. It's a mirror image of the first 50 subjects that we reported to the FDA. No statistically significant differences between the groups. There were only a few inconsequential complaints in both groups with no signs or symptoms of addiction or withdrawal within 72 hours of the last dose. These data support that Narcogesic is nonaddictive as predicted by the animal studies and the initial cohort of volunteers."

"Marv let me ask about the few complaints," Mark said. "I know they were considered inconsequential and unrelated to addiction but what was their nature?"

Marvin jumped to a data table that listed the diary entries of all 200 subjects and highlighted the few complaints. "Looks like we have some runny noses, sneezes, watery eyes, and a couple of headaches. Sounds like common cold or flu stuff."

"Is that your statistical or medical opinion?" Mark jabbed.

"Sorry," Marvin said abjectly, as he searched and found the table of remarks made by the anesthesiology residents assigned to the clinic visits for these patients. "Here it is. The evaluating clinician indicated that each of these cases were consistent with rhinovirus infections or seasonal allergies. I stand corrected," he said with a smirk.

"Of course, the only way to definitively establish whether a reversible side effect is drug related is with a positive de-challenge and rechallenge," Mark said. "That is, does it resolve when we stop the drug, and does it re-emerge when we reinstitute it? Regardless, I would agree that none of these were related to the study drug."

"Next are the results from the Phase II-III efficacy study of 400 patients split 50/50 between Narcogesic and oxycodone to manage post-operative pain," Marvin continued. "Table I shows fewer doses taken by the Narcogesic group (26 vs. 42 mean average of total caplets/patient) and this difference was highly significant at an alpha level of $p<0.005$. Similarly, Table II shows lower average pain scores (2.3 vs. 5.6 out of 10), also highly significant. In terms of efficacy then, we can say that Narcogesic is at least equivalent to oxycodone."

"It was more effective," Mark pounced. "And significantly so. But this just means that the doses were not equipotent. A lower dose of Narcogesic or higher dose of oxycodone and the drugs would have been equivalent pain relievers. So, Narcogesic is more potent than oxycodone, which is consistent with the animal data suggesting that its equivalent to fentanyl. Superb! ... as long as the safety profile was acceptable."

"And it was!" Marvin replied rabidly. "Table III shows a higher incidence of numbness, lightheadedness, euphoria, and other complaints or side effects with oxycodone, whereas these were essentially nonexistent in the Narcogesic group. Finally, Table IV shows that, while there were no patients in the Narcogesic group with signs or symptoms of withdrawal within 72 hours of the last dose, there were 24 of 100 oxycodone patients with two or more such symptoms.

"So, if we pool the results from both of the blinded comparative trials, we have a total of 300 Narcogesic subjects with essentially no side effects, and no addiction," Mark concluded. "And what about the 700 patients enrolled in the Phase-III open-label safety study?"

"More of the same," Marvin answered as he displayed the relevant data table. "Exactly more of the same in terms of safety and, importantly, not a single case of addiction in this cohort of post-operative outpatients. Of course, pain relief was not formally assessed because this was not a comparative study of efficacy."

Mark and Mia embraced at the table without standing and that started a series of fist bumps, high fives and hugs around the room.

"Let me see if I have this right," Mark said scholarly, as the others took their seats and recomposed themselves. "Compared to oxycodone, one of the most prescribed narcotic analgesics in the country, Narcogesic required less drug to deliver more pain relief with fewer side effects and no addiction over a four-week treatment period following major surgery. Unless I'm mistaken, that should put a dent in the number of prescription opioid users graduating to heroin!"

Be sure to visit the Vasa while you're in Stockholm, Mia thought.

Robert Taylor heard the celebrations coming from down the hall the moment he walked through the glass front doors of the DCOR building. As he entered the conference room on the first floor, Mark introduced him to Anne and Marvin as they were leaving. Mark then established a wireless connection between his phone and the external speaker in the center of the conference table then dialed Grant Sawyer at Goldman Sachs and placed his phone on the table.

"Hello, Grant. Bob Taylor here together with Mark Oberon and Mia Reinhardt. What's the good word?"

"We were hoping you had one," Grant quickly retorted. "I'm here with all the important people on our side and I'm sure Marcus Goldman and Samuel Sachs are here in spirit. You said the call would be right after your internal review of the pivotal trial results. Well? Do we have ourselves a drug? Do we have an IPO?"

"Grant, this is Mark. Bob just walked in and hasn't heard the results yet either, so allow me and Mia to bring everyone up to speed at the same time. First, we didn't expect to see this with Narcogesic but let me just ask everyone. How many drug-related suicides would be too many?" he asked, then covered his mouth and looked at Mia as Bob groaned.

"One!" Grant blurted out. "Unless it's Bob!"

They all laughed at Bob's expense, and Mark when on to describe the safety and efficacy results of the clinical trials. At the end of Mark's monologue, the Goldman representatives were pleased to hear that TORX had a drug, and an IPO.

Grant informed the group that his team had worked tirelessly and were nearing completion. The Form S-1 registration statement was ready to be filed with the SEC and a draft of the red herring prospectus was awaiting insertion of the trial results before distribution to prospective investors.

"We'll send you a copy of the red herring for your approval prior to distribution," Grant said. "For your edification, a red herring prospectus does not specify a price or number of shares, although it may indicate a preliminary range for one or the other. It also cannot be used to take orders but gauges the level of market interest in the security."

"I thought a red herring described something that was misleading or distracting," Mia questioned.

"In essence, this is the same," Grant explained. "It's a precursor to the final prospectus that gets priced with the actual number of shares to be sold once the SEC approves of the offering. Then the prospectus is no longer a distraction but the real deal!"

"We talked about needing $500 million or so to execute our plans," Bob said. "Grant, what are you thinking in terms of number of shares and price at this point?"

"Subject to market interest, we're thinking maybe 20 million shares to be authorized by the SEC with six million shares to you three as the insiders and six million to be sold to the public, leaving eight million in reserve for future use, such as an incentive stock option (ISO) plan, stock-in-lieu-of-cash transactions or a secondary public offering. Based on our assumptions and five-year forecasts for worldwide sales of Narcogesic, we can easily support an initial market valuation of $1.5 billion using a discounted cash flow model. That would put the IPO price at $75 per share. You would sell six million shares of NASDAQ: TORX to pocket $450 million, less our fees and reimbursable expenses."

"Given the current cap table, that would be 1.5 million shares each to Mark and Mia, and 3.0 million to me and my partners," Bob said. "This means the insiders would own 50 percent of the outstanding shares; essentially a controlling interest."

"Assuming that all the outstanding shares are voting shares," Grant answered, "But we might get some pushback on that. Some institutional investors want to see the insiders holding some nonvoting shares which wouldn't change your monetary stake but could cede control to the outsiders and institutional shareholders. Given the critical importance of Mark and Mia to the understanding and success of this miracle molecule, I doubt control will be an issue. In fact, I wouldn't be surprised if they insist on key-person insurance on both of you. Now let me ask if there's been any resolution on the organizational structure."

"There has," Bob replied. "We agreed that I will serve as the Chief Executive Officer and Chairman of the statutory Board of Directors. Mark will serve as the Chief Scientific Officer and Chairman of the Scientific Advisory Board, and Mia will be the Chief Operating Officer. Finally, as you suggested, we will hire Norm Brady from Keystone Capital as our Chief Financial Officer once the IPO is in the books. We will also hire Anne McCarthy as our Regulatory Affairs officer and we will continue to retain Richard Blair as outside legal counsel."

"That's solid," Grant remarked. "All good choices. Finally, a few words about the strategic plan and use of proceeds. We spoke with Hank Watson who will stay on as CEO after the merger between RxFactor and TheraPeuTex. Subject to your review and approval he has agreed to a commercial supply agreement to manufacture Narcogesic under very reasonable terms. He is also open to discussions of a merger, especially if we acquire a commercial sales, marketing, and distribution capability. Like us, they have an interest in becoming a fully integrated company."

"How do we acquire those capabilities?" Mia asked the obvious.

"Thank you," Grant said as if the question had been planted. "We have a short list of small drug companies in the business of pain management that we believe would be open to a merger. One that's high on our list happens to sell branded injectable and transdermal analgesics that are manufactured by TheraPeuTex. Such formulations would be obvious line extensions for Narcogesic. They also have a well-trained salesforce that calls on anesthesiologists and pain specialists. I had a nonconfidential discussion with the CEO and he would be open to a merger of equals, or an acquisition if they are the smaller and less-valuable company. We think this is an excellent target and, without naming any names, we wrote the prospectus with such an acquisition strategy clearly stated, so it won't be a surprise to the financial markets. If anything, it will be an expectation."

"Would the CEO of the small analgesic drug company accept a lesser role in the new entity? Bob asked but with his ego in check.

"He would, or we'd send him packing," Grant said. "We control the terms. I had that discussion with him quite frankly, and he said, 'if you have a guy with a company and a strategy that can make my shares worth more than I can, I'll gladly step aside.' He certainly has the right attitude. It's the guys that aren't motivated by money that scare the hell out of me! What he doesn't know is that the launch of Narcogesic will bury his company, so he'll look like a genius and well-deserving of a golden parachute if that's his choice."

Grant wrapped up the call by telling everyone that final copies of the IPO documents would be distributed internally the next morning, with comments due by the end of the day. The S-1 would be submitted to the SEC the following day and the red herring prospectus would then go out to Goldman's targeted list of potential investors. He said TORX should put out a press release as soon as possible on the pivotal trial results to prime the pump, and it should mention that the NDA submission is imminent. Grant said they should all plan on a roadshow to pitch the IPO to interested investors and be ready to leave in a week or so. The plan would be to visit a dozen different cities, and three to four times that many investors, over a grueling two-week period. He would accompany them, together with Norm Brady as an outside financial analyst, and they would all charter a private plane to maximize the flexibility of the schedule.

34

New York City, NY

He positioned his monocle over his right eye, then began to scan up and down shining a penlight at various oblique angles to the canvas. Henri Beauchamp was a renowned French purveyor of impressionist art, and Geoff Fischmann had invited him to the Pinnacle Penthouse to have a look at the original Claude Monet that hung on his side of The Bar. When he purchased the piece at a Sotheby's auction last year for $26 million, he knew it was one-of-a-kind and had outbid two other art collectors. One from Europe and the other from Japan. But lately, some had implied it was not a singular masterpiece. He hired Henri to retire the question. Karl, the other half of the infamous Fischmann Brothers, stood nearby and listened with more than a passive interest since their wealth was shared.

"Ah, Monsieur," Henri said discerningly, as he backed away from the painting. "It's definitely a Claude Monet original from late 1890 or early 1891, and it is most valuable." Geoff sighed with relief but continued to hang on every word. "However," Henri continued.

Shit, Karl thought. He almost always hated the word 'however' because of what usually followed.

"It is not the only *Haystacks* painting," Henri said as Geoff gasped. "Rather, it is one in series of paintings by the master that used various haystacks of wheat, oats or barley and explored the subject under various conditions of light, times of day, seasons and weather. Mind you, it *is* the only one of its kind painted under *these* conditions, but it is only *one of twenty-five* accurately referred to as *Haystacks*."

"One of twenty-five!" Karl fumed. "Geoff, you're a damned idiot. Easy come, easy go. All you need to do now is spend $26 million on each of the other twenty-four, then set them on fire. Shit! I need a drink!"

Geoff reluctantly thanked Henri for his time and indicated that he could pick up a check for the appraisal and his travel expenses at the receptionist's desk across the lobby from Cody. Then he wandered over to Karl's side of The Bar and joined him for a late morning that-didn't-go-so-well Bloody Mary.

"Geoff," Karl said, using all the concentration he could muster to redirect their focus. "In my email this morning was a red herring prospectus from Goldman Sachs."

"Yeah, I received one as well," Geoff said as he pulled the celery stick out of his drink and snapped off a bite. "We don't do IPOs, so I trashed it."

"Goldman also knows we don't do IPOs," Karl replied. Kingsley had made his drink to his liking with Worcestershire sauce, Texas Pete, a dill pickle slice, and three bleu cheese stuffed olives. "In fact, everyone on the damn Street knows we don't do IPOs, so I figure there must be something special about this one. The company is Theta Opioid Therapeutics. Drs. Robert Taylor, Mark Oberon and Mia Reinhardt are the principles."

"Never heard of them," Geoff dismissed as he took another big swig of his Bloody Mary.

"Yes, you have," Karl said. "Those are the folks from Duke that filed that patent Wally Cooper called us about. Some non-addictive narcotic."

"Oh, that's the one I read about in that press release the other day," Geoff said as he found the relevant text message and read aloud. "Here it is. 'TORX announces positive results from its pivotal trials of Narcogesic, a nonaddictive opioid pain reliever. The company expects to submit a New Drug Application to the FDA very soon. It has registered with the SEC for an IPO to raise the capital needed to take Narcogesic to market. Analysts are calling the drug revolutionary and predicting that it will quickly cannibalize the $30 billion global market for opioid analgesics.'"

The Brothers agreed they should not dismiss this one out of hand, even though investing in an IPO was outside their wheelhouse. This was precisely the reason they had hired Carlos Martinez, MD, as their in-house medical expert and analyst for scientific investments. As a physician, he had struggled with betting against medical technologies and scientific advances in pursuit of short-selling financial gains, but the paydays had anesthetized him to the irony, and he soon became very good at finding creative ways to short a company. Karl called him down to The Bar to join in their discussion of TORX.

"What'll ya have, my friend?" Kingsley asked Carlos.

"I'll have a big mug of that Black Rifle coffee," Carlos replied. "Make it that Murdered Out extra-dark roast. Just black," he said as he joined Karl and Geoff at a high-top table on Karl's side of The Bar. He was aware of the barstool recently renamed the *Janie O* and chose another stool.

"Guys, I read the TORX press release the other day and scanned the red herring from Goldman this morning," Carlos said. "I've been keeping my eye on this one and I can tell you there's a ground swell building in the medical community. They believe that Narcogesic will revolutionize pain management and eliminate a major source of drug addicts. This won't be good news for prescription opioid manufacturers or for the drug cartels."

"Once TORX closes on its IPO in a couple of weeks, I don't see a downside to bet on," Geoff observed, licking some salt from the rim of his glass before taking another sip. "If anything, they've orchestrated a string of good news events. They just announced positive trial results to support the red herring. Next, they'll have an NDA submission and patent issuance to support closing on the IPO. Then they'll have the market breathlessly awaiting the NDA approval and product launch to support the aftermarket performance of the stock. Textbook!"

"Let me give it some thought," Carlos said, enjoying his hardy breakfast coffee. Not only did he like the coffee, a lot, but he liked supporting the 100 percent veteran-owned company that was doing so well. About that time a burner phone in his pocket rang out. Caller ID read OTD, so he answered. He did not use the external speaker, so he elaborated as necessary for the benefit of Karl and Geoff.

"Hello Ty. How's life treating you these days?" Carlos asked as he covered the microphone and whispered, "Ty Dixon." After a long pause he repeated some of the conversation. "So, the FDA has decided to use an Advisory Committee to guide their review of the Narcogesic NDA when it's filed, and the Reviewing Division has asked you to chair the committee. Nice. What's in it for us?" After another long pause. "So, you think we should short the big pharma companies that manufacture opioids because losing that product line will reduce their revenues and hurt their stock prices. What companies did you have in mind?" Carlos hammered down some more Black Rifle coffee, then whistled. "Goodness, those are two of the biggest drug companies in the world. Thanks. We'll think about it. By the way, give me a call when the Narcogesic NDA is filed, and you have a date for the Advisory Committee meeting." Ty agreed to do that and ended the call.

"Ty Dixon," Karl huffed. "That's the sonofabitch that screwed us on the ViroSelect short call. Lost $16 million on that one. Now his bright idea is shorting two of the biggest drug companies in the world because a fraction of their business is at risk. Billions in additional revenue from new monoclonal antibodies awaiting approval with billions more in the pipeline and this clown thinks we should short them." Karl quickly chewed his celery stick from one end to the other and somehow managed to avoid phalangeal involvement. "Someone needs to throw a dead fish in the backseat of that guy's car!" Karl raged as he stood and stormed back to his office.

"Isn't that what the mob used to do when they targeted one of the wise guys for a hit?" Carlos asked Geoff rhetorically.

Geoff left The Bar and went around the corner into Karl's office. He was hoping his brother had simmered down about Ty and would be ready to talk about some new short-selling schemes.

Carlos finished his Black Rifle coffee and decided to call his brother Miguel from his office down the hall. As he walked across the atrium lobby and past the Big Boards of the Pinnacle Penthouse, he noticed that XMED was trading at $98 per share and VSLT was at $185 per share.

Could have made more holding XMED a while longer ... and could have lost a lot more holding VSLT any longer!

"Hola!" Miguel said as he answered the call from Carlos. "I was just thinking about you, bro. Are you ready to leave that petty peso job of yours in New York yet and join me down here for some serious Mexican bean counting? I know you would find the tequila refreshing, the señoritas exciting, and the beans rewarding! C'mon. What do you say?"

"Listen, Miguel," Carlos said with all seriousness. "We've recently become aware of an experimental drug here in the U.S. that threatens to destroy the market for legal narcotics around the world and, in time, the market for your *products*.

"What sort of experimental drug? Maybe I'll have El Cocinero switch from making fentanyl to that!"

"I'm sure with the recipe he could do that, but your *customers* would not get *hooked* on it. They would take it or leave it. This experimental drug is a *nonaddictive* opioid pain reliever.

Fentanyl without the habit. Won't be long and, poof, there goes your business, booze, and broads!"

"Shit, you say!" Miguel blustered. "Carlos! You gotta help me, bro!"

35

San Diego, CA

Wearing a pair of pink rubber gloves, Brantley Corbin reached over to the assembly line and removed an amber plastic medicine bottle from the conveyor belt. He tilted it upside down over his palm and dispensed a single white film-coated caplet embossed on one side with dark blue lettering that read *TORX*. Then he flipped it over to reveal the same dark-blue lettering that spelled out *NARCOGESIC.*

"Duke blue and white," Mia pronounced. "All that's missing is the Blue Devil logo! We never specified the color scheme, so our hats are off to your creativity and attention to detail."

"You'd be surprised how often the color scheme of a prescription drug matches the school colors of its discoverers," Brantley said. As President and CEO of TheraPeuTex, he prided himself in going the extra mile to please the companies that contracted for his formulation development and manufacturing services. In addition to Bob Taylor and Mia Reinhardt of TORX, Brantley had invited Paul Harris from RxFactor to join them on a tour of the drug production facility since Paul had been instrumental in facilitating the merger of their two companies.

The clean room at TheraPeuTex was alive with all manner of human and robotic motion as technicians monitored every step of the production process from raw material to packaging and labeling. Now coming off the line was the last of the first commercial batch of Narcogesic that would be the subject of the FDA's preapproval inspection of the facility. Paul had not been through that regulatory hoop before because RxFactor was not a drug manufacturer, but Brantley and his team had been through several. It was not uncommon for such facilities to be cited by the Agency for an inadequately labelled bottle of solvent here or a missing notation in a record there, but they had never received an FDA Form 483; a deficiency requiring correction prior to FDA approval and product launch. For Brantley, this was another source of pride.

Bob had seen Mia in her white laboratory coat at the Duke Center for Opioid Research (DCOR) on a few occasions but there was something even more appealing about the way she looked now wearing a pink face mask, hair net and gloves. The same could not be said for Brantley, Paul, or himself.

After their morning tour the four gathered in the executive dining room for an early lunch. It was already a little past 11 a.m., and Brantley had scheduled the foursome for a 1:18 p.m. tee time at Torrey Pines Golf Course just up the road. Mia had been on her high school golf team up in Valencia, but she had never played Torrey.

"I hope you both had a chance to look over the red herring for TORX that we sent in advance of this meeting," Bob said as he selected a lettuce-wrapped sandwich from the serving platter on the table. "We think Grant Sawyer and his team at Goldman Sachs did a great job describing our commercial plans for Narcogesic. With the clinical trials in our rearview mirror, and the NDA in its final stages of preparation, we are here in San Diego on the last leg of our IPO roadshow to raise the capital we will need to make, market, and sell the drug worldwide."

"Indeed," Brantley replied. "We both had a chance to review your plans and discuss them between us. I mentioned to Grant that RxFactor and TheraPeuTex have merged their operations to provide a full range of drug discovery, formulation, and manufacturing capabilities using state-of-the-art technologies and automation. Since we were the acquiring company, our shareholders elected to retain the TheraPeuTex name, though I personally favored RxFactor." Paul smiled since he was the one who had conceived of the name. "Fee for service on a contract basis served us both well over the years, but we believe greater growth and value can be achieved by expanding our capabilities across the board. We now aspire to become a more fully integrated biopharmaceutical company."

"And we share your aspiration," Bob remarked. "Grant mentioned that you might be amenable to a discussion that could bring Theta Opioid Therapeutics and TheraPeuTex together. In this case, TORX would be the acquirer, and you would focus exclusively on Narcogesic with a host of potential new formulations and line extensions."

"And we share your enthusiasm," Paul said. "The idea of having the world's only nonaddictive narcotic analgesic is exciting, and subsequently introducing injectables for acute use, transdermal patches for convenient chronic use, even lollipops for pediatric oncology, would be contributions to medicine worthy of our efforts."

"Together, the only thing lacking would be distribution, sales and marketing," Mia added.

"I mentioned to Grant that we know a small analgesic drug company that could bring those capabilities to the table," Brantley shared. "Have you heard of Dolomedicus Pharmaceuticals? They have a couple of branded drugs in their detail bags. Mostly nonsteroidal anti-inflammatory pain relievers. The company has a good distribution network, and a well-trained salesforce that is well-regarded by the anesthesiology and pain management communities. I had a chat with their CEO Jim Burroughs not long ago and he was more than open to a discussion of synergies. He even mentioned they were contemplating a venture into cannabidiol (CBD) topicals with a focus on pain relief, so I'm sure he would find your patented nonaddictive opioid even more to his liking."

"Brantley, I hate to interrupt you when you're on a roll," Paul said, "but we have a tee time soon, and I've been dying to get Mia on the links." Bob raised an eyebrow and resisted the temptation to look at Mia for any sign of simpatico.

Everyone must have found the discussions engaging because only Bob put much of a dent in the platter of sandwiches. Brantley thanked his kitchen staff for lunch and offered to drive the foursome to the North Course at Torrey Pines. Their clubs had been delivered to the course in advance.

"If you've never played the North Course at Torrey, then you're in for a treat. It was recently redesigned by Tom Weiskopf," Paul said.

Their bags were waiting on the golf carts when they arrived and Bob was a little irritated that Mia had been paired with Paul, though he didn't let on. He admitted to himself that riding with Brantley would probably be more productive at least from a business perspective. As the players climbed into their respective carts, one of the bag boys approached Paul.

"Sir, if you don't mind my asking, is that your white bag with the navy-blue trim on the back of your cart?"

"No," replied Paul. "That's Mia's bag. She's not a Duke alum but she's a big fan now."

The bag boy whistled then looked at Mia. "Mind if I take a closer look at those clubs, ma'am?"

"Not at all," Mia responded, "but we do need to head to the first tee box shortly."

The young man selected her 7 iron and withdrew the club slowly and carefully from the bag. Whistling again he expounded, "Mizuno blades! You don't see those around here much unless the tour is in town. You must be a scratch golfer?"

"Once was," Mia said demurely, as she looked down at her golf shoes in a sincere gesture of humility.

Bob didn't understand all the fuss and left Brantley in the driver's seat of their cart as he approached the bag boy. "What's the big deal? I have a nearly new set of Mizunos in my golf bag and I don't hear you asking me if I'm a scratch golfer!"

"But these are blades, sir. No cavity back. Same as the ones some of the pros use. Very difficult to swing consistently. Microscopic, sweet spot. I once bought a set and couldn't hit the broadside of a barn. Then, after seven or eight holes, I connected with a 7-iron that flew about 175 yards. Normally my 150-yard club. I was amazed, but one good shot every 15 or 16. Not the odds I prefer. My hat's off to you, lady. Enjoy your round."

Bob walked sheepishly back to his cart, and having overheard the bag boy Brantley remarked, "Guess we won't be playing for skins today!"

Paul drove Mia to the first tee box and stopped beside the blue tees. Brantley pulled up behind them and chuckled to himself when it occurred to him that the blue tees at Torrey Pines were misogynistically referred to as the *men's tees*. He was just thankful that Mia had passed up the black tees which everyone regarded as the *pro tees*. In retrospect, it would have been less embarrassing for everyone had she played from the blacks.

Mia had ducked into the clubhouse lounge and changed into a navy-blue blouse with white shorts that showed off her long shapely legs. Now addressing her ball on the first tee box, Brantley and Paul knew she resembled one of the pros on the LPGA tour but didn't follow women's golf close enough to know her name.

Lexi, Bob thought as if he were reading their mind. "Nice drive. I'm guessing you'll get tired of hearing us say that. Maybe I'll just wait and make a snide remark when you hit one fat."

"I don't think you can stay quiet that long," she said with a flirtatious grin.

36

Los Angeles, CA

The gauze patch over his right eye was held in place by an elastic bandage that encircled his head just above his ears. His right cheek and jaw were badly swollen and a deep shade of purple. Sitting at the breakfast table at the Chateau Marmont just off Sunset Boulevard, Grant Sawyer was in obvious discomfort and finding it difficult to speak.

"What in the world happened to you," Mia asked quite surprised as he had been perfectly fine the night before when they all left the hotel bar and retired for evening around 10 o'clock.

"When I returned to my room last night, after a little light reading, I decided to take a hot shower. I finished up, towel dried, walked out of the bathroom and tripped over the desk chair that I had left too far out in the room. My face planted itself on the massive wooden bedpost as I crashed to the floor. No blood, but a great deal of pain. I managed to make it down to the front desk and they called EMS. The team arrived in minutes and transported me over to Cedars-Sinai Medical Center where I spent the next couple of hours in the ER. As you might imagine, I didn't get much sleep last night, but I think I can make it through the investor meetings we have scheduled here in L.A. today and San Francisco tomorrow."

Mia and the others had no reason to disbelieve his story, but the truth was far more harrowing. After a couple of Fireball whiskies and ginger ale, Grant had said goodnight to the others and had indeed gone to his room. However, one look in the mirror at his bloodshot eyes had sent him to his bag of toiletries to retrieve a bottle of Visine. It was then he remembered that his Afrin spray bottle was empty. Not that it contained oxymetazoline or any other nasal decongestant. Rather it contained his home-grown concoction of fentanyl in saline. He had graduated from prescription Vicodin to street-sourced fentanyl years ago and no longer enjoyed the high it once imparted. Now he only sought to avoid the dreadful feelings that occurred from even the shortest periods of abstinence. Driven by forces beyond his control he had left his room and wandered out onto Sunset Boulevard.

Several hours had passed since his last fix, so Grant had been unable to make the right decision. The right decision would have been to Uber over to the nearest clinic and admit to his addiction. Instead, he had walked a few blocks down the street to The Comedy Store where he was sure he could score a little China white from one of the locals. A whisper here and a redirect there and it wasn't long before he had made a play.

Grant had followed the seedy character out the front door of the club and up a ramp beside the building, then out behind the parking lot of the Andaz West Hollywood hotel next door. Under the flickering light of the small-time dealer's Bic, Grant had bought just enough to make it through the final days of the roadshow until he could get home to his own stash. Unfortunately, his alligator-skin wallet full of Presidential portraits had been more than the scumbag could resist. A strong blow from the man's left fist had put Grant on the ground and a Beckham-style kick to his face had finished the job.

Grant had told the truth to his clients about the treatment he had received at Cedars-Sinai Medical Center, but he had been less than frank about the circumstances surrounding his visit. When he had returned to the hotel, he had discovered that his wallet was still in his back pocket sans any currency and his fentanyl purchase was no longer in his front pocket. The only thing now standing between his pain and misery was a seven-day supply of Percocet dispensed by the hospital outpatient pharmacy and he knew it wouldn't last two days.

Cursed tolerance.

Grant managed to finish his breakfast though it had been little more than orange juice through a straw. Mark and Mia remained oblivious to Grant's addiction despite their expertise and Bob believed his good friend from Duke was viceless. Norm, on the other hand, had lost his 23-year-old daughter to a cocaine addiction and his antennae were fully extended.

It had not escaped Norm's attention that they were staying in the same hotel where John Belushi died of a cocaine and heroin or *speedball* overdose years ago. Norm knew little of medicine, but his personal tragedy had driven him to learn much about cocaine and drug addiction. He knew that cocaine was a stimulant and heroin was an opioid, and he knew both were illegal street drugs with no FDA-approved medical uses. He also knew that fentanyl was the prescription opioid that had claimed the life of Mia's brother, Warren. Ever the reserved financial analyst Norm quietly shared the same passion as Mia and for the same reason.

The drive to their final investor presentation of the day had been a short and comfortable one in the Carey Town Car. The five roadshow warriors were seated in the conference room of the L.A.-based managers of the California Retired Teachers investment fund. Mia had just wrapped up another dazzling pitch and the fund representatives were ready to ask a few questions.

"Thank you, Mia," the lead manager said. "And thank you all for coming today. It is a very compelling story and a very worthy endeavor. Regardless of whether we participate in your IPO, we truly wish you the best. We've done our homework and there's little doubt in our minds that you will soon file your New Drug Application for Narcogesic and even less doubt that the FDA will approve the drug. But our questions go to your plans after the drug is approved. Since we're all hoping and expecting demand for Narcogesic to be profound, how do you plan to produce enough drug to satisfy the demand in a timely manner?"

Bob took the question. "As outlined in our prospectus, most of the proceeds will be used to acquire targeted companies that will give us the operations we will need to quickly become a fully integrated company with a therapeutic focus on analgesics. Of course, I can't name any names at this point, but none we're considering would be a disappointment to the financial markets."

"Since Narcogesic will certainly generate global demand, and we all like Euros and Yen as much as we like Benjamins, do you plan on acquiring some foreign companies?" she followed up.

"Probably not," Bob replied. "Our current thought is to license the patent rights outside the U.S. to foreign partners. This could be one multinational company with a global reach or more than one depending upon their regional strengths and weaknesses. Of course, those with the most favorable terms would be given special consideration," he said with a wink. The gesture might have made Mia jealous, but she knew it was just Bob's way of baiting the hook.

"Do you have any revenue forecasts that you can share with us?" one of the fund managers asked.

"Unfortunately, it will be the policy and practice of the company not to make financial projections or to give guidance to potential investors. This will afford us the greatest protection from shareholder suits that benefit no one, except perhaps the lawyers. Since Goldman Sachs is the underwriter, their analysts will not be permitted to cover the company during this quiet period ahead of the IPO. However, with us today is Norm Brady, the financial analyst at Keystone Capital, a firm with no position or interest in TORX at this point. However, in full disclosure, we might bring Norm onboard after the IPO as our Chief Financial

Officer, provided he doesn't demand the lion's share of the net proceeds!"

Everyone chuckled and Norm blushed a bit but quickly gathered his composure. "Our independent research indicates that the global market for prescription opioids last year was $28.9 billion, of which the U.S. held 69 percent or $19.9 billion. Despite the markedly superior profile of Narcogesic with its near absence of side effects and no reported cases of addiction, we have used a conservative estimate of market potential. Further, we blunted the rate of market penetration as an offset for the time it will take the company to engage its corporate partners in the U.S. and overseas, and we discounted all the estimates by 40 percent to factor the market's typical resistance to premium pricing."

"Can we get a copy of your slides?" one of the managers begged as he was busy taking copious notes.

"One better," Norm replied. "I'll leave behind a copy of our report titled the *Global Prescription Opioid Market Over the Next 5-Years*, which assumes a Narcogesic launch in the U.S. by the end of this year and overseas introductions over the next two years. We believe this forecast more than supports Goldman's pricing range of $70-75 per share for the 20 million shares to be authorized, including the six million shares to be offered to the public. No charge for the report!"

The lead manager said she had no further questions and confirmed that the others were satisfied as well. She thanked the five of them for their time and indicated how impressed she was with the performance of the drug, the novelty of its discovery and the professionalism of the plans for its global launch. She mentioned that she would bring the opportunity to her investment committee immediately and was confident they would concur with her favorable recommendation. She said the group's Carey Town Car was waiting outside to take them to the Atlantic Aviation FBO at the Bob Hope Airport in Burbank for their chartered flight on to San Francisco.

WONDERFULLY DREADFUL

The passenger lounge at the FBO facility was comfortably furnished with black leather recliners and they all agreed to rest a few minutes before boarding their late-model King Air 350.

"I could get used to this treatment," Mia said as she starred out the window of the general aviation facility at the collection of private aircraft on the tarmac. "And the best part is, they don't leave without us!"

"And they don't leave until *we're* ready!" Bob added. He had been on roadshows before, raising money for his own ventures, but he had not been through the grueling schedule of an initial public offering. "While some might say that chartering a private plane is an unnecessary extravagance, I must admit, Goldman does it right. It really did make our visit of fifteen cities in thirteen days not only doable but tolerable. I can't imagine having done it commercially."

"Attention to detail," Grant said. "And I'll share with you that the lead manager of the Teacher's Retirement fund pulled me aside as we were leaving. She said that she had called ahead and confirmed that our plane had been refueled and was ready to go. She also mentioned that she was a private pilot and complimented us on our choice of the twin turbo prop. Slower for sure, but much more economical than a business jet. *Prudent* was the word she used with a pat on my shoulder. If she wasn't sold already, our providence sealed the deal. I can tell you that institutional investors hate extravagance on the part of the executives of their public companies."

"Well, there's an advantage to staying private that you didn't tell us about," Mark said as he lowered the leg rest of his recliner. The rich black leather shrilled as he arose from his seat, and it sent a subliminal message to the others that he was the one in charge of their discretionary schedule and it was time to leave.

Bob led everyone through the lounge and out the automatic sliding glass doors to the King Air waiting just outside. Their pilots were already in the cockpit going through the preflight checks, and the cabin stairs had been lowered for their embarkation. They had come to appreciate the lack of TSA scrutiny and delay on their private flights that had become the new normal in commercial air travel. The aircraft was configured for eight passengers. Grant and Norm sat together on the three-seater couch and Mia sat in a recliner across from them. Mark and Bob selected a pair of opposing seats just forward of the others.

The sun was setting as the ground crew secured the cabin door. The aircraft taxied down the runway and lifted imperceptibly off the ground, traveled west over Thousand Oaks, then banked north up the coast. Mia had her nose to the window as she watched the last sliver of sun disappear behind the Channel Islands. It reminded her of the celebration on Mallory Square nearly every evening in Key West. She had grown accustomed to the King Air flights, this one now en route to its fifteenth city in nearly as many days, but she never tired of the magnificent hawkeyed views of the planet.

Grant rubbed his jaw, disappointed by the continuing degree of discomfort. During the last investor presentation, he had excused himself and ducked into the men's room for his fourth dose of Percocet in seven hours. It reminded him that it was his growing tolerance of Percocet that had led him to street fentanyl, the source of his current misery. With nowhere on the small plane to escape for another discreet dose, he settled back for an hour of pain.

Mark pulled the highly polished burlwood tray up from its resting place beside his seat and unfolded it between himself and Bob. Then he lifted his phone from his jacket pocket, launched a PDF from his cloud file and handed the phone to Bob.

"As you know, we are submitting the Narcogesic NDA to the FDA tomorrow," Mark said to Bob. "That's a draft announcement that we can release in the morning. Have a look. In addition to the usual media outlets, Goldman has an extensive list of email addresses and social media accounts of high-net-worth clients and potential investors that should receive the news directly."

"Read it out loud, so we can all hear and comment," Mia said as she overheard their discussion. Bob took Mark's phone and resized the screen, then read aloud.

"Theta Opioid Therapeutics (TORX) - a private biopharmaceutical company based in Research Triangle Park, North Carolina, announced today that it has submitted its New Drug Application (NDA) to the U.S. Food and Drug Administration (FDA) seeking approval to market Narcogesic. The results of the pivotal trials of the drug were recently disclosed and support the company's claim that Narcogesic is the world's first nonaddictive opioid analgesic. Analysts have predicted it will rapidly capture a substantial portion of the world's $30 billion annual market for opioid pain relievers. TORX has retained Goldman Sachs as its investment banker and has filed an S-1 registration statement with the Securities and Exchange Commission (SEC) to sell six million shares of stock in an initial public offering expected to close very soon. Proceeds from the financing will be used to acquire the operations necessary to commercialize the drug."

"Nice," Grant replied in a ventriloquistic effort to avoid aggravating his jaw.

"We should add the news about the patent office recently issuing the Narcogesic patent," Mia suggested.

"Oh, that's a good idea," Bob agreed. "Some public companies might separate the two announcements to get more bang for their buck in terms of stock price. But that's just a short-term trading inefficiency. The markets quickly value the contribution of each component event and arrive at a price that reflects their combined value. When the dust settles, it's no different than if the news had been released simultaneously."

Bob handed the phone back to Mark and he added a sentence or two about the patent. Then he attached the file to an email and sent it to the working group at Goldman with a request to distribute the document first thing in the morning.

"Ladies and gentlemen, please return your tray tables to their original upright and locked position," Mia said mockingly as she lampooned the announcement of commercial flight attendants. Mark complied with a smile and settled back for the remainder of the short flight.

The King Air flew in low over San Francisco Bay and glided smoothly down the well-lit runway of the Hayward Executive Airport in Oakland. It was a short drive from there across the Oakland Bay Bridge to Union Square in the Financial District. The entire group preferred to stay at historic old hotels rather than their more contemporary counterparts. Bob had voted for the Sir Francis Drake, but had lost out to the others, so they checked into the Westin St. Francis, around the corner from the Drake. As the bellman stacked their bags on his cart, Mark dazzled the group with some trivia.

"Even I'm not old enough to remember when the St. Francis Hotel was a favorite haunt of the Hollywood stars of the roaring twenties. Stars like Douglas Fairbanks, Mary Pickford, and Charlie Chaplin. It was even the subject of one of Hollywood's first sex scandals when Roscoe "Fatty" Arbuckle, a silent movie comic that rivaled Charlie Chaplin, hosted a party in a series of suites here and was later accused of raping and killing another hotel guest. Ultimately, after a high-profile trial, he was acquitted. Everyone thought the film industry would clean up its act consequently, but it didn't."

"And it hasn't to this day!" Mia added.

37

San Francisco, CA

Grant and Norm were already seated at a breakfast table in the main dining room of the Westin St. Francis when Mark and Mia came down to join them. The white tablecloth that flowed over the edge was as sharply pressed as the white gloves of the waiter that poured the coffee. His white tuxedo with black lapels, bowtie and pocket square added a touch of class that defined the St. Francis. Mia noticed that the purple discoloration of Grant's facial injuries had turned a slight greenish yellow and was a clear sign of healing. Norm observed that Grant was speaking with much less discomfort than just the day before. Perhaps another sign of healing or, as Norm suspected, a sign of medicating with something stronger than Tylenol.

"Morning troops!" Bob said in a cheerful tone as he bounded into the dining room and took a seat next Mia. The waiter instantly appeared and offered him coffee from a sterling silver pot. Bob turned his coffee cup right side up and the rich aroma wafted around the table as the waiter poured a full cup. Bob held the saucer under his cup all the way to his lip to catch any accidental spill. It was just another of his many social graces that Mia found charming.

"So, today we have three meetings scheduled," Grant said like the Tin Man asking Dorothy for oil. "We will be visiting with the managers of some specialty healthcare funds based here in

San Francisco, including the Blue Star Fund at 9:30 a.m., a lunch meeting with Roan Capital at 11:30 a.m., and Golden Gate Health Ventures at 2:30 p.m. I've scheduled dinner at Kim Sung Lee's in Chinatown for 5:30 p.m., and we can leave in the morning whenever we're ready. The drive to Hayward will take about an hour, allowing for some all-day rush hour traffic, and the pilots have informed me that our flight time to RDU will be about five hours given the usual tail wind."

"Have you had any feedback from the investors we've met with to date?" Mark asked as he carefully forked another bite of egg, Canadian bacon and English muffin dripping with Hollandaise sauce.

"You'll be pleased to know that the book is oversubscribed!" Grant replied with a grin no bigger than he could manage.

"Pardon me, Grant," Mia said taking another sip of her Constant Comment. "What do you mean by oversubscribed?"

"We have more demand for the shares than we had planned to sell. This means we have the good fortune of being able to increase the number of shares we offer, or to raise the price per share, or some combination of both. In any case, we can raise more money than we had originally planned and, as I always say, 'raise it when you can.' Nothing hurts worse than needing to go back to the well when your stock price is down."

Between ravaging his pecan pancakes drizzled with real maple syrup and glancing over at the digital copy of the *Wall Street Journal* on his phone, Bob managed to keep one ear on the conversation. He was at least as good as Mia at multitasking. "I don't have the firsthand experience you do in newly issued securities," Bob said with deference to Grant. "But I don't think we should try to squeeze every nickel out of the market at this point. I'd be inclined to raise the price a bit without offering more shares."

"I agree," Grant said. "The original price target was $70-75 per share and our guys in the backroom tell me the book would now support a price of $95 per share. I suggest we keep the offer at six million shares and reset the price to $85 per share. That would still leave some on the table as a hedge against a selloff when the securities start trading in the secondary market."

"Leaving $10 per share on the table is a $60 million cushion," Norm observed. I'm generally not a fan of leaving money on the table, but in this case it's a sound practice to avoid a selloff that can feed on itself. Given no near-term risks other than the ones we've described in the prospectus that are not likely to occur, I think $60 million is a reasonable hedge."

With everyone in agreement, Grant called his associates in New York and told them to proceed with the sale of six million shares of TORX at a final price of $85 per share. The thought of soon depositing over $500 million was a sobering one for Mark, Mia, and Bob, but it would give them the horsepower they needed to bring Narcogesic to bear on the opioid crisis. As they all pushed back from the breakfast table, ready to lean into the last day of the roadshow, they silently went through the mental exercise of what their stakes would be worth after the closing. Finishing her tea, Mia multiplied her 1.5 million shares by $85 then reflected on the remark that Jillian had made after Bob had invested the first $500,000 in the company. It seemed like eons ago.

Little Miss One Million ... bah humbug, she thought.

Grant passed on calling their Carey driver since it was just a short walk from the Westin St. Francis through the Financial District to the Triple Nickel building formerly known as the Bank of America Center. Although Mia found the morning view of the San Francisco skyline from the 42nd floor of the building distracting, her presentation to the Blue Star Fund managers was a cakewalk and it was like preaching to the choir.

"Very nice presentation, Dr. Reinhardt," the lead manager remarked on behalf of the fund. "Unless my colleagues have any questions, I'll just say right up front that we're already onboard. The red herring was clear and concise. Mr. Sawyer, we called your associates in New York yesterday and committed to 100,000 shares."

"Thank you for your support," Grant said, feeling no pain after having taken three doses of Percocet before breakfast. Since the scumbag dealer in L.A. had taken his money and the fentanyl he had purchased, he was hoping the Percocet would last until he got home tomorrow but it was looking doubtful.

"Our appetite for your shares actually exceeds our allocation from your investment banker," one of the other fund managers acknowledged. "We fully expect to purchase more in the open market, assuming the price doesn't get away from us. On the other hand, if Narcogesic can put an end to the opioid crisis, there is probably no price we wouldn't pay."

"In any event it would be far less than the price already paid by too many," Norm said. His staid remark was understood by all and heartfelt by Mia.

The elevator doors of the 42nd floor closed slowly as Mia and Norm eased over to one corner. Mark and Bob positioned themselves near the elevator control panel and bantered with anticipation about the group's upcoming lunch meeting with Roan Capital. As the elevator jerked to begin its decent, Grant felt a bolt of pain shoot through his jaw. He was disappointed but not surprised that his morning dose of Percocet was wearing off quickly. Before the roadshow he knew little about opioid addiction other than the fact that he was an addict. Now he knew all about tolerance and was terrified to have learned that 80 percent of heroin addicts were first addicted to prescription opioids. Maybe retreating from street fentanyl back to prescription Percocet would at least be a move in the right direction.

Once at ground level the group doubled back down Kearney Street three blocks to Montgomery Tower. Their meeting there on the 28th floor with Roan Capital had gone very well and lunch in the conference room had been over the top. Roan had declared their commitment to purchase 80,000 shares and intent to accumulate more in the aftermarket. Grant had thanked them for their $6.4 million pledge and assured them that their investment would be financially and altruistically rewarded.

Conveniently located two floors below were the offices of Golden Gate Health Ventures. The receptionist had escorted the group into the conference room and Mia had made the necessary connections to her laptop in preparation for her 29th and final investor presentation. The thought occurred to her that by now, in the event of laryngitis, any one of her associates could probably give the talk verbatim.

Rather than sitting down with the others to wait on their host, Mia strolled over to the large plate-glass window that spanned the entire length of the room from floor to ceiling. Bob assumed it was nervous energy in anticipation of her last sales pitch, but it was the uneasy feeling of being 26 floors above the San Andreas fault. In the distance she could see the iconic Coit Tower positioned atop Telegraph Hill and wondered if the Christopher Columbus statue that had been removed due to recent social unrest would ever be returned to its majestic position at the foot of the tower.

"Never a boring view," the woman announced as she entered the room alone and approached Mia with her hand extended palm out. "I'm Paris Skye, the lead manager her at Golden Gate Health Ventures, and you must be Dr. Reinhardt."

"I am and very pleased to meet you. These are my colleagues at Theta Opioid Therapeutics," she said with a gesture in their direction. "Dr. Robert Taylor our CEO, Dr. Mark Oberon our founder and CSO, Mr. Grant Sawyer our investment banker with Goldman Sacks, and Mr. Norm Brady a healthcare analyst at Keystone Capital who will be joining us as our CFO after the IPO closes."

Everyone took their seats and Mia took Paris through the discovery of Narcogesic, the clinical trial results and submission of their New Drug Application. She also reviewed the manufacturing, sales and marketing plan. Paris had listened carefully without interrupting but was eager to ask a few questions when Mia concluded.

"It goes without saying, but a very elegant piece of work," Paris regarded, acknowledging Mark as well. "As you know, San Francisco is infamous for drug addiction, so perhaps it's fitting that you end your roadshow here."

"The reputation is unfortunate," Mark said. "And undeserving. Addiction is a biochemical disturbance in the brain. A compulsion not a choice. With Narcogesic, people will finally have a choice between pain relief and addiction."

"Mia, during your presentation you mentioned that the FDA had decided to empanel an Advisory Committee to review your NDA and recommend its approval or rejection by the Agency."

"That's right," Mia replied. "It's typical for the FDA to seek the advice of an outside independent scientific Advisory Committee when considering a *first-in-class* application for marketing and Narcogesic would be the first *nonaddictive* opioid pain reliever."

"So, what are the chances the committee will reject the NDA?" Paris asked flippantly. "Not to be heretical but such a rejection would be devasting to new investors."

"I guess there's no guarantees when dealing with the FDA or any other government agency for that matter, but I can tell you that they have been atypically forthright in their guidance on the approvable path for Narcogesic. In effect, they said they would approve the drug, if the pivotal trial results are positive. With analgesic efficacy comparable to fentanyl and not even a hint of addictive potential, it's hard to imagine a committee that would be anything other than favorably inclined."

"Despite my client's enthusiasm, I'm obliged to mention the Risk Disclosure Statement in the prospectus," Grant added.

"A little cold water never hurt anyone, except the Wicked Witch of the West," Mark jeered, "The fact is, my work is well regarded by the entirety of the world community of *opioidologists,* as I like to call them, and the Advisory Committee is simply a subgroup of these colleagues of mine. I assure you they all share our enthusiasm for the clearance of Narcogesic as soon as possible."

"I'm aware of the unanimous opinion shared by your colleagues," Paris remarked. "Consequently, I've pledged to purchase 200,000 shares at a minimum. Rejection of your application by the Advisory Committee would put the FDA in a very awkward position and would make for a very bad day at Golden Gate Health Ventures."

Her words hung the air as Norm did the mental calculation of a loss involving 200,000 shares purchased at $85 per share. Ouch! With no other drugs in their pipeline, the selloff would be exsanguinating.

THE DINING ROOM AT Kim Sung Lee in Chinatown was dimly lit by colorful shaded lanterns. Trickling sounds from a see-through water feature in the center of the room subliminally relaxed its patrons. The group dined on Peking Duck that Grant had ordered before their arrival, and the chef carved it at their table. As the others enjoyed their fruity drinks with little tissue-paper umbrellas, Mark cracked open his fortune cookie and read the saying aloud.

"You don't always have to take the bad with the good," he read.

Wonderful without dreadful, Mia thought.

"Any after dinner plans for a night on town?" Bob asked, looking at Grant and Norm.

"I think I'll just spend a quiet evening at the hotel," Norm said. None were surprised that the Certified Financial Analyst had no plans to tear up the town.

"I'll likely do the same and retire early," Grant followed. "My jaw is still pretty sore and the medication they gave me doesn't seem to last long. Early to bed and early to rise may be just what the doctor ordered."

"What exactly did they give you at Cedars-Sinai?" Mia asked with genuine concern for its apparent inefficacy.

"Something called Percocet," he replied, feigning that he knew little about narcotics.

"Well, I'm meeting with some of my old buddies from UCSF," Bob conveyed. "There's a great little coffee shop near campus in the Haight-Ashbury with an open-mic tonight. Maybe I'll borrow someone's guitar and try out one of my new songs on a friendly crowd."

THE ATTENDEES OF THE private fund-raising event at the Monterey Bay Aquarium were among the most affluent and philanthropic in the Bay Area, and Mia was not surprised that Mark had been invited. She was pleased he had asked her to join him since Bob had not extended her an invitation to the nightclub. Mark graciously introduced her to several of the benefactors, including some he seemed to know quite well. After parting words with another couple, he and Mia headed to a food station that was positioned near the Sea Otter exhibit. The waiter there in formal attire offered them an assortment of sushi and sashimi that had been freshly prepared by the station chef. Mia selected a piece of salmon nigiri drizzled with Ponzu sauce and topped with chopped scallions while Mark chose the flying fish roe wrapped in seaweed. He preferred the tiny orange caviar over the much larger red salmon roe and demonstrated his familiarity with the cuisine by adding a quail egg.

"Hey Mark, would you look at that," Mia said with her nose near the glass of the otter tank. "Do you see how that one is using a rock on his chest as an anvil for opening shells to extract the meat from inside? I'm told they store their favorite rock in a skin pouch."

"When I was in high school, more than a few years ago, the use of tools was thought to be unique to humans and a defining characteristic of intelligence. Now we know that many different species share this trait, whether learned or inherited."

"I know that chimpanzees have been observed using twigs to extract termites from their mounds," Mia noted. "And a dolphin will wrap its nose in sponge to prevent abrasions when hunting on the sea floor."

"Of course, both species are now well known for their intelligence, but even some lower-order creatures use tools. Alligators have been observed floating sticks on their nose to attract unsuspecting birds, crows use rocks to crack nuts, and the coconut octopus will gather coconut shells for protection on the sea floor."

In Mia's opinion, the jellyfish exhibit on the second floor was the most amazing and beautiful. Watching the *jellies*, she was overcome with a sense of calm and wonder at the sight of the delicate sea creatures. She focused on one individual in a jet-black tank that glowed an iridescent green as it moved slowly by with rhythmic muscular contractions of its bell-shaped body.

"That particular species is *Aequorea victoria* more commonly known as the crystal jelly," Mark said without referring to the placard on the wall nearby. "You probably learned that it produces flashes of blue light when intracellular calcium ions activate the photoprotein aequorin which is then converted to green light by resonant energy transfer in the presence of green fluorescent proteins, or GFP. The discovery and sequencing of the jellyfish gene encoding for GFP was the subject of a Nobel Prize in chemistry and has become a valuable tool in molecular biology and biomedical research."

"I do recall," Mia replied. "I read the history of GFP when I learned it was the source of the green fluorescence in our Fluoropioid assay."

"Your memory serves you well," Mark said as he gave her a squeeze that he hoped would not be unwelcome.

"That's because I take a memory enhancer," Mia said coquettishly. "It's a nutritional supplement containing apoaequorin which is a modified version of the crystal jellyfish photoprotein. The makers claim this protein taken orally has been clinically shown to improve memory and cognition, which is appealing to older consumers with age-related memory loss."

"I believe the clinical trial results were questionable," Mark said. "We know that proteins taken orally or consumed as a part of our diet are degraded by proteases in the gastrointestinal tract and absorbed as their component amino acids. Whereas small molecules can be given orally, proteins and macromolecules like insulin and monoclonal antibodies must be injected directly into the bloodstream. In addition, all large molecules and most small molecules are denied entry into the brain by the so-called blood brain barrier, or cerebral capillary epithelial cells. So, any claim of a protein influencing the brain or memory when given orally should be viewed with considerable skepticism."

"I was actually teasing you about taking the jellyfish supplement," Mia confided. "I'm dubious of the claims, as well. That leaves only my superior intellect to thank for my memory!" Mark playfully gave her a dismissive look, then suggested they should and get back to the St. Francis.

"I'll call for an Uber," Mia said as she raised her phone to launch the app.

"Nonsense. I'm the one that invited you to this little soiree and I'm the one that will get you home."

"So, you use Lyft rather than Uber?" Mia said looking over his shoulder as he launched the app. "That may be the *only* thing we don't have in common."

38

San Francisco, CA

The continental breakfast at the Westin St Francis had been far more pleasurable than the rush-hour ride to the airport despite the comfort of their Lincoln Town Car. Fortunately, their flight to RDU had clocked in at just under five hours thanks to a 140-mph jet stream. Gathering their luggage and exiting the King Air they thanked the pilot and co-pilot for their professionalism and efficiency throughout the roadshow.

Once inside General Aviation, Norm and Grant headed straight for the restroom while Mark, Mia and Bob drifted off into the passenger lounge. Norm silently cursed a mild case of benign prostatic hypertrophy that left him with the bladder capacity of a bullfrog. Grant similarly cursed a tolerance for opioids that left him with no pain medication just two days into a seven-day supply of Percocet. He had scored a single-dose packet of fentanyl from a friend of the bellman before leaving the St Francis that morning but hoped he could make the last leg on to Teterboro without hitting it.

Norm returned from the men's room and found Bob stretched out in one of the black leather recliners resting with his eyes closed but not asleep. Mark and Mia sat beside one another at the walnut conference table in the middle of the room and Norm pulled out a chair across from them.

"I'm guessing we'll hear very soon from Goldman Sachs that the IPO has sold out," Norm said to no one in particular. "I've already cleaned out my desk at Keystone Capital and I'm looking forward to leaving the Big Apple to start anew with you all here in the Research Triangle Park."

"It's pronounced *y'all* by the natives," Mark said. "But even the transplants like Mia and Bob over there have adopted the phrase. Isn't that right, y'all?"

"Actually, the term is grammatically redundant," Bob said opening one eye. "The second person pronoun *you* can be either singular or plural, so the addition of *all* to the plural use is redundant and contracting the two is even more ridiculous!"

Suddenly the door to the men's restroom burst open and Grant staggered into the hall beside the lounge. The group looked in horror as he fell to his knees then collapsed face first on the tile floor. Mark was the first to his side and quickly assessed his status. Mia with her phone already in hand dialed 911. Even more productively, the receptionist at the front desk had witnessed Grant's collapse and summoned the EMS unit stationed at the facility.

Moments later, two well-equipped paramedics stormed into the hall and began attending to Grant with Mark's assistance as Norm approached. "It may be an opioid overdose," Norm offered. He had seen Grant go into one of the stalls in the restroom and assumed he was taking care of business. What Norm did not know was that Grant had exhausted his supply of Percocet and had ducked into the stall to reluctantly snort the powdered dose of fentanyl he had procured that morning. What Grant failed to consider was that straight fentanyl is much more concentrated than the dilute concoction to which he was habituated.

"Your suspicion is consistent with his presentation," Mark said as he kneeled alongside Grant. "Pinpoint pupils, loss of consciousness, labored breathing."

"I have no medical training, but I did have a daughter that died of a cocaine overdose. Though cocaine and opioid addicts differ in many ways, they share the same drug dependence and drug-seeking behavior that Grant indiscreetly revealed on occasion."

"That would explain his agitated state at some of our meetings," Mark noted.

"And complaints of only transient pain relief with Percocet," Mia added.

The senior paramedic wasted no time retrieving a vial of Narcan from his equipment bag. He grabbed a small syringe prefixed with a needle and removed the plastic cap with his teeth. Then he jabbed the needle through the gray rubber stopper of the vial, carefully withdrew three cc's and administered the 1.2 mg dose intravenously. Within moments Grant regained a degree of consciousness with his vital signs improved. A couple of minutes later he was given a second dose and gradually became more alert and responsive.

"The drug of Lazarus," the junior paramedic remarked.

"It also confirms that our friend here is an opioid addict that just dodged a bullet," Mark said. Grant looked sheepishly at him through pupils that were now more reactive to light and accommodation. The men helped Grant into one of the recliners nearby and Mia fetched a glass of ice water from the refreshment center. With Grant resting comfortably in a recliner the paramedics asked whether he was willing to be transported to the nearest hospital or clinic. They knew it was not uncommon for patients to refuse further care after a Narcan rescue.

"I'll be fine," Grant said but his bruised and battered jaw belied the pronouncement.

"Listen," Mark said caringly as he placed a hand on Grant's knee. "As you've heard from us on the road *et. nauseum*, addiction is not a choice, and it should not be an embarrassment. Importantly, it cannot be ignored without dire consequences.

There are plenty of fine treatment centers in New York to be sure, but there is none finer than the Duke Center for Opioid Addiction and Rehabilitation right here in Durham." Grant raised an eyebrow and was about to object when Mark continued. "I'll personally attend to your care and let me invite Mia to close deal."

"Grant, I'm sure you've struggled with the symptoms of withdrawal, whether by accident, when you've run out of drugs, or intentionally, when you've tried to quit. However, under medical supervision, we can use drugs like methadone and buprenorphine to suppress the symptoms of withdrawal," Mia explained. "Unfortunately, these are addictive opioids as well, with the same constellation of withdrawal symptoms as the others, though less severe. It's simply substituting the lesser of two evils, while the patient is weaned off narcotics. Since Narcogesic is a nonaddictive opioid, lacking any withdrawal phenomenon, we believe it may be an ideal replacement for methadone or buprenorphine. To test this hypothesis, we have recently initiated a study of Narcogesic as an adjunct to opioid withdrawal and rehabilitation. You would be an ideal candidate."

"Doctors orders," Grant said submissively, as he nodded his head in the affirmative. The sense of dread that had burdened him for so long was suddenly lifted from his soul. He had come to respect and appreciate the medical prowess of his clients and felt lucky to know them in an unlucky sort of way.

"If Narcogesic can get me off fentanyl, I'll buy your ticket to Stockholm," Grant said, aware of the rumor as he looked at Mark through hopeful eyes.

"So, you're Dr. Oberon," the senior paramedic surmised from Grants remarks. "Very pleased to meet you sir," he said as he shook Mark's hand. "Word on the street is that your little company here in the Triangle is about to go public to raise money for the worldwide launch of Narcogesic. Though I don't have much money, I'm prepared to bet what I have on your stock as soon as it's available."

"And I have even less," his junior partner admitted. "But I'm a more sophisticated investor, and I intend to short the maker of Narcan. Once Narcogesic hits the market, Narcan is DOA!"

They all chuckled as the paramedics headed out the front door of the FBO with their emergency medical equipment in tow. Mark and Mia agreed to escort Grant to Duke for immediate enrollment into the Narcogesic study of addiction and rehabilitation, and the group waved through the window at Norm as he boarded the King Air 350 for his flight on to Teterboro without Grant.

"I'm not that familiar with his CFA credentials, but the guy is clearly a financial wizard," Bob said as he watched the cabin door close behind Norm and the plane taxi down the runway.

"It stands for Chartered Financial Analyst," Grant said with his condition improving. "Whereas a Certified Public Accountant, or CPA, is widely recognized in the tax and accounting world, a CFA is considered the equivalent of an MBA in world of finance, not unlike our MBAs from Duke."

"Well, I think he'll make a great CFO, and his experience as a healthcare analyst at Keystone is a bonus," Bob added. "Not only is he familiar with the global opioid markets, but he knows the players in the space and will be a tremendous asset as we evaluate potential partners."

Mia wasn't sure if the others had picked up on Norm's revelation about his daughter's fatal overdose, but it hadn't been lost on her. Kathleen Brady was Norm's motivation, and Warren Reinhardt was hers.

39

New York City, NY

Dr. Mark Oberon gazed at the gigantic plastic button embedded in the podium overlooking the floor of the NASDAQ stock exchange at One Liberty Plaza. Standing beside him at the podium were his colleagues Drs. Mia Reinhardt, Robert Taylor, and Jillian Saunders, as well as Anne McCarthy and Norm Brady, together with the Chairman of the exchange. As he glanced up at the digital clock displayed high above, Mark thought about the many titans of business that had stood there before him to ring the opening bell. The group verbally counted down from ten seconds and at the stroke of 9:30:00 a.m. local time Mark depressed the button with the middle finger of his right hand crossed over the index finger in a gesture of good luck. Mia was the only one on the stage that noticed the gesture and winked at Mark as the bell rang loudly for the next several seconds amid deafening applause from the podium and the trading floor. It was a moment the two would treasure for years to come.

"And there you have it," the business news anchor announced live on television just after nine-thirty. "The opening bell of the NASDAQ stock exchange as Theta Opioid Therapeutics, Inc. (NASDAQ: TORX) begins its first day of trading. The company's founder and Chief Scientific Officer, Dr. Mark Oberon; the bell ringer. TORX is the discoverer and developer of Narcogesic which promises to be the first nonaddictive opioid pain reliever. The company's marketing application is under review at the U.S. FDA and its imminent approval is widely anticipated. The company raised $510 million on the sale of six million shares at $85 per share to fund the global commercialization of its drug. As you can see, the stock opened at $90.50, up $5.50, a strong signal from the market that Narcogesic promises to put an end to the opioid crisis that has plagued the world."

Geoff and Karl Fischmann watched the opening bell on their nine-panel 4K OLED TV beside the Big Boards of the Pinnacle Penthouse. Their offices and residence were on the top floors of the Old Woolworth Building at 233 Broadway, a mere five blocks from the NASDAQ exchange. Their healthcare analyst, Dr. Carlos Martinez, stood with The Brothers as the news anchor completed his summary of TORX.

"I just got off the phone with one of my classmates from St. George's medical school," Carlos said as he saw the ticker cross the bottom of the screen that read *TORX $95.50 up 5.50*. "He happens to be the Chief Surgical Resident up at St. Luke's Roosevelt and a day trader in between cases. He's been tracking on this Narcogesic drug and believes it will indeed secure Dr. Oberon a place among the Nobel Laureates."

"Well, this may be another sterling example of a stock we should have played long and jumped on when the IPO shares were offered to us," Geoff said with some regret.

"Nonsense," Karl countered. "I haven't seen a stock yet when an irrationally exuberant herd hasn't created a terrific opportunity for a short and this one has all the markings. We just need to find the right angle."

The three men left the Big Boards and wandered down the hall past the two-story garden atrium and into Karl's side of The Bar. Their full-time bartender paused from wiping down a crystal martini glass and addressed them in his native Jamaican tongue.

"May I interest you gentlemen in your favorite morning alcoholic beverages?" Kingsley asked.

"We'll have a pot of that Arabica coffee from Arusha," Geoff said as they passed up the bar stools and high-top tables. He and Karl had been introduced to the delightful brew during their stay at the Arusha Coffee Lodge on a 2-week East African safari through Tanzania and Kenya a few years back. The Brothers settled into a soft black leather couch, and Carlos pulled up a matching chair that complemented the dark Gothic motif of The Bar.

"So, how do we play this fiddle?" Karl asked as Kingsley brought over a large pewter pot of the dark-roast coffee with service for three. He poured each man a cup prepared to their liking from memory. Heavy cream, no sugar for Geoff, a teaspoon of honey for Karl, and black for Carlos. The rich aroma triggered an urge that Carlos had not experienced since his days cramming for the medical boards. Nicotine. Fortunately, it was fleeting.

"I'm no Charlie Daniels, rest his soul," Carlos said. "But this may rosin up your bow. I think the answer is Ty Dixon."

"Isn't that the dumb sonofabitch that suggested we short the biggest manufacturers of prescription opioids?" Karl blustered rhetorically. "Some of the world's largest drug companies with opioid sales that pale in comparison to their earnings!"

"That's him," Geoff recalled. "He's also the biostatistician from the University of Michigan that suggested we short ViroSelect on an inside tip. That one cost us $16 million bucks!"

"Right artist, but wrong tune," Carlos declared.

Karl listened intently as he stirred another dollop of honey into his coffee. "I'm all ears."

"I spoke with Ty yesterday," Carlos said as Geoff leaned into the conversation, setting his coffee cup aside. "Of course, this goes no further than the three of us." Karl gave him a goes-without-saying look. "Ty informed me that he was asked to empanel the Advisory Committee to the FDA for the Narcogesic marketing application. He has selected an impressive body of scientists and physicians, highly regarded in their field, along with one consumer advocate. The members of the committee have received their copies of the relevant documents, including the clinical trial results, and TORX is scheduled to present and defend its application before the committee a week from this Friday. The meeting will be held promptly at 1:00 p.m. in the Great Room of Building 31 on the White Oak Campus of the FDA in Silver Spring, MD."

"Why on a Friday afternoon?" Geoff wondered.

"Many of the companies seeking an Advisory Committee's blessings are public, and committee actions, whether positive or negative, can be market-moving, especially for smaller companies. Since the proceedings usually take all afternoon, announcements are typically made after the markets close at four-thirty. This gives analysts and investors time to digest the relevance of the ruling and implications for the future value of the sponsoring company before the markets reopen. Fridays are often reserved for companies and drug products likely to create the most noise, providing the entire weekend for dissemination of the news."

"So, the FDA is expecting Narcogesic to be noisy," Karl said with no clue as to where Carlos was going with this. "I just don't see the short play here. TORX presents its flawless clinical trial results, its manufacturing partner defends the pristine production of drug product, the Advisory Committee recommends approval with accolades to the company founders and its well wishes for a Nobel Prize, and NASDAQ: TORX heads for Mars! What am I missing?"

"You're missing the part where the committee rejects the NDA for Narcogesic and recommends that the FDA issue one of its infamous 'nonapprovable' letters!" Carlos said as he leaned back in his leather chair with a look of content.

"Well, that would certainly make for an exciting Monday morning on Wall Street," Karl said like a lion that had just taken down a zebra on the plains of the Serengeti.

"What if the FDA overrules its Advisory Committee and issues an approvable letter?" Geoff pondered. "If the committee's recommendation is not binding on the FDA, the market will likely wait until the FDA itself rules one way or the other."

Kingsley came over to ask the men if they needed anything more from the bar. With everyone satiated, Carlos waited for Kingsley to retreat before he answered Geoff.

"The Advisory Committee's recommendation is not binding on the FDA per se," Carlos replied. "But I'm not aware of a single case where the Agency has ever overruled the committee, regardless of whether their recommendation was favorable or unfavorable. The FDA does not want to be in the awkward position of rejecting a drug that the medical community is demanding or approving a drug it considers to be unsafe or ineffective. No, I assure you, if the committee rejects the Narcogesic NDA, for any reason, it will trigger a TORX selloff the likes of which has not been seen since the collapse of the Dutch tulip market in 1637!"

"Just exactly how do we engineer the committee's rejection of a drug the world is expecting will put an end to the opioid crisis?" Geoff asked Carlos with more than a modicum of skepticism.

Someday you'll want to make something happen ... or keep it from happening ... and I'm your man! Carlos recollected the words of his brother.

"This is where Ty Dixon comes in," Carlos said.

"There's that name again," Geoff moaned. "The only one that made money on him was that Goth girlfriend of Karl's. What was her name? Oh yeah, Jayne Gillis. ViroSelect. Makes me want to puke over there on the *Janie O* barstool!"

I should call her, Karl thought salaciously.

"Well, this one isn't Ty's idea. This one's all mine," Carlos said as he leaned forward and spoke softly. "In fact, when my cards are played out, we will have gotten even with Ty!"

"Now you're talking," Karl said. "Assuming it involves a beheading!"

"I wouldn't rule that out," Carlos replied not even half-jokingly. "Your HR department must have missed this when you hired me, but I'll let you in on a little secret. Have you heard of the Sinaloa drug cartel?"

"Only the most notorious drug gang south of the boarder," Karl answered. "I'm liking it already!"

"My brother Miguel happens to be The Enforcer for the kingpin of the cartel. Miguel is one very bad hombre. I know. I've seen him do some things that would make a man give up his own mother. He told me if there was anything I needed to make happen, or to keep from happening, to give him a call. If we want to keep the Advisory Committee from recommending approval of Narcogesic, Miguel's our man!"

"How does Ty figure into this," Geoff asked Carlos.

"If there's anyone that can get the physicians and scientists on the committee second guessing the results of the clinical trials, it's the statisticians. Most panelists will have had a course or two in biostatistics, but few will have anything more than a basic appreciation for modern statistical methods like multivariate regression analysis using SPSS Statistics or SAS software. The physicians and scientists rely of the statisticians to tell them when they can be reasonably confident that the results are due to the drug or intervention and not to chance."

"How does Miguel get Ty to persuade the committee members that they can't believe their lying eyes?" Karl queried.

"We can leave that to Miguel. Given nine committee members, I'm sure he knows at least 900 ways. I don't think we want to know or need to know the details. I can only say that I wouldn't want to be in Ty Dixon's shoes when Miguel Martinez sets his plan in motion."

"It's been our experience that Ty doesn't respond well to carrots," Karl said. "So, I'm glad to hear that we're using a stick this time, and I wouldn't object to a baseball bat!"

"I suggest you both head to the War Room. Get Max on the phone over at the NASDAQ and start short selling as many shares of TORX as you can borrow." Carlos tapped on the home screen of his phone to launch the stock app and check the most recent stock price. "$89.75 +4.75. Up 5.6% percent in the first hour of trading! We better get moving. You have some trading to do, and I have a phone call to make!"

The Brothers stood synchronously, like a matched pair of bookends. "After you," Karl said, gesturing for his brother to go ahead. "It's the second mouse gets the cheese!"

The two men ordered a pair of Bloody Mary's from Kingsley as they left The Bar and headed to Karl's office, affectionately referred to as the War Room on an active trading day. By the time Kingsley delivered their drinks, they already had their NASDAQ floor trader Max on the phone and had instructed him to short as many shares of TORX as he could manage to borrow.

Max called back just after the close of the market to inform The Brothers that they were now short 250,000 shares of TORX at an average price of $91.25 per share, representing just a fraction of the first day's volume, and less than 5 percent of the float. The Brothers' ledger for TORX now had a first-day entry of $22,812,500 in black ink and 250,000 shares in red ink. It paired nicely with their Bloody Mary's.

40

Los Mochis, Sinaloa, Mexico

The sun shone brightly through the bedroom window and its rays glistened on the coconut-oiled bronze body of the former Miss Mexico as she basked in the afterglow of a passionate morning in the arms of Miguel Martinez. His wife Margarite and their young son Pedro had abandoned him weeks ago, which was probably best for everyone concerned. Now he had their beautiful seaside villa to himself, although Salma Flores was a frequent guest when she was not bedding his boss El Enterrador, head of the Sinaloa drug cartel. Miguel was one tough hombre and the cartel's chief enforcer. Salma knew he was cold. Stone cold. But she also could not resist the lifestyle she had as a trinket of the cartel. As she slowly ran the tip of her warm wet tongue in circles over his tight abdomen, she could sense his arousal as she attempted to coax him into another rough go round. It wasn't their first encounter, by far, but they always knew it could be their last.

Suddenly Miguel's phone vibrated on the nightstand and played out the instrumental theme song to *Miami Vice*. "Ah, shit," he said grabbing the phone and holding it so that he could see the caller ID screen.

"Don't answer it!" Salma purred.

Slapping her bare backside, Miguel leaned over the edge of the bed for a closer look and could see that caller ID read *unknown*, so he let it go to voicemail. Even when the caller was known, unless it was El Enterrador, he would let it go to voicemail just so that he could listen to the full ten second clip of the pounding beat of his favorite song. Shortly after the novel ringtone ended, a chirp signaled that the caller had left a voicemail. To Selma's chagrin he played it back immediately.

Miguel, it's Carlos. Call me back the moment you get this message. It's very important to both of us.

Forsaking his animal instincts and further stoking Salma's insatiable desires, Miguel climbed out of bed and slipped into a pair of gray cotton sweatpants. He then retrieved his Kimber EVO SP Raptor 9mm from the nightstand and slipped it into the back waistband of his pants. Everyone knew if they ever found Miguel dead his Kimber 9mm would be nearby.

"I need to return this call. It's my brother Carlos and he said it was urgent. I'll tell the staff to bring us breakfast by the pool."

Selma pulled the rose-colored bamboo sheets off the length of her toned physique and lingered long enough for Miguel to look back. When it was clear that his interests were no longer carnal, she donned a sheer orange silk robe and followed him out to the pool where they sat beside one another in a pair of Spanish Equipal chairs.

"Carlos. How are you, bro?" Miguel said after dialing the number that had been left on voicemail. Carlos was still holding the burner phone in his hand when the call came through.

"Miguel. Thanks for calling back so soon. Listen, I'm here in my New York office and just left a meeting with my partners. Do you remember that drug I told you about that is pending approval here in the U.S.?"

"The one you said will destroy our business down here?" Miguel questioned but knew the answer. "Narcogesic. Sure. I remember. I told El Enterrador about it and he ordered all the resources of the cartel to be at our disposal to eliminate the threat. Maybe we just find out where they're cooking the shit and set the kitchen on fire. We could even lock the doors first and make sure we bake the chefs."

Selma peered over the top of her pink-framed sunglasses at Miguel with an inquisitive look.

"Maybe you can go find out what's keeping the staff from bringing our breakfast," Miguel snarled. "Sorry Carlos," he said into the phone as she took the not-so-subtle hint and left him alone. Miguel was not a man to ask twice.

"I'm guessing the company has a contingency manufacturing plant, so burning the primary production facility would not solve our problem," Carlos said,

"Maybe we should ask El Enterrador if he has a good idea. Over the years I've learned he has some very creative ways of dealing with people."

"It may be helpful to involve him with the details, which I'm not sure I want to know, but let me give you an angle that I know will work."

Selma returned to the poolside with two of the kitchen staff trailing close behind. Each of the waiters was carrying a handwoven wicker tray of fresh fruit, juices, and croissants. Miguel's tray included a cup of black coffee with two shots of Clase Azul tequila on the side. The staff knew he liked to add them both to his first cup of coffee in the morning and left the trays on a teak table next to him. After the staff had retreated to the kitchen, Selma dropped her orange robe on the Mexican-tile deck and slowly, teasingly, entered the pool. Miguel paid her no attention. Almost. Then he drank down both shots of tequila without the coffee and chased them with a glass of fresh-squeezed orange juice. It wasn't that he needed to chase his tequila with anything. Ever. He just loved fresh orange juice. Nearly as much as aged Clase Azul.

"So, Miguel," Carlos continued over the burner phone. "The FDA must approve a drug before it can be legally marketed in the U.S., and in the case of Narcogesic, it has assembled a panel of experts to help make the decision. It's called a scientific Advisory Committee."

"Well, if they're anything like your DEA, it won't be easy to push them around," Miguel said as he watched every side stroke that Selma took.

"Actually, the DEA is a law enforcement branch of our government within the Department of Justice, whereas the FDA is a public service branch of our Department of Health and Human Services," Carlos explained. "The FDA has its own campus security, as well as local law enforcement, protecting its campuses near Washington, D.C., but it's not an extensive force."

"How do we keep this committee of experts from approving the drug?" Miguel asked.

"Ah, that's where you come in," Carlos prodded. "You see, the medical experts on the committee will defer to a single statistician on the panel to tell them if the favorable clinical trial results are due to Narcogesic or to chance. It's called the *null hypothesis* and it's the key statistical question of every controlled clinical trial. If the statistician says the appropriate level of statistical rigor was not met, his opinion would be unchallenged by the others and drug approval would be denied."

"What's the name of this statistician," Miguel asked as he withdrew the Kimber from his waistband and waived it in the air. "I'll just put a bullet in his head."

"I like your enthusiasm, Miguel, but it's not that easy. The FDA would simply replace the statistician on the panel as often as necessary!"

"What do you propose?"

"I'm not the one with the criminal mind, here," Carlos said knowing the term would flatter his brother and not offend him. "I remember you telling me that if I ever needed to keep something from happening that you were my man. Well, we need to keep the statistician from recommending approval. He will use whatever arguments he must to convince his colleagues and you just need to apply enough pressure to keep him focused.

"What's the name of this sonofabitch?" Miguel asked.

"Funny," Carlos replied. "My boss calls him the same thing! His name is Ty Dixon. The Advisory Committee meets a week from Friday at 1:00 p.m. in the Great Room of Building 31 on the White Oak Campus of the FDA in Silver Spring, MD. The outcome of this meeting will determine whether Narcogesic is approved and whether you will need to find a new line of work!"

Carlos ended the call on his burner phone and tossed it into the wastebasket of his New York office just as two shots rang out at Miguel's seaside villa in Los Mochis. A double tap. Miguel never fired just once. Fortunately, the bullets from his Kimber 9mm passed through a burnt-orange terracotta pot full of purple Mexican petunias and fell harmlessly into the ocean beyond. The beautiful former Miss Mexico was not certain whether the shots were fired in anger or delight. Stone cold.

"C'mon, babe," Miguel said to Selma. "Get out and get dressed. We need to take the chopper over to El Enterrador's. I need his opinion on how to handle a little situation north of the border."

41

Romulus, MI

The early Friday morning temperatures were below the dewpoint, so the driver turned on the heater and rolled down his window to clear the condensation from the windshield of their black Cadillac Escalade as they departed from the Enterprise Rent-A-Car lot at Detroit Metropolitan Airport. They had left in the early morning hours from Los Mochis aboard the cartel's Hawker 800XP and Miguel Martinez had brought three of his most trusted henchmen with him. The blacked-out vehicle rounded the interchange loop off Merriman Road just before dawn then headed westbound on I-94 following a GPS-guided route to an address that Miguel had been given by his brother Carlos.

"According to Google Maps we'll be there in about 30 minutes," Miguel said, using the navigational app on his phone while talking to one of the men he had sent two days earlier to stakeout the location of their target. "What's your status, Mario?"

"We're parked on Barton Shore Drive across the street from the house. We're in a vacant lot well hidden among a group of trees. The broad got in about eight o'clock last night and has been alone in the house ever since. I think the side driveway will be your best bet."

"Our ETA is 6:32 a.m. Keep your eyes open because if this thing gets sideways, I'll close them for you. Permanently."

Barton Hills was an affluent suburb of Ann Arbor and just a short drive from the airport. Ty and Kayla Dixon had a lovely estate there off Barton Shore Drive with the privacy of three wooded acres and no visible neighbors. It wasn't the salary of a tenured professor that afforded them the luxury as much as it was the consulting fees that Ty commanded from the FDA and pharmaceutical industry as one of the most highly regarded biostatisticians in the country.

Kayla poured herself a cup of Starbucks Breakfast Blend from the Keurig one-cup coffee maker and added half a spoonful of powdered creamer with no sweetener. Standing at the Brazilian granite countertop of their gourmet kitchen she closed her eyes and savored the first sip of the morning. As she opened them, she recalled Ty mentioning that his Advisory Committee meeting that day at the FDA would start with a planning session around ten-thirty and a short break for lunch followed by the public portion of the meeting in the afternoon. Whenever Ty was out of town, they would call one another every morning and it was a bit of a game as to who would place the call first. Looking at the bright blue LED clock on the microwave oven she could see it was still too early for the call.

Suddenly, the doorbell to the service entrance rang out. It wasn't unusual to receive parcel deliveries, any time of the day, but she instinctively checked the security app on her phone. As she sat her coffee cup down and headed for the side door, she looked at the 2x2 matrix of live video feeds from the security cameras around the home. She wasn't bothered that one was blacked out and dismissed it as a bad connection. She had also been oblivious to the notification of motion detected by the driveway camera. Afterall, her life as the wife of a successful statistician at the University of Michigan was generally uneventful and far removed from the sinister world of drug cartels.

The moment Kayla turned the knob that retracted the deadbolt, the door burst open and slammed into her right shoulder. As she fell hard on the tile floor, she was aghast to see her cherished new iPhone bounce on its edge then slide across the room. Fleetingly, she thought about the screen protector she should have purchased, then quickly and more appropriately redirected her attention to the invaders. Before she could scream, the larger of the two men grabbed her by the arms, stuffed a sock in her mouth and secured it behind her head with a strip of white linen.

"Put her little ass over there in that chair," Miguel barked from a distance revealing to Kayla that there were at least three attackers, though she could not see the third. Miguel's men needed no further guidance. They dragged Kayla across the floor by both arms with no regard for her torso or lower limbs. Shoving her down hard onto a chair at the breakfast table they used large plastic cable ties to bind her wrists and ankles to the arms and legs of the chair. Kayla guessed that both men were Hispanic. She still could not see her third captor, but she surmised from his accent that he too was Hispanic and apparently the one in charge. She then noticed a colorful set of full-sleeve tattoos on both arms of one man and a pair of ragged old black tattoos on the neck of the other. She shuddered to think they made no attempt to conceal their identities.

"Would one of you morons mind getting me her phone from over there on the floor?" Miguel berated.

"I'll get it, boss" the one with the colorful tattoos replied. Miguel grabbed it from him and could see it was a more recent model iPhone than his own. He was familiar with most of its basic features and functions but feared it was capable of much more than he understood and handled it like a venomous snake.

"Would this be your phone, bitch?" Miguel asked without needing an answer as he held it up to her face. He used his own phone to send a text message to his driver ordering him to bring the rental car around to the side of the house for a quick departure. Then he used Kayla's phone and entered the number that Carlos had given him. He punched in the last number and before sending he noticed that a name had appeared on the line below the number.

Honey Bun

42

Silver Spring, MD

Ty Dixon had just finished his morning shower and was shaving in front of the bathroom mirror of his Bethesda Marriott hotel room when his phone rang. Looking at the screen he could see that the incoming call was from his wife Kayla. *She beat me to the call*, he thought.

"Hello, sweetheart," he answered.

"Well, I'm sure as shit not sweet, and I'm told I have no heart, Honey Bun," Miguel said, requiring nothing more than his usual intonation to strike mortal fear in the recipient of his call.

"Who is this?" Ty demanded, not yet having connected the dots that would have put a crosshair on Kayla.

"You don't need to know who I am. You just need to know that I'm your worst nightmare. A regular Federico Krueger!" Miguel said with a hideous little laugh. He lowered Kayla's phone from his ear and looked at the screen then launched FaceTime and reversed the camera without disconnecting the call.

Accepting the switch to FaceTime, Ty looked at his screen and could see his wife bound and gagged and squirming in a chair. He recognized the breakfast room of his house but not the shadowy figures that were moving about. Hearing her muted cries, he fought back a profound sense of helplessness and hopelessness.

"Do you recognize this bitch?" Miguel blurted out. "Of course, you do!" Then he moved the phone in for a closeup of the heart-shaped locket around Kayla's neck. Reaching out he snatched it off, breaking the clasp of the delicate gold chain, then opened the locket and held it up to the phone. "Looks like a photo of your wife here on the left although maybe not sweating as much as she is right now. And, Oh! Look! That must be your dumb ass on the right!"

Ty stumbled backwards and fell onto the hotel bed as his legs buckled beneath him. "Don't hurt her. Please, don't hurt her. What is it you want?"

"I want you to go into that FDA meeting of yours today and tell your committee members to reject Narcogesic."

"And how am I supposed to do that? Every doctor on the panel and the FDA is looking forward to its approval."

"You're a smart guy. You'll figure it out. But if you don't, I might let my boys here have a little fun with your wife ... before we cut her head off!

"Oh my God!" Ty muttered almost incoherently. "No! I'll do as you say. Just don't hurt her."

"If you convince that committee of yours to vote against that stupid drug by three o'clock this afternoon, we'll release your wife unharmed. And we'll have someone in the room there, so we'll know if you're behaving. But failure is not an option. If the meeting is canceled, or postponed, or rescheduled in any way, or ends with anything other than a no vote," Miguel said, cracking his jaw. "Well, let's just say, that's when the fun begins!"

As the caller disconnected, Ty lowered the phone from his ear with a trembling hand and stared mindlessly at the screen. It took him a few moments to note the time in the upper left corner of the phone. 7:06 a.m. He thought about calling 911, but quickly concluded the local authorities in D.C. would be useless in helping to save his wife in Michigan.

Still staring at his phone in disbelief, Ty spotted the *Find My* app. Launching it, he watched as the icons for each of his Apple devices began to populate on a map in satellite view. A bright blue dot showing the current location of his cell phone hovered over Washington, D.C. while a collection of other device icons appeared over Michigan. Using his thumb and index finger he zoomed in and watched as the icons for his iMac and iPad appeared over Ann Arbor, and he was thrilled to suddenly see Kayla's iPhone appear among them. Zooming in further, he could see that his iMac and iPad were stationary at his home in Barton Hills, and that Kayla's phone was nearby, but on the move!

He watched as the position of the icon updated frequently on the map. It moved slowly south down Barton Shore Drive and paused briefly at the intersection of Whitmore Lake Road then merged onto Business South US-23. Moments later he watched as the icon moved just beyond the Barton Drive overpass then drifted off US-23 and settled motionless.

In the Huron River!

A myriad of worse-case scenarios raced through his mind as he stared at the hauntingly still icon for several minutes hoping it would move. Praying it would move. Ty could picture Kayla's phone lying on the bottom of the Huron and tried desperately not to imagine that her body was anywhere nearby.

"Dr. Armstrong. This is Ty Dixon," he said hurriedly, as he called the FDA Commissioner. "Sir, I'm sorry to bother you, but I just received a ghastly phone call from some men who have kidnapped my wife. Their only demand is that I convince our committee today to vote against the approval of Narcogesic. They said if that doesn't happen by three o'clock, they will kill her, and they will have someone in the audience to keep them informed of my cooperation."

"Oh my God! I'm so sorry Ty. Listen, I'll call the FBI Director this moment. I know him personally, and he'll send some agents over to your hotel posthaste. In the meantime, don't go anywhere and don't call anyone."

FBI Special Agent in Charge Frank Hughes together with two other agents arrived at Ty's hotel room within 15 minutes. For the next half hour, they questioned him about the call from the kidnappers and he provided as many details as quickly as he could. Upon learning the highlights, Agent Hughes asked if he could make a phone call or two from the bedroom. With permission he made the calls then rejoined the group.

"Okay" Agent Hughes announced. "I have engaged our Ann Arbor bureau and they are assembling a team of divers to search the river near the bridge where your wife's phone stopped tracking. I hate to say this Dr. Dixon, but there is some chance that your wife's hand is wrapped around that phone of hers." Ty's face contorted and he recoiled from a grotesque underwater vision of Kayla's hand holding tightly to her phone.

"That's it!" Ty said desperately. "The committee meeting can go on without me. I'm going back home to help find Kayla. Alive!"

"No, Dr. Dixon, you mustn't," Agent Hughes said. "At this point you need to do everything you can to comply with the demands of the kidnappers. Your wife's life depends upon it."

"I can't possibly get the committee to vote against Narcogesic," Ty said. "There's just too much favorable data and support."

"You're free to do whatever you'd like, of course, but here's what we suggest," Agent Hughes said. "Since the kidnappers claim they will have an associate in the audience, which may or may not be the case, you need to make sure the meeting starts on time. We will call the FDA Commissioner and confidentially bring him up to speed on the details. No one else will be involved. The two of you should be able to steer the discussions in the direction of a no vote well enough to convince everyone in the audience and long enough to buy us the time we need to locate and rescue your wife."

"I wonder why they gave me a three o'clock deadline?" Ty asked, and the word made him cringe.

"Follow the money," Agent Hughes replied. "Always follow the money. TORX is a public company and there is a great deal of money to made or lost betting on the stock of the company. We'll certainly pursue that angle too as we turn over every rock looking for Mrs. Dixon."

"How will I know when you find her?"

"We will keep you and the FDA Commissioner abreast of our progress by text messages," Agent Hughes replied.

"And what if you haven't found her by three o'clock?"

"Then a vote against the drug would be most helpful," Agent Hughes said pensively.

"We'll find her. And we'll find her alive and in time. Don't you worry about that," one of the other agents said with bravado, as he put a reassuring hand on Ty's shoulder.

43

Ann Arbor, MI

FBI Special Agent in Charge Nick Fernetti watched from the shore along with a few of his agents as a hand emerged from the frigid waters of the Huron River wrapped in black neoprene rubber. Then a head rose above the waterline and the gloved hand removed the mask of his most senior search and rescue diver.

"Pretty murky down there, sir," the diver shouted to Agent Fernetti as he slowly made his way to shallower water. "Nothing, sir. Nada. No phone and no body."

"Damn," Agent Fernetti cursed.

"Excuse me, sir," one of his agents said, taken aback by the suggestion that his boss was disappointed that they hadn't found the woman dead.

"The phone, not the body," he corrected. "I was hoping we'd find the phone. Send it to the FBI lab. Maybe recover some prints or DNA or some helpful information from the last several minutes of its use."

"Any word yet from Apple on the phone records?" the agent asked, doubtful the phone itself would be functional if recovered.

"Yep. Got a text message a few minutes ago. They pulled their copy of the FaceTime video file from the call between the Dixon phones and ran it through the facial recognition database they share with Google and Facebook. More extensive than ours. International, in fact. Of course, they identified Dr. and Mrs. Dixon on their respective phones, but the other FaceTime images on Mrs. Dixon's phone were unidentifiable."

"What about the audio?" the same agent asked.

"The primary unidentifiable voice on Mrs. Dixon's phone was given a 97 percent probability of being that of a Hispanic male and his dialect a 76 percent probability of being from the Mexican state of Sinaloa."

"Cartel!" the third agent exclaimed. "That's not good!"

"You think?" Agent Fernetti replied sarcastically.

"Over here, sir," another diver yelled ashore from a boat that was hovering over a spot further downstream. "Sir, over here. We have the signature of an object on side-scan sonar consistent with that of a body on the river bottom. Pulling it up now to have a look."

As the winch on the USCG response vessel slowly turned, two more divers went over the side with no splash. Moments later, air bubbles churned in the water like a boiling caldron as the men surfaced.

"Just the body of a dead St. Bernard, sir. Appears he's been down there a while. Probably fell through the ice over the winter."

Agent Fernetti reconnoitered with his agents and divers on the north bank of the river. "Well, fellas, we've been up and down this river on both sides of the bridge. It's not that deep, not that wide and not that swift, but we're coming up empty handed. No phone and no body. Correction. No human body. She's either dead further downstream, or she's ..." he said but was interrupted.

"Sir, what side of US-23 runs along this side of the bridge where the phone signal cut out?" one of the more junior agents asked.

"The southbound side, I believe, right?" Agent Fernetti said with uncertainty, but the others reassured. "Why do you ask?"

"Look over there on that utility pole. South side of the bridge. Right where the bridge meets the shore. What's that look like to you?"

"Well, I'll be damned," Agent Fernetti said. "It sure looks like a security camera to me, too!"

"Facing oncoming southbound traffic. Front license plates should be a snap to read. With or without a zoom."

"What are you waiting for?" Agent Fernetti shouted as he playfully shoved the shoulder of the junior agent. "Find out who owns that camera then what vehicle tossed a phone over the bridge from the southbound lanes at approximately seven-thirty this morning."

"Yes, sir," two of the agents said as they spun on their heels.

"Oh, and fellas," Agent Fernetti called out as the men looked back. "I'll bet you a dozen donuts when you locate the vehicle that it's a late-model luxury SUV. These Mexican drug cartel guys all have the same taste in wheels!"

44

Silver Spring, MD

Ty had joined his other Advisory Committee members and FDA representatives in the café of Building 31 for lunch, but he had no appetite and ate nothing. As they departed for their meeting in the Great Room, his phone vibrated without ringing and he noticed an incoming message from Special Agent Nick Fernetti in Michigan.

THE BAD NEWS IS - WE DIDN'T FIND YOUR WIFE'S PHONE. THE GOOD NEWS IS - WE DIDN'T FIND YOUR WIFE EITHER. DOESN'T MEAN SHE'S NOT DEAD, JUST THAT SHE'S NOT WHERE WE'VE LOOKED SO FAR.

Whose team is this guy on? Arthur Armstrong thought.

The FDA Commissioner was the only other one to receive a copy of the text message from Agent Fernetti. He hoped beyond hope they would find Kayla Dixon soon. Preferably alive. But the Agency could only play along with Ty and the FBI for so long. A few hours. Maybe over the weekend at most. But the fact was 130 citizens were dying every day from opioid addiction and the tradeoff for one life today would not be a difficult decision.

In no mood to mingle, Ty walked briskly along the wall of the Great Room then climbed a short flight of stairs to the dais up front. He acknowledged no one as he moved swiftly along the backside of the conference table and sat near the middle behind the nametag that read, *Dr. Ty Dixon, Chairman.*

Given the enthusiasm for Narcogesic it was standing room only with every seat in the house occupied by industry titans, media moguls, stockbrokers, and day traders.

Carlos Martinez, MD was seated near the back of the room along a side aisle. Looking at his phone he could see that TORX was now trading at $125.25, up 1.25 on the day. The volume was very light compared to the heavy trading of the security over the last two weeks since its public debut. Apparently, the bets were in, and everyone was awaiting the outcome of this meeting. The Fischmann Brothers had sent their chief medical advisor to bear witness to the news that the scientific Advisory Committee had voted against Narcogesic!

Carlos had planned to make two calls, probably after the close of the market. The first would be to The Brothers to deliver the good news, at least from their perspective. The second would be to his brother Miguel to congratulate him on a job well done.

Dr. Mia Reinhardt arrived at the Great Room promptly at one o'clock. She was never a minute early or a minute late. Her obsessive-compulsive personality would never permit such lackadaisical timing. Dr. Mark Oberon on the other hand had been since shortly before noon.

The crowd quieted as the FDA Commissioner rose from his seat in the front row and took to the podium.

"I would like to welcome everyone to our Advisory Committee meeting for Narcogesic. Importantly, I would like to welcome our guests from Theta Opioid Therapeutics and in particular Dr. Mark Oberon, its scientific founder whose pioneering research has led us to this moment. Finally, I would like to thank our committee members for their time and dedication to our mission of ensuring the safety and efficacy of every drug that enters the U.S. market. With that, let me invite Dr. Charlene Hopkins, the head of the reviewing division, to say a few words."

Cool as a cucumber, Ty thought. *But then, it's not his wife!*

"I know we are all anxious to get started, so let me just briefly outline the program for today," Charlene said into the microphone at the podium. "First, representatives of TORX will summarize the key components of their NDA, including the Chemistry, Manufacturing and Controls (CMC) for Narcogesic along with its preclinical pharmacology, toxicology, and clinical trial results. Then perhaps a few words from Dr. Oberon about the role of Narcogesic in pain management from his perspective. Finally, we will open it up to questions by Dr. Dixon and his committee."

Even before she could return to her seat, Ty seized the microphone at the conference table and began to address the audience. "I think I speak for the entire committee when I say that we've all read the NDA and I think we're as familiar with it as we need to be. As such, and in the intertest of time, I'd like to make a motion that we skip the presentations by the sponsor and move right to Q&A. Do I have a second?"

The committee members were dumbstruck by the unusual request, as were the FDA administrators, and more than a moment went by before one of the members slowly raised his hand and hesitantly seconded the motion.

"Any objections?" Ty asked. "Fine then," he said, waiting for no one. "I'll begin the questioning. I read there was a total of 200 volunteers in the first pivotal trial, only half of whom received Narcogesic. The other half received placebo. There was also a total of 400 patients in the second trial, only half of whom received Narcogesic while the other half were given oxycodone. That means that a grand total of a measly 300 subjects have been exposed to Narcogesic in the comparative trials. Now then, I realize there were *no reported cases* of addiction among these 300 subjects, but what statistician at Theta Opioid Therapeutics thinks that zero out of 300 supports the claim of having a *nonaddictive* opioid?"

His shot across the bow echoed through the room like a Howitzer as a young man in the audience with wire-rimmed glasses timidly raised his hand. "Give that man a microphone," Ty barked at one of the audiovisual technicians circling the room. "Stand up young man and tell us your name!"

"Goldberg, sir. Marvin Goldberg. I'm not an employee of the company, but I am a statistician. PhD research statistician at Duke University and the company's statistical consultant."

"You look familiar," Ty said, but he couldn't place the face.

"I was a student of yours at the University of Michigan."

"Ah. Indeed. I remember. In that case, I know you're familiar with the statistical Rule of Three. Why don't you take a moment and describe it for us, Marv?" Ty asked pejoratively.

"Well, sir, it means that, if there are no cases of a particular event in a sample size of n, then one can be 95 percent confident that the real incidence is not more than one in n/3."

"Very good. So, in this case, we have n=300 Narcogesic subjects divided by three, which means there could be as many as one in 100 patients that become addicted to the drug. Is that right?" Ty was giving the theatrical performance of his life and could only hope that the kidnapper's plant in the audience was duly impressed.

"Yes, that's correct," Marvin replied knowing where this could lead.

"Now I'm no physician or expert in pain management, but if one in 100 patients becomes addicted to Narcogesic, I wouldn't call that a *nonaddictive* drug, would you? Would any of you?" Ty demanded as he looked up and down the table at the panelists. "That's one percent for heaven's sake! If the mortality rate of a disease state is one percent, I wouldn't call that a *nonfatal* disease, would you? Would any of you?" Ty said as he slapped his hand on the table for dramatic effect.

"You're right, Dr. Dixon," one of the expert physicians agreed. Ty was taken aback that anyone found his argument compelling enough to agree but was certainly pleased. "That would actually be a disturbingly high incidence of addiction. In my hands, addiction to oxycodone or even fentanyl is far less than one percent."

"That's because you don't follow your patients long enough or close enough to know who's becoming addicted!" Dr. Oberon cried out from his seat loud enough to be heard without a microphone.

For the next hour Mark and various committee members argued back and forth about the incidence of opioid addiction and the statistical rigor of the clinical trials.

Carlos checked his phone and noticed that the share price of TORX was beginning to slide. The quote was now $119.75, down 4.25 at 2:17 p.m. He had no idea what scheme his brother Miguel had deployed but it was working. He looked around the room and noticed lots of folks on their phones. No doubt calling their brokers. Some were even broadcasting live video of the raucous.

Carlos called Karl and Geoff with an update and The Brothers were delighted to learn that things weren't going well for the drug. They were short a total of 660,000 shares of TORX owed to various brokers, having sold them short over the last two weeks at an average share price of $95. A nearly $63 million leveraged bet. They would start buying back the shares at a profit as soon as the stock price dipped below $95. With the committee voting to reject Narcogesic, probably after the close of the market, they would have the weekend to celebrate before the massive selloff Monday morning that would enable them to begin covering their position at a handsome profit. They wouldn't be surprised if it opened south of $25 and they certainly wouldn't be disappointed.

45

Ann Arbor, MI

Kayla was stretched out on a stained mattress lying flat on a dirty old pinewood floor with her arms and legs bound by long black cable ties. The cotton sock that had been stuffed in her mouth was now soaked with saliva and the strip of linen that held it in place had not loosened a smidge. She watched as the man across the room with the menacing black tattoos on his neck sat quietly scrolling on his phone. Whatever was occupying his time was the farthest thing from her mind. Her only friend was the early afternoon sun that beamed brightly through the glass window above her head, and she dreaded what its disappearance might bring in the hours to come.

After crossing over the Huron River bridge, her captors had driven just a couple of more miles to a very plain-looking two-story bungalow on Sixth Street in the Old West Side of Ann Arbor. There were at least six degrees of separation between the house and El Enterrador. A local dealer in the cartel's long supply chain had offered it up as a safe house for his quarry. Miguel was pleased that his boss had stepped up to work out the details of their plan to save the cartel.

Miguel's forward patrol team had gone ahead from Barton Hills to confirm that the safe house was indeed vacant as promised and had moved to a position further up the street to keep lookout. He had instructed three of his men to take Kayla into the house while he stayed back in the lookout vehicle. Two of the men were to keep watch of the front and rear entrances from inside the first floor while the third man was to guard their victim on the second floor.

Special Agent in Charge Nick Fernetti had taken cover with a tactical team of six men in the backyard of a home on Fifth Street directly behind the bungalow. He had also positioned a sniper unit on the second floor of the house directly across Sixth Street.

"Black Cadillac Escalade with Michigan license plate GFY-864," one of his agents reported quietly over the two-way radio.

"Looks like you boys owe me a box of donuts!" Agent Fernetti said speaking softly.

It was the same vehicle and plate number they had seen on the video from the security camera at the Huron River bridge. The plate had been clearly visible as the vehicle passed by at 7:16 a.m. and it only required a little zooming to observe an object being tossed out the rear passenger window at precisely the time and location that Kayla's GPS phone signal had departed from the bridge. The vehicle belonged to Enterprise Rent-A-Car and the firm had been cooperative in sharing its current GPS location on Sixth Street.

One of the men in Miguel's lookout vehicle had been monitoring the bungalow by split-screen video on his phone. Two camera phones had been positioned inside the bungalow with one on the first floor and one on the second. Miguel had no idea the FBI was in the neighborhood and, lucky for him, they had no idea he was there either.

The *Miami Vice* ringtone broke the silence inside the lookout vehicle and caller ID indicated it was their plant in the audience at the FDA meeting. Miguel checked the time. 2:37 p.m.

Almost the witching hour.

"Sir, the meeting seems to be going our way, but the committee has not yet voted," the man reported. "I'll call you back at three. Sharp."

Miguel pulled his Kimber 9mm with the rosewood grips from his waistband. He released the magazine and counted seven rounds.

Full.

Then he slammed the clip back into the gun and racked the slide.

Locked and loaded.

He would return shortly with just five rounds in the magazine.

Double tap. In the forehead.

Miguel slipped the Kimber back into his waistband, stepped out of the car and headed up the sidewalk toward the bungalow. In his trademark white leisure suit and baby-blue T-shirt he was obviously not from the neighborhood.

"What do you see?" Agent Fernetti quietly asked the sniper over the two-way radio.

"There's a mirror on the back wall of the second floor and I can see the reflection of a woman bound and gagged. She's lying on a mattress with its head against the opposite wall just below the window. There's also a man with hideous black tattoos on his neck sitting in a chair across the room playing on his phone."

"That's her. Do you have a clear shot at him?" Agent Fernetti asked.

"Like a buck eating corn in the backyard of my farm up in Grayling."

"We're ready to take the house from the rear. You got the ball."

Suddenly, two shots rang out.

Double tap.

Uncertain as to the origin of the shots, Miguel looked inquisitively at the muzzle of his Kimber. The simultaneous sounds of glass breaking and the beating wings of sparrows taking flight caused him to flinch and turn quickly back to the car.

"What the hell was that?" he shouted to the man in the backseat with the split-screen videos on his phone.

"There's shattered glass all over the broad on the mattress," the man said to Miguel. "I think somebody just popped our guy upstairs. Who the hell? Holy shit! A bunch of feds in camo with assault rifles just crashed through the backdoor of the house. Oh my God! They just capped both our guys downstairs!"

Agent Fernetti stepped back outside the rear door of the bungalow and pulled his phone out of his tactical vest pocket. He smiled as he noted the time. 2:57 p.m.

Safe and secure by three o'clock, he thought.

Having optimistically drafted his text message before the assault, he simply pressed the icon to send.

46

Silver Spring, MD

MRS. DIXON SAFE AND SOUND. YOU'RE FREE TO VOTE. ANY WAY YOU'D LIKE.

Ty Dixon and Arthur Armstrong both received the text message simultaneously.

"That's it! I've heard enough," the FDA Commissioner announced as he stood up with a microphone that he had taken from one of the floor technicians. Like the seasoned engineer of a runaway train heading down the wrong track, it was now in the capable hands of Art Armstrong to reverse course while preserving the credibility of his Advisory Committee and his Agency.

"Dr. Dixon," the Commissioner began. "I think it's time we hear from the FDA's statisticians about this little concern of yours. I believe you know the senior statistician of the reviewing division, Dr. Milton Warner, seated next to me here with six of his statisticians behind him. If I'm not mistaken, Dr. Warner was *your* professor at Stanford before you became gainfully employed at the University of Michigan. So, let's ask him. Dr. Warner, what is your opinion on the matter?"

"Of course, Dr. Dixon is quite right about the Rule of Three," he began as he took the microphone from Dr. Armstrong. "But whether the sponsor is allowed to claim that Narcogesic is a *nonaddictive* opioid is a matter of labeling and advertising, not a question of safety or efficacy. The comparative trials have demonstrated that Narcogesic is effective beyond any statistical or clinical doubt. Superior to placebo and at least equivalent to oxycodone as a pain reliever. Additionally, there were essentially no side effects. So, safety is not an issue."

"Thank you, Dr. Warner," Dr. Armstrong regarded as he retrieved the microphone. "To be clear, whether a drug is acceptably safe and effective is the question we pose to our Advisory Committees. Whether a particular term is permitted for the purpose of labeling or advertising is strictly the purview of the reviewing division and the Agency."

"But sir," Mia stood up at her seat and was handed a microphone. "Safety and efficacy are required. I'll give you that. But whether Narcogesic is *nonadditive*, and the first among opioids in this regard, is paramount. Whether it is a *life-saving pain reliever*, or just another *life-threatening narcotic*, is the very reason we're here today." Mia was reminded of her brother as she drew the stark contrast. She remained standing as if waiting for an answer, though she had posed no question.

"Dr. Armstrong, if I may, let me address the term *nonaddictive*," Charlene Hopkins said as she was handed the microphone. Mia slowly sat back down in her seat. "Of course, the true incidence of opioid addiction varies with potency or dose and duration of treatment, and there may be genetic predispositions and interindividual variabilities that may increase one's risk. But using Dr. Dixon's Rule of Three ..."

"Excuse me," he interrupted. "It's not *my* rule, it's a statistical rule."

"I'm sorry," she said. "Using the *statistical* Rule of Three, we can be 95 percent confident that fewer than one in 100 patients will become addicted to Narcogesic. However, if we include the cohort of 700 patients from the Phase III open-label safety study in which there we also no cases of addiction reported, we now have n=1,000 and a maximum incidence of less than one in

333. The question is whether this is adequate for labeling the drug as *nonadditive*, or whether we need fewer than one in 1,000, or one in 10,000, or some other such lower limit to permit the claim."

Mark Oberon promptly stood at his seat and gestured with a dismissive hand. "Despite what some of my *esteemed colleagues* on the committee have claimed, one in 100 would be a welcome reduction in the incidence of opioid addiction in the hands of anyone competent, and one in 333 would be even more impressive. But I would not be surprised if it's fewer than one in 10,000. In fact, I would not be surprised if a single case of opioid addiction were *never reported again!*"

The crowd began whispering like celebrities at the Academy Awards, and several in the audience jumped on their phones to send a text message or place a quick call. Carlos raised his cuff-linked shirt sleeve and peered at his Presential Rolex. 3:14 p.m. He doubted that the committee would put the question to a vote before the close of the market.

"Well, then," Charlene said, looking at Mark and Mia. "Perhaps the company would agree to conduct a Phase IV study to continuously surveil the incidence of addiction *after* approval. With such a commitment, perhaps we could allow the advertising of Narcogesic as *nonaddictive* until the first reported case of addiction occurs, at which time we could revisit the claim. Does that seem reasonable to those on my staff?" she asked and watched as they all nodded in unison. "And would that be acceptable to you, Dr. Armstrong?"

"Indeed, that would be a most appropriate course of action."

"Let me ask the company. Would that be ..." Charlene continued but was interrupted.

"Yes. Yes, it would be," Bob Taylor said, uncertain as to whether he should remain seated, stand, or go blind. The CEO wanted to add his two cents, and if any sort of contract was required, he was ready to sign.

"Then let's put this NDA to a vote right now," Ty Dixon announced from the dais. "Are there any opposed to the approval of the drug?" he asked as he looked up and down the conference table. With no show of hands and no verbal objections, he quickly remarked. "There you have it!"

The crowd roared like a pride of lions. Mark and Mia stood and embraced as nearly everyone else jumped on their phones or rushed for the exits. Narcogesic was on its way to FDA approval.

Carlos quickly placed the first of his two planned calls as he checked the TORX share price at 3:17 p.m. It was already $158.40, up $34.40, and climbing rapidly. Not unexpectedly, The Brothers answered the call on the first ring.

The second call, to his brother Miguel, went unanswered.

Unfortunately, The Brothers were not in for a long celebratory weekend. Rather, they had forty-three minutes before the close of the market to prevent whatever blood loss they could. They were now among the frenzied buyers pushing the stock price higher with every trade. By the time the closing bell rang, Max had bought back all 660,000 shares the boys were short. At an average price of $278.25, The Brothers had lost more than $120 million in forty-three minutes.

47

Washington, D.C.

The trademark fragrances of the White House Rose Garden were unmistakable to the Cabinet members and heads of federal agencies that had gathered there many times before. However, on this particular and glorious spring afternoon, it was a first for Drs. Robert Taylor, Mark Oberon, and Mia Reinhardt as invited guests of the President of the United States. The walnut wood podium that stood stately in front of the crowd was adorned with the Presidential Seal on a field of navy blue and the White House press corps had been notified of the scheduled joint press conference. Everyone stood as the President rounded the corner of the West Wing and made his way down the steps to the podium.

"Ladies and gentlemen," the President began as he adjusted the microphone. "It is with great pleasure that I have asked you here today to share in what promises to be the beginning of the end of a great casualty that has besieged our nation and indeed the world for generations. Today we are making a series of announcements that I believe will bring an end to the opioid crisis in America. A crisis that has overwhelmed our criminal justice system, stolen the vitality of our young people and robbed this nation of its full economic potential. Let me begin by asking our great FDA Commissioner, Dr. Arthur Armstrong, to come forward and make the initial announcement. Art, please."

"Thank you, Mr. President," Dr. Armstrong said courteously. "First, this will probably come as no surprise to anyone after the great work last week of our Advisory Committee to the Division of Anesthesiology, Addiction Medicine and Pain Medicine. It is with pride and great hope that I announce the FDA's approval of Narcogesic as the world's first and only nonaddictive opioid analgesic."

A polite but robust round of applause rose from the audience. Sitting in the front row, Mark beamed with pride and Mia sobbed with satisfaction knowing that her brother Warren's overdose and untimely death had not been in vain.

"Now a few announcements of my own," the President said stepping back over to the microphone. "First, since Theta Opioid Therapeutics received government funding in the form of NIH grants to support some of its earliest drug development efforts and since the opioid crisis is a declared national emergency, the federal government acting in the best interest of this nation's public health has decided to exercise its rights under the Narcogesic patent that was issued to Duke University and later assigned to TORX. From this day forward, the government will control the supply and distribution of Narcogesic, and we intend to provide it free of charge to the healthcare marketplace. This will remove any economic incentive to prescribe or use anything else. I suspect this one will get me in hot water with the Congressional Budget Office!"

Austin Crammer, the company's patent attorney at Duke had also been invited and was sitting directly behind Robert Taylor. Austin leaned forward and whispered in Bob's ear, "I knew the government had that right under U.S. Code 28, Section 1498, but I don't recall that it's ever been used."

"Second," The President went on. "We are hereby ordering that all other oral opioid analgesics previously approved by the FDA are to be withdrawn from the U.S. market over the next 60 days and reclassified as Schedule I controlled substances with no approved medical uses. And I suspect this one will get me in hot water with Big Pharma, but I think they'll get over it!"

The President paused briefly for effect then continued. "Next I'd like to introduce Dr. Robert Taylor the CEO of Theta Opioid Therapeutics and invite him up to make an important announcement of his own. Bob, please."

Bob was sitting in the front row between Mark and Mia when the President motioned for him to come forward.

"Thank you, Mr. President," Bob said proudly, as he took to the podium and adjusted the microphone. "Sir, it would be my distinct honor and great pleasure to make this next announcement, but I'm afraid I must delegate the task to someone far more eloquent as an orator, and far more deserving as a co-founder of the company and codeveloper of this great drug. Let me invite to the stage my colleague and dear friend, Dr. Mia Reinhardt."

Mia stood and gracefully approached the podium, her blonde locks blowing gently in the breeze like the U.S. flag on the pole behind her. Pausing briefly before she began to speak, she took in the fragrances of the historic garden and relished in the moment, flanked by the CEO of her company to her left and the CEO of the country to her right. For the first time in a long time, Mia was uneasy in front of an audience, but summoned the courage to overcome her anxiety.

"Mr. President, Dr. Taylor, if you don't mind, I'd first like to invite my colleague and very dear friend, Dr. Mark Oberon, to the podium to present him with a very special gift."

The President gestured for Mark to come forward. Once he was on stage, Mia reached into the base of the podium and withdrew a beautifully gift-wrapped box about one cubic foot in size. Not at all sure what to expect, Mark gently untied the ribbon and peeled back the wrapping paper. He lifted the lid, reached in, and slowly raised a three-dimensional tissue paper model of the Narcogesic molecule. "I thought it would be a fitting replacement of the tetracyclozine model you have back at your office!" Mia said.

"Thank you so much, Mia. You have no idea how much this means to me. And now I have a little something for you," Mark said as he reached into his pocket and pulled out a black key fob, then handed it to Mia. "It's the key to a new Subaru Outback. And if you'd rather have a Tesla Model S, I'd be happy to swap it out!"

As Mia gave Mark a big hug, and wondered how he knew she liked Tesla, she whispered in his ear. "I wouldn't trade it for the world!" Mark left the podium with moist eyes, and Mia continued.

"It is now my honor and privilege to announce that, rather than penalize our shareholders by exploiting its rights to our patents with no consideration, the federal government has decided to exercise its powers of imminent domain and acquire all the assets of Theta Opioid Therapeutics for the fair market value of $6.2 billion. This is a slight premium to its price when trading was halted by the SEC earlier this week, and the equivalent of $310 per share outstanding."

Bob Taylor quickly did the math on his stake and arrived at $930 million, though much of it would be shared with his investors. Mark and Mia shared $930 million fifty-fifty, though that calculation was the furthest thing from their minds.

"Mr. President," Mia continued. "My good friends Mark and Bob, and all of you who have embraced our cause. I wish you could have known my brother Warren. He would have been so proud of what we have accomplished here today. Warren called opioids his *wonderfully dreadful* vice, and I'm just so pleased we now have a *wonderful* pain reliever devoid of the *dreadful* curse of opioids. There's nothing I can do to bring back my brother, but my soul is less tormented knowing that his legacy has been fulfilled.

You could have heard a heart break as many in the audience thought about themselves, or their family members, or their friends touched by the opioid crisis.

EPILOGUE

The gray woven paperboard box was lined with pigskin suede and contained a red leather-bound document of handmade paper on the right and a wildly colorful work of art on the left. He was not literate in Swedish and could not read the beautiful calligraphy of Annika Rücker, but he could certainly read his name in the middle of the diploma ~ *Mark James Oberon*. The much smaller white box contained a palm-sized gold medal with the bust of a bearded gentleman on one side and the Genius of Medicine on the other, holding an open book in her lap as she collected water pouring from a rock to quench the thirst of a sick girl. After walking slowly across the stage to *Pomp and Circumstance*, Dr. Mark Oberon was handed the awards for the Nobel Prize in Medicine by a representative of the Royal Swedish Academy of Sciences. His white tuxedo and tails paired nicely with his smile as he immediately refocused his attention on Dr. Mia Reinhardt sitting in the audience. She would not have missed the event for the world despite their long flight to Stockholm in December.

Dr. Robert Taylor had not been seen nor heard from in the weeks that followed the government's buyout of TORX. He had indulged himself with the purchase of a 132-foot Feadship that he had christened *Drug Money*. Of course, the U.S. Coast Guard found little humor in the name, but he had been given special dispensation by the U.S. President, and the vessel was not to be boarded anywhere in the waters of the U.S. or its territories. The ship was last spotted anchored in Rendezvous Bay just off the shore of St. John in the U.S. Virgin Islands, and the paparazzi was finding it difficult to keep track of the many celebrities he entertained onboard.

The last hour of trading in NASDAQ: TORX had raised red flags at the SEC, and subpoenas of trading and phone records were passed out like candy. Karl and Geoff Fischmann were the only ones to report losses that day. Heavy losses. Their consistent use of burner phones had put some distance between them and most of their securities manipulations, but Carlos Martinez had failed to use one when he had made his two calls that afternoon from the Great Room at the FDA.

Transcripts of his first call led to federal grand jury indictments of The Brothers and Carlos for securities fraud in the illegal trading of NASDAQ: TORX. Since they had been on the wrong side of the trading this time, it only added insult to injury. The second call had led to names like Miguel Martinez, Ty and Kayla Dixon, and Hector Morales, and resulted in additional charges for kidnapping and endangerment. The Brothers had no knowledge of the kidnapping, and Carlos give up his brother Miguel in exchange for a lighter sentence and forfeiture of all his ill-gotten gains, including the Rolex.

Karl and Geoff Fischmann each received 99 years for securities fraud, money laundering, and a host of other white-collar crimes. They were assigned to a cell together at the Federal Correction Complex in Butner, North Carolina and were in good company with the likes of Bernie Madoff. Not surprisingly, the only ones to visit them were two colorfully dressed gentlemen that fancied the attention they received from the male prisoners that whistled as they passed by. Their requests for conjugal visits were denied by the warden, and by The Brothers.

Hector "El Enterrador" Morales successfully denied any knowledge or involvement in the escapades north of the border. The release of Narcogesic and its rapid adoption worldwide, coupled with the relegation of all other opioids to Schedule I status, had driven a spike through the heart of his empire. Prison, whether in Mexico or the U.S., would have been far worse than simply becoming accustomed to having far less.

Miguel Martinez was another story. His brother Carlos had thrown him under the bus, and the U.S. Attorney General wanted more than a pound of flesh. He was indicted by a federal grand jury for kidnapping and drug trafficking, as well as a host of charges under the RICO Act. However, the Mexican government was not cooperating with extradition since he was also wanted in Mexico for first-degree murder involving pig roasts and feline feasts.

Miguel stood alone on the front porch of his seaside villa, his wife Margarite and son Pedro long gone. He watched as the beautiful Salma Flores climbed into his vintage white Ferrari Spyder and drove slowly down the driveway and out of his life. He could not have cared less. Stone cold. As she disappeared beyond the trees, he retreated to the poolside patio out back.

Abruptly cresting the ridge just beyond the seawall of the compound rose six Seahawk helicopters with their U.S. Navy insignias clearly visible. Flying in formation and closing quickly, they prepared for landing. With a click of his jaw, evoking the memory of that rusted old Cadillac Eldorado from long ago, Miguel reached into his waistband, withdrew his Kimber EVO SP Raptor 9mm, put the barrel of the gun in his mouth, and pulled the trigger.

It was the second time in his life that he didn't hear the shot.

AUTHOR'S NOTE

The parallels and contrasts between the COVID-19 and opioid crises are striking. COVID-19 is accurately characterized as an infectious disease pandemic, whereas opioid addiction is not widely accepted as a neurological disease epidemic. An ideological chasm has caused many to reject the science of COVID-19 vaccinations and the advice of the CDC/FDA, while sociological differences have prevented many from accepting the neuroscience of addiction and the faultlessness of its victims. It's been said that COVID-19 does not discriminate between rich and poor, black and white, or Christian and Buddhist, and the same can be said of drug addiction.

While we justifiably focus on the morbidity, mortality, and economic destruction wrought by COVID-19, let's not forget the generations of death and lost productivity attributable to drug addiction. It is not improbable that a powerful nonaddictive narcotic analgesic may someday be discovered. In the interim, let's elevate the political and social dialogue concerning the decriminalization of drugs and the provision of medically supervised rehabilitation for all. The return on this investment would far outweigh those of many given a higher sociopolitical priority.

ACKNOWLEDGMENTS

A special thanks to my friend Larry for his time,
attention, and thoughtful review, and without whom
I would have made a small fortune on Bitcoin.

With gratitude to my cousin Debbie for her assistance,
and I hope she enjoyed the tacos!

ABOUT THE AUTHOR

Roger Blevins, Pharm.D., is the former cofounder and CEO of two biopharmaceutical companies, including one he listed on the New York Stock Exchange and one he funded in the private equity markets. He is the coauthor of two New Drug Applications for cardiovascular drug products approved by the U.S. Food and Drug Administration, both on the market today, and the author of more than 40 original research publications in the medical literature.

Born and raised in suburban Detroit, and a graduate of Wayne State University, Dr. Blevins was an assistant professor and cardiovascular researcher at Sinai Hospital of Detroit prior to leaving academia for the pharmaceutical industry. During his business tenure, he was credited with the development of adenosine as an anti-arrhythmic agent and as an adjunct to stress testing in nuclear cardiology, as well as the automation and development of a fluorescence bioassay for drug discovery.

Dr. Blevins is a former resident of Los Angeles, CA, Raleigh-Durham, NC, and The Villages, FL. Now retired and living in Charleston. SC, with family throughout the Carolinas, when he's not reading or writing about scientific fact or fiction or enjoying a glass of cabernet on his back porch overlooking the Cooper River, you can find him on the golf course or traveling the countryside with his wife Sandy in their motorcoach or playing his Taylor guitar for his grandchildren.

Made in the USA
Columbia, SC
26 November 2021